LILY'S LIGHTHOUSE

DEE MARKWITH

Table of Contents

Chapter One

"Well, it looks like it's your lucky day," Jose grumbled, walking past her without a glance.

"What's that supposed to mean?" she asked, her eyebrows raised quizzically.

Jose had called her the night before, asking her to meet him alone in his office at 8:00 am sharp. She'd spent most of the night tossing and turning, unable to sleep for fear of what the meeting was about. He'd offered no details, and since staff meetings always took place on Monday mornings, his request for a one-on-one Friday morning meeting was an unsettling surprise. His "lucky day" remark slightly assuaged her anxiety, yet she steeled herself for bad news, regardless. *OCD Cleaning* had a high turnover rate, in part due to Jose's mercurial nature, and she hoped she wasn't next on the chopping block.

"You're taking over the Matson account," Jose replied, taking a seat at his desk and opening his laptop.

"Oh, thank God," Lily sighed quietly, the tension releasing from her body.

"Don't thank God, thank me," Jose snarled.

A portly Hispanic man in his mid-fifties, Jose's pneumatic office chair sunk under his weight. As always, his thin hair was combed over in a poor attempt to hide his bald crown. He'd clearly begun balding years ago, and she suspected he'd been sporting that same desperate comb-over for the last two decades. She'd never seen him without his mustache, and she figured that was just as old, if not older, than his wispy head of hair. He sat with his plain white t-shirt tucked in, his large belly spilling over to hide the belt he was wearing. Jose always had the same unenthused look, as if life had beaten every ounce of joy from him. He was a no-nonsense man who never seemed to smile and likely hadn't laughed in years. She never felt comfortable around him, as he was ill-tempered and prone to angry outbursts, often berating his employees over minor infractions. She'd once seen him make a worker cry just for showing up three minutes late. Lily tried to keep her interactions with him brief, for fear he'd lash out at her as well.

"That's Jeanine's account," Lily said, confused.

"*Was* Jeanine's account," Jose corrected. He still hadn't looked at her. Powering on his laptop, he sat with his arms crossed, his eyes fixed on the screen as he waited for it to boot up.

"What do you mean?" she asked, fearing she already knew the answer.

"I fired her yesterday. Caught her stealing from the storeroom."

Lily didn't want to poke the bear, so to speak, but curiosity got the better of her. "Stealing? What did she steal?"

"What does it matter?" Jose spat. "She stole, and that's it! I have no tolerance for thieves."

"You couldn't just give her a warning?" Lily questioned cautiously, knowing there was nothing of any great value in the storeroom. It was mostly just mops, brooms, buckets, and other various cleaning supplies. She braced herself for one of Jose's tantrums, but to her surprise, it didn't come.

"Somebody steals once, they're going to steal again. Like I said, I have no tolerance for thieves." He paused to finally make eye contact with her and added, "Let this be a lesson to you."

Offended, she felt her face grow warm and her heart began to race. She'd never stolen anything in her life and didn't appreciate Jose's warning. This wasn't the first time he'd cautioned her against theft, and she couldn't help but feel it was because of her skin color.

"Look, I'm not a th—" she started, only to be cut off by Jose.

"Yeah, yeah. You're not a thief. I get it. That's what they all say. Look, do you want the Matson account or not? You'll be taking over Jeanine's shifts, 9:00 am to 3:00 pm on Mondays and Fridays. It comes with a nice pay raise. An extra two hundred dollars a week in your pocket, and you only have to work two days a week. Pretty sweet deal, if you ask me."

Desperately needing the money, she swallowed her anger and calmed herself with a deep breath. "Yes, yes, I do. Thank you."

"Good, because you start today," Jose said, turning his attention back to his laptop.

"But what about the Hilton?" Lily asked, referencing her current obligation. The *Hilton* hotel next to Tucson's airport was where she'd been cleaning since she first took the job six months prior. While she initially hated the position for the memories she had there, she'd grown numb to it and found herself going through the motions in a sort of daze five days a week. This would be her first time cleaning an actual home, and if the rumors were to be believed, it wasn't your average house.

"We have enough people there as it is," Jose replied, typing away on his keyboard. Lily assumed he was replying to emails, which was his typical morning routine. "They won't miss having you there." He paused to pull a small notepad from his desk drawer and jotted something down. "Here," he said, tearing off the sheet and handing it to her. "It's the address. Be there by 9:00 am. Tell security you're with OCD Cleaners. They should let you in. I already called to tell them about the change."

"Okay…" Lily trailed off, noting the address scribbled on the paper.

"And remember what happened to Jeanine," Jose said flatly, returning to his keyboard.

Just because I'm black doesn't mean I'm a thief, you racist piece of shit, is what she wanted to say. It took every ounce of restraint she could muster not to lose her cool.

"Yes, sir," she replied, turning to leave.

She hurried to the parking lot, eager to put distance between her and her boss, and breathed a sigh of relief when she sank into the familiar seat of her 1998 Toyota Corolla. Cosmetically, it was nothing to look at, but it was mechanically sound enough to get from Cleveland to Tucson nine months prior, and it had been getting her around the city just fine since her arrival.

Tucson, Arizona. She still couldn't believe she was there, and all for a man she'd met online. They'd found each other through an online dating website, which she wasn't proud of, but given her busy schedule as a full-time nanny to a spoiled seven-year-old boy, she didn't have much free time to meet people in the real world. It didn't help that at only twenty-six years old, she didn't care for the bar or club scene. An avid reader since childhood, she preferred to spend what little time she had to herself with her nose in a book. Her small social circle had stopped inviting her out, knowing she'd rather spend the night in with whatever work of non-fiction had caught her eye. She wasn't much for alcohol and leaned toward the intellectual side, tearing through anything historical or scientific to sate her appetite for knowledge.

Further complicating any attempt at a dating life, she still lived at home with her parents. They didn't mind having her, and for the most part, she didn't mind their arrangement. She made decent money as a nanny to an affluent couple's bratty son, so they let her stay, knowing it would help her save for her schooling faster. As much as she loved learning, she also loved teaching and had aspirations of teaching children someday. For years, she couldn't decide what she wanted to do with her life. It wasn't until twenty-five that she finally realized her calling. With her mother a librarian and her father a mechanic, they didn't make enough money between them to help further her education. Lily believed that guilt was why they welcomed her to stay for free, refusing her attempts to pay rent. Regardless, it was their house and their rules, and she was sure the last thing they wanted was for her to bring home a man. She respected that, but also found herself missing companionship. She'd never had a serious boyfriend, and at her age, she knew that probably wasn't healthy. Online dating seemed like a way for her to possibly connect with somebody like-minded; somebody who might fill that inherent human desire for affection.

As an attractive yet modest woman, her online dating profile garnered much interest, though it was usually from the wrong people. She'd lost count of the crude messages she'd received, or messages from men who appeared to be functionally illiterate. She'd all but given up on the online dating when she received a message from Ryan Carter, a handsome thirty-two-year-old white man from Tucson, Arizona who had taken the time to read and appreciate her entire profile. Most men didn't seem to bother, only messaging her based on the eight photos she'd been allowed to upload. Ryan immediately piqued her curiosity, as his message was so well-written and composed. A look at his profile revealed that it was worded just as well, and that he was a man with substance and depth. He'd listed his hobbies and interests, which mostly mirrored hers, but his distance made her reluctant to reply. She'd been hoping to find somebody local, not somebody 2,000 miles away. She told herself that he was simply too far, and intended to tell him that in her reply, which she felt he was owed since his introduction had been so sweet. In it, he'd chosen to compliment her mind instead of her looks, noting what a remarkable writer she was, and how he'd found her through their shared interest in learning. He'd even recognized the distance between them, apologizing in advance if he was too far away. In her reply, she thanked him for his kind words and gently told him that their distance was just too great. That should have been where it ended, but it wasn't. Ryan had replied with a joke, and she'd responded with a laugh. He'd messaged her again with a question, and she'd returned it with an answer. Their back-and-forth messaging went from days to weeks, and from weeks to months, inevitably leading to phone and video calls that quickly turned romantic. They told each other everything, openly sharing their strengths and their weaknesses. He told her he had "small vessel disease," which was a shrinking of the blood vessels in his brain, causing him to occasionally slur his words; the slurring worsening as the day progressed. She didn't mind, however, as it didn't detract from his allure. In return, she confided that she had a benign tumor removed from her right breast three years earlier, resulting in a small scar that had left her a bit insecure when it came to intimacy. It could have been worse, she'd told him, as her aunt had a similar tumor that was cancerous. It had claimed her life after she'd wasted away to nothing from the chemotherapy, and although she was quite young at the time, Lily remembered how sick and frail she looked before she passed. Of course, Ryan had assured her that the scar didn't bother him in the least, and if anything, made her even more unique. At that moment, she thought that loving somebody you'd never met face-to-face might just be possible.

Lily found herself reading less, as their daily calls often lasted for hours. With their differing time zones, they settled on 8:00 pm Eastern Standard Time, since it worked well for them both. They usually stuck to phone calls, but once a week, they'd make it a video call so they could see each other. With every video call, Ryan would be sitting on a small bench just outside of his apartment, claiming it gave him a chance to enjoy the fresh air. He would occasionally duck out of frame, saying he was trying to pick up a lizard he'd spotted, or that he'd found an interesting rock. Even with the scorching Southwest summer heat and the heavy monsoon rain, he would invariably take his position on that same bench while she curled up in her favorite reading chair. She asked for a tour of his apartment more than once, but he'd always insisted it was "a little messy" and would quickly change the subject. She didn't press the issue since she hadn't given him a walk-through of her home out of respect for her parents' privacy. He was also so charming that she allowed herself to ignore any red flags she might have otherwise lingered on.

She'd surprised herself by being the first to suggest meeting each other in person. A year earlier, she would have never considered such a thing, yet there she was, nervously ready to meet the man she'd become so enamored with. Ryan was quite receptive to the idea, but given his position as a regional manager for the *Circle K* chain of convenience stores, he couldn't get the time off from work. He explained that his duties were quite important and that he'd already exhausted both his sick and vacation days taking care of his ailing mother, who lived just around the corner from his apartment complex. He had brought up his mother's poor health shortly after they'd started talking and had addressed it several times since. She'd taken him at his word, even though she didn't recall him mentioning any time off from work.

With Ryan traveling to Cleveland out of the question, along with the possibility of meeting halfway, Lily knew the only real option was for her to make the bold move of heading to Tucson. She had more than enough money saved up, and with the holidays approaching, she knew she'd have a few days off from work. With a little planning, she was sure she could pull off a brief trip to Tucson and be back just in time to spend Christmas with her family, but the decision didn't come easily. She did trust Ryan, and talking to him was always the highlight of her day, but there was still a niggling doubt in the deep recesses of her mind that she could never quite shake. As well as she thought she knew him, she had to remind herself that she'd never truly know him until they spent time together. What if he'd been hiding things from her? She tried her best to shake that thought from her mind, replacing it with the regret she'd have if she didn't go and missed out on what could have been a beautiful—and possibly lifelong—romance. She believed there was a very good chance he was the man she was destined to be with, and with that belief guiding her, she finally made her decision. After an entire week of deliberation, she told Ryan that she had enough faith in him to make the journey. To her surprise, Ryan pushed for her to simply pack her car and drive there, insisting they were ready to live together. He'd promised her his commitment and assured her she'd have no problem landing a good job that would allow her to quickly recover the money she'd spend relocating. He'd already told her about the University of Arizona, and he reiterated that it would be the perfect place for her to pursue a degree in teaching. He painted a beautiful picture of the life they could live together, but despite Lily's strong feelings, there was no way she was going to move across the country for a man she'd never met in person. She found a gentle way to convey that to him, and although he sounded disappointed, he understood where she was coming from.

Her parents knew about Ryan since he'd become such a big part of her life, but they were quite opposed to the idea of her risking her money and safety on a 2,000-mile flight to visit a man she'd met online. Of course, she couldn't blame them since it did sound ludicrous, but she knew she'd spend the rest of her life wondering what could have been if she didn't take the gamble. He could be a disappointment, or he could be everything she wanted. There was only one way to find out.

With Ryan sharing her nervous excitement, she booked the flight during one of their evening phone calls. She booked it two weeks in advance so it would be cheaper, and Ryan had promised to pick her up at the airport, going on about how thrilled he was to finally hold her in his arms. They continued their daily phone calls as usual, both giddy with anticipation and counting down the days until her arrival. Ryan would go over his ideas for their time together, and Lily would delight in hearing all the fun, romantic things he had planned. A trip to the Desert Museum, a drive up historic Mt. Lemmon, horseback riding at Tanque Verde Ranch, a picnic in Agua Caliente Park… the list went on, and she was on board with it all. She had no idea what or where any of these places were, so she'd Google them while he spoke, grinning wide as she envisioned them together at each spot. She'd throw in her own ideas as well, like dining at an authentic Mexican restaurant and touching a real, live cactus, and he was more than happy to indulge her every whim. She would only be there for four days, and in those four days, they wanted to do as much as possible.

The evening before her flight, Ryan had unexpectedly asked that she book a hotel for her stay. She felt a wave of disappointment and confusion since she'd planned on staying with him like they'd discussed. He explained that his mother was temporarily staying at his place as her illness had grown worse, and that they'd be better off avoiding the situation entirely. He would still have to work and check in on his mother, he told her, but would spend every free moment he had with her. She was fine with that, but baffled when he asked her to rent a car. His car had been acting up, he said, and was likely going to end up in the shop. This sudden change didn't sit right with her, but she ignored her instincts and booked both a hotel and a rental car anyhow. The trip had just grown more expensive, dipping further into her savings account. Still, she woke early the following morning, and with her bags packed, slipped into the outfit she'd carefully selected for her first encounter with Ryan. Around her neck, she'd clasped the silver lighthouse necklace her grandmother had given her shortly before she passed. Lily would often rub it when she was nervous, and as the only sentimental piece of jewelry she owned, she rarely left the house without it.

After a double-check to make sure she hadn't forgotten anything, she had requested an Uber since her parents couldn't drive her to the airport. They earned a meager yet respectable living, and neither of them could afford to take time off from work. Lily had seen them before they'd left for the day, and they'd pleaded with her to remain cautious, insisting she call them the moment she landed. She promised she would, and once she'd reached the airport, she sent Ryan a short text message informing him that she was boarding the plane and would see him soon. He texted back that his car had ended up in the shop after all, but assured her that he would find a ride and meet her at the airport as planned. With that, she anxiously departed for Tucson, hoping he wouldn't let her down.

She'd only flown twice before, and those were short flights to visit her grandmother in Tennessee before they'd found a nursing home for her in Cleveland. She spent most of the flight nervously rubbing her lighthouse pendant for good luck, and when the plane began its descent, she craned her neck to look out the window at the Southwestern landscape below. She didn't realize just how mountainous the area was and sat with her jaw agape as she took in as much as she could.

After deboarding, she made her way to the baggage claim, worrying that Ryan wouldn't be there. A sense of panic began to set in as she played out possible scenarios in her mind, all of them bad. What if he had just been playing her, or got cold feet and backed out? The panic heightened, but she managed to shove it down deep.

Needing a moment to calm down, and remembering her promise to her parents, she stepped aside to let them know she'd made it safely, and knowing they were still at work, sent the same "Just arrived in Tucson!" text message to both of their phones. As eager as she was to find Ryan, she waited for a moment, giving them time to reply. It only took a few seconds for her mother to respond, thanking her for the update and once again reminding her to stay cautious. She was in the middle of replying "will do" when Ryan messaged her to let her know he'd found a ride and was there waiting for her. Her father wasn't big on texting and rarely checked his phone while working, so she didn't wait for his reply. She knew he'd get around to it when he could.

Stuffing her phone back in her handbag, she felt her heart begin to race as she continued toward the baggage claim. To say she was nervous would be an understatement, but that nervousness vanished the second she saw Ryan standing by the baggage carousel with a single red rose in his hand and a backpack slung over one shoulder. She immediately picked him out of the small crowd that had gathered to scoop up their luggage, and the moment their eyes met, they both smiled wide. She'd hurried into his waiting arms, feeling his warm embrace while noting his faint smell of cigarette smoke. He'd told her about the smoking early on, which would usually have been a huge turn-off for her, but he insisted he only smoked when he was nervous, which wasn't very often. She was able to overlook the smell, telling him how surreal it felt to be in Tucson with the man she'd spent every day talking to for the last year. If she were being honest, the smell helped lend to the reality of the moment, which was quickly setting in.

She'd accepted the rose and had paused to hold it to her nose, inhaling its sweet scent. They both took a step back to look each other over while they continued to process the excitement of finally being together. He was every bit as handsome as she expected, and by how many compliments he'd heaped on her as he looked her up and down, she knew that she'd lived up to his expectations as well. Standing 5'6" with flowing black hair that fell to the small of her back, her curves fit nicely into the light pink sundress she'd decided to wear after Ryan had reminded her that a Tucson winter was *not* the same as a Cleveland winter. As an accent, she'd managed to find a light pink flower hair clip that matched her dress, and she'd chosen to wear it above her right ear. For earrings, she'd selected white hoops, and her lighthouse necklace glimmered under the bright airport lights. Although she'd been told a few times over the years that heels made her legs look even sexier, she'd opted to wear white flats with light pink laces, completing the theme she'd settled on.

Lily had always been busty and could tell Ryan was trying not to glance at her cleavage, which was on full display thanks to her dress riding down. She discreetly hiked it back up as she soaked in Ryan's charm. His hazel eyes locked onto her big, brown eyes, and a genuine smile painted his boyish face. He was a bit scruffy, which she didn't mind, and she could tell he'd attempted to style his short, dark brown hair. It also appeared he'd tried to dress up, wearing a red button-up shirt—that looked one size too big—tucked into a pair of faded blue jeans, which were conspicuously missing a belt. It was clear that fashion wasn't his top priority. Still, he was undeniably handsome, and the way he was looking at her tugged at her heart.

After Lily pointed out her luggage, Ryan insisted on grabbing it and carrying it for her while they walked toward the rental car agencies, his backpack still slung across his shoulder. Lily had felt a bit of nervousness return as they made idle chit-chat, and she suspected he was also on edge. They were still getting used to the real-world versions of each other, but by the time they'd reached their rental car, they were joking around like old friends. Since he knew his way around Tucson, she'd offered to let him drive, but he'd reminded her that the rental car policy only allowed her behind the wheel. That made sense to her, and as they stuffed her luggage and his backpack into the trunk, he once again apologized for his car trouble. She assured him she understood and reminded him that her father was a mechanic. As a child, she'd spent a great deal of time in his shop and knew all about car trouble.

She couldn't believe how warm and sunny the Southwest was in December and understood why Ryan had told her to dress accordingly. While it was 6:00 pm in Cleveland, it was only 4:00 pm in Tucson and there was still an abundance of daylight. She was just as much in awe of the weather as she was of the cacti and palm trees she'd been greeted with when she'd pulled out of the parking lot. He affectionately placed his hand on her right thigh, and she found herself smiling wide again as he guided her to the nearby Hilton, where she'd reserved a room for the following four days. He assured her he'd be spending as much time with her as possible, so she'd secured a room with two beds and hoped he wouldn't find it awkward. Thankfully, he seemed just fine with it, and after dropping off her luggage and his backpack, Lily took a few moments to freshen up. Ryan fished around in his backpack for a bottle of water, and she listened attentively while he told her more about the city.

They'd decided on dinner together at *Amelia's Mexican Kitchen*, an authentic Mexican restaurant that was a bit of a drive, but it gave her a chance to bask in the overwhelming beauty of the Catalina Mountains. Lily had only been in Tucson for a little over an hour, yet she'd already fallen in love with the place. Seventy degrees in December was definitely something she could get used to. Over dinner, they'd grown more comfortable with each other and she delighted in spending time with someone so well-spoken and intelligent. Although she'd already asked him this over the course of their long-distance courtship, she once again questioned why he was working for Circle K when he was capable of so much more. He was used to it there, he'd shrugged, and he liked how close it was to his home. She felt the same ache of disappointment she had the first time she'd asked him this, and wished he had greater aspirations. He seemed to lack drive and motivation, but she felt that was something she could help him develop in time.

After dinner—which Lily had paid for since Ryan had mistakenly left his wallet in his backpack at the hotel—she had excused herself for a moment and made her way to the bathroom where she sent a follow-up text message to her mother letting her know that she felt safe around Ryan. She also noted a text message from her father, who had replied with only a thumbs-up emoji to the "Just arrived in Tucson!" update she'd sent earlier. At fifty-five years old, her father wasn't very savvy when it came to modern technology. He was a mechanical whiz and could fix any car problem imaginable, yet could barely type a sentence on a cell phone. Shaking her head with a smile, she slid her phone back into her handbag and returned to Ryan.

On the short walk to the car, Ryan had asked if they could quickly stop at a store to pick up a few drinks for the night ahead. It would loosen them up, he'd said, and even though she generally avoided alcohol, Lily had agreed that some social lubricant was a good idea. She was comfortable around him, though not fully, and felt she could open up completely if she were more relaxed. He directed them to a *Fry's* supermarket and had followed her inside to point out what he wanted for alcohol, wasting no time finding a large bottle of vodka. Liquor didn't sit well with her, so she'd carefully selected a bottle of white wine, but Ryan had insisted a box of wine was a better choice since it would last through her stay. She certainly hadn't planned on drinking the entire trip, but Ryan persisted and she'd reluctantly buckled to his pleading, puppy dog eyes. Since his ID was back at the hotel in his wallet, he told her he'd pay her back for the drinks and waited for her outside.

Back at the hotel, Ryan hastily poured himself some vodka using one of their room's complementary plastic cups. Lily was surprised by how much he'd filled it, and that he didn't use a mixer or need a chaser. She poured herself half a cup of the boxed wine, sipping it slowly as they sat at the small round table situated in the corner beside their beds. Alcohol always made her sleepy, and she was already tired from her long day of traveling. She knew she needed to pace herself or she'd end up spoiling the night by falling asleep too early. Ryan, on the other hand, took big swigs of his vodka, and soon had to refill his cup. The alcohol did loosen them both up, however, and the conversation flowed, though not as freely as Lily would have liked. She was comfortable around Ryan but hadn't quite reached the level of comfort she'd hoped for. When she'd asked Ryan if he was worried about a hangover since he had to work the following day, he once again surprised her by announcing he'd managed to get the following four days off. She was mildly irked by this since she'd traveled to him under the pretense he wasn't able to take any time off.

Lily drank more than she'd intended, which might have been a subconscious effort to keep up with Ryan. She had a good buzz going, but she refused to cross over into drunk territory, wanting to keep her senses and guard up just in case things went awry. She felt safe around Ryan, yet remained alert, knowing his demeanor could change as he grew increasingly intoxicated. She'd seen people go from warm and friendly to cruel and violent when they were drinking, and she didn't want to end up in a bad situation.

They had sat for hours, talking about anything and everything before calling it a night. When she changed into her white silk pajamas and climbed into bed, Ryan—fully drunk at this point—had climbed into bed with her. Although it was uninvited, she found she didn't mind and allowed him to curl up next to her. He'd stripped down to just his boxers, and she'd enjoyed feeling his warmth pressed against her. It had been three years since she'd slept next to a man, and she hadn't realized how much she'd missed it. She was also impressed by Ryan's restraint, as he made no attempt to advance on her sexually, remaining respectful as he quickly fell asleep holding her. She could hear him snoring faintly, but the sound was somehow comforting and helped lull her to sleep as well.

Over the next three days, they spent their time together exploring Tucson and checking off everything planned on their list. Each day was filled with something new and exciting and ended with them having drinks back in their hotel room. Ryan's words would slur as the night went on, and he'd occasionally space out, but she'd grown used to it by now and knew it was due to the small vessel disease he'd told her about. It was on the third day during their picnic at Agua Caliente Park when Ryan finally made his move. Leaning in to kiss her, she didn't shy away but wished she'd felt more of a spark. She had also smelled something on his breath that she couldn't quite identify, but it wasn't enough to stop another kiss.

She enjoyed Ryan's company immensely, but as their third full day together drew to a close, she still wasn't sure if the chemistry was really there or if she was just fooling herself into believing it was. One thing she was sure of, however, was that she'd completely fallen for the Southwest. The culture and landscape radically differed from what she'd grown up with, and she still couldn't get over the mild winter temperatures. She found herself sweating in the sun on a few occasions, which wasn't something she'd ever experienced during the winter. Claiming it was to avoid how dehydrated he'd get during the bone-dry winter months, Ryan carried a large water bottle with him at all times and suggested she do the same. That seemed a bit overboard to her, but she did carry a small bottle in her handbag.

It was her final night there, and they'd spent the latter part of the day stealing kisses from each other. She had readied herself for him to at least try to seduce her sexually—which she wouldn't have allowed anyhow—yet he'd simply drifted off to sleep holding her the same as he had the previous nights. Perhaps he was just being a gentleman, she thought, or he wasn't ready to be intimate with her yet. A part of her worried he wasn't interested, but the kisses he'd showered her with throughout the day seemed to say otherwise. She tried not to let it bother her since they'd known each other in person for only four days.

The following morning, she began packing her things while Ryan watched with a look of sadness. She was scheduled to leave that evening, meaning they still had several hours left together, but she needed to check out of the hotel by 11:00 am. Making sure they hadn't left anything behind, Ryan had slung his backpack over his shoulder, grabbed her luggage, and just like he had at the airport, carried everything to their rental car while she lingered in the lobby to check out. She'd met him at the car and they'd once again stuffed her luggage and his backpack into the trunk before settling into the vehicle. He leaned over the center console for a kiss before asking how she'd like to spend the remainder of their time together. Since he hadn't offered to show her his apartment yet, Lily took it upon herself to ask if she could see it but Ryan quickly shot the idea down. His mother was extremely old-fashioned, he'd explained, and wouldn't appreciate anyone seeing her in her weakened state. She was the kind of woman who would dress to the nines and tidy up her home before having company over, he went on. Lily had met people like that before, so she understood and didn't press the issue. Throughout her visit, Ryan had been good about checking up on his mother through text messages, stepping away a few times to call her, and Lily adored him for it. Family was important to her, and by his actions, she could tell it was important to him as well.

With time to kill before her flight home, Lily had suggested grabbing a bite to eat since they'd slept through the hotel's complimentary breakfast yet again. Over the course of her visit, Ryan had expressed concern over his vehicle's repair costs a handful of times, worrying he wouldn't be able to afford it, and in doing so, had guilted Lily into paying for every meal. The restaurants he'd chosen for them were quite pricey, and she hadn't been thrilled about pulling more money from her savings, but she'd convinced herself the memories they were making were worth it. This time, however, she asked that they go somewhere a bit cheaper since she'd already gone so far over budget. Ryan had pointed the way to *Eegee's*, a local Tucson favorite specializing in sandwiches and salads, and it was halfway through their meal when Lily decided to ask Ryan how he truly felt about her. Even though they'd shared dozens of kisses by now, Lily still couldn't gauge his feelings, and if she were being honest, she was bothered that he hadn't tried to move on her sexually. She worried he wasn't attracted to her in that way and was just stringing her along with kisses until she left, but he assured her that he found her incredibly sexy, claiming she was easily the most beautiful woman he'd ever met. She'd blushed at this while he went on to explain that he'd been tamping his sexual urges, fearing she'd think he'd asked her there just to get laid. He wanted more than sex, he continued, and thought it best to wait until they were ready to take the next step. When she asked what that next step was, she couldn't stop smiling when he replied, "A committed relationship." He'd given her the answer she'd been hoping for, and they spent the rest of their meal discussing the logistics of building a future together. As predicted, she was left to foot the bill with Ryan promising he'd pay her back with his next paycheck. If his car repair ate that paycheck up, he told her he'd pay her back with the next one. Either way, he assured her that she would definitely be getting reimbursed. She'd felt a pang of skepticism every time he said this, but it always melted away when she looked at his boyish, almost innocent face. He was easy to trust. Too easy.

With another two hours to kill before her flight, they'd agreed to window shop at the *Park Place Mall*, walking hand in hand while stopping for an occasional kiss. They weren't ready to let each other go, but both knew the time had come, and with emotions running high, began heading toward the airport. In a final attempt to at least catch a glimpse of Ryan's apartment complex, she'd offered to drop him off there since his car was still in the shop, but he was adamant about seeing her off properly and assured her he could find a ride home. Reaching the airport, she returned the rental car and he helped her with her luggage again, his backpack hanging from one shoulder as they made their way through the terminal. Of course, they had to part ways just outside of the security checkpoint since he wasn't allowed to wait with her at her gate, and she'd fought back tears as they stood holding hands, sharing a few final kisses as they said their goodbyes. She'd felt a sense of relief that Ryan hadn't dropped the "I love you" bomb because, as much as she cared for him, she wasn't ready to say those words back. She promised to let him know when she landed in Cleveland, and with that, she had turned to await her flight home.

They resumed their daily phone calls and weekly video calls, often reminiscing on their wonderful time together. Lily had returned to her nanny position and had begun recouping the money she'd spent on her tryst with Ryan, who still hadn't sent her a dime of what he owed her. The nanny job paid well, and without any rent to pay, it didn't take long for her to rebound financially. She forgave Ryan's debt when he told her his car had crapped out completely. He claimed he'd been pinching pennies to buy a new one, and she thought it best that he focus solely on that.

As the weeks wore on, she grew increasingly frustrated by Cleveland's bitter-cold winter temperatures and gray, gloomy sky. She'd been spoiled by Tucson, missing its sunshine and warmth, and couldn't imagine ever tiring of its scenic mountain views. Unlike Cleveland, you could see for many miles in the Southwest, and she'd found the openness liberating. Cleveland now seemed restrictive and claustrophobic to her, feeling more like a frigid, snowy prison. Ryan had been pushing for her to move in with him, and the idea proved too hard to resist. When she'd broken the news to her parents, they hadn't fought her on it like she'd expected. She'd spent so much time going on and on about Tucson and Ryan, they'd explained, that they had already braced themselves for the inevitable. She had their blessing as long as she kept in weekly contact and enrolled at the University of Arizona as promised. They were sure to remind her, however, that should something go wrong, they couldn't afford to bail her out of trouble. Lily had offered to pay them rent dozens of times over the years to help ease their financial burden, but they'd insisted she keep every penny of her earnings so she could further her education like they wished they had done. A part of Lily wondered if they were looking forward to finally having an empty nest.

She'd miss the money from her job as a nanny but wouldn't miss the spoiled child, that much she was sure of. Her parents asked that she stay until the end of May since they didn't want her driving across the country in the winter, but knowing the weather wouldn't take long to improve once she started driving South, she insisted on leaving as soon as she finished her final two weeks as a nanny. Those two weeks gave her time to plan for the long trip ahead; a trip that both frightened and excited her. Anything could go wrong on a 2,000-mile drive alone. In contrast, there was the thrill of the open road and seeing more of the country. She wished Ryan could make the trip with her, but he'd made a good argument for a flight to Cleveland being another unnecessary expense. Since she'd become so reclusive, she didn't have any friends willing to make the journey, either. As always, her mother and father couldn't afford the time off of work to help her with the drive, and they worried about such a pretty girl traveling the country alone. When she'd told them about the move, they assumed it would be in the early summer and would involve a moving truck with Ryan as co-pilot. Her cramming what little she could into her car and making the drive herself in the winter was not what they'd had in mind, but she'd made her decision, and whether or not they approved, that decision was final.

Her father had fully inspected and serviced her car, giving it a thumbs-up for the long-distance drive, and when the big day finally arrived, Lily woke before sunrise to fill her vehicle with as much as she could fit. She told her parents she'd reimburse them if they shipped the rest, or would just come back to get it at some point, hopefully with Ryan since it would give them both a chance to finally meet him. She was leaving early so they could see her off before heading to work, and as they took turns embracing her outside in the cold winter air—each planting a kiss on her left cheek—they'd sternly instructed her to call them with an update every chance she got. They would be worried sick, her mother had said with tears beginning to flow, and Lily could feel them shivering as they both hugged her one more time. She was shivering too, and welcomed the warmth of her car, which she'd left running to defrost her icy windshield. She'd already entered the address Ryan had given her into her cell phone's GPS, and as she backed out of the driveway, she rolled down her window to wave a final goodbye. She hadn't told them that she'd hidden one thousand dollars in a kitchen drawer as a thank you for their support and generosity over the years. Had she simply presented it to them, she knew they wouldn't have accepted it, and she planned on telling them where to find it when she arrived in Tucson.

Heading toward the interstate with a tank full of gas, she couldn't help but think of how crazy it was for her to be moving across the country for a man she'd met online. She shook her head in disbelief, asking herself what she was doing as doubts began to creep in. It was too late to back out now, though. She was doing it. She was heading to Arizona.

Chapter Two

She snapped out of her recollections with a shudder and looked at the paper in her hand. The last thing she needed to be thinking about was Ryan. Pulling her phone from her handbag, she entered the address Jose had scribbled into the same GPS that had guided her to Tucson and had been helping her around the city for the last nine months. She was slowly learning to navigate the area on her own, but given its enormous size, she still relied heavily on her GPS. When Jose had asked to meet with her, she never expected to be given such a heavy responsibility. This was her first home cleaning assignment, and if Jeanine's stories were to be believed, it was one heck of a job. It also meant that Jose trusted her over the rest of his crew, even though she'd only been with the business for six months. Then again, she mused, six months was fairly long given how fast he went through cleaners. Still, she felt honored that he'd trusted her with such an important account.

Jeanine, a fiery Latina, had gushed about Austin Matson so often that Lily had grown tired of hearing his name and often rolled her eyes whenever it was mentioned. She'd heard all about his lavish four-story estate in the foothills that boasted an elevator, a collection of expensive cars, an auditorium-size home theater, an ornate rosewood wet bar stocked with the finest liquors and wines, and a helipad for his own private helicopter. Jeanine was prone to embellishing stories, however, so Lily never knew what to believe and took her co-worker's word with a grain of salt. Jeanine was the only person Lily might consider a friend in Tucson, but they weren't very close by any means and were still getting to know each other. Getting fired is never fun, so with her phone mounted to its usual spot on her dashboard, she dialed Jeanine to see how she was holding up.

"Hey, girl," Jeanine answered. "I'm assuming you heard the news?"

"I did," Lily replied. "Jose just told me. I'm so sorry."

"Am I on speaker?" Jeanine asked.

"Yeah, sorry. I'm driving."

"To the Hilton?" Jeanine questioned in a puzzled tone. "Aren't you way late?"

"Well…" Lily began. She hadn't thought about how Jeanine would react to her taking over her job. Not wanting to lie, she decided to come clean and let it out. "Jose asked me to take over the Matson account."

To her relief, Jeanine didn't sound upset. "Good for you, girl," she replied. "Try to get in on that action. He's one *fine* lookin' white boy!"

"Stop!" Lily laughed. "Not interested."

"You should be," Jeanine rocketed back. "He's hot and rich as fuck!"

"So you've mentioned," Lily replied. *So you've told me a million times*, she wanted to add but held back. Even though she knew the answer, she wanted to change the subject. "Why did Jose let you go? I don't get it."

Jeanine groaned and explained, "He said I stole some shit. I don't know. He's stoopit."

Lily always chuckled whenever Jeanine pronounced "stupid" as "stoopit" in her thick Latina accent.

"Well," Lily started, still chuckling, "did you?"

"Okay, I took *one* roll of toilet paper. Just one roll! Like, who cares about one fucking roll?"

"*Just* one roll?" Lily questioned skeptically.

"Alright, it might have been an entire case," Jeanine confessed. "Still… who cares, right? It's just toilet paper. He's such a cheap piece of shit!"

"It's still stealing," Lily pointed out. Realizing she sounded like a moralistic prig, she regretted letting the words escape her so quickly.

"Oh my God, I can't believe you're siding with him," Jeanine hissed.

"I'm not siding wi—"

Jeanine cut her off with, "Ah, you can get fucked too, you goody-two-shoes bitch."

With that, she hung up, abruptly ending the call and severing the only friendship Lily thought she had made in the city.

"Well, there goes that," Lily groaned. Even though they weren't very tight, it still hurt losing the one person she'd connected with. She tried not to let it dampen her mood and continued on her way to Austin Matson's address, which, according to her GPS, was located at the foot of the Catalina Mountains to the north. After a thirty-minute drive that took her to the outskirts of the city, she approached the security checkpoint leading to Austin Matson's residence, stopping just before the gate to announce herself to the guard.

"Name?" the man asked flatly, taking one step out of his booth to carefully look her over.

"Lily Ward," she replied with a warm smile. "From OCD Cleaners."

"And you're here for…" the guard trailed off, reaching for his clipboard and trailing his eyes down what she assumed was a residency list.

"Austin Matson," she answered, suddenly feeling a sense of nervousness even though she was supposed to be there.

"Okay," the guard said with a smile. He pressed the gate release and motioned for her to freely pass through. "Welcome to Eleven Arches Estates. You're good to go."

Lily had expected the winding uphill road to lead solely to Austin Matson's home and hadn't known she'd be entering a small community of what appeared to be Tucson's most affluent socialites. As her GPS guided her on, she passed one multi-million dollar home after another, struggling to remain unimpressed. She'd only seen houses like these in movies and magazines, and now that she was seeing them in the real world, she found it hard not to stare in awe.

Despite growing up in a low-income household, Lily had never been impressed by fortune or fame, nor had she wished for that lifestyle herself. She was raised to be humble and modest, and although the extra income would have helped, she had even turned down several modeling offers over the years. She felt she was a bit too thick to make it as a model anyhow, and suspected the offers had been from men with ulterior motives. Either way, if she was going to find success, she wanted to find it using her mind, not her looks. It was character that mattered the most in life, not the material or superficial. Still, she couldn't pry her eyes from these lavish homes and decided it was okay to admire them as long as that admiration didn't turn into envy.

She slowed her speed to a crawl so she could soak in their extravagance, and snapped out of her awe when her GPS instructed her to turn into a wide, freshly-paved driveway on her right. Shortly after turning, she was greeted by a mechanical wrought-iron gate that opened as she approached, seeming to invite her in. As she pressed on down the long driveway lined with high shrubbery, the Austin Matson residence came into full view and trounced the homes she'd just seen. This wasn't a house, it was a four-story adobe mansion that stretched into the surrounding foothills and high into the sky, radiating wealth and reflecting the importance of the owner.

The property's meticulous landscaping was rife with flourishing trees and flowers, but she wasn't versed enough in dendrology or botany to identify them. She did, however, recognize the saguaro and prickly pear cacti—the two cacti names she knew—that had also been strategically placed alongside a variety of decorative rocks and stones.

The upkeep on the landscaping alone must cost a small fortune, she mused as she rolled to a stop. The spacious driveway ended in a circle with a large fountain in the middle, shooting water from its center like a geyser. Parked on the outside arc of the round driveway was a black Ferrari that had likely come from one of the three garage doors on the far right of the sprawling estate. She tried to resist, but she couldn't help but marvel at its sleek curves reflecting the late morning sun. It had been positioned in front of the home's tall double doors, leading her to believe the owner would be taking it for a spin soon. She had a feeling that owner was Austin Matson.

Such a waste of money, Lily thought. It was the most expensive vehicle she'd ever seen by far. She tried to pry her eyes from it but there was an almost magnetic pull making avoidance impossible. *A beautiful waste of money, though.*

Lily settled on a place to park opposite the Ferrari where the water of the flowing fountain hid her car. She knew her old Toyota Corolla looked conspicuously out of place in such an opulent setting and was hit by an unexpected feeling of embarrassment. She scolded herself for it, reminding herself that there was nothing wrong with her vehicle and that it had more character than any luxury vehicle ever could.

She never wore much make-up, having heard her entire life that she was a natural beauty who didn't need any. Still, her current situation was making her a bit self-conscious, which was something she rarely felt since she was usually so confident in herself, though that confidence never crossed into arrogance. Amid such decadence, she felt woefully plain and fished around in her handbag for the small make-up kit she rarely used. For a moment, she didn't think it was in there. She had to dig deep to find it and used her car's sun visor mirror to apply a quick coat of eyeshadow, eyeliner, and mascara. A touch of blush was used to accentuate her prominent cheekbones, which was a trick she'd learned from her grandmother. She knew she had some red lipstick somewhere in her handbag, and was about to give up looking when she found it. Noting that she'd still managed to get there five minutes early, she stepped out of the car and readjusted her black polo work shirt that had *OCD Cleaners* embroidered in red lettering on the left breast. With the hot September sun beating down on her, she bent down to check her hair in her side-view mirror and noticed that her red lipstick coincidentally matched the lettering on her shirt.

Lily left her handbag in her car and slipped her cell phone into her pocket. Swallowing her nerves, she made her way around the fountain, briefly pausing to admire the Ferrari again. She took in the palatial estate one more time, looking up at its many windows and wondering how many rooms it boasted.

You'll find out soon enough, she reminded herself while heading up the three steps leading to the estate's grand double doors. They were made of solid wood and each featured a narrow glass window running down the center, allowing for a degree of visibility inside and out. Instead of a traditional lock, one of the tall doors was fitted with a keypad, allowing for keyless entry, and some sort of small black screen she decided was a fingerprint scanner. Two large terracotta vases were seated on both sides of the doors, and while empty, they still added a great decorative touch. Her eyes quickly found the doorbell and pressed it to signal her arrival. If the Sonoran Desert mansion was this luxurious on the outside, she couldn't begin to imagine what awaited her inside.

As she waited for an answer, she smoothed out her black work pants and added a bit of fluff to her hair, trying to give it a bit more life. It took a moment for one of the two doors to crack open, and when it did, she was greeted by an older man whose short, perfectly parted hair had turned completely white. He stood wearing thick horn-rimmed black glasses, and she could see the prominent wrinkles under his eyes behind them. He appeared to be in his seventies and stood wearing a burgundy three-button vest over a white dress shirt tucked into black slacks. His freshly polished burgundy penny loafers matched his vest splendidly, telling her he had a good eye for fashion.

"Mister Matson," Lily began before the man had a chance to speak. Offering her hand, she continued, "I'm Lilian Ward."

With a look of befuddlement, the man shook her hand and replied, "It's nice to meet you, Lilian Ward, but I haven't the faintest idea who you are."

Detecting the English accent in his soft voice, Lily broke the handshake and pointed at the embroidery on her shirt. "I'm with OCD Cleaners."

"Ah, yes," the man said, adjusting his glasses and leaning in closer to read the lettering. "And where, may I ask, is Jeanine?"

Confused and uncomfortable, Lily cleared her throat and explained, "I'm her replacement." She paused and added hesitantly, "Her permanent replacement, Mister Matson."

She hadn't expected Austin Matson to be so... old. Jeanine had painted him as youthful with rugged good looks, and although the man before her still had a charm to him, he was far from youthful or rugged. Her former coworker had clearly taken some creative liberty with her description.

"In the fifteen years I've been with him," the man said with a smile, "this is the first time I've ever been mistaken for Mister Matson."

He threw his head back and laughed while Lily covered her face in embarrassment, recognizing her mistake.

"Oh my goodness, I'm so sorry. I don't know why I assumed you—"

Still laughing, the man cut her off and dismissed the mix-up with a wave of his hand. "It's fine, my dear! I needed a good laugh today!"

The man's genuine laughter was infectious, and she burst into laughter as well. "I feel so stupid."

"Let's try this again, shall we?" the man asked with a kind smile. This time, he offered his hand to her and she accepted with a smile of her own. "Please, call me Winston. I'm Mister Matson's butler, but he prefers to call me his assistant."

"Well, it's nice to meet you, Winston," Lily replied with a playful curtsy.

"And you as well. Now, please, do come in."

When he stepped aside to motion her in, she could feel the estate's cool air-conditioning and welcomed the change from the desert heat outside. It had been so bright out that it took a moment for her eyes to adjust to the home's interior, and when they did, she let out an audible gasp as her jaw dropped.

Winston had guided her into an enormous open foyer with flooring that appeared to be sienna-brown marble tile with burnt umber veins. A large cream-colored rug with a dark tribal Aztec pattern—likely hand-woven and very expensive—covered a large portion of the floor and kept with the adobe mansion's Southwestern theme. Slightly larger than the ones outside by the front doors were two more terracotta vases positioned on both sides of a long bifurcated staircase with wooden steps and a black metal handrail leading to the second floor. The same marble tile flooring continued down a long hallway to her left, and down another long hallway to her right. The foyer was home to two rusted metal sculptures, both standing about her height; one, a seated coyote howling up at an implied moon, and the other a saguaro cactus with two arms, one shorter than the other. Between the two sculptures were steel elevator doors, again lending credibility to Jeanine's stories. So far, her former coworker hadn't seemed to exaggerate anything.

"I'll be damned," Lily muttered to herself. She returned her attention to the foyer, noting what appeared to be a full louver door beside the elevator, and walls had been faux-painted with three shades of clay using impressive sponge work. She counted at least six matching end tables placed against them, all topped with black metal lamps and various pictures. Several glass display cases also showcased what appeared to be a careful arrangement of items, but they were so far away that she couldn't quite make them out. Whatever they were, she was sure they were valuable. Along with end tables and display cases were more vases—these a dark brown—that contained a variety of plants she believed were real. A collection of paintings hung from the walls as well, all of them depicting familiar Southwestern scenery. She recognized the silhouette of the Catalina Mountain Range and a desert landscape peppered with cacti and vibrant flowers, but the others hung just out of view.

A look at the high ceiling above revealed six large skylights that filled the room with natural light and a giant wagon wheel chandelier. Like the lamps and stairway railing, it was also made of black metal and lined with a dozen lights inside frosted glass shades. She noticed security cameras mounted to the ceiling in every corner, keeping a watchful eye over the room. She had a feeling there were plenty more to be found around the property.

Although Lily had only seen a fraction of it, the enormity of the estate made her feel small. Such extravagance also made her feel out of place and even a little intimidated, which she chastised herself for with the reminder that none of these riches mattered; it was all superficial and didn't define a person. Her thoughts were interrupted by Winston, who had given her a moment to soak it all in.

"Beautiful, isn't it?"

"It's lovely," Lily replied with a polite smile, trying not to act or sound too impressed.

"I shall inform Mister Matson of the changes," Winston said, heading toward the elevator doors with a noticeable limp. "I'm sure he'll want to meet you."

"You mean he doesn't know?" Lily asked.

Reaching the elevator, Winston pressed the call button beside its doors and turned to face her. "I don't believe either of us were notified."

"Oh, I apologize. I thought my boss had told you."

"No worries, my dear. Please, wait here while I fetch Mister Matson."

With that, the elevator doors parted and closed after he stepped inside. As Winston disappeared from her sight, his words replayed in her mind: *I'm sure he'll want to meet you.*

It made sense that he'd want to feel her out before giving her free rein of his home. Left by herself, she stepped further into the room and daringly made her way to one of the glass display cases she'd seen. Inside, she found a carefully arranged selection of gems, all varying in size, shape, and color, crystal figurines, some sort of award for technical innovation, framed photographs of people she didn't recognize, a few vinyl records—presumably rare—and an antique pistol. Even though the display case appeared to be locked, she kept her hands clasped behind her back as a way of telling the watchful security cameras that she had no intention of stealing anything.

Moving to the other display case, she found similar items, but this one featured two more awards for technical and scientific achievements along with a framed copy of *Technology* magazine with the cover reading, "Billionaire Austin Matson's Quest for Quantum Processing." Rather than featuring a picture of Austin Matson, however, it featured a large stylized image of some sort of processor overlaying light blue binary code. Next to the magazine was an appreciation plaque from the mayor, propped up by a gold picture easel, recognizing Austin Matson for his sizable donations to the various hospitals in the area. Two more plaques from the fire and police department sat next to it, thanking him for his additional funding.

Slowly continuing around the room, she paused in front of each painting to admire the artwork. None of them were paned with glass, making it easier to see the brush strokes. She recognized the paint as oil and that each piece shared the same style, leading her to believe they were all created by the same artist. A painting opposite the stairway caught her eye. From where she'd been standing when she'd entered the estate, she hadn't been able to see it. This new vantage point brought it to her attention, and she moved in for a closer look. It was of Kokopelli, the Hopi figure known for his rounded back and flute, playing his tune under a moonlit desert sky. Her favorite of the paintings she'd seen, she got so lost in its artistry that she hadn't heard anyone approach her. A deep voice from behind her made her jump.

"Beautiful, isn't it?"

She turned to find a man towering over her with the most incredible steel-blue eyes she'd ever seen. They belonged to a face so handsome she immediately felt a fluttering sensation in her belly. She'd always thought the "butterflies in your stomach" thing was nonsense, but now that she was experiencing it for the first time, she finally understood the idiom. A strong, square jawline and high, pronounced cheekbones were that of a model, and his immaculately coiffed dark hair had a few strands hanging over his forehead in a curl, reminding her of the comic book Superman she'd grown up with. He appeared to be freshly shaven and stood looking at her with a warm smile, dressed to the nines in a black business suit over a crisp white dress shirt and a silk burgundy tie. A matching silk burgundy pocket square peeked out of the breast pocket of his suit jacket, and unable to break away from his piercing eyes, she had to assume his shoes were on point.

She guessed his height to be 6'2", and his broad upper body led to a narrow waistline, giving him that classic V-taper she'd always loved. He looked powerful, and his wide chest told her that a good amount of muscle was hiding under that suit. Fearing she'd be staring into his eyes a few seconds too long, it occurred to her that he'd been staring into hers just as long. She shook herself out of her daze and managed to find her voice.

"Yes, it is. I'm sorry, you startled me."

"My apologies," he replied in the same deep voice. He offered a big hand, and she could feel his strength when she shook it. "I'm Austin Matson."

"Lilian Ward," she returned, the butterflies still fluttering in her stomach. She realized she'd introduced herself using her full name, which is something she never did, and wondered if it was a reflexive attempt to sound more sophisticated. Although she was fighting it, she did feel outclassed in this man's home and presence. "It's nice to meet you."

"And you as well," he said, adding with a coy smile, "You've just become the most beautiful piece of art in here."

Did he just hit on you?

Unsure of how to react, she clumsily blurted, "I'm with OCD Cleaners."

"Yes, Winston told me. You're Jeanine's replacement, right?"

"I am," Lily replied, still stuck on his seemingly flirtatious remark. "Her permanent replacement, if you approve."

"Can I ask what happened?"

"It's probably best if you don't," Lily shrugged, not wanting to make Jose's business look bad. After all, he'd let a thief into a mansion loaded with valuables.

"Fair enough," Austin replied, looking her over. She used the time to look him over again as well, this time making her way down to his Italian leather loafers, their sheen suggesting a recent polish. Yes, his shoes were indeed on point. Lily wasn't sure if he was assessing her for the job or checking her out, but it felt like the latter.

The moment was interrupted by a chime, followed by the elevator doors parting. Winston limped his way out and made his way over to them.

"Forgive me," he said as he approached. "I had to use the little boys' room before I begin the tour. There's a lot to show, and I'm afraid I can't hold it like I used to."

Austin covered his eyes with his hand and chuckled as he shook his head. "Too much information, Winston."

"Oh, yes, I apologize, sir. Now, shall I begin the tour, or would you like more time with Miss Ward?"

"You know what? I think I'll give the tour today," Austin replied.

Winston seemed surprised by this sudden change. "I thought you were leaving for a meeting with—"

Austin put his hand up and stopped him. "The meeting can wait. Call Henry and reschedule for noon."

"Yes, sir," Winston nodded, limping back to the elevator. Before stepping inside, he turned to say, "I do hope you enjoy the tour, Miss Ward."

"Thank you," she replied, amused by the old man with the English accent.

When the doors closed behind him, Austin returned his attention to Lily. "He's something else, isn't he?"

"I love him," she smiled. "He's adorable."

"I had the elevator put in for him. His hip's shot and his prostate's in rough shape," Austin explained. "Poor guy's in and out of the bathroom every thirty minutes."

"How old is he?"

"He's eighty-two, believe it or not. I've been trying to get him to retire for years now but he refuses. Says he wouldn't know what to do with himself otherwise. He tells me working for me gives him a sense of purpose. His wife died twenty years ago, and he doesn't have any kids, so I'm sort of all he's got."

Lily was moved by Austin's compassion and loyalty. Instead of forcing the man out and hiring somebody younger, he spent what was likely a small fortune having an elevator installed in the home just for him.

"It's like the old saying goes," Lily began, "'when you slow down, you go down.'"

"I've never heard that before," Austin replied with a smile. "I like it."

"They say keeping busy is the key to living longer," she shrugged. "I'm not sure if there's any truth to it."

"I'm sure there is," he said, still smiling.

Austin asked her a few short questions about her employment history with OCD Cleaners before gently prying into her background. Cautious, she only shared that she was still new to the area, having moved from Cleveland, but didn't delve into what had brought her to Tucson. Aside from herself and her parents, nobody knew the reason, and that's the way she wanted to keep in fear of looking both stupid and naïve. As expected, he also asked about her criminal record, and he laughed when she jokingly told him she was wanted in ten states. She was sure to add that, no, she had no criminal history, and had never even received a parking ticket. He seemed to trust her, and knowing she'd likely be left alone with him for the duration of the tour, she was relieved to find she trusted him as well… to an extent. She still had to keep her guard up.

"Now, let me show you around," he said, gesturing to the long hallway to her right.

Lily seemed to have passed Austin's test, and she couldn't stop smiling as they walked side by side; in part due to the energy he exuded, and in part because of the money the position came with. Landing this job was important as it offered her a chance to slowly rebuild the savings account Ryan had bled dry. This was her opportunity to fix her life and pursue her degree as planned. She couldn't screw it up.

Conversation flowed easily between them as he guided her past a gorgeous bathroom tiled in white followed by four large carpeted bedrooms; all the same size but varying in layout. The hall opened up into a gourmet kitchen as big as her apartment, and she covered her mouth to gasp as she took it all in.

The flooring had changed to a cool gray slate with hues of earthy blues, greens and burnt reds, keeping with the Southwestern theme. What looked like pure white marble topped the counters running down the length of every wall—only interrupted by the latest stainless steel appliances—with beautiful wooden cabinetry placed above them. Two large kitchen islands, each featuring its own sink and topped with the same matching white marble, were stationed in the middle of the room and surrounded by wooden counter stools, all upholstered in golden-brown leather. Smaller versions of the wagon wheel chandelier she'd spotted earlier hung above the two islands, and she appreciated that subtle touch. They weren't needed now, as the room was well lit by four large windows dressed with rust-colored curtains pulled aside by black metal holdbacks. The countertops were home to smaller appliances, cutting boards, bowls of fruit, and flowers arranged perfectly in glass vases.

"You've got to be kidding me," she said, her words gushing out uncontrollably. "Your kitchen looks like a set for some sort of cooking show."

Austin laughed and invited her to help herself to anything in the fridge should she get hungry during her shifts. From there, he led her to another huge, open room housing the magnificent wet bar Jeanine had told her about. It was longer than described and ran down the wall to her left. Behind it, rows of top-shelf liquors and liqueurs had been neatly placed on glass shelving with a mirrored backing. The beer and wine were kept in coolers under the bar, Austin explained, along with an ice dispenser and glassware. The bar top was made of quartz, which she'd have never known unless he told her, and the row of stools lining the bar front matched the stools found in the kitchen.

The flooring had returned to the same marble tile found in the foyer and hallways. In the middle of the room were two identical brown leather sectional sofas that served as seating for guests, both placed facing each other. Between them sat a large wooden coffee table with a crystal top, and under it, a smaller version of the same hand-woven carpet she'd seen upon entering the estate. In the back corner of the room was a black Steinway grand piano, adding an air of sophistication, and in the other corner, a billiard table topped with red felt. More vases of differing sizes and colors were placed around the room, all of them spilling out a selection of plants and flowers. As with the kitchen, several large windows poured in daylight while offering a view of the foothills outside. More daylight spilled in through a large sliding-glass door that opened to reveal a stunning rear courtyard garden boasting a prodigious kidney-shaped swimming pool in its center. A series of large, smooth rocks had been stacked in the middle of the pool, rising up above the water to allow a flowing waterfall to run down them. An in-ground hot tub complimented one side of the pool, and on the other side, a fire pit and grill sat next to a fully stocked covered outdoor bar with ample seating. As with the front yard, the rear courtyard's landscaping was a diligently upkept arrangement of trees, flowers, and cacti surrounded by an arrangement of decorative stones and gravel. Noting the lights running alongside the pool and outer perimeter of the courtyard, she envisioned how incredible it must look when illuminated at night. Her heart sank a bit, knowing she'd never get to experience it since her shift didn't extend beyond sunset.

You don't need to see it, she told herself. *You just need to do your job and go home.*

Back inside, the tour continued and their conversation quickly turned to playful banter that helped put her at ease, though not fully. On top of being remarkably handsome, he was proving to be quite charming and funny as well, but she'd learned the hard way that people aren't always what they seem. She told herself to stay wary, and this time, not ignore any red flags like she had in the past. So far, he hadn't raised any, which seemed promising.

He led her into his home gym that rivaled any commercial gym she'd seen, and given the sheer weight of it all, he didn't have to explain why it was on the first floor. It housed high-end equipment ranging from machines to free weights, and included a cardio area with a row of treadmills in front of a row of stationary bikes, followed by a final third row of ellipticals. Flat-screen televisions were mounted above each piece, offering users entertainment to pass the time. Positioned in the back left corner of the estate, the two outer walls were made almost entirely of glass, providing a breathtaking view of the Catalina Mountains.

As they stood among the equipment, she caught herself admiring his strong body again. She'd sworn off men after Ryan, but Austin Matson was proving hard to ignore.

"This explains that physique."

Instead of allowing his ego to swell from the compliment, he once again surprised her with his modesty. "I try to keep fit."

"It's working," she said. Her eyes continued to roam his body, wondering what it looked like under that expensive suit, and unaware that she was flirtatiously biting her lower lip. Lily felt a palpable energy between them as he stood looking her up and down.

"You have quite the body as well, if you don't mind me saying so," he replied with a sly grin.

"Thank you," she blushed, her heart beginning to race.

He's totally checking you out. No, he's not, don't be stupid. The guy probably dates rich white supermodels. Why does it matter? He's trouble. Just do your job.

Snapping back to reality, she shook her head and cleared her throat, breaking the moment between them. "I'd love to see some more of the home."

He cleared his throat as well and agreed they should move on.

Having seen the first half of the bottom floor, he guided her through the second half and didn't protest when she asked to peek inside the three-car garage she'd noticed when she'd arrived. She was treated to a collection of vehicles new and old, all of them polished to perfection, but could only identify a handful. Even though she'd spent a considerable amount of time in her father's shop, vehicles of this caliber never passed through it. They were reserved for the richest of the rich, and only serviced by authorized dealers.

She noticed an empty spot, and what belonged there wasn't much of a mystery.

"So, I take it that *is* your Ferrari outside."

"It is," he nodded. "It's my newest addition."

"It looks like you were about to leave when I showed up," she said, subtly steering the conversation to the question that had been gnawing at her since their introduction in the foyer.

Austin nodded and explained, "I had a business brunch scheduled with an investment banker just around the corner."

Feeling they'd established enough of a rapport, Lily asked, "And you rescheduled just to give me the tour when Winston could have done it?"

"Whoa, is it hot in here?" Austin replied, his face turning red while jokingly tugging at his shirt collar.

She laughed at his deflection and playfully swatted his arm, taken by how solid it was. Batting her eyes, she prodded, "Come on, spill."

Did you just flirt with him? Oh, God, I think you did. Stop! Remember Ryan.

"Maybe I was just curious how you ended up pushing a mop and a broom," he shrugged, and was quick to add, "Not that there's anything wrong with that. Women of your immense beauty are typically high-profile models or actresses."

Immense beauty, she repeated in her mind, the butterflies returning to her stomach.

"You're sweet, but I'm *far* from model material," she countered humbly, keeping the modeling gigs she'd been offered over the years to herself. "I'm way too curvy."

She saw Austin's eyes trail down her body. "You have curves in all the right places, believe me."

Okay, he's definitely flirting with you.

Lily tried not to read too much into it, figuring he was likely a flirt by nature, yet, she couldn't resist returning the flirtation, convinced it was all lighthearted fun. Well aware of how long it had been since she'd had any of that, she granted herself permission to play along.

"And you have muscles in all the right places," she said. "You're the one who could be a model, especially with that jawline."

"I wouldn't want to take the pay cut," he joked.

They both shared a laugh, and when the laughter subsided, their eyes met for a long moment that teetered on awkward. Lily was the first to break the silence. Looking down at her work clothes, she blurted, "It's just to get me into school, you know? The cleaning thing."

"There's no reason to be ashamed of it," he assured her with genuine sincerity. "It's a respectable way to make a living."

"I'm not ashamed, I'm just…" she trailed off, realizing she did feel a slight sense of shame in the presence of someone so accomplished.

"What will you be going to school for?" he asked, seeming to sense her sudden discomfort and wanting to redirect their exchange.

"I want to be a teacher. Third grade, I think."

"A commendable goal," Austin nodded. "We need more educators." Smiling, he continued, "I knew there was more to you. I could see it in those eyes of yours."

She blushed and shyly looked away. "Thank you."

"I'd love to hear more of your story," he said.

Lily hesitated, fearing she'd opened up too much already and had flirted a bit too heavily. She defensively raised her guard again and chose her reply carefully.

"It's not worth missing your meeting over, believe me."

"Maybe I'm just not a fan of brunch," he laughed, cutting the slight tension that had formed between them.

She chuckled with him and looked around the garage again at his collection of expensive toys, using it as a way to turn the tables on him.

"Alright, I have to ask…"

"Go on."

"What the heck do you do for work? I mean, I know it's something in the tech industry, right?"

"Indeed," he nodded. "I'm the founder and CEO of Tomorrow Tech. We manufacture and distribute cutting-edge microprocessors worldwide. We have factories in five locations here in the States, and five more overseas. We're also the only company with the resources to produce a surplus, which we keep in two warehouses in undisclosed locations. Whenever there's a global shortage of microprocessors, everyone comes to us."

"And you make a huge profit by marking the prices up," Lily said.

"Smart girl," Austin nodded with a grin.

"So, how did you get started in the industry? I can't imagine it's an easy one to break into."

"Come. I'll tell you more while we walk," he replied.

Her deflection had worked. Following him out of the garage, she found herself glued to every word he spoke.

"When I was a kid, my neighbor was this huge computer geek." He paused and smiled as he recalled his childhood friend. "Aaron Mosely. Since we lived right next to each other, it didn't take long for us to become best buddies, and I spent a good deal of time at his house. His bedroom was cluttered with computers and computer parts. I mean, they were *everywhere*. He'd carved out enough space for a bed, but the rest of the room was just computers, computer parts, and books about computers." Austin looked at her and joked, "Did I mention he liked computers?"

"You did," she laughed.

"Anyhow, he introduced me to my first microprocessor. He described it as 'the brain of the computer' and that was it for me. I was hooked. I just found them so fascinating, they became all I could think about. You know how most kids are obsessed with dinosaurs or trucks? Yeah, well, I was the kid who was obsessed with processors. In most cases, a childhood obsession fades fast and is replaced by another."

"But not with you," Lily said.

"Not with me," he agreed. "I tore through every book I could find, trying to learn everything I could about how computers work and how microprocessors function. The internet was still fairly new back then, but widespread enough for me to gather more information. I'll spare you the details, but I was eventually able to create a microprocessor of my own using the small workstation I'd built in my parents' basement. Granted, it was a piece of crap, but still," he chuckled. "I discovered it was easier to modify existing processors. Reverse-engineering them also helped me learn a lot. I found ways to improve existing technology and eventually landed a job with IBM. They were so impressed by my work that they promoted me. The pay increase allowed me to save up some money, and with the help of a loan from my bank and some friends who believed in me, Tomorrow Tech was born."

"And now you're a millionaire," Lily smiled.

"Well, a billionaire, but who's counting?" Austin replied with a sly smirk.

Sweet Jesus, he's a billionaire… and he's brilliant.

She tried to remain unfazed by the money, but she couldn't deny how attractive she found his mind. Men this good-looking and smart were a rare breed.

They made their way to his colossal home cinema furnished with four ascending rows of black leather theater seats facing a fourteen-foot screen, and a faint moan of desire escaped her when he confessed that he'd never even used it, explaining that he preferred to read and had built the cinema mainly to entertain guests.

He's a reader, she thought. *Of course, he's a reader. God, that's sexy.*

On the second floor, Austin invited her to share more of her life, but she was only willing to give him the broad strokes. She trusted him enough to dive a bit deeper into her upbringing in Cleveland, and outlined her plan of earning her bachelor's degree in teaching, but didn't dive into her private life. As captivating as he was, she'd only known him for a little over an hour and had to remain wary. She was already upset with herself for returning his flirtation. When he asked why she'd decided on Tucson of all places, she danced around any mention of Ryan and claimed her move was for the climate and positive things she'd heard about the University of Arizona.

Austin didn't divulge much about his personal life, instead choosing to listen. He seemed genuinely interested in her as a person and what made her tick, and having lacked any real attention in almost six months, she couldn't help but bathe in it. She'd never been one to seek recognition, but recent months had proven that everyone needs at least a little. When he looked at her with his honest blue eyes, she'd swear there was some sort of chemistry between them, but she wrote it off as just her imagination—and perhaps wishful thinking— reminding herself that a man of such wealth and importance would want nothing to do with a penniless cleaning lady who lived in one of Tucson's most impoverished neighborhoods. The socially-elite looked down their noses at people like her, didn't they? That's what she'd always believed, but Austin's actions seemed to say otherwise.

He'd been treating her as an equal, and as the tour progressed, he'd even started treating her like an old friend. Along their walk through the mansion, he instructed her how he'd like each room cleaned but worded it to sound more like a suggestion than a command. He didn't want to come across as her superior, and it didn't go unnoticed by her.

Two more hallways lined with fine artwork gave way to eight more bedrooms and two more bathrooms, with each hall leading to spacious common areas with similar layouts. Brown leather seating and a large flat-screen television could be found in both, along with more decorative items that had been carefully selected and positioned around the rooms. It was the third floor, however, that held the biggest surprise, and where Austin began opening up about his own life. Passing even more bedrooms, he once again led her down a long hall

ending in a pair of tall wooden pocket doors with flush brass door handles. The doors disappeared into the surrounding wall as he parted them, and what they revealed left her speechless. She stood frozen with wide eyes, unable to move, and unable to form words.

"Are you okay?" he chuckled, seeing her reaction.

"Holy shit," she finally breathed, standing in complete awe of his exquisite home library. She rarely cursed, but the word had come tumbling out before she could stop it.

Towering bookcases hugged every wall, and rows of them ran down both sides of the room with walking space in the middle. Each completely filled from top to bottom, they held a collection of books so vast, it would take several lifetimes to read them all. Armchairs with matching ottomans had been placed throughout the library, but unlike the rest of the seating in the house, these were upholstered in a fabric she couldn't identify but looked inviting. A small end table with a brass reading lamp had been positioned next to each chair, making for the perfect reading environment.

"This is... I can't... I..." Lily stammered, stepping into the library and looking around the room in pure astonishment.

She rushed to the closest bookcase that she quickly identified as revered American classics and trailed her finger along the spine of each, rattling off the great authors she'd grown up with.

"Twain, Melville, Salinger, Hemingway, Steinbeck," she gushed. "This is incredible!"

"You know them?" Austin asked, sounding surprised.

"Know them? I grew up on them!"

"Ah, a fellow reader," he beamed, grinning wide. "I knew I liked you."

"I just can't believe this," Lily said, stepping back to soak in the massive collection again. "You must have a million books in here!"

Austin chuckled. "Well, I don't think it's *that* many, but it's a lot, yes."

"There's no way you could have read all of these," she said, walking slowly through the library.

"I wish I had that much free time," he sighed. "I travel a lot and always pick a book to bring with me. They're great for a long flight."

"I bet," Lily replied, her eyes continuing to scan each shelf.

"Whenever I find a book that looks interesting, I can't stop myself from buying it," Austin said. "I always tell myself I'll read it, but it often gets left on a shelf to collect dust."

"Compulsively buying books?" she laughed. "I know all about that. I still have a ton I haven't read."

Lily stopped to brush her hand along one of the chairs, noting its softness, and could see herself spending countless hours in it with a good book.

"Shearling," Austin said, identifying the material for her. "Faux shearling, of course."

He followed behind her as she moved around the room and seemed to enjoy watching her explore every bookcase. The shelves were arranged by category, with four of them devoted entirely to computing. She looked over a few of them before moving on, lingering in his non-fiction section before making her way to the back of the library. He'd reserved it for fiction, and almost an entire shelf had been devoted to Stephen King, making it hard to miss.

"A King fan, I see," she commented.

"Well, I grew up in Maine, so it's kind of a requirement," he smiled.

"Wait, you grew up in Maine?" She excitedly turned to face him and got lost in his eyes again. She was taken by his deep voice and the way those blue eyes looked at her.

"I did," he replied. "In a small town off the coast."

"Have you seen a lot of lighthouses?" she asked eagerly.

"Just a few." His eyes moved down to her neckline. "Don't think I didn't notice that lighthouse necklace."

Her heart felt like it skipped a beat, and the butterflies returned in full force. In the time they'd known each other, Ryan had never asked about—or even acknowledged—the necklace.

"Oh, yes," she said, gently touching the pendant. She'd been so surprised by Austin's comment, that was all she could think to reply.

"You don't see many of those in Arizona," he laughed. "I assume there's a story behind it?"

"There is," she nodded. Suddenly aware of how long they'd been together, she followed with, "but I've already taken up enough of your time."

Austin tugged up a sleeve to look at his wristwatch. Shining silver, she couldn't tell if it was a Rolex, but she knew that it was expensive. "I still have forty-five minutes. We're good. Please, go on."

"Are you sure?"

"I'm sure. Please, sit," he said, motioning to one of the chairs.

Sinking into the seat, she found it even more comfortable than it looked. He pulled another chair closer and sat facing opposite her, his eyes locked onto hers attentively.

Conflicted, Lily hesitated while weighing her two choices. She could either lower her defenses enough to share this important moment in her life with him, or continue to shield herself from men and the heartache they could bring. Deciding she was being irrationally overprotective, she dropped her guard to allow him brief entry into her world.

"My grandmother loved lighthouses. She saw one when she was just a child and thought it was beautiful. It really stuck with her. We all lived in Tennessee at the time, and since my parents both had to work, she would babysit me five days a week. We were really close," Lily explained. "Her home was decorated with lighthouses, which wouldn't have made sense to most people since there aren't any lighthouses in Tennessee."

"Yeah, landlocked states aren't exactly known for their lighthouses," Austin chuckled.

"Exactly. She had small replica lighthouses everywhere. Magnets, pins, stickers… you name it. Anything lighthouse, she just had to have."

"I know all about obsessions," Austin said in a callback to his lifelong love affair with computer processors.

"Right? You get it. At some point before I was born, she took a trip up the coast of New England with my grandfather, stopping at as many lighthouses as they could along the way. I only have vague memories of him since he died when I was very little. I remember him being very sweet. Anyhow, she took pictures of every lighthouse they'd seen along the way and kept them in a photo album on their coffee table. She'd insist on showing anyone who came over. Around the time my grandfather died, my dad had been offered a job at a manufacturing plant in Cleveland, which is how I wound up there. I guess a friend of his knew how good he was with vehicles and recommended him," Lily shrugged. "It was supposed to pay great, but the job ended up falling through when he got there. He found a job at a small repair shop and my mom wasn't pleased since it meant she still had to work. Things were tight since they had to afford daycare for me. I hated it and really missed my grandmother. She'd stayed behind in Tennessee and gave me her lighthouse necklace before we left." She reached for the pendant and rubbed it affectionately while she continued. "I was just a kid, but I knew how much she loved it, so it's always meant a lot to me. She'd call me every week without fail until the dementia got worse. We knew we had to do something since she couldn't take care of herself anymore. My mom found a nursing home in Cleveland and we moved her there. Even with her dementia, she insisted on bringing as many of her lighthouses as she could. We put them around her room to comfort her when she had moments of clarity, which weren't often and eventually stopped altogether."

"That's awful," Austin said, seeming to hang on every word. "I'm so sorry."

Lily let the pendant rest on her neck again and placed her hands on her lap. "I visited her as often as I could after she'd been moved to hospice. I was by her side when she passed. I'll never forget it. She was completely unresponsive, and I was told she didn't have much longer. I didn't expect her to open her eyes, but she did. She opened them wide and was looking at the ceiling, but I swear she was looking at something else entirely. A memory. Which one, I don't know, but a memory. Then she got this big smile on her face and she said, 'I see it. I see it. The lighthouse. It's beautiful. I see it. I see it.' At that moment…"

She stopped and sniffled, feeling a tear fall down her cheek. Austin was quick to offer his silk pocket square, and she accepted it, softly dabbing her eyes.

"Thank you," she sniffled. "At that moment, she looked so happy. At peace. Her eyes shut and she was gone, just like that. I watched her slip away."

"Oh, Lily," Austin said, taking one of her hands in his. "I am so sorry."

Lily sniffled again and blotted away more tears. "I'm just glad she went with a loved one by her side, thinking about that lighthouse."

"Not a bad way to go," Austin pointed out.

"God, I'd love to see a lighthouse again. A real lighthouse. It's been so long. I saw one when I was a child, but I barely remember it."

"You will," he smiled.

"Look at me," she sniffled. "Blubbering over here like a fool. I shouldn't have even told you any of this."

"I'm glad you did. Thank you for sharing it with me," he replied, gently squeezing her hand.

"It's been five years, but it still hurts," Lily sighed. "I think it always will."

"To fully appreciate the beauty in life, you have to experience the pain."

Wiping away the rest of her tears, she found him looking at her with earnest compassion. It wasn't like her to open up like she had, especially with somebody she'd just met, but his kind eyes and warm smile made it too easy. He'd proven to be unlike anything she'd expected, and beyond anything she could have hoped for. Even with that, she had to remind herself that she didn't really know him, and that she'd been burned before by her trusting nature. Suddenly feeling uncomfortably vulnerable, she raised her guard again and refocused on the task at hand.

"Okay," she said, taking a deep breath and handing him back his pocket square. "Let's finish up this tour. I'm not getting paid to cry, and you have a meeting you need to get to."

The tour of the third floor finished on the opposite side of the estate where Austin showed her "The Classroom," as he appropriately called it since that's exactly what it was. Rows of student chair-desks sat facing a teacher's lectern with a huge whiteboard behind it, and the back of the classroom was lined with workbenches topped with a wide spectrum of electronics that looked to be computer parts and small tools. Austin explained that once a month, he'd fly in children from across the country to impart some of his knowledge in a three-day hands-on workshop that he taught completely free, even providing on-site room and board. Regardless of socioeconomic status, Austin went on, if a child showed an interest in computer electronics, they were welcome to enroll with their parents' help and permission, of course. He personally selected the twenty new students each month and enjoyed getting to know them as they worked together. Lily now understood why there were so many bedrooms and such a large kitchen. In his own way, Austin was a teacher. As if he wasn't attractive enough, he'd just managed to become even more so. She'd always written the wealthy off as disgustingly materialistic, considering their excessive lifestyles a reflection of their greed. Austin's giving nature, however, flew in direct opposition to that belief and was slowly changing her opinion.

The fourth and final floor had been scaled back to accommodate an open terrace on the roof of the third floor. Located on the back of the estate, the terrace delivered another intoxicating view of the mountains above and foothills below. The rooftop had been arranged with durable, weather-resistant furniture, and tan patio umbrellas protruded through the center of each table, offering refuge from the hot desert sun. More decorative vases had been placed against the high black metal safety railing running along the three side edges of the roof, and she couldn't miss the long, wide telescope angled upward for viewing the nighttime sky.

After a brief walk around the terrace, they stepped back inside where Austin showed her the remainder of the estate. The same familiar elevator doors she'd seen on each floor didn't come as a surprise. What did surprise her, however, was this floor being built for just two rooms. They were separated by a spacious common area filled with another brown-leather sectional sofa and more Southwestern decor, with four big picture windows lining the front wall of the estate. Looking out, she could see the city in the distance, and hadn't realized just how high the uphill drive through the posh community had taken her.

The imposing wooden double doors to each room were shut for privacy. They were both matching master bedrooms, Austin told her, with the western room being his, and the eastern room belonging to Winston.

"I'm sure there's more I could have shown you, but that will have to do for now," Austin said, glancing at his watch.

"Well, I appreciate you taking the time out of your busy day to show me around," Lily smiled, but couldn't resist asking the question that had been on her mind since stepping into the estate. "Who decorated this place, anyhow? They did an incredible job. It's gorgeous."

"That would be me," he answered with a look of pride. "I appreciate the kind words."

"Wait... the decor is all you?" she asked, looking at him skeptically.

"What?" he chuckled. "A guy can't have a good eye for home decor?"

"I have a feeling you're a man of many surprises," she smirked.

"Would it surprise you to learn that I designed the place, too?"

"Not one bit," she laughed. "But don't you think it's a bit…" she trailed off, worried she might offend him. However, Austin wasn't about to let it go.

"A bit what?"

"Excessive?" she blurted. "I mean, this place is like a luxury resort."

He looked impressed and studied her for a moment. "You really are a smart girl. I designed it with that in mind."

"Really?"

"Really. If I ever decide I've had enough Tucson or if I'm ever in a tight spot financially, I can either rent or sell this place as a foothill resort. I know a big-time hotelier who wants it and has already made me a few generous offers."

"If you've ever had enough of Tucson?" Lily questioned, puzzled. "I thought you love it here? I mean, this entire home is like one giant ode to the Southwest."

"And I do love it here," Austin said. "But at some point, I'd like to settle down and start a family. I'd like to do that back in Maine."

"So you can be close to your own family?"

"Well, that, and because I want my children to experience all four seasons like I did. It builds character. I hate snow and ice now, but as a kid? I loved it! Snow days were the best. You're from Cleveland. I'm sure you know all about snow days."

"Sitting in front of the TV, waiting to see if school's been canceled?" Lily laughed. "Yes!"

"See?" Austin chuckled. "You get it."

"I do," she agreed, following him to the elevator doors. As they waited for them to part, she looked at his bedroom door and curiosity got the better of her. With a sly grin, she asked, "You mean, I don't get to see your bedroom?"

Oh, God, that came out wrong. Way to sound like a tramp, Lily.

Thankfully, Austin didn't take the question as suggestively as it sounded. He returned her sly grin with one of his own as he told her, "I need to leave at least a little mystery."

She understood and respected that. It made sense that he'd want to maintain a bit of privacy, so she left it alone and continued to the elevator with him by her side. On the ride down, she complimented his beautiful home and thanked him for the tour, which was her way of making small talk to avoid any awkwardness. She swore she could feel an attraction between them, but once again dismissed it, believing a man of his class couldn't truly be interested in the broke black woman who was about to scrub his floors.

When the doors parted, they slowly walked side-by-side to the estate's front double doors. Austin checked his watch again and gave her a few last-minute ideas for the cleaning, still dancing delicately around his phrasing.

"I was thinking you could just start with vacuuming and dusting today," he began, "and maybe wipe down the kitchen counters and islands. How about you just focus on the bottom two floors today and worry about the top two on Monday?"

"I can do that," she nodded. "Let me just grab my supplies from my trunk and I'll—"

"No need," Austin said, stopping her mid-stride, and he redirected her to the full louver door she'd noticed upon entering the home. It proved to be a closet where he kept an assortment of every cleaning solvent she could possibly need, all neatly arranged on metal wire shelving along with feather dusters, sponges, rubber gloves, and everything else she'd grown too familiar with thanks to OCD Cleaners. In the back of the closet, a floor buffer for the tile sat beside a vacuum for the carpeted bedrooms, both looking far too expensive for her comfort. Tucked away in the corner was a mop bucket with a mop sticking out of it, which was something else she knew all too well, as was the broom and dustpan next to it.

"I'd say this should do it," she remarked, looking everything over.

"Okay, great," Austin said from behind her. "And don't worry about laundry. I'm sure you know I use another service for that."

"I do now," she replied with a sigh of relief. She'd changed enough bedding working at the Hilton.

"Listen, I really need to run, and I don't know when I'll be back."

Lily turned to face him with a polite smile. "That's fine. I can see myself out."

"You see this here?" he asked, pointing out the small silver intercom recessed into the wall to the right of the front doors. "Hold the first button and tell Winston you're ready to go. He'll come down and see you out."

"I'm fully capable of opening and closing a door," she chuckled.

Austin looked a bit uncomfortable and cleared his throat. "It's more to let us know when you're done for the day."

"So you can track my hours," she said, embarrassed that he'd had to explain that. It made sense that they'd want to know when she left so he could pay her accordingly.

"It's nothing personal," he assured her. "Remember to help yourself to anything in the fridge, and if you're gone by the time I get back, I'll see you Monday morning."

"Sounds good," she said with another polite smile.

"It's been a pleasure," he replied, grinning wide. His steel-blue eyes remained fixed on hers for a moment, and a rush of excitement coursed through her. She had just spent nearly three hours with this man, yet she wasn't ready for him to go. A slight disappointment hit her when he slowly turned to leave, adjusted his suit jacket, and stepped out the door, leaving her alone in the foyer.

Get yourself together, she told herself. *You need this job, don't screw it up.*

She knew her inner monologue was right and doubled back to the supply closet. Fishing her cell phone out of her front pocket, she noted that it was 11:50 am, giving her a little over three hours to work. In that time, she resolved to do the best job possible in hopes of leaving a good impression. While it wasn't even a drop in the bucket to Austin Matson, the extra two hundred dollars a week on top of her usual salary was big money to her. With him gone, she was able to break from the mesmeric spell he'd cast on her and focus all of her attention on the estate. Three hours wasn't long, but she was determined to prove she was the right fit for the position. She set the alarm on her phone for 3:00 pm, wheeled the vacuum cleaner out of the closet, and wasted no time getting to work.

Lily tuned out the steady whir of the vacuum by replaying the tour in her mind, trying to visualize elements of the mansion rather than Austin Matson. Of all the wondrous things she'd seen along the way, the library was easily the highlight of the home. Jeanine didn't strike her as much of a reader, so she wasn't too surprised she hadn't heard about the vast collection of literature. Austin unexpectedly appeared in her mind, bending her over in the library and taking her from behind while her hands clenched a bookcase shelf, causing the entire thing to rock and sending books tumbling to the floor. With his big, strong hands on her hips, he thrust in and out of her, filling her completely with his thick co—

She shook the thought from her mind, upset with herself for having it, and reminded herself that she didn't really know Austin.

Yes, he was handsome, and, yes, he seemed kind, but so did Ryan in the beginning. Remembering the nightmare with him, she suddenly felt foolish for allowing Austin into her thoughts. She needed to keep her guard up or her life could be ripped apart again. Burying him deep and covering him with memories of her family, Lily tore through the bottom half of the estate, cleaning like a woman on a mission.

When her alarm sounded, she stood proud of what she'd been able to accomplish in the short time she'd had, foregoing food to get the job done. As much as she wanted to see those blue eyes again, she told herself it was a good thing that Austin hadn't resurfaced. After making sure she'd returned everything to the supply closet, she held the first button on the intercom as instructed.

"Okay, Winston, I'm done for the day."

She was beginning to think he hadn't heard her when his reply finally sounded through the speaker. "Yes, Miss Ward, I shall be right down."

His definition of "right down" and hers differed, as it took almost ten minutes for the elevator doors to chime, announcing his arrival. When the doors parted, he limped his way over to her with a smile on his face, looking around the foyer as if inspecting her job. Lily found his charade amusing since the foyer had already been spotless before she began.

"Good, good," Winston said. "I'm sure Mister Matson will be quite pleased."

"I hope so," Lily sighed. Three hours of non-stop cleaning had left her exhausted and hungry.

Winston moved by her and opened the front door to guide her out, but stopped her with a raised finger before she could step outside.

"Courtesy of Mister Matson," he said, handing her a folded one-hundred-dollar bill he'd pulled from the breast pocket of his vest.

The unexpected gesture left her momentarily stunned. She hesitated to accept the money, unsure if it was a tip or charity. If it was charity, her pride certainly wouldn't allow her to take it.

"It's customary to tip the help," Winston smiled, seeing her confusion.

"This is way too much," Lily said, shaking her head in disbelief.

"Nonsense, my lady," Winston replied. "We shall see you Monday morning at 9:00 am sharp, yes?"

"You shall," Lily beamed, playfully using his parlance.

"Good day, then," Winston replied with a slight bow, closing the door behind her.

Forty minutes later, she pulled into her run-down apartment complex, and just as she always did, nervously hurried to her unit, hastily bolting the door behind her. An old, neglected building in the city's most notorious neighborhood, it was the only housing she'd been able to find on short notice and with little money to her name. She dropped her handbag to the floor and groaned as she looked around her tiny one-bedroom dump. It felt like something you'd see in a war-torn third-world country compared to Austin Matson's estate and was a harsh reminder of the disparity between their social classes.

Just be thankful you have a roof over your head, she told herself. *Don't be ungrateful.*

She'd scrubbed and shampooed the stains on the torn Berber carpeting a dozen times since moving in, but every attempt to remove them had been futile. In no position to spend money, she'd learned to live with them until she could afford an area rug big enough to hide them all. The living room had visible drywall patches on the walls in several places, likely the result of a former tenant's fists, and the small kitchen was a complete disaster. The linoleum flooring—once white but now yellowed by age—was cracked and peeling, and the wood laminate surface of the warped cabinets was all but gone. Mold and mildew stippled the walls of the cramped bathroom that was too small for a bathtub, with only enough room for a shower stall that was beyond cleaning, just like the toilet beside it. To the apartment's credit, the lone bedroom was a decent size, but the carpeting was just as stained and torn as the living room, and the walls had also been noticeably patched in a few areas.

The whole place was embarrassing, but without any friends in the area, at least she didn't have to suffer the humiliation of anyone seeing it. In the six months she'd lived there, nobody else had stepped inside the apartment, and that's the way she intended to keep it. It was temporary, she'd routinely remind herself, and when she financially recovered from the Ryan ordeal, she'd begin searching for a nicer place. That financial recovery would come faster thanks to her new position. She didn't expect one-hundred dollar tips to be a regular occurrence, but the two-hundred dollars added to her paycheck every week was going to add up quickly. Knowing she couldn't blow the opportunity she'd been given, she vowed to keep her distance from Austin Matson. Everything about the man was a distraction, and distractions led to sloppy work. She needed to do the best job possible for the security of her employment, even if that meant keeping her exchanges with him to a polite minimum.

Lily's attempt at pushing the gorgeous billionaire from her mind lasted until she crawled into bed that night and succumbed to desire, revisiting her library fantasy from earlier that day. After bringing herself to a powerful orgasm while thinking about Austin ramming in and out of her from behind, only one thought flashed through her mind in the darkness of her room:

Oh, goddammit.

Chapter Three

"Just make sure a room's empty before you go in," Jose growled, scolding Brenda for a mistake she'd made the previous week. Lily had expected him to fire her for walking in on a couple having sex, but it seemed he was in a forgiving mood for once.

After going over the previous week's report, the Monday morning staff meeting came to an end and all twelve cleaners began shuffling out of Jose's office. During the meeting, Jose announced that Lily had taken over the Matson account, which they'd all figured out by now anyhow and was the reason they'd been shooting nasty glares her way. He'd asked Lily to stay behind, and as she stood waiting by his desk for the room to clear, she began to worry he was reassigning her. Perhaps her cleaning hadn't lived up to expectations after all, and Austin Matson had requested someone else.

"People these days," Jose said, tilting his chair back and propping his legs up on his desk. "Why is it so hard to find good fuckin' help? I swear, every week it's something else." He paused to look around his small office and added, "Jesus, I can't wait to be done with all of this. I hate this shit."

"I'm sorry you feel that way," Lily replied nervously. She didn't know what else to say, and was unsure of where this was going.

"I got a buddy in California. We go way back. Real smart guy. Says he invented some new type of computer processor thing," Jose said. "Tells me it's made out of some sort of plastic and doesn't get hot or nothin'. He claims it's going to change the world. I don't know," he continued, shaking his head. "I'm not a tech guy. All I know is he just registered the business and needs an investor."

Lily expected him to pressure her into asking Austin Matson to invest. To her surprise, he went a different direction.

"I've been doing this a long time," he told her with a sigh. "I've managed to save up some good money doing it, too." A big, devilish grin spread across Jose's face. It was the first time Lily had seen him smile. "I'm going to invest in his business, and we're both going to make a fortune."

"That's… great…" she muttered slowly, realizing that at this point, Jose was just thinking out loud.

"'PlastiCPU.' That's the name of it." Jose waved his hand and added, "Pretty stupid name if you ask me, but he swears it's going to make us millions."

"I hope it does," Lily replied politely. "It sounds like a great opportunity for you."

Of course, she didn't believe any of this would ever really happen and dismissed it as pure fantasy, but Jose sounded convinced.

"I'll be living in those foothills like your tech guy. I'll buy me a million-dollar home with a pool on the roof. Sexy women in bikinis everywhere. You just wait."

"Well… you'll have to invite me over," Lily joked, playing along. "I'll be sure to bring my bikini."

"Hey, speaking of your tech guy, how did it go on Friday?" Jose asked, returning to reality.

"At the Matson estate? It went really well… I think. Did you hear anything?" Lily asked.

"I didn't," Jose replied, resting his hands on his belly. "That's a good thing."

"I suppose it is,' Lily agreed.

"No complaints… always a good thing," Jose continued. "You know, you're the only worker I've had who hasn't had any complaints?"

"Really?"

"Really. It's why I trusted you with the account. Speaking of which," Jose said, pointing at the analog clock hanging on his office wall, "you better get to it."

"Yes, sir!" she smiled, itching to get out of his office. Jose's unpredictable temperament always made her nervous.

On the drive to the Matson estate, Lily reminded herself to focus solely on her job and only speak to Austin Matson when needed. She'd impressed herself over the weekend by thinking about him far less than she thought she would, distracting herself with one of the books from her collection. Believing it might send the wrong message, she'd even resisted the urge to wear make-up that morning so it wouldn't appear as though she'd dolled herself up for him. Arriving at the estate, however, she was informed by Winston that Austin wasn't even there. Apparently, he was out of town handling business and would be gone for the remainder of the week. This was a good thing, she told herself, yet she still felt a brief moment of disappointment.

Winston vanished and stayed out of sight while she cleaned the top two floors, and it was in one of the many bedrooms that she made a curious discovery. Sticking out from under a dresser was a roll of cash bound by a rubber band that appeared to have landed there accidentally. She picked it up and resisted the urge to count it, placing it in her pocket to give Winston later. When 3:00 pm rolled around, she called for him to see her out and he appeared sooner this time, once again handing her a crisp one-hundred-dollar bill on her way out the door. Like before, she protested that it was far too much, but he insisted she keep it for a job well done. The tip reminded her of the money she'd found, which she promptly handed over while explaining where she'd discovered it. Winston seemed surprised and thanked her for her honesty, surmising that it was likely left behind by a guest.

She left with a smile that remained on her face the entire walk to her car, but faded as she made her way home. With the drive giving her time to think, it occurred to her that Jeanine had never mentioned one-hundred dollar tips, and that's certainly something she would have bragged about. The more thought she gave it, the more unusual it seemed. Either way, if she continued receiving an additional two-hundred dollars a week on top of the extra two-hundred the position came with, she'd easily be able to afford a better apartment in a safer area soon while continuing to shove money into her savings account.

Only working two days a week left her with a bit too much time for Austin to creep into her thoughts, and books could only distract her for so long. She had a lengthy list of things she still wanted to see and do in the area but, unfortunately, most of them cost money, and since her pay increase wouldn't be reflected in her paycheck for another two weeks, she really had nothing to spend. She'd been able to squirrel away a little thanks to OCD Cleaners, but it wasn't anything substantial, and she'd sworn on her grandmother's Bible to never touch it, even in times of crisis. That money was to be protected at all costs, since her future depended on it. She could add to it, but taking from it was out of the question.

To eat up some of the free time that came with the Matson account, and to earn even more money for her savings, Lily asked Jose if she could return to the Hilton two days a week. He told her the timing was perfect since he'd been about to fire Brenda anyhow for being "a fuck-up," as he put it, and needed help filling her shifts. He scheduled Lily for the following day, and since she was all too familiar with the job, she picked up right where she'd left off. She could tell the other cleaners weren't thrilled about it but she ignored their scowls and went about her business. Jose scheduled her for that

Thursday as well, and Friday saw her back at the Matson estate, where the striking billionaire was still conspicuously absent. Again, Austin Matson's faithful assistant handed her another one-hundred-dollar bill on her way out the door, but this time, it made her feel uneasy

The following Monday, Winston greeted Lily with his usual smile but made no mention of Austin, leaving her to clean just as he had the previous two occasions. Assuming Austin was still gone, she set to work cleaning the first floor again, grabbing a small folding step-stool from the storage closet to reach the estate's higher shelves. She was dusting in one of the bedrooms with her back to the door when a commanding voice startled her from behind.

"Lilian Ward, it's good to see you again."

She yelped in surprise and stumbled off of the stool into the strong arms of Austin Matson, who was wearing a business suit again, this one a dark blue with a red tie. As she looked up into his enchanting blue eyes, she felt her heart begin to race and her face grow warm.

"I didn't mean to frighten you. My apologies," he said, gently setting her down.

"It's okay, it's just, it's," Lily began, flustered. "I just didn't know you were home."

"I got back into town on Saturday," he replied, looking at her with his perfect smile.

She swallowed nervously and turned to pick up the feather duster that had fallen to the floor, using it as a reason to break from his eyes. She climbed back onto the step-stool and continued dusting, though it was more of an act at this point. "Did you have a good trip?"

"Not really. I had to fly to Michigan to handle a small hiccup in our production line."

She kept her back turned to him in an effort to resist his charm. "You got it straightened out, I take it?"

Don't look at him. Don't you dare look at him. You don't need to look at him.

"I did," he answered. "We had a small problem with our silicon wafer supplier and—" Austin cut himself off and sighed. "I won't bore you with the details, but it's settled now, yes."

"Well, that's good," Lily replied politely. There was a long moment of silence, and she could feel his eyes on her. Known to be a nervous talker, she felt she needed to fill the quiet. "My boss was telling me about his friend in California who invented some sort of a plastic processor. It doesn't produce any heat or something, I don't know. Sounded interesting, though."

"Plastic doesn't conduct electricity," Austin pointed out.

"I'm just repeating what my boss said," Lily shrugged, keeping her back to him. "He's not a computer guy, so I'm sure he got it wrong."

"Did he say anything else about it?" Austin asked, sounding genuinely curious.

"Just that the guy registered the business and is looking for an investor or something. It's called…" Lily paused, struggling to recollect the name. "Damn, what was it called? PlastiCPU! Yeah, that was it."

She returned to dusting, still trying to avoid his gorgeous face and impressive build.

"That does sound interesting," Austin replied. "Anyhow, I was wondering if you've eaten yet. It just turned noon."

"I'm good," Lily answered, suddenly aware that she'd dusted the same picture three times now. "I ate right before I got here."

"Well… if you'd like to join me for lunch, I'll be in the kitchen."

"Thank you," she replied, "but I think I'm going to finish up this floor."

"Very well, then," Austin said with a hint of disappointment in his voice.

When she was confident that he'd left the room, she let out a heavy sigh and stepped down from the step-stool. She was proud of herself for showing such restraint, but a bit worried she'd come across as rude. The last thing she needed was to lose the job because she'd overdone it trying to push him away. Fighting the urge to join him in the kitchen, she moved on to the next bedroom instead.

At 3:00 pm, the alarm on her phone sounded, signaling that it was time to call it a day. Never one to stop in the middle of a task, she stayed another fifteen minutes to finish the room she'd been working on before returning the cleaning supplies to the foyer closet. Austin answered the call to let her out, surprising her in a pair of black athletic shorts and a white tank top soaked in sweat. A black towel was draped around his neck, and beads of perspiration were visible on his forehead. His damp hair was a bit mussed, yet his "Clark Kent curl," as she liked to call it for its alliteration, still hung over his brow in perfect form.

"Forgive me," he said, using the towel to blot away the drops of sweat that had begun to run down his face. "I just got done working out. Is it three o'clock already?"

Alone with him in the foyer, there was no turning her back to him this time. She tried to fight it, but it was impossible to avoid his pronounced muscles that were still glistening with sweat. The timing of his workout seemed a bit too coincidental, and she wondered if it had been orchestrated to gauge her reaction to his strapping physique.

Clever man, she thought. Had it been anyone else, she would have found the ruse cringey, but Austin had somehow found a way to make it work. Finding amusement in his theatrics, she couldn't help but play along.

"Why, Mister Matson, if I didn't know any better, I'd think you were trying to catch my attention," she said, smiling wide.

"Why, Miss Ward, I have no idea what you're talking about," he returned with a mischievous grin.

Her eye roll turned into a laugh. "You're something else."

"I missed you, too," he smirked.

Their flirtatious exchange was interrupted by the elevator's chime. The doors parted and Winston limped over to them, shaking his head apologetically.

"Yes, yes, I'm coming, I'm coming!" he said, breathing heavily from his hurry. "I was in the loo."

"I already beat you to it," Austin said with a look and tone of annoyance.

Winston stopped and looked them over, taking a few seconds too long to recognize that he'd just intruded on whatever moment they'd been having.

"So sorry, Mister Matson. Shall I leave?"

"I was just on my way out," Lily said before Austin could answer. She realized she'd been dangerously close to getting sucked into Austin's charm again and was grateful for Winston's sudden appearance. She moved toward the front door and Austin brushed by her to see her out.

"Allow me," he said. His smile looked forced, and Lily could tell he was still frustrated by Winston's unintentional interference.

She flashed him a polite smile as she stepped by him. "Thank you."

"Oh, before I forget," he said, stopping her. He reached into the small right pocket of his shorts and pulled out a one-hundred-dollar bill.

Lily looked at it and sighed. "Okay, I have to ask. What's with all of this money?"

"What do you mean?" Austin asked, looking confused.

"Look, I'm not trying to be ungrateful, but Jeanine never said anything about these big tips, and believe me, she would have."

"Maybe Jeanine didn't do as good of a job as you," he grinned.

She kept her eyes on the bill in his hand so she wouldn't get lost in his blue eyes again. "I just don't want anybody's pity, is all. I'm no charity case."

Austin's face abruptly turned sullen, and if she wasn't mistaken, he looked wounded by her words. "Is that what you think this is?"

"It feels like it, yes."

"Well, since we're having a moment of honesty here," Austin said, "I love that you want to be a teacher. We need more of them. I know school isn't cheap, and—"

"So this *is* charity," she groaned, cutting him off.

"Look, I'm just trying to help."

"And I appreciate that, but I didn't ask for help," Lily rebutted. "I can do this on my own."

"I don't doubt that for a second," Austin replied, "and I apologize if I offended you, but help isn't always a bad thing. You think I didn't get help along the way?" He gestured to his estate and continued, "I wouldn't have any of this if I didn't accept a little help here and there."

"Yeah?" she asked, thinking over his words.

He's right, she told herself. *Don't let foolish pride get in the way of a good thing.*

"Yeah," he repeated with a smile. "Maybe this is just my way of paying it forward." He paused and added, "And maybe someday you can pay it forward, too."

Lily allowed herself to look into his eyes and was greeted by a warm sincerity that immediately replaced her skepticism with appreciation.

"Thank you," she said, smiling back. "And I will. I promise."

"I know you will," he replied, grinning.

"I'll be back Friday morning," she called over her shoulder while heading to her car. He saw her off with a friendly wave, which she returned before driving off, satisfied with how they'd left things.

The following day saw her back at the Hilton, dodging more glares from jealous coworkers. The long shift gave her mind far too much time to wander, and as hard as she tried to fight it, she couldn't stop it from wandering to how unbelievably sexy Austin had looked in his tight tank top. Her thoughts drifted to trailing kisses down his hard body, and with her vivid imagination, she could almost taste the salt on his skin. She knew she shouldn't be fantasizing about the man who was, in an indirect way, acting as her boss. The majority of her paycheck came from the money Austin paid OCD Cleaners every month, and after Jose took his cut, the rest was all hers. She didn't need to be daydreaming about the devilishly handsome magnate who was her ticket to the future she'd mapped out for herself.

When Friday morning came, she was greeted by Winston and told that Austin had traveled to California for a business meeting. Again, she felt a small stab of disappointment, but knew it was for the best. He'd returned by Monday and greeted her wearing a dark blue polo shirt that showcased his muscular arms and chest. It was tucked into a pair of gray dress slacks with a black leather belt that matched his black leather Oxford shoes, and when he motioned her inside, the elegant watch on his wrist didn't go unnoticed. They made small talk in the foyer, with Lily asking how the meeting went and Austin replying that it had gone very well. Their eyes lingered on each other for a moment too long, which seemed to have become the usual with them, and Lily was the first to break away. As she pulled the vacuum cleaner from the storage closet, Austin informed her that the twenty students he'd selected would be arriving Friday afternoon, but shouldn't interfere with her cleaning. When noon rolled around, he found her tidying up a bedroom on the second floor and once again invited her to join him in the kitchen for a bite to eat. Like she had the week before, she declined by politely telling him she'd stuffed herself at a drive-through before her shift, insisting she would be just fine until she got home. He persisted, but soon acquiesced with a frustrated sigh, leaving her to her duties.

At a little past 3:00 pm, she rang to be let out and Winston's voice replied from the intercom that he was on his way. She braced herself for Austin to appear, rushing to beat Winston to the door, and felt foolish when he didn't show. Why would he? He was an important man who had much bigger things to deal with than letting a cleaning lady out of his home, and his mild flirtations had surely just been in jest. Worse, she feared they may have even been in her head; a creation of the loneliness she'd felt in recent months. These thoughts and more ran through her mind as Winston handed her yet another one-hundred-dollar bill, and the thoughts stayed with her on her drive home.

Austin wasn't kidding about the students. When Winston answered the door Friday morning—inviting Lily in with the same warm grin as always—he reminded her that the children would be getting there a bit later in the day. She likely wouldn't see much of Austin, he went on to explain, since he would be busy with last-minute preparations for their three-day stay. Winston had barely finished speaking when Austin dashed into the room, startling them both with his unexpected appearance.

"Lily!" he said, rushing over to her with a desperate look in his eyes. "How much do you love me?"

She chuckled in confusion, shaking her head. "What? Why?"

"The mother of one of the boys waited until now to tell me the kid will only eat chicken nuggets. Apparently, he's autistic and extremely picky when it comes to food."

"Oh, no," Winston interjected. "This again?"

Lily shot him a look and Austin recounted the nightmare they'd had a year prior with a girl who would only eat hot dogs. She knew where this was headed and didn't have to wait for him to ask.

"Let me guess… you don't have any chicken nuggets and need me to pick some up?"

"Would you?" Austin asked, pleadingly. "I know it's not in your job description, but Winston can't drive and I still have way too much to do. I just don't have the time to—"

"Alright, alright," she laughed. "Lily Ward, to the rescue."

She saw Austin's strong chest heave as he breathed a heavy sigh of relief. "You're a saint." Reaching into the back pocket of the casual khaki slacks he was wearing, he pulled out a black leather wallet and hurriedly pulled out a one-hundred-dollar bill. "Here, this will have to do. I think there's a Fry's supermarket about twenty minutes from here on—"

"Relax," she smiled, admiring how impressive his arms looked in the light blue polo shirt he had on. "I'll find it."

"I could kiss you," he smirked, looking at her with those steel-blue eyes she loved. "Grab a few bags and throw 'em in the freezer when you get back. There should be room."

"I'm on it," she assured him with a playful salute.

She was heading for the door when Austin called out from behind her. "Oh, and keep the change."

Looking over her shoulder, she replied, "If you insist."

"I insist," he smiled. Snapping his fingers, he added, "Oh, and grab some ketchup while you're at it."

"Aye, aye, captain," she said, stepping out the front door Winston had opened for her.

Lily arrived back at the estate nearly an hour later carrying four grocery bags filled with the requested chicken nuggets and ketchup.

Winston followed her to the kitchen, where she managed to make just enough room for the nuggets in the freezer and had no problem finding a place for the ketchup in the enormous pantry.

"There," she announced, closing the pantry door. "Crisis averted."

"I'm sure Mister Matson will be quite pleased," Winston smiled. "Oh, and he would like for you to meet him in the courtyard."

"Right now?" she asked.

"I believe so, yes," Winston replied.

As Lily watched him limp out of the kitchen and disappear down the hallway, she wondered what Austin Matson had in store for her now. As instructed, she made her way to the courtyard, where she found Austin by the pool, using an electric pump to inflate a colorful array of pool toys, tubes, and rafts.

"Ah, you're back," he said in his deep voice, standing to face her. "Did you manage to find them?"

"I did," she grinned. "Nuggets in the freezer, ketchup in the pantry."

"You're a lifesaver," he replied, kneeling down by the electric pump.

"I was a nanny to a fussy eater, so I totally understand," she told him.

Breaking from the inflatable dolphin he'd been working on, he looked up at her with his brow raised in curiosity. "You were a nanny?"

She hadn't meant to tell him that, but the words had spilled out. The relaxed environment and his casual attire were making it too easy to open up. She decided she was fine with him knowing about her time as a nanny, but reminded herself to be a bit more careful with her words. The last thing she needed was to blurt out anything related to Ryan.

"I was," she replied. "Before I moved here."

"How long did you do that?" he asked with sincere interest.

"Five years," she answered. "Five very long years."

Austin chuckled and returned to the dolphin. "I take it you didn't like the job?"

"The kid was insufferable," she said. "A spoiled brat who would throw the worst tantrums when he didn't get his own way.

"How old?"

"Seven. I started when he was only two. He was okay then, but it was all downhill after four. I tried to work with him, you know? I tried teaching him that you can't always get what you want, but it was pointless since his parents always got him everything he wanted."

"Do you like kids?" Austin powered off the pump and looked at her again. He seemed to be studying her face in an attempt to gauge her real feelings on the subject.

"Oh, don't get me wrong, I love kids!" Lily replied earnestly. "I wouldn't want to teach them if I didn't like them."

"Hey, you never know," he chuckled. "I swear a few of my teachers hated kids." Rising to his feet again, he gently kicked the inflated dolphin into the pool. "Do you ever want kids of your own?"

"Absolutely!" she answered. "I just want to wait a few more years. You know, after I have my degree and everything."

"Smart," he smiled, pulling a deflated neon green raft over to the pump.

"What about you?" Lily asked, turning the question around on him. She remembered him saying he'd like a family of his own someday, but she wasn't sure how serious he was about it.

"Do I ever want kids?" He paused with a look of lamentation and a sigh. "I do. If I'm being honest, I thought I would have had them by now. Maybe it's just not in the cards."

"What makes you say that? You're still young. Mid-thirties, right?"

"Thirty-six," Austin said. "Good guess." He shrugged and continued, "I just haven't found the right woman yet. It doesn't help that I've been busy building my business for almost two decades now. I've been on the go pretty much non-stop since I was only eighteen. Most kids are working at a fast-food joint at that age. I was trying to devise a global distribution system for the new processor I'd created."

Lily stood quietly, listening while he spoke. She hadn't opened up much to him, and conversely, he hadn't opened up much to her. His thoughts seemed to be flowing out unfiltered, and she didn't want to interrupt.

"About two years ago, I finally reached a point where I could slow down and take more time for myself. I started dating, thinking it was time for me to meet somebody and settle down. Do the whole family thing, you know?"

Still kneeling, he began to inflate the raft.

"And?" she probed over the low hum of the pump's motor.

"And I met a woman I thought might be the one." A curious mix of emotions crossed his face. He looked disappointed, sad, and upset all at the same time. "Let's just say I thought wrong."

She tried to gently pry more out of him, but he'd already retreated behind his own walls. It suddenly hit her that she wasn't the only one with her guard up. "What happened?"

"We went our separate ways, and that was that," Austin shrugged.

Lily could tell he was uncomfortable. Pointing at two small inflatable arm floaties that had already been filled with air, she joked, "I don't think those are going to fit you."

"Very funny," Austin laughed, the smile returning to his face.

"Pool party?" Lily asked while the pump continued to whir.

"Pool party," he repeated. "Most of these kids are traveling a long way for this. I like to let them have some fun before class begins. It also gives them a chance to mingle and get to know each other."

"That's sweet," Lily said, noting the defined muscles of his vascular arms. She imagined them pulling her in for a kiss and could feel the butterflies return. In an effort to shake them, she resorted to the world's most mundane topic. "The weather's perfect for it."

For being the middle of November, the weather really was perfect, however. An unusually warm day, the temperature was already sitting at seventy-five degrees and would likely hit a high of eighty. With how cool the desert got at night, Lily expressed concern over the water being too cold, but Austin pointed out that the pool's heater was on. He invited her to test the water herself and she knelt down beside the pool to run her hand through it, feeling its inviting warmth. An uninvited vision of Austin pinning her naked body against the wall of the pool shot through her mind; her legs wrapped around his body while he lifted her with his strong arms, holding her up with a firm grip on her ass while he slid in and out of her.

She abruptly stood and turned to the estate. "I need to get to cleaning."

"About that," Austin said, shutting off the pump. "How would you like to make some extra money today?"

Lily stopped and faced him again. "I'm listening."

"Twenty kids is a lot to handle. Well, nineteen kids since one got sick and couldn't make the trip. I have a few parents tagging along, which is normal. Some people aren't comfortable letting their kid travel alone to spend three days with a man who's essentially a stranger."

"Understandable," Lily nodded.

"Every parent has to sign a waiver," Austin continued. "I also provide security camera footage from all three days to any parent who asks for it. That's more for my protection."

"I don't blame you there," she replied, knowing how litigious people could be. Given Austin's net worth, it only made sense that he'd want to protect his reputation and his bank account.

"There are usually five or six parents here," he explained, "but this year, there are only four. I could use another chaperone to help out with everything today."

"Just for today?"

"Just for today," he nodded, and nudged the neon green raft into the pool with his foot. "I've been hosting these classes for the last five years and haven't had an incident. I'd like to keep it that way. The pool party and cookout require the most attention. Winston offered to help, but there's only so much he can do. I'm pretty sure he's half blind now but doesn't want to say anything."

"So, what are you thinking?" Lily asked.

"I set a strict bedtime of 9:00 pm for all of the kids. I know it's a lot to ask, but I was hoping you could skip the cleaning today and help out until they hit the sack. There's an extra hundred in it on top of your usual tip."

"Done," she smiled. She would have done it for free just to fill out her Friday for a change, and, admittedly, to spend more time with the gorgeous man who was now smiling back at her. Dressed up or dressed down, he always knew how to look good, and she admired the effort he put into his appearance. Her own appearance, however, left a lot to be desired. Looking down at her black work pants and work shirt, she knew she'd look a bit out of place for the day's events.

As if reading her mind, Austin looked at his watch and did the easy math in his head. "Feel free to run home and get changed if you want. It's not even 11:00 am and the kids aren't scheduled to arrive until 2:00 pm. I'm sure you don't want to stand around in the Tucson sun wearing all black. Oh, and bring a bathing suit if you want to hit the pool."

"Are you sure?" she asked.

"I'm sure," he smiled.

"Thank you!" she beamed, eager to slip into something lighter and more colorful. With the drive to her apartment complex taking forty minutes, she debated stopping at a store somewhere closer to buy an outfit but told herself she didn't need to spend any money. The real reason, however, was because all of her make-up was at home and she wanted to fancy herself up a bit.

She arrived back at the estate at 1:45 pm, having underestimated how long it would take her to get ready. She'd chosen to wear the teal sundress with a vibrant floral pattern that she'd found at a *Ross Dress for Less* shortly after arriving in Tucson. Sleeveless and long with a draped open back, it was certainly colorful and fit the occasion perfectly. Figuring she might be chasing kids around, she chose white flats instead of the white heels she'd been considering. Of course, her lighthouse necklace was on display, and she'd put extra work into her makeup. She didn't need to do much with her hair other than running a brush through it, and she let it fall down her back.

Winston let her in and commented on how beautiful she looked, but it was Austin's reaction that she was waiting for. It had occurred to her that he'd never seen her outside of her work clothes, and she was curious how he'd respond to it. Winston told her Austin was still outside setting up for the party that was scheduled to begin when the kids arrived, which should be soon. Lily took a deep breath before stepping into the courtyard, where she was surprised by how much work Austin had done in the time she'd been gone. Tables and chairs had been placed about, each table topped with stringed balloon bunches floating upward. Paper plates and plastic utensils were arranged neatly on each table as well, and a large banner welcoming the students hung from the poolside bar. The alcohol had been stripped from the bar and replaced with bottles of juice, soda, water, and snacks, making for a kid-friendly hangout. Other festive decor had been placed around the courtyard, and a large sound system had been positioned by the rear of the pool.

It took a minute for Lily to find Austin, who was placing cans of soda in the mini fridge under the bar. Crouched down with his back to her, he didn't see her approach from behind, yet wasn't startled when she announced herself.

"Hello down there," she said, smiling.

"Welcome back," he replied, continuing to load the fridge. "Hey, would you mind handing me that last case of—" Austin fell on his butt mid-sentence after turning to face her, causing Lily to erupt with laughter.

"Are you okay?" she asked, still giggling. She couldn't tell if his fall had been real or staged, but the look on his face seemed genuine.

"Lilian," he gasped, standing up and brushing off the seat of his pants. He stood there for a moment, looking her up and down with wide, blue eyes, his jaw slightly agape and appearing lost for words. "Lilian," he finally said, "you look breathtaking."

She was inclined to believe him since she sincerely seemed to have taken his breath away, albeit momentarily.

"Thank you," she blushed, batting her eyes. He stepped closer to her, still looking her over, and her heart began to pound.

Bad, Lily, bad! What are you doing?

"You're exquisite," he said, with a lustful look in his eyes. When he moved even closer, she realized she was returning the same look.

"That's a nice color on you," she replied, gently pulling on his shirtsleeve. She let her fingers run down his arm, and her breathing intensified as she felt his skin. His body close to hers, she could smell whatever cologne he was wearing, and the scent was inebriating. Her heart beat faster as he seemed to lean in for a kiss, and—

"Mister Matson, the children have arrived!" Winston's voice interrupted from the courtyard doors.

Austin quickly pulled away from her and cleared his throat. With heavy, frustrated sarcasm, he replied, "Yes, Winston, thank you! Your timing is always great!"

Lily covered her mouth with one hand and chuckled, the other hand playfully swatting Austin's hard chest.

"I shall see them in," Winston said, oblivious to the moment he'd ruined. He disappeared from sight, and Austin looked at his watch.

"They're a few minutes early," he groaned. "But it's okay. I think we're good. Can you do me a favor and finish loading the fridge while I greet the kids?"

Lily shook her head to clear away the conflict she was feeling. "Of course. Go do your thing."

"Thanks," he replied, and paused for a second. It looked like he had something else to say but decided against it, moving past her instead.

Kneeling down, she tore open the last case of soda and began stuffing the cans into the fridge while trying to process what had just happened. She'd been hoping for a reaction, but didn't expect *that* kind of a reaction. She was supposed to be keeping a polite distance from the man, yet she'd done herself up for him and had almost let him kiss her at a pool party she shouldn't even be at. She was disappointed and embarrassed by how weak she was. For all she knew, Austin could be lying about his love life and have a woman waiting for him in every state. She didn't need to be seduced by some silver-tongued Lothario.

Or maybe he really likes you.

She finished loading the fridge but remained kneeling for a moment.

And maybe you really like him.

The sound of the children's joyous screams overtook her thoughts. They burst into the courtyard, overwhelmed with excitement by the sight of everything awaiting them. Austin trailed behind with the four parents he'd mentioned, who looked almost as excited as the kids, but for an entirely different reason. While the children got to play, the parents—all women—got to spend time with the one and only Austin Matson in his multi-million dollar estate, which felt more like a resort than a home.

Lily watched from the bar as Austin gathered the kids into a semi-circle to lay down the rules for the pool party and the estate before setting them loose. While they were changing into the bathing suits they were asked to bring, he used the brief moment of quiet to walk the parents over to Lily, who smiled wide when he introduced her as his friend rather than his cleaning lady. They were exchanging pleasantries when the children bounded into the courtyard again, all heading straight to the pool to get the afternoon festivities started. The air was filled with cries of exuberance and the kid-friendly music Austin had put on; every child's face painted with pure delight as they darted about, and turning devilish when they found the squirt guns Austin had hidden for them to find.

Lily didn't think it was a coincidence that all four parents happened to be women, and it didn't slip past her that none of them were wearing wedding rings. As she watched them fawn over Austin, she couldn't help but wonder if they'd taken them off before entering the estate. Two of the mothers were quite attractive, the other two not so much, but Austin didn't return any of their flirtations. She had to chuckle at how desperately they were trying to win Austin's favor, each working hard to outdo the other.

"I love computers!"

"Nobody loves them more than me. I have, like, five of them."

"I built a computer myself once."

"*Pfft*, I build computers all the time."

Lily covered her mouth to giggle at the amused looks Austin was shooting her, tacitly suggesting he knew what they were doing. One of the mothers, who had been going overboard with her niceness, accidentally revealed her true colors when hit by the squirt-gun of a passing child.

"You little shit!" she snapped with gritted teeth, her face twisted in rage. Instantly recognizing her mistake, she tried to recover with a fake grin and a lighthearted shrug. "Kids will be kids," she added with an equally fake chuckle, but the damage had already been done.

"Yeah, maybe don't say that to a child," Austin said with a fake smile of his own, but a stern look in his eyes.

Even with her faux pas, she continued to relentlessly flirt with Austin along with the others. Most men would have sopped up the attention, but Austin seemed more annoyed than anything. Aside from their introduction filled with feigned niceties, none of the women had bothered speaking to Lily, choosing to focus only on the man of the hour. Waiting for the right moment, he mouthed the words "save me" to Lily, who was happy to oblige.

"Sweetie?" she interrupted. Taking his hand in hers, she looked at him with an affectionate smile that she didn't have to force. "Let's go have fun with the kids."

"I like that plan," he replied, raising her hand to delicately kiss the back of it. Smiling politely, he excused himself from his sycophants, who stood in a frozen stupor, likely feeling very foolish for their behavior. Lily guided him to the other side of the pool where she was confident the women would be out of earshot, and their words drowned out by the gleeful sounds of the children.

"Lilian Ward, to your rescue again," she said, well aware of the daggers being shot her way from across the pool.

Austin leaned in with a smirk. "Really? That's what you came up with?'

"It's the best I could do on the spot," she shrugged.

His smirk turned into a broad smile. "Hey, I'm not complaining."

She realized they were still holding hands. Looking down at them, she found beauty in the contrast of his white skin against her dark mocha complexion. She waited to see if he would pull away, but he seemed to be enjoying their connection.

"So," Lily began, admiring his modelesque face in the warm afternoon sun. "Are you getting in?"

"The pool?" he asked. "No. It's against my policy. I keep my entire body visible at all times," he added, pointing out the security cameras placed throughout the courtyard, all peering down with an ever-watchful eye. "You can never be too safe these days." He didn't have to explain for her to understand. A parent could convince a child to say anything for a chance at his money. With a sigh, he added, "It's easier to rebuild a bank account than it is a reputation."

"Very true," she replied. His reasoning was sound, but she'd been expecting to see him with his shirt off and was sure her face reflected her disappointment, if only for a second.

"You can go in, though," he told her, motioning to the pool.

"I didn't bring a swimsuit." She left it at that, leaving out that she wasn't ready for him to see her in the only swimsuit she owned, which was a skimpy bikini top with matching bottoms Ryan had picked out and insisted upon. She also didn't want to get her hair wet, but with the number of squirt guns she was seeing, she had already braced herself for it.

Lily thought she saw a look of disappointment flash across Austin's face as well and found amusement in how they'd both been trying to get each other shirtless. Two of the mothers approached to ask Austin where the "adult beverages" were, as they put it, and looked upset when he reiterated that it was a strictly alcohol-free retreat. He'd already told them that several times, he reminded them, and wouldn't be reminding them again. Grumbling, they rejoined the other mothers, and the four sat with sour faces, paying little attention to the children they were supposed to be looking out for.

"Wonderful chaperones," Austin scoffed, shaking his head.

"Does this happen often?" Lily asked.

"More often than I'd like," he sighed.

Writing the mothers off as useless, Austin and Lily spent the afternoon watching after the kids themselves, even getting involved in a squirt gun fight that had escalated into an epic backyard battle. Lily's hair ended up getting wet, but she'd been so caught up in the fun that it didn't bother her. Given Austin's imposing stature and deep, commanding voice, it was quite a sight seeing him so playful. He was the quintessential alpha male, yet fiercely intelligent with a sensitive heart, and was proving to be surprisingly good with kids, despite having none of his own.

When the sun began to set around 5:30 pm, Austin fired up the grill, and with both Winston and Lily helping, he made sure everyone had plenty to eat. After the cookout, the kids were herded into the cinema, where they were treated to a movie as planned. The four mothers, having given up on seducing the great Austin Matson, chose to accompany the children into the cinema rather than help tidy up the courtyard. Winston had been tasked with chaperoning the movie since Austin didn't trust the mothers to do the job, and Lily stayed to lend a hand cleaning. Austin told she was free to go, but with no other plans for the night, she insisted on helping. The kids had been extremely well-behaved throughout the day, but they were still kids and had managed to make quite a mess that took almost the length of the movie to clean.

Satisfied with the job they'd done, Lily excused herself for the night. The movie was almost over anyhow, meaning the kids would be heading to bed soon. Austin walked her to her car, thanking her again for the tremendous help she'd been, and for rescuing him from the mothers. He handed her two hundred dollars, which she fought him on, but he assured her she'd earned every penny and persisted until she accepted it. As they hovered by Lily's car, her heart began to race with anticipation of the kiss she sensed was coming. Yet, as much as she wanted it, she wasn't sure if she could bring herself to allow it. The day had shown that Austin wasn't some womanizing playboy who required adoration and attention. He could have had all four of those women if he'd wanted—likely at the same time if he'd pushed for it—yet their advances had meant nothing to him. It left her questioning if he really did have a romantic interest in her, or if she was merely some sort of fetish. She hated that thought, but had to ask herself why, out of all the women in the world, he'd want the broke one cleaning his toilets.

Standing with her back resting against the driver's side door of her car, the moment finally came. Austin appeared to move in for a kiss, but when he did, Ryan's face unexpectedly rushed into her mind, causing her to panic.

"I should get going," she blurted, abruptly turning and opening the car door. She'd managed to evade the kiss, but had left Austin standing in confusion.

"I'm sorry if I—" Austin began, only to be cut off by Lily, who had swiftly settled into her driver's seat.

"It's just been a long day and I'm sure you're just as tired as I am," she continued, steamrolling over Austin's words. She didn't even know what she was saying at this point, she just knew she needed to get out of there and fast. "And I have such a busy day tomorrow. I have to get up early to meet a friend for breakfast, and then we're going shopping, and I have to clean my own place, and…" Realizing her rambling was only making the awkward situation worse, she took a deep breath and regained her composure. "Thank you for a wonderful time," she said, smiling up at him. "I hope your weekend goes well with the kids."

"Thank you," Austin said, still with a look of utter bewilderment. "I hope you have fun with your friend tomorrow. I'll see you Monday?"

"You'll see me Monday," she nodded.

Closing her door, she sped away from his estate every bit as confused as she'd left Austin. He was everything she could ask for in a man and more, yet instead of welcoming his kiss, she'd completely freaked out and, in doing so, had just made things very uncomfortable between them. With his Sonoran mansion out of sight behind her, she pulled over to let her emotions come pouring out, sobbing uncontrollably while asking herself how she'd allowed this to happen. She'd wanted nothing more than to feel his lips on hers, yet Ryan had shown up to ruin the moment. Thanks to him, she'd developed a distrust of men that she'd unfairly been projecting onto every man who crossed her path, including Austin.

Lily sat in silence, weeping. Only now was she beginning to understand the extent of the psychological damage Ryan had caused her. Because of him, she realized she may never be able to give herself to another man, and she hated him for it. She reached up and gently brushed her left eye with her fingertips, remembering how swollen it had been in the days following his fist. The emotional pain had hurt far worse than the physical.

Tears streamed down her cheeks in dark rivulets from the eyeliner she'd been wearing. It took her nearly twenty minutes before she could continue on her way, unable to forgive herself for ruining what would have been a perfect day with an incredible man who seemed genuinely interested in her. Lily hoped Austin would show her the forgiveness she couldn't offer herself. She didn't know how she'd be able to face him again after how she acted, and finished her drive home upset and embarrassed.

In the confines of her ramshackle apartment, she crawled into bed and listened to her neighbors fighting as she wept, perseverating over how the scene with Austin had unfolded in contrast to what it could have been if her past trauma hadn't chosen that exact moment to make an appearance. There would be no getting up early for breakfast with a friend—that nonsense story had come tumbling out of her as an excuse to leave. She had no friends in this city and had probably just blown the chance she'd had at making one. She was all alone here, and filled with a chasm of emptiness, fell asleep with her face stained from tears.

Chapter Four

Winston greeted Lily the following Monday morning, and she took his warm invitation inside as a good sign. It meant she hadn't been replaced by somebody who wasn't a neurotic mess, but she knew she easily could be if she didn't get her act together. She'd spent the entire weekend beating herself up over what had happened, and was hoping Austin would answer the door so she could offer both an explanation and an apology.

"Is Austin home?" she asked Winston as casually as possible while making her way to the supply closet.

"He is, Miss Ward, but he will be busy for the remainder of the day."

"I see," she replied, trying not to appear bothered. "Well, if you happen to see him, tell him I say hello."

"I'll be sure to pass that along," Winston smiled.

When 12:30 pm hit and Austin still hadn't sought her out for a lunch invitation, she began to suspect that he was intentionally avoiding her. By 3:00 pm, she was sure of it, but held out hope that he would surface to see her out. Her heart sank when Winston arrived instead, and as she stepped out the door, she took another desperate look over her shoulder for those incredible blue eyes. Realizing she may never see them again, she thanked Winston for another generous tip and fought back more tears as she made the walk to her car.

Sinking into her driver's seat with a sigh, she told herself to be thankful she still had a job. Yes, she royally blew it with Austin, but as long as she still had a paycheck and a roof over her head, she knew she would be okay. She tried to convince herself that things had unfolded for the best since the last thing she needed was the distraction of a man. Right now, she just needed to worry about saving enough for her tuition, which shouldn't take long thanks to the Matson account.

You're okay. Everything is going to be okay.

Starting her car and putting it into drive, she began to head down the long driveway, but her old Toyota Corolla just wasn't having it. It lurched forward and seemed to seize up, making a series of loud knocking noises before dying.

"Please," she pleaded. "Please, don't do this to me."

Lily placed the car back into park and turned the key again, feeling her face turn hot when nothing happened. Trying to remain calm, she closed her eyes and took a deep breath, assuring herself that everything was okay and that the car just needed a minute. Holding the breath she'd taken, she turned the key and completely lost it when the car still refused to start, screaming so loudly that several birds took to flight from the trees they'd been perched in on both sides of the driveway. She began pounding on her steering wheel while unleashing a string of profanity so deafening, she couldn't hear her car horn sounding as her fists pummeled it with such force that the old, dry rubber began to crack. When she finally ran out of punches, she sat with her chest heaving in anger, asking herself what else could go wrong with her life.

Too emotionally drained to even cry, she rested her forehead on the steering wheel that her hands were now gripping so hard, her red knuckles had turned white. As she reflected on the mess she'd made of her life, a chuckle escaped her that soon became an almost maniacal laughter. Her hysterical cackling was interrupted by a knock on her window that made her jump, and she groaned at the sight of Austin, who was looking her over in concern. Covering her eyes in embarrassment with one hand, she rolled down the window, but couldn't bring herself to look at him.

"Car trouble?" he asked.

She sniffled and tried to collect herself. "How long were you standing there?"

"Long enough to know you're not okay," he replied.

"Great," she muttered. "Now you really must think I'm crazy."

"What? No, that's not what I meant," he said in a gentle tone. "I'm just worried about you."

She wiped her eyes and looked up at him. He was just as gorgeous as ever, dressed in a charcoal button-up shirt tucked nicely into a pair of black slacks.

"I'm okay," she told him. "I just want to go home."

"Yeah, about that," Austin began. "I'm thinking your car isn't on board with that plan."

"I have no idea what's wrong with it," Lily groaned. "I just hope it's not something major. I need it to get around. I'm screwed without it."

"Well," Austin said, unbuttoning his shirt to reveal the white cotton undershirt below, "let me take a look at it." He gently set his charcoal shirt on the roof of her car and asked her to try the engine again. When nothing happened, he dropped to his back on the ground and crawled as far underneath the car as his large build would allow.

"You know how to fix cars?" Lily asked, stepping out to observe.

"I'm no mechanic," his muffled voice answered flatly from below the car, "but I know enough to tell you that your engine block is cracked. There's oil everywhere down here."

"No… no… oh, God…" Lily gasped, beginning to hyperventilate as she felt the panic attack coming. The daughter of a certified master mechanic, she knew what a cracked engine block meant.

"Yeah, your engine's shot," Austin said, sliding out from under the car. "This thing isn't going anywhere. We'll have to—"

He stopped short when he turned to see Lily's condition. She stood shaking, her breathing labored and her eyes welling with tears.

"I… I can't…" she stammered, knowing the money she'd been working so hard to save for school would now be going toward a new car. "I… can't… I can't afford…" Dropping to her knees, the tears she didn't think she had left in her began to flow. *"Why?"* she wailed. *"Why is this happening to me? What the fuck did I do wrong?"*

Austin rushed to her side, dropping to his knees as well, and wrapping her in his arms. She fell into them, weeping against his chest while he tried to soothe her.

"Shh… it's okay," he told her softly. "It's okay. I promise you, everything is okay."

"Everything is not okay!" she cried. "This can't happen right now. I can't afford to buy a car. I just started saving money. I need it for school. I don't even have enough to buy a car. This is… I… I… I can't believe this is happening…"

Her thoughts came out in fragments that Austin seemed to easily piece together.

"Hey," he said, gently lifting her chin and turning her face to his. "Look at me."

"I can't," she sniffled, resisting his eyes. "I'm so ashamed. I can't believe I let this happen to me."

"Lilian. Look at me," he repeated in his powerfully authoritative voice. She hesitantly met his eyes, and although her vision was blurred from her tears, she could see his look of compassion. "Everything is going to be fine. This isn't the end of the world. You don't need to buy a new car. I have a great mechanic who can probably weld that crack and get you up and running again in no time."

"You don't get it," she said, sniffling again. "I barely have any money saved. I doubt it's enough to even cover the weld. This isn't a cheap fix. I'm going to be starting all over again for the second time now."

"My guy owes me a favor," Austin smiled. "Just let me handle this. We'll have your car back on the road by the end of the week."

"You're sweet, but this is my mess," Lily replied. "I'll figure it out. I have AAA and can get—" She cut herself off when she remembered she'd let her AAA membership expire two months earlier in an effort to save more money. "Never mind. I never renewed it. Of course, I didn't. Just my luck."

"Look, do you remember what I said about accepting help?" Austin asked.

Lily wiped her eyes and nodded. "Yes."

"Then let me help you." He paused and looked at her car. "I mean, what else are you going to do, push this thing home?"

She laughed and leaned into him, feeling safe in his strong arms. Austin had managed to pacify her, but her anger had been replaced by the shame of her meltdown. He always came off so calm and collected, she had to wonder if he ever let his emotions get the better of him.

"I don't know why you'd want to help me with how I've been acting lately. You must think I'm a complete lunatic," she groaned, covering her eyes with her palm.

"Stop," he said, playfully nudging her. "Here's the plan. We're going to leave your car here. I'll call my mechanic and have him over to take a look at it. I'll drive you home, and if all goes well, your car should be ready in just a few days. Sound good?"

"Okay," she conceded. A few days was manageable. The pay raise that came with the Matson account had begun appearing in her paycheck along with the extra income from working the Hilton two days a week, and with it, she could afford a ride service until her car was patched up. "Thank you."

After helping her to her feet, he gave her a warm hug and repeated that everything was going to be just fine. Enveloped in his muscular physique, she couldn't help but believe him. He seemed to have a way of making her feel protected and safe, which was surprising given how long they'd known each other.

Let him in, she told herself. *Stay cautious, but let him in. At least a little. You owe him that much.*

"Let me just grab my keys," Austin said. "Wait right here."

"Where else am I going to go?" Lily joked.

"Good point," Austin replied over his shoulder, hurrying into the estate.

Lily used his absence to scoop her handbag from her car and remembered to grab Austin's shirt as well, fighting the urge to smell it while she waited. Knowing she didn't have the willpower to resist, she stuffed it into her purse and reminded herself not to forget about it. A minute later, the center garage door opened and the black Ferrari came rolling out. When he'd offered her a ride home, it hadn't occurred to her that it would be in one of his many luxury vehicles. Just as she had when she'd first seen it parked in the driveway weeks earlier, she tried telling herself that it was little more than an excessive waste of money and nothing to get excited about. That sentiment was short-lived, however, vanishing the moment Austin pulled up alongside her. In true gentlemanly fashion, he hopped out to open the passenger door for her and carefully helped her inside, making sure she was seated comfortably before gently shutting the door for her. He resumed his position behind the wheel and paused to watch her face as she looked around the interior of the Ferrari, admiring its craftsmanship while taking in the scent of the new vehicle.

"If my father knew what I was sitting in right now, he'd totally flip out," Lily said, looking at the fine leather stitching seen throughout the vehicle. She refused to touch anything, gripping the handbag on her lap to prevent her hands from wandering.

"Feel free to take a picture."

She was tempted, but didn't want to come across as materialistic. The allure of the Ferrari wore off quickly anyhow, and within minutes, she found herself admiring Austin rather than the vehicle. His tight white undershirt shirt hadn't suffered too badly from his crawl underneath the car, and it showcased every sculpted muscle, his hypnotic blue eyes looking ahead as they took off down the driveway. He truly was a remarkable man, both mind and body, and she hadn't forgotten about the apology and explanation she still owed him. The drive gave her the opportunity to clear the air between them, and it was an opportunity she wasn't going to waste.

"Can we be honest with each other?" she asked.

"I'd like for us to always be honest with each other," he replied.

"Were you avoiding me today?"

"I was," he nodded. "After how badly I embarrassed myself Friday night, I figured I'd lay low for a while. I can take a hint."

"No, it's not like that. You didn't—"

"It's fine," Austin interrupted. "I misread the situation and was humbled. I apologize."

"What? No," she said, shaking her head. "I'm supposed to be the one apologizing. I don't want you to think that I was leading you on, or just playing with you. It's not that at all."

"No?" he asked, his brow raised skeptically. "It sure felt that way."

"And I'm sorry, I really am," Lily replied with an almost pleading tone. "Believe me, I think you're incredible. I just don't know what you could possibly want with me. You probably have a thousand women lined up at any given moment. I see the way they look at you. Hell, those moms were practically worshiping you."

"I don't know about that," Austin laughed.

"Oh, come on. You're, like, the world's most eligible bachelor and I'm this complete nobody. You have everything and I have nothing. I don't even have a car now."

"That's temporary," he pointed out. "And you're *not* a complete nobody. I really hope you don't think that."

"It's hard not to feel that way compared to you…"

"Then stop comparing yourself to me," he shrugged.

"I know, I know. I guess I've just been a bit confused by your intentions," she sighed.

"What, you don't think I could be genuinely interested in you?"

"It's a bit hard to believe…"

"Because of your job, or your social standing? You realize how silly that is, right?"

"Is it?"

"Look, I can see where you're coming from, but I hope you know I'm not like that. All that matters to me is a person's character, not how much money they make or what they have or don't have. I'm not that superficial, you know."

"Says the guy driving a Ferrari," she pointed out in jest.

"Very funny." He paused, and his face showed a hint of agitation. "I can't believe you'd think that of me. Ouch."

Realizing she'd offended him, she knew she needed to address her past. "It's not your fault, it's mine. I have some trust issues when it comes to men. I shouldn't have taken that out on you. You've given me no reason not to trust you. You've been wonderful, actually. I'm sorry."

"Can I ask about the trust issues?" Austin prodded.

There was a long moment of silence while Lily considered her words. She wanted to tell him about Ryan but didn't know where to begin and feared she might lose whatever respect she'd gained by sharing too much.

"My last relationship wasn't good." Sullenly looking down at her handbag, she continued, "It ended very badly."

That was all she could bring herself to say. Thankfully, it seemed to be enough for Austin, who looked like he had pieced the rest together himself.

"I'm sorry," he said, seeing the pained look on her face. "If it helps, I can relate."

"Yeah?" she asked, surprised by this revelation.

"Oh, yeah," he replied, followed by a heavy sigh. "It also ended very badly."

Another long moment of silence followed as they both reflected on their past, neither of them willing to share any details. Feeling they'd each said enough about a subject that was obviously still a sore spot for them both, Lily broke the silence by asking about Austin's weekend with the children. He welcomed the redirect, and his face lit up as he recounted the time he'd spent with the kids.

She guided Austin to her apartment complex as they talked, enjoying a much lighter conversation. Before reaching her building, he asked if she'd like to stop for food or groceries somewhere, pointing out that he'd never seen her eat during one of her shifts. She told him she wasn't comfortable helping herself to his kitchen, but the snacks she'd bring in her handbag were always enough to cover her until she got home. Emotionally drained and frazzled from her tantrum in his driveway, she politely passed on his offer and had him continue on.

As they made their way into her seedy neighborhood, she began to notice the looks Austin's Ferrari was getting. She always tried to avoid attention, especially in this part of the city, but a vehicle of this class was impossible to miss and was turning heads left and right. She was thankful for the tinted windows providing her with a degree of anonymity, and reminded Austin to keep them rolled up at all costs.

Even with them up, she could still hear the hoots and hollers coming from Tucson's less reputable citizens and found herself wishing they'd chosen a more discreet car.

He doesn't own a more discreet car, she realized.

When they came to a stop at the intersection before her complex, she was rattled by a shabby man who'd approached the vehicle to cup his hands against her window, trying to peer inside and flashing a toothless smile when he caught a glimpse of her. She covered her face with her hand and cast a glance at Austin, who seemed unfazed by the scene.

"Austin," she hissed through gritted teeth, still using her hand as a makeshift shield. "Please tell me you're seeing this."

"I am," he replied flatly. "It's okay. Just ignore him."

More people appeared on both sides of the street to get a look at the vehicle, and with them came shouts and whistles.

"This was a bad idea…" Lily muttered. "I probably should have warned you about my neighborhood."

"Grant and Alvernon?" Austin scoffed. "Please. I've seen far worse."

His confidence quelled her anxiety, yet she was still relieved when the light turned green. Grant and Alvernon was widely regarded as Tucson's worst area for its concentration of vagrants and drug addicts, with gunshots routinely ringing out in the night. After experiencing firsthand just how quickly a person's life can fall apart, she tried not to judge these people, but they didn't make it easy. Daylight drug use and deals were a common sight here, as were bus stop fights, and she feared what she'd come home to if she ever made the mistake of leaving her apartment unlocked. She didn't feel safe here, and had already been searching for an apartment in a better part of the city, but that search would have to wait now that she had a cracked engine to deal with.

Lily directed Austin into the parking lot of her complex, worried that the minefield of potholes might do damage to the Ferrari given its low ground clearance. However, he maneuvered around them with expert precision, safely reaching her parking spot without incident. Before she could thank him for the ride, he sprang from the car and rushed around to the passenger side to open her door for her, offering his hand to help her out.

"No way is that a fuckin' Ferrari," a voice spoke as Lily stepped out of the vehicle.

Lily and Austin turned to see a man in urban wear approaching from behind, his straight-brimmed hat cocked to the side and chains hanging from around his neck. He appeared to be a heavily tattooed Hispanic man in his mid-twenties, and he'd taken his sunglasses off to get a better look at the vehicle. Lily nervously stepped closer to Austin and grabbed his arm, feeling it tense as he assessed the situation. She could feel him ready to spring into action, yet outwardly, he looked just as relaxed and composed as always.

"It is," he said in a welcoming tone.

"Damn, man! The fuck's a Ferrari doin' in this neighborhood?" the man said, moving in for a better look.

"We don't want any—" Lily was cut off by Austin before she could finish with "trouble."

"I figured I'd give her a tour of Tucson," Austin told the man, motioning to the Ferrari.

"Yeah, maybe not the best hood to tour," the man joked, smiling wide. "You mind if I take a peek inside?"

"Sure, have a look," Austin replied, stepping aside to let the man by. "She's beautiful, isn't she?"

"She is," the man agreed. "You're one lucky son of a bitch. I've never seen one of these up-close. Still got that new car smell and everything."

Lily squeezed Austin's arm, and he shot her a wink that told her everything was okay. She listened as the two men spoke about the vehicle, both sprinkling in little pieces of their lives and finding a few comment interests. After several minutes passed, the man apologized for taking up so much of their time and shook Austin's hand, introducing himself as Peter and thanking him for the opportunity to look over the vehicle. At that moment, Lily felt a wave of guilt for having judged such a nice person. That guilt was quickly overshadowed by admiration for how Austin had handled the situation, treating the man like a friend instead of a threat. Not only did Austin have book smarts, it was clear that he had street smarts as well.

"Allow me to walk you home," Austin smiled, gesturing for her to lead the way.

Lily had expected only to be dropped off and hadn't planned for this turn of events. Afraid of Austin seeing her apartment, she tried using his car to avoid the embarrassment. "You don't want to leave a Ferrari in this parking lot unattended, believe me."

Austin looked around and shrugged. "It'll be fine. I'm not worried about it."

The car had been her only excuse, and it hadn't worked. With a sigh, she allowed Austin to walk with her to the second floor, stopping outside her apartment door.

"237," he said, noting her apartment number.

"That's me," she replied. "Thank you so much for the ride home. I know it was a long drive. I owe you."

"It was a pleasure," he smiled, "and you owe me nothing. I'll call my guy on the drive home and have him come over to look at your car."

"You're a sweet man," Lily told him with sincerity, reaching up to softly brush his cheek with the back of her hand. Austin closed his eyes for a moment, seeming to enjoy the sensation of her touch. Opening them again, he took her hand in his and kissed it, looking at her intently with his steel-blue eyes.

"Take this," he said, releasing her hand to pull his wallet from the back pocket of his slacks. He thumbed through it and handed her a business card. "My cell phone number. If you need anything at all, day or night, just give me a call."

"Thank you. I will."

"So… feel like giving me a tour?" Austin smiled, pointing at her apartment door.

"Raincheck?" Lily asked. "After the day I've had, I think I just need to lie down for a bit. I'm exhausted."

She felt bad for dashing his hopes, but she couldn't bring herself to show him the squalor she was living in. What she'd told him hadn't been a lie, however, as she'd been hit by a bout of fatigue so severe, she was struggling just to keep her eyes open.

"Raincheck," Austin agreed. "Go rest up and feel better. Text me, so I have your number."

"I will," she replied. "Get home safely."

Thanking him one more time, she slipped into her apartment without him catching a glimpse inside. She told herself that when she did move, it would be somewhere she wasn't ashamed of and could entertain guests without fear of judgment. For now, she just needed to get past this setback with her car, and hoped Austin's mechanic would quote her a fair price.

Feeling lightheaded and weak, she made herself something to eat but lost her appetite after only a few bites, deciding to cover it with plastic wrap to finish later. Instead of food, she chose sleep, curling up on the tattered couch she'd found online for only fifty dollars and had talked the seller into delivering for an additional twenty. It wasn't much to look at, but draping a blanket over it had helped, and for the price she'd paid, it was surprisingly comfortable. She was out within minutes.

Lily awoke in complete darkness to the sound of her phone ringing from inside her handbag. Feeling her way around her dark living room, she found her bag by the front door where she'd left it and frantically dug through it for her phone, thinking the call might be from Austin. Still half-asleep, it hadn't occurred to her that she hadn't given him her number yet. She'd made a mental note to text him like he'd asked, but had fallen asleep instead, figuring the text could wait. Finding her phone, she was shocked to see how long she'd slept. She'd only planned on taking a short nap, but had slept for nearly four hours, and felt like she could have slept another four if her phone hadn't rung. When she saw the call was from Jose, she tried not to panic, telling herself that he was likely calling to ask if she could pick up another day at the Hilton.

"Hello, Jose. Is everything okay?" she answered in her usual fashion.

"You... you fucking bitch!" Jose screamed so loudly Lily had to pull the phone away from her ear. *"You backstabbing fucking whore! I can't believe you did this to me!"*

"What? What are you even talking about? I think you've made some sort of mista—"

"You ran your slut mouth about my guy in California! We were going to make millions together, but he sold the entire business on me. I'm fucked now! That was my ticket out of this shitty cleaning business and you took it from me!"

Lily's heart pounded in her chest while her mind raced in confusion. "Jose, I don't know what you're talking about!"

"He sold the entire business!" Jose repeated, continuing to shout angrily. *"And guess who he fucking sold it to? Your little billionaire fuck buddy, Austin Matson!"*

Lily swallowed nervously as the pieces of Jose's story came together. "What? Are you sure—"

"Yes, I'm fucking sure!"

"Jose, please, calm down. Stop screaming!"

"Fuck you!" Jose spat loudly. He took it down a notch and explained, *"Matson flew to California to check out the processor my guy invented. He bought everything! The processor, the business, the name... everything! He owns it all now, and I know it's because of you!"*

Lily knew it, too. She groaned as she recalled telling Austin about the processor, and how he'd flown to California a day or two later. "Jose, I am so, so sorry. I just mentioned it casually and didn't think he'd take it seriously. You have to believe me, I'd never intentionally screw—"

"Screw me over? Well, you did! And after how good I've been to you, too. I hope his dick was worth it because you're fucking fired."

"Jose, please, don't do this," Lily pleaded. "Can't your guy in California give you some of what Austin paid him?"

"Why the fuck would he do that?" Jose countered. "I hadn't even invested in the business yet. He doesn't owe me shit! I already got your shifts at the Hilton filled, and I told Matson he can get fucked. I don't need his account that badly."

"Jose, please," Lily pleaded again. "Please, just calm down. I'm sure we can all work this out somehow and—"

"Fuck you! If I ever see your bitch face, it'll be too soon!"

With that, the call abruptly ended. Lily collapsed to the floor, staring up at the ceiling as her eyes adjusted to the dark. This time, she really was too drained to cry, and laid motionless on her worn carpet in an almost catatonic state, replaying Jose's words in her mind.

I told Matson he can get fucked.

She had no way of knowing if Jose had conveyed that sentiment to Austin through a phone call, text message, or email, and supposed it really didn't matter. She'd stuck her nose where it didn't belong, and in doing so, she'd cost herself the job she so desperately needed while severing OCD Cleaner's long-standing relationship with the Matson estate. She'd made a complete mess out of things yet again and had nobody to blame but herself. Sitting up, she braced her elbows on her knees and rested her forehead against the palms of her hands. She remained in that position for quite some time, reflecting on her life and wondering what she did to turn the universe against her.

You did it to yourself.

She couldn't argue with that thought. A series of bad decisions had led her to this moment—sitting alone in the dark living room of an apartment she could no longer afford. She might have enough money set aside to fix her car, but she knew she didn't have enough to cover the repair and the following month's rent. Even if she did forgo the car to pay her rent, there was no guarantee she could find a job within walking distance before the rent was due again. If she couldn't, she'd be left homeless with no money, and that was a gamble she wasn't willing to take. Life had kicked her in the gut and dealt her an uppercut when she was doubled over, turning her life upside down in just one day.

Slowly making her way to her feet, she flipped on the living room light and returned to the couch, this time to sit in anxious contemplation. She needed to find a way out of the situation she'd landed herself in, but with no job, no car, and limited money, there seemed to be no viable solution for staying in Tucson. She loved the city and had her heart set on attending the University of Arizona, but at this point, it was time to give up on that dream. From the moment she'd arrived here, everything had gone wrong and had continued to go wrong, as if some sort of force or entity was telling her she didn't belong here. The money she'd managed to save left her with only one option, and that was to sell her car for scrap and buy a plane ticket back to Ohio. She knew her parents would take her back in, no questions asked, and although it would be a blow to her pride, at least she would be safe. She could mail her few belongings back to Cleveland and—

Sudden, unexpected tears began to fall as she realized her entire life could fit into just a few boxes. She was twenty-seven now, yet had almost nothing to show for it. An overwhelming sense of despair overtook her, proving once again that she still had more tears left in her. Of all things, she found herself thinking about Austin Matson, and how she'd never see his blue eyes and perfect smile again. He'd treated her better than anyone in this city had, yet she'd done nothing but push him away. She'd had a chance to apologize to him, at least, but would have to live with the regret of never offering a real explanation.

She wiped a runaway tear from her cheek and sat in silence for a moment, debating her next move. Ohio was her best bet, and if she was going back, it would have to be soon. The end of the month was coming quickly, and she'd have to be out of her apartment by then. There was no way she could afford another month of rent and a flight home. She wasn't thrilled about breaking her lease, but had made such a disaster out of her life that there was no other way around it.

Using the same boxes she'd moved in with and had saved for her eventual move out, she began packing the few things she cared about. Shipping heavy boxes full of books wasn't going to be cheap, but she couldn't bring herself to part with any of them. She'd need them to help forget about the last ten months of her life. Most of her household items had come from dollar stores and weren't worth bringing, nor would they be needed since she'd be living with her parents again.

She could donate those things and drag her bed and couch to the dumpster with a "free" sign where they'd be gone within hours.

In a testament to what little she owned, it only took her thirty minutes to pack. Taking a seat on her living room floor next to the eight boxes she'd filled—six with her personal belongings and two with donations—she buried her face in her palms and tried calming herself with a series of deep breaths. She was still worked up from Jose's phone call, and replaying his words in her mind wasn't making things any better.

I hope his dick was worth it because you're fucking fired.

Clearly, Jose thought she'd been sleeping with Austin, and that a plot against him had been formed out of pillow talk. Her mind circling back to Austin, it occurred to her that when she'd dug through her handbag for her phone earlier, she'd brushed aside the shirt she was supposed to have given back to him. She'd been so exhausted that it had slipped her mind, but she still had every intention of returning it, even if she had to mail it. Crawling over to her handbag, she gently pulled out the shirt and buried her face in it, taking in the faint scent of the wonderful man she'd be leaving behind. Forgetting to hand the shirt over to him earlier proved serendipitous, as it gave her a bittersweet way of saying goodbye to him. Moving to the couch, she laid down with his shirt clenched against her chest, wishing things could have been different between them. His excessive lifestyle would have been a turn-off if he hadn't countered it with his giving nature. She recalled the plaques and certificates she'd seen in his foyer, each thanking him for his contributions to the city. She knew travel arrangements for his monthly students weren't cheap either, yet he'd been footing that bill for years so he could share his knowledge with the children in his hands-on workshops. He really was a good man, and she had a feeling she was going to spend the rest of her life regretting how things had unfolded between them. If she hadn't been so guarded, there was a chance they could have had something beautiful together. She'd only known him for a few weeks, yet she knew she was going to miss him for a lifetime.

Lily was wiping more tears from her eyes when she was startled by a soft knocking on her apartment door. She froze, unsure of how to react. In the seven months she'd lived there, nobody had ever knocked on her door, and it seemed odd that somebody would be knocking now. Her mind went to Jose and how angry he'd been on the phone. Chills ran down her spine as she envisioned opening the door to find the barrel of a gun pointing in her face. Given how upset she'd made him, it wasn't beyond the realm of possibility.

More knocks sounded, these louder than the previous, but not aggressive. Rising from the couch as quietly as possible, she slowly crept across the room without making a sound, hoping to catch a view of the person through her door's peephole. Suddenly, more knocks.

"Lilian? Are you in there? It's Austin."

She exhaled the deep breath she'd been holding as relief washed over her. She wiped her eyes, cleared her throat, and opened the door.

"Hey," she greeted meekly. "What are you doing here?"

She had a feeling she knew, but she still had to ask. He was still wearing the same black slacks from earlier, but had changed into a dark red button-up shirt.

"So that's where that went," he said, looking at the shirt Lily had forgotten she was holding.

"Oh, I'm so sorry," she said, handing it back to him. "I meant to give it back to you earlier. I put it in my bag and totally spaced." She paused and added, "I wasn't trying to steal it, I promise."

"It's fine," Austin smiled, accepting the shirt. "May I come in?"

"Sure," she sighed, motioning him inside. At this point, there was no use hiding her living situation from him. He stepped past her and stood in her living room, saying nothing while he looked around the apartment. "Welcome to my empire of dirt."

"It's nice," he shrugged. "Not a bad little place at all."

She knew he was just being nice and adored him for it.

"Try not to be too jealous," she joked.

He turned to her with a somber look on his face. "How are you holding up?"

"After being fired for being a backstabbing whore?" Lily asked, swallowing hard. "Oh, I'm doing just fine, Austin, thank you for asking. I have no car and no job. No place to live come the first of the month. I'm just winning at life over here, aren't I?"

"Lilian, I am so sorry," Austin began, his eyes wide and apologetic. "I had no idea Jose was looking to invest in PlastiCPU. If I had, I would have never—"

"It's okay," Lily stopped him by holding up her hand. "It's not your fault. It's mine. I shouldn't have even mentioned the damn thing, I just didn't think there was any way you'd take it seriously."

"Did Jose really call you that?"

"What? A backstabbing whore? Those were his exact words, yes, along with a few others I won't repeat."

For the first time, she saw a look of anger in Austin's eyes. "He should have never spoken to you like that. He owes you an apology."

"Yeah, well, I'd fly off the handle too if somebody screwed up my chance to make millions," Lily replied.

Austin turned to look at the boxes she'd seen him notice. "What's this all about?"

"That's my entire life. My entire life, reduced to just eight boxes. And two of them are just things I'm donating, so it's really like my entire life reduced to just six boxes. Pathetic, right?"

"Lilian, what are you—"

"I'm leaving," Lily interrupted. "I'm going home."

"Tucson *is* your home," Austin parried, visibly upset by her announcement. "I know how much you love it here. You don't have to leave."

"I don't want to go," Lily said, taking a seat on her couch. "But this city doesn't seem to want me. Everything's gone wrong since the moment I got here."

"You're just upset, which is understandable right now. Don't make any decisions until you've had time to calm down."

Lily shook her head and chuckled sarcastically. "Time? I have no time, Austin. I have to be out of here in a week. My car dying was bad, but losing my job wrecked me. I have just enough money saved up to mail those boxes and fly back to Ohio."

"Please," Austin said, taking a seat by her side. "We can figure this out. You don't have to go."

"Even if I start applying for jobs tomorrow, who's going to hire me? I can't use Jose as a reference now, and I don't even have a working vehicle." She stopped to sniffle and wipe away a tear before explaining her situation. "Let's say I do pay December's rent, but can't find a job before rent is due again in January. Then what? I'll have no money and no way back to Cleveland. I'd be homeless, Austin. Homeless. I don't know anyone in this city I can stay with. I don't even have any friends here. If my car was working, I'd consider living out of it for a few weeks, but I don't even have that as an option now."

"It does seem like quite the predicament," Austin agreed. "But you're forgetting something."

"And what's that?" Lily asked.

Austin put his hand on her knee and looked at her with a grin. "You know me."

Lily covered his hand with hers and squeezed it gently. "Yeah?"

"Yeah. So here's what's going to happen," Austin said, bolting to his feet to take charge. "You're going to stay with me. You can have your pick of whatever room you'd like and stay as long as you want. We're going back to the estate tonight and we'll pick up your things tomorrow."

She sat in stunned silence for a moment. She'd later reflect on how attractive she found his authoritative tone and his ability to assume control, but for now, she needed to address his offer.

"Austin… that's… wow," she gasped, shaking her head in disbelief. "That's incredibly sweet, but I wouldn't feel right about that. You've already done way too much for me as it is."

"You're in this mess because of me," Austin reminded her, "and you can't tell me you're not. If I hadn't bought PlastiCPU, you'd still have a job right now. That's a fact. I know it, and you know it. Now it's up to me to make things right. You're staying with me and I won't have it any other way."

Lily nervously tapped her foot while she considered Austin's offer. It really hadn't been his fault since she'd never told him that Jose had a vested interest in PlastiCPU, and he really had done more than enough for her as it was. She didn't want to be an imposition, but she also knew it would buy her the time she needed to find work.

"Okay," she sighed. "Okay, but it's only until I find another job and can lock down a new apartment. Deal?

"Deal," Austin smiled, reaching for her hand and helping her to her feet. "Grab what you need for tonight and we'll get everything else tomorrow, I promise."

"I can't thank you enough for this," Lily said as she rooted through the boxes she'd packed and pulled out anything she might need for the night and the following day. Austin stood with his hands folded in front of him, waiting patiently while she rummaged. "I will find a way to repay you for your kindness, I swear."

Shoving her essentials into two plastic shopping bags she stored under her kitchen sink, she took one last look around the apartment and sighed.

"Are you going to miss this place?" Austin asked.

Fuck no.

"Not one bit," she replied, choosing a more ladylike response.

Confident that she had everything she needed, she followed Austin to the parking lot where his silver Aston Martin convertible sat waiting for them. There were no admirers this time, but Lily found her defenses raised nevertheless. The sun had long since set, and in this part of town, one could never be too sure of what was lurking in the shadows. Always a gentleman, Austin helped her into the car before taking his seat beside her, and with that, they were off.

Chapter Five

They reached the estate by 10:30 pm, and although this was late for both of them, neither Lily nor Austin were ready for bed. Lily was wide awake thanks to unexpectedly sleeping through the afternoon and the better part of the evening, and Austin appeared to be running on a mix of emotions, one of them excitement. He seemed genuinely overjoyed to have Lily as his house guest, and wasn't surprised when she chose the bedroom on the third floor closest to the library.

"Would you care to join me downstairs for a drink?" he asked after seeing her to her room. While innocent enough, the question caused a flood of painful memories to wash over her, triggering a panic that she tried to hide. Austin, however, was far too perceptive and somehow managed to see it. "Scratch that idea. Maybe some other time."

"No," Lily said, stopping him as he turned to leave. Her instinct had been to decline the offer and excuse herself to bed, but if she was ever going to trust a man again, she couldn't keep running away. "I'd love to join you. Can you give me just a few minutes to freshen up?"

"I can do that," he smiled. I'll meet you at the bar?"

"I'll be there in twenty, if that's not too long."

"Perfect," he replied. "I look forward to it."

She waited until she was sure he was gone before bolting to the bathroom, shedding her clothes along the way and putting her hair in a bun. If she was going to spend time with him, she at least wanted to feel clean and hurried into the shower to rinse off the day's sweat. With ten minutes left, she knew she wouldn't have time to get dressed and do a full make-up job, so she settled for throwing on just the purple satin bathrobe she'd brought and just redoing her eyeliner and eyeshadow. For taking only eighteen minutes, she thought she'd done an impressive job, and still had just enough time for the long walk through the mansion. She used the elevator to save time, and on the ride down, nervously rubbed her lighthouse pendant as she played out the two ways the night could go. Unbeknownst to Austin, this was his big test, and he could either pass or fail. As she discovered with Ryan, alcohol could pierce through any veneer, exposing a person's true character, and oftentimes, their real intentions. If Austin's gentle demeanor and charm were nothing more than a clever facade, a few drinks could reveal what was really lurking beneath. That thought terrified her, but she needed to know if he had a dark side that could potentially bring trouble. If she caught even the slightest warning sign, she'd be on the first flight back to Ohio. She paused before entering the barroom and took a deep breath, hoping this wasn't yet another mistake. Shaking her hair loose from the bun she'd tied it in and placing the hair tie around her wrist for safekeeping, she kissed her lighthouse pendant and stepped into the doorway, stopping there to await his reaction.

"Right on time," Austin smiled, noticing her in his peripheral vision and looking at his watch. "I swear, you're the most punctual woman I've ever—" When he turned his head to give her his full attention and saw what she was wearing, he stopped short and his smile turned into an approving grin. He sat on one of his elegant leather bar stools, looking her over with a hint of lust in his eyes. "I'm loving the choice of wardrobe." He looked down at his button-up shirt and dress slacks and joked, "I suddenly feel overdressed."

"You like?" she asked, doing a little twirl for him.

"Oh, I definitely like," he said, rising to his feet while continuing to look her over. "You're strikingly beautiful, Lilian Ward."

"You always know how to make a girl feel special," she blushed, crossing the room to him.

"Please, take a seat," he said, helping her onto the bar stool next to his. "What would you like to drink?" he asked, moving behind the bar.

"Do you have any Moscato?" she replied, worried she sounded uncultured. As somebody who seldom drank, she wasn't versed enough in wine to know if she'd be looked down on for her choice.

"Good call," Austin said, disappearing from sight to dig through the wine cooler under the bar. "I've never been much of a wine guy. Moscato's the only wine I even like, honestly." There was a pause as he continued his search, and she could hear the clinking of bottles being pushed aside. "I drink so rarely that I don't even know what I have back here." Another pause, this time followed by, "Ah, here we go!"

He resurfaced holding an unopened bottle of Moscato, and carefully uncorked it for her. She was relieved to find he wasn't exactly a sommelier either, but more relieved to hear he wasn't much of a drinker.

"And what will you be having?" she asked.

"I think I'll join you with the Moscato," he smiled. Pulling two wine glasses from under the bar, he delicately poured them each a glass. "Cheers."

"Cheers," she repeated, raising her glass to his. She took a small sip, followed by a larger one, noting that this Moscato tasted much better than the others she'd tried over the years, likely due to its expensive price tag. "I needed this after the day I've had."

"You and me both," Austin agreed, returning to his seat next to hers.

"I take it Jose called to chew you out, too?" Lily asked.

"Boy, did he," Austin chuckled. "I could barely make out what he was saying, he was screaming so loud. He had a few creative insults, I'll give him that."

"I got the same treatment," Lily said, taking another sip of her wine. "He was convinced that processor was going to make him rich. I do feel bad for ruining his retirement plans. He's a jerk, but he was good to me… mostly."

Austin took a sip of wine as well, seeming to match her pace. "Well, don't feel too bad. He wasn't going to make a dime off of that thing."

"No?"

"Please," Austin scoffed, rolling his eyes. "The guy told me Jose wanted to invest fifty grand. That's nowhere near enough money for what he had planned. I mean, this guy was talking about a manufacturing plant with global distribution. On the off chance he did find a few more investors, the guy's a terrible businessman and would have run the entire operation directly into the ground. He's a brilliant guy, don't get me wrong, but he has no business sense whatsoever."

"So you just bought the entire business?" Lily asked, genuinely intrigued by the machinations of Austin's mind.

"That's just the thing. There *was* no business to buy. The guy had a vague business plan, that was about it. He hadn't even registered the business with the state of California or applied for a trademark on the name. Hell, he hadn't even filed a patent on the processor. The guy's living proof that you can be very smart, yet very dumb."

"Ah, so you just bought the processor?"

"Bingo. And for dirt cheap, I might add. He didn't even negotiate. He accepted the first offer I spit out. Goes to show what a lousy businessman he is."

"Dare I ask how much you paid him?"

Austin laughed and finished his glass of wine. "One million."

"That does seem cheap," Lily agreed, finishing her glass as well. She was already feeling the effects of the alcohol, but after the day she'd had, she welcomed it. Still, she knew to stay in control should the alcohol bring an undesirable change in Austin.

"I would have paid twenty," Austin said with a devilish grin. "I didn't even want the name. PlastiCPU? Stupid. The processor, however, is a stroke of genius and something I've been trying to accomplish myself for the last few years. I was almost there, but this guy beat me to it."

Lily took a gulp of her wine and Austin followed suit. She knew just enough about computing to follow along, but on a never-ending quest for knowledge, she had to know more.

"So if plastic can't conduct electricity, is it just replacing the silicon? Forgive me if that's a silly question."

"I see why you're not a model now. You're too smart," Austin smirked. "Yes, that's right… sort of. The plastic is mixed with a conducting filler. A plastic polymer holds the filler in place so it carries the electric current straight through the polymer. Does any of that make sense?"

"It does," Lily nodded. She was thoroughly captivated, but more by how excited Austin got while talking about his passion. As he continued on, explaining the more technical side of things, she sat admiring his jawline and the way his mouth moved when he spoke. Hovering over his brow, his Clark Kent curl barely moved despite his animated enthusiasm, and his blue eyes were alive with energy. Her eyes trailed down to the dark red button-up shirt hugging his body and showcasing the muscular physique underneath.

God, he's so fucking sexy.

A sudden silence fell, and she realized Austin had caught her wandering eyes. He salaciously ran his eyes down her body as well, as if to let her know they were on the same page.

"One more?" Austin asked, noting their empty glasses.

She could tell by his flushed cheeks that he was feeling the first glass of wine, which came as a relief, as it proved he really wasn't much of a drinker. Feeling much safer, she allowed herself to drop her guard so she could enjoy the night with no restraints.

"Fill me up," she smiled, only aware of the double entendre after his smirk brought it to her attention.

"I'd love to."

Her fantasy of Austin taking her in the library shot into her mind, bending her over and filling her completely as she pleaded with him not to stop. She shook the thought away and cleared her throat.

"So… tell me again how a guy like you is single?"

"A guy like me?" he asked, chuckling.

"Oh, you know. Brilliant. Gorgeous. Funny. Kind. Would you like me to go on?"

"I notice you didn't include 'rich' in there," he said.

"That's because I don't care about your money," she shrugged, raising her filled glass to his. "Cheers."

"Cheers," he returned, taking a sip. "I know you don't, and I have to admit, I find that hugely attractive."

"Oh?" she asked, taking another sip as well.

"Most women look at me and see dollar signs and a ticket to fame. They couldn't care less about me as a person. They just want my money and a chance to share my spotlight. It's beyond old," Austin explained. "I could tell the moment I met you that you had absolutely no idea who I was."

"Guilty," Lily giggled. "I actually had to Google you."

"Why is that such a turn on?" Austin laughed.

She laughed along with him and flirtatiously swatted his arm. "Silly. So, come on, spill. Why are you single?"

"Like I told you before the pool party, I just haven't met the right woman yet." He took a sip of wine and smiled at her. "Or maybe I have."

"You're smooth, Austin Matson," she smirked. "But not that smooth. You told me you thought you'd met the right woman but thought wrong."

"Boy, women really never forget, do they?" he playfully grumbled.

"That's right," she grinned. "So what happened?" Austin's face turned dour, and Lily feared her prodding had extinguished their spirited repartee. "I'm sorry," she said, shaking her head and taking a nervous sip of her wine. "I shouldn't have asked. I didn't mean to ruin the mood."

"What? No," Austin said, quick to reassure her. "You didn't ruin anything. You have every right to ask. It's just…" He trailed off and lifted his wine glass, finishing most of his drink in one big gulp. "It's a bit painful. And embarrassing."

She saw the look of pain in his faraway eyes as he seemed to relive some sort of trauma, and in that moment, she realized they may have much more in common than she'd thought.

"Hey," she spoke softly, placing her hand on his knee. "You don't have to talk about it. Not now. Not ever."

He covered her hand with his and squeezed it gently. "No, no, it's fine, really," he told her. "You'd find out sooner or later anyhow."

"Okay," she said, "but if you can't get it out, I understand."

"I met a woman at a lecture I was giving at MIT. We hit it off, one thing led to another, and we got serious. She seemed perfect… in the beginning. Everyone always does, don't they?"

Lily rolled her eyes and finished her wine. "Boy, ain't that the truth."

"She told me everything I wanted to hear. Well, everything she thought I wanted to hear. She was living in Boston, so we did the long-distance thing for a while. I'd fly her here, and I'd fly there." Austin paused to finish his wine as well. "Long story short, the long-distance thing got old fast. She kept pushing for us to live together, but really, she was just pushing to live *here*," Austin explained, gesturing to the estate. "I didn't think we were ready for that, but against my better judgment, I allowed it and she wasted no time making herself comfortable. A little too comfortable. She'd walk around here like she owned the place, have people over without asking me… I never knew who was coming or going. Call me crazy, but I should at least know who's coming in and out of my home, right? I mean, it would be one thing if it was a close friend of hers who she'd known for years or something, but she'd meet random people at a club and bring them back here without asking me first."

"Yeah, that's really not okay," Lily agreed. She listened with rapt attention as he continued.

"I figured since she was new in town, she was just going out to try and make friends. I wanted to give her the benefit of the doubt. She'd ask for my credit card since she hadn't found a job here yet, and I'd give it to her, thinking she might build at least one or two real friendships. The clubs she was going to weren't cheap, either. I had to put my foot down when she racked up a six thousand dollar tab in one night."

"Six thousand dollars?" Lily gasped. "*Six thousand* dollars?"

"That was my reaction, too. Apparently, she decided it would be fun to buy everyone's drinks the entire night."

"Basically, a bunch of strangers were getting drunk on your dime."

"That's right." Austin stopped to refill his glass of wine and poured Lily another at her request. "Anyhow, we got into a huge fight about it. She kept insisting that I was being a cheapskate who didn't want her to make friends. I told her she shouldn't be making friends at a bar or club at her age anyhow. I reminded her that she was twenty-nine and needed to start acting like an adult. Yeah, that didn't go over well. She accused me of calling her old, and that led to another massive fight. A few of my things didn't survive. Let's just say that she had a damn good throwing arm."

"Oh, Austin… Did she ever hit you?"

"She didn't," Austin sighed. "But there were a few times I really thought she was going to. I think she'd remember that I was her meal ticket and stop herself."

"How long were you two together?" Lily asked, shocked by the parallels between their lives.

"About a year. Don't get me wrong, things weren't always bad. We did have some good times. I knew she didn't love me, though. She loved my fame and money, and she loved using that fame and money for attention. She was always bragging about being my girl, which would have been sweet if she wasn't doing it for all the wrong reasons. Everywhere we went, she had to get a picture of us together to post on her social media."

"Look at me, I'm with Austin Matson," Lily said, waving her hands around mockingly.

Austin got a chuckle out of that. "Exactly. Everyone needed to know that she was with me. I wouldn't be surprised if she told strangers on the street."

"Did you love her?" Lily studied his face while he deliberated for a moment.

"No," he finally answered. "I thought I did in the beginning. Like I said, the first few weeks were great. I hate to say it, but I think I saw myself getting older and convinced myself that she was a good fit for me." Taken aback by how similar their stories were, Lily hung on every word Austin spoke, listening quietly as he continued. "It was about ten months into our relationship when my accountant noticed a good chunk of money missing from one of my business accounts. I'm talking seven figures. Gee, you'll never guess who took it."

"She stole a million dollars from you?" Lily blurted much louder than she'd intended.

"Two million, to be exact," Austin replied, taking another sip of his wine.

"Please tell me you didn't let her get away with that," she said, shaking her head in disbelief.

"Unfortunately for her, no, I did not let that one slide. She was smart enough to withdraw the money in dozens of small chunks so my bank wouldn't alert me, but she was far from a criminal mastermind. Tracing the transactions back to her was easy."

"Pardon my language, but… holy shit! What happened?" Lily was on the edge of her seat, fully engrossed in this unbelievable drama that rivaled any work of fiction.

"I confronted her about it, of course. She admitted it, but claimed she'd only done it because I'd cut her off financially, which I had. I figured by that point, she should have had a job. When we met, she told me all about her plans of becoming a software developer. Looking back on it, I don't think she even knew how to use a computer. I'm convinced she attended that lecture just to meet me and had memorized just enough developer lingo to answer the questions she knew I'd ask. I have to admit, she did a good job. She got one over on me. See? Not so brilliant after all."

"Everyone makes mistakes," Lily said, reaching for his hand. "Everyone."

"Yeah," he replied, their clasped hands resting on his knee. "I know. I didn't let her get away with it, though. I recorded her whole confession and handed it over to the police. That part was easy.

Keeping it out of the press, however, was the trick. I knew if the media got wind of it, I'd look like a complete idiot. Investors would lose faith in me. My company's stock would take a major hit. It would have been all bad."

"Well, I certainly didn't see anything about it when I searched your name," Lily assured him.

"And you never will. I had to grease some palms to make that happen, but the incident is buried deep. You saw how cautious I was with the kids. I can't afford any scandals. Scandals can ruin a person's business and their life."

"What happened to her?"

"She's currently serving five years in a federal prison right here in Tucson, actually."

"Did you get your money back?"

"Surprisingly, I did manage to get most of it back. Not all, but most."

"Austin, I… I don't even know what to say. I'm so sorry that happened to you." She took a moment to reflect on his story, and he seemed to know the question that was coming next. "You let this girl you barely knew move in and she stole two million dollars from you. Why would you open your home to me after that? You barely know me, either."

"It doesn't seem very smart, does it?" Austin laughed.

"Not really, but I do appreciate it, and please know that I would never steal. Not from you, not from anybody," Lily said, gently squeezing his hand.

"I know you wouldn't," he smiled, but there seemed to be something hiding behind it.

"Wait a minute," she said, remembering the roll of cash she'd discovered her second day at the estate. "The money I found in the bedroom… that was a test, wasn't it?"

"One you passed with flying colors," he smirked. "I had to know you if you were as honest as I thought you were. You're not the only one who has to be cautious, you know."

"Oh, you sneaky devil," she replied, glaring at him with mock anger. She had to admit, it was a shrewd trick that she might have used herself if the roles had been reversed. "Do you ever visit her?" she asked, steering the conversation back to his ex-girlfriend. "In prison, I mean."

Austin shook his head in disgust and took another sip of his drink. "God, no. I washed my hands of that mess. You know, the whole ordeal could have left me bitter and cynical, but I refused to let it. It would have been easy to lose all trust in people. To build walls around my heart and not let anyone in. I guess I just didn't want to end up..."

"End up?" Lily asked, her brow raised curiously.

He looked at her and shrugged, "Like you."

"Ouch," she said, pulling her hand away from his. "Do I really make it that obvious?"

"I see the hurt in your eyes. Not all the time, I just catch glimpses of it, usually when you begin to open up just to retreat behind your walls again." He pulled her hand back to his and held it firmly. "I won't ask what happened. You can tell me when you're ready. I just know that he hurt you deeply."

"He did," she replied meekly, avoiding Austin's gaze. He was perceptive, she'd give him that.

"Look at me," Austin said. "Please." She hesitated for a second before meeting his intense eyes. He caressed the side of her cheek with the back of his fingers. "I'm not him. I will never hurt you, Lilian, I promise you that. I'm far from perfect. You know that now. I screw up. I make mistakes. I'm human. But I'll never intentionally hurt you, and will always treat you with the respect and dignity you deserve."

"What do you want with me?" she asked, wiping away the tears his words had brought to her eyes. This was her chance to address what had been weighing so heavily on her mind. "You could have anyone. Why me?"

He smiled wide, his blue eyes locked onto hers. "Because I think you're the most beautiful woman I've ever seen."

"Oh, Austin," she blushed, looking away sheepishly.

"But you're not just beautiful. You're also smart, honest, and tough."

"Tough?" she chuckled. "You did see me fall apart in your driveway earlier, right? I don't know how you could find me attractive after that." She sniffled and joked, "I'm an ugly crier."

"Stop," he laughed. "And you're a lot tougher than you think. I know your family is back in Cleveland and you don't have any friends here, yet you've been out here making it all on your own. You've been working hard to save up for school, and I'm sure living in that neighborhood hasn't been easy, either."

"Yeah," she said, choosing not to push back on the points he'd made. Currently unemployed with no running vehicle, she didn't exactly feel like she was making it.

"I know you've had some setbacks," he continued, as if reading her mind. "But you would have figured everything out, even without my help."

"Maybe," she sighed. She really hadn't wanted to return to Cleveland, and after having time to calm down, might have figured out a way to stay in Tucson, if anything, just to avoid telling her parents the truth. She'd been too humiliated and ashamed to tell them what had really happened, choosing to keep them in the dark about Ryan. As far as they knew, she was happily living with him and about to enroll at the university.

"You would have," he smiled. "On the drive to your place earlier, you called me incredible. You're the incredible one." His smile turned into a smirk as he added, "Maybe we can be incredible together if we stop getting in our own way."

"Oh, Austin," she said, floating from both his words and the alcohol in her system. She thought he might lean in for a kiss, but he surprised her by hopping off his stool and moving behind the bar.

"I have something for you," he said, reaching under the bar and pulling out a small gift bag. He returned to his seat next to her and handed it to her with an explanation. "I actually made this for you a couple of weeks ago, but never gave it to you."

"You made me something?" she asked, feeling the butterflies return to her stomach again.

"I mean, it's nothing fancy or anything…"

She looked at him for a moment before carefully reaching into the bag and pulling out something solid that had been wrapped in tissue paper.

"Austin… what is…"

"Open it and find out," he smiled.

Delicately removing the tissue paper, what she found left her speechless, and so overcome with raw emotion that it took her a moment to find her words. "Oh my God. Oh my God," she breathed. "You made me a lighthouse?"

Tears formed in her eyes as she looked at the small wooden lighthouse Austin had made for her, even taking the time to paint it and decorate its base with real shells. The words "Lily's Lighthouse" were painted above the lighthouse's front door with a precise hand, and the bottom featured a small switch that illuminated a light atop the lighthouse tower.

"I made you a lighthouse," Austin repeated, nervously awaiting her reaction.

"You made me a lighthouse," she said again. Without thinking, she leapt into his lap and kissed his soft lips. "I can't believe you made me a lighthouse."

"I take it you like it?" he smiled, wrapping his arms around her.

"I'm... I'm sorry," she said, realizing she'd thrust herself onto him.

"You can apologize by giving me one more," he smirked.

She gently set the lighthouse on the bar and ran her fingers through his dark hair, staring deeply into his eyes and realizing that she was head over heels in love with him. What followed was a kiss so passionate, it eclipsed anything she'd experienced before. She loved the feeling of his mouth on hers and made the kiss last, finally breaking it to address his remarkable gesture again.

"Did you really make this?" she said, returning her attention to the lighthouse.

"I'm not the best craftsman, but, yes, I did. You told me you wanted to see a lighthouse. The first day we met. In the library, remember?"

"I remember," she smiled. "I just can't believe that you did."

With an almost limitless amount of money, he could have simply bought her a decorative lighthouse piece. Instead, in the most romantic gesture imaginable, he took the time to handcraft her one.

"I know it's not exactly what you had in mind," Austin told her, "but I want you to consider it a placeholder, so to speak. It's my promise to take you to a real lighthouse someday."

"Austin... this is the sweetest thing anyone's ever done for me. Nobody's ever made me anything before. I can't believe you waited so long to give it to me!"

"I was going to give it to you sooner, but thought you might find it silly. Then things got a bit weird between us and I almost didn't give it to you at all."

She admired the artistry and attention to detail again. "Oh, Austin, this is anything but silly. I love it. I really do."

And I love you, she would have added if it hadn't felt too premature. For now, she just wanted his soft lips on hers again and leaned in for another kiss, feeling his tongue dance against hers. His low, fervid moans and heavy breathing reflected his desire for her, and she was sure she was sending back her own signals.

"You're so unbelievably sexy," he growled, feeling the curves of her body through the thin fabric of her robe.

"I could say the same," she panted, unbuttoning his shirt while kissing him hungrily. He took over, undoing the last few buttons, and shrugged the shirt off, tossing it over his shoulder. This time, there was no undershirt, and she was finally treated to a view of his sculpted physique.

"Jesus," she breathed, taking in every powerful muscle.

As with the wine, he matched her pace by tugging her robe open as their mouths met again, and just like he had with his shirt, she shrugged the robe off, letting it fall to the floor. He broke the kiss to see what had been hiding underneath it, and by the look in his approving eyes, she could tell he liked what he saw. Having forgone a bra or panties, she sat naked on his lap, surprised by how secure she felt with him.

"My God," he gasped, looking her up and down. "You're perfect."

He trailed kisses from her neck down her breasts, showering each one with equal affection. For a brief moment, she worried he might ask about the small scar on her right breast, but he didn't seem to notice it, and if he did, he obviously didn't mind. With a hand on his shoulder and the other hand on his chest, she closed her eyes and moaned at the sensation of his tongue swirling around one nipple before making his way to the other. Big and full, yet still perky for their size, her breasts had always drawn attention, and with how much consideration Austin was giving each, she sensed that he was quite pleased by them. She always enjoyed having them touched, and could feel how wet she was getting as he continued to kiss and suckle them.

Sliding a hand up his thigh to his crotch, she could feel how hard he was through his slacks and could tell right away that he was very well-endowed, which was fitting, given his large stature. She squeezed his cock, and he moaned, writhing in his seat as his body begged for more. Their lips met for another kiss and their tongues mingled as she blindly unclasped his belt, pulling it off completely and dropping it to the floor. Their chests both heaving with desire, they stayed locked in a heated kiss while she worked to unbutton his pants, but Austin stopped her, seeming to have something else in mind. With lustful eyes, he pushed the bottle of wine aside and brushed their wine glasses off of the bar, sending them crashing to the floor behind it where she heard them both shatter.

"What are you doing?" she giggled as he hoisted her onto the bar top and positioned himself on his stool between her legs.

"I need to taste you," he breathed, placing her legs on his shoulders.

Lily had a moment of panic when she realized that she was sitting fully nude on his bar in plain view of anyone who might enter.

"Wait! What about Winston?"

"It's way past his bedtime," Austin assured her. "We're safe."

"Are you sure?" she asked, glancing at the doorway.

"Shh…" he replied, silencing her. Slowly kissing his way up her inner thigh, he looked up at her with a burning lust in his eyes that made her quiver with anticipation. Leaning back on her elbows, she watched as he ran his tongue up her wet slit, moaning loudly as pure pleasure coursed through her body. He held onto her hips with his strong hands, delicately kissing and sucking her clit, and she lost all control of her filter when she felt him slide a finger inside of her.

"Oh, fuck!" she cried. *"Oh, fuck!"*

She'd never been much for oral sex, but Austin was proving she'd simply never had it done properly. Other men fumbled around blindly, unaware that they were missing every mark, whereas Austin had immediately honed in on her sweet spot and took full advantage of it. She could hear how wet she was as he slid his finger in and out of her, his mouth working her clit in a way she'd never experienced before. Resting her feet on his shoulders, she closed her eyes and dropped from her elbows to lie with her bare back on the bar, squirming in ecstasy as he continued to work his magic.

"Oh my God! That feels so fucking good," she said, running her fingers through his hair.

"Mmm… you like that, baby?" she heard him purr.

"Yes… holy shit, yes. Don't stop."

"You're so wet," he said. She stole a glance as he pulled away to wipe his face with the back of his hand.

"I'm sorry," she breathed, worried it was too much.

"Don't be," he smirked, looking up at her. "I love it. You taste so good. I want more."

Grabbing the back of his neck, she pushed his head back down, feeding it to him while he hungrily mouthed her again, his finger sliding in and out of her even faster while her moans filled the room. Lily never thought she'd be able to reach an orgasm this way, and was surprised to feel herself getting close. Austin seemed to feel it as well and eagerly invited it.

"That's it, baby," he said from between her legs. "I want you to cum for me. I want you all over my face and in my mouth…"

The moment arrived when Austin slid another finger inside of her. Her back arched and her fists slammed into the bar top as the powerful climax rocked her to her very core.

"H-h-holy fuck!" she cried out, her voice quivering and her feet pressing into his strong shoulders. "I'm.. I'm…"

He buried his face in her, his mouth locked onto her pink slit while she came. She fell back onto the bar again, her chest rising and falling as she fought to regain control of her breath.

"God, that's hot," she heard him say. She opened her eyes just enough to see him licking his fingers, his chin soaked with her cum.

"What… the fuck… was that?" she panted. "That was… that was…"

Still recovering from the most explosive orgasm she'd ever experienced, she couldn't finish her thought and signaled to Austin that she needed another minute. He smirked as he ran kisses down one shaking leg before running them down the other.

Austin had found a way to impress her yet again. Not only had he made her cum using just his skilled mouth and two fingers, she couldn't believe how quickly he'd been able to do it. She looked to her left and smiled at the lighthouse he'd made for her. In the course of just one day, her life had been turned upside down but set right-side up again thanks to this magnificent man.

"Are you okay up there?" he asked, and chuckled when she replied with just a thumbs-up.

It took her a few more seconds to find her voice. "That was amazing. I don't know how you did that." She propped herself up by her elbows again and smiled at him. "A little help down?"

Austin effortlessly lifted her onto his lap again and she nuzzled his neck, breathing in his scent.

"You always smell so good," she purred, kissing her way down to his chest. Her hands explored his body, feeling every hard muscle, and he let out another moan when she returned to his cock, picking up where she'd left off earlier. This time, he didn't stop her when she began to unbutton his pants, and she could see the ache of desire in his eyes as he watched her pull his zipper down. Realizing her current position wasn't going to work, she climbed down from his lap and spread the fly of his pants, his sizable erection quite visible through his athletic boxer-briefs. A slight tug on the underwear was all it took to free it from its fabric confines, and it came springing out in full force. She could see the pre-cum seeping from his tip, and taking his hard shaft in her hand, began stroking him as he continued to watch.

"Lilian… on my God…" he breathed, his voice shaking. He closed his eyes and gripped the bar with one hand, his moans growing louder as she stroked him faster.

"You like that?" she whispered into his ear. His answer came in the form of a series of groans, each in sync with the movement of her hand. When she paused, he opened his eyes to find her looking at him while seductively biting her lower lip. That move always seemed to drive men wild, and Austin was no exception. She used the hair tie she'd placed around her wrist to put her hair in a ponytail, and his impressive member twitched with the anticipation of what he knew was coming. Bending down, she swirled her tongue around the head of his cock, tasting the salty pre-cum coating it.

"You're so big," she said, wrapping her hand around the base of his shaft. She wasn't just playing to the male ego, she really was taken by his size, and for a brief second, worried she wouldn't be able to manage it. She never considered herself particularly good at it, nor did she particularly like doing it, but was going to try her best. She owed him that much.

Here goes nothing, she thought, taking him in her mouth. One hand glided up and down his shaft while she sucked him, and judging from his moans and body language, she knew she was doing something right.

"God, that feels good," he groaned, rubbing her back with his free hand. "You're amazing."

"Yeah?" she asked, glancing up at him while she licked her way up his throbbing cock.

"Jesus!" he burst when she took him in his mouth again, this time so deep she almost gagged. She'd never been with anyone so vocal before, and to her complete surprise, she found herself enjoying it. Her jaw was beginning to ache from his size, but she was so taken by his responses—both verbal and physical—she wasn't about to stop. His commanding voice added an excitement to the act and brought out a side she never knew she had.

"You taste so good," she told him, using his own words from earlier.

"I love watching you do that," he replied gruffly.

Lily looked up at him with a smirk, using both of her hands to stroke him. "Watching me suck your cock?"

"Yes, baby." Almost pleadingly, he continued, "I want more. I want to feel your mouth again."

Baby. It was the second time he'd called her that now, and she loved the sound of it. He let out a loud groan when she took him back into her mouth, sucking him harder while her hands twisted up and down his shaft. She'd never worked this hard to please a man but was driven by his reaction, and when his hips began to thrust in his seat, she knew he was nearing orgasm.

"I love your cock," she panted, licking it from the bottom to the top before taking him as far into her mouth as she could handle. This time she did gag when he hit the back of her throat, but she didn't let it stop her and continued on, determined to make him cum.

"Not yet," Austin said. Breathing heavily, he pulled himself out of her mouth and gently stroked his cock, looking down at her with eyes full of carnal hunger. "I want you," he growled. "I have to have you."

It wasn't in her nature to be intimate with a man she'd only known for a few weeks, but with arousal clouding her judgment, her traditional convictions had flown directly out the window.

"I want you too," she said, feeling how wet she was again.

Hopping down from his stool, Austin slid his shoes off and pulled his pants and boxer-briefs down, stepping out of them and kicking them aside. Naked now, he closed the gap between them and drew her into his big arms, kissing her passionately as his hard cock pressed into her. She'd already decided she was going to let him take her, it was just a matter of where it would be happening at this point. The hard tile floor didn't look too inviting, and with how uncomfortable leather could be on bare skin, the two matching sofas beside them didn't seem very fun, either. As much as she wanted to live out her library fantasy, it was a bit out of the way for how impulsive she was feeling. By the time they'd both made it naked through the estate, she feared the moment would be gone. She wanted him now, and she knew he didn't want to wait, either. She did have another fantasy she wanted to act on, but before she got a chance to suggest it, Austin spun her around and bent her over the stool she'd been sitting on before she'd jumped onto his lap.

Okay, this works.

She cried out in a mixture of pain and pleasure as he worked himself inside of her, but the pain quickly vanished as she stretched to accommodate his girth. All pleasure now, she gripped the stool tightly and felt it rock as he began to thrust in and out, her wetness audible even with their moans. With his strong hands holding her hips, he picked up the pace, ramming her harder and faster from behind.

"You feel so good," she heard him pant.

She wanted to reply with something smoothly sexual, but all she could manage was a crude string of, *"Fuck me, baby! Fuck me, baby! Fuck me, baby!"*

The two hind legs of the stool banged against the tile floor in rhythm with Austin's thrusts. When his moans grew louder, she glanced over her shoulder and almost came again just by the sight of his incredible body.

"Oh my God, you're so fucking hot," she said through clenched teeth. "Don't stop."

He slapped her ass—a first for her that she found oddly enjoyable—and gave it to her harder, plowing into her with such force the stool began to inch its way across the floor.

"You hear that, baby?" he asked, bending over to speak into her ear while he continued to thrust every inch of himself in and out of her. "You hear how wet you are?"

"Yes," she breathed.

"I fucking love it."

It was the first time she'd heard him curse, and in its context, it drove her wild.

"You like it?"

"Yes."

"You like how wet I get for you?"

"Yes!"

"It's all for you, baby," she said, "every drop."

She'd always been so demure, she couldn't believe the words coming out of her mouth, nor could she believe how easily they were flowing. She'd never been this vocal with any man before and found it exhilarating in a taboo way.

"That's right," he growled, "that's my girl."

That's my girl, she repeated in her mind. *My girl.* She could get used to that. She took another look over her shoulder and saw that his eyes were closed in concentration, his brow glistening with sweat. She could tell he was close, and in that moment, she realized she was close again, too.

"D-d-don't stop," she sputtered. "I'm… I'm…" His grip tightened on her hips as he thrust himself into her, and that's all it took to push her over the edge.

"Cum for me again," he said, giving it to her harder and faster.

"Oh, fuck!" she cried out loudly as the orgasm hit, surging through her with an intensity she didn't think possible. *"I'm cumming! Oh, fuck! Oh my God!"*

It was rare for her to cum once with a man, but Austin had just managed to make her cum twice, leaving her shaking and winded. She hugged the stool while Austin continued on, racing toward his own finish.

"Baby," he moaned, grunting with each forceful thrust. "I… I'm…"

He didn't have to say it for her to understand that he was seconds away from erupting. In the moment of clarity following her orgasm, Lily was suddenly aware of how careless they'd been, neither of them having stopped to consider any form of protection. Despite her strong feelings for him, she wasn't about to let a pregnancy derail her dreams and worried that in his current state, he might not take that into consideration. They'd already risked it by allowing things to get this far, but she wasn't about to increase that risk by letting him release inside of her. Thinking fast, she spun around and dropped to her knees, holding her breasts up and together as an open invitation for him.

"Do it," she said, looking up at him pleadingly. "I want you all over me."

You do? Girl, what are you even saying?

"Yeah?" he grunted, his eyes locked onto hers.

"Yeah," she replied with an impish grin.

She could see how wet his cock was from her cum as he stroked himself, and it didn't take long for him to burst. He let out a long groan as he covered her chest with his warm load, surprising her by how much he had in him. She could feel it dripping down her breasts and caught a drop with a finger before it could fall to the floor. He watched her lick it off, and she hoped it looked as sexy as intended.

"God, that's hot," he breathed, winded from his visibly strong orgasm.

"You made a mess," she smirked. Looking down, she realized just how drenched she was. This was another first for her as she'd never let a man finish on her before, nor did she ever think she would. However, because she'd asked for it and it hadn't been done out of disrespect, she found she didn't mind. If she were being honest, a part of her even liked it.

"That was a lot," he chuckled. "I'm sorry."

"I'll take it as a compliment," she giggled, still feeling the effects of the wine. "Any chance you have a towel?"

"You know what? I actually do," he said. "I'll get it for you when my legs stop shaking. I just… need a second."

Lily nodded and laid down on her back to stop his cum from making it to the floor. The cool tile floor felt nice against her warm body. "I'm with you there. You fucked me so good, I couldn't walk if I tried."

Language, Lilian. You're supposed to be a lady.

Austin stood with his chest heaving, looking down at her naked body, half of it covered with his mark. "That was amazing."

"It was," she agreed. "And I think we both needed it."

"Definitely," he said, slowly making his way behind the bar in search of a towel. Finding one, he returned to her side and knelt down to wipe her clean. "When I woke up today, the last thing I expected was this."

"To be wiping your cum off of my tits?" she joked.

Austin threw his head back and laughed. "You have a way with words."

She let a silence fall as he delicately cleaned her. Looking up at him, she couldn't believe how the day had unfolded. As he gently dabbed away his mess, she found herself admiring him again. "You're gorgeous, you know that?"

"You're the gorgeous one," he returned. He stopped and looked at her with a deep affection she dared to think might be love. "I'll never forget the first day I saw you. You were standing in the foyer looking at that painting, and I just thought you were breathtaking. I couldn't take my eyes off of you." He finished wiping her clean as he continued, "When I saw your reaction to my library, that's when I knew you were truly special. You know my ex never stepped foot in there? Not even once. She had no interest in it at all."

"Not much for literature, I take it?" Lily asked.

"I think I saw her read a magazine once," Austin smirked. "But I'm pretty sure she was just looking at the pictures."

Lily laughed and playfully batted his arm. There was another moment of silence that was broken by her honesty.

"That library is how I knew you were more than just good looks and charm. There's a big, beautiful mind in there, too," she told him, reaching up to brush his cheek.

Austin looked around the room in contemplation. "This really doesn't do much for you, does it? The money, I mean."

"It's nice," she said, propping herself up on her elbows and looking at the elegance surrounding her. "But I could take it or leave it."

"Really?" he asked, studying her face.

"Really," she said. "Money makes life easier, I'll give it that much, but it's not like we can bring it with us when we're dead."

"Speak for yourself, I'm lining my coffin with gold," Austin joked.

"You're something else, Austin Matson," Lily chuckled, brushing a stray lock of hair from his face. She suddenly remembered the idea she was about to suggest before he had decided to have his way with her. "Is there any chance the pool heater is on?"

"It is," Austin nodded. "Want to go in?"

"Can we?" she asked excitedly, sitting up and wiping away a small spot he'd missed.

"I'd love to," he smiled, reaching for her hand and helping her to her feet.

"I'd say we could bring our wine glasses but I don't have the glue or the patience," Lily joked, referencing the wine glasses she'd heard shatter when Austin had pushed them off of the bar.

Austin erupted with laughter. "Yeah, I'll clean that up tomorrow. I take it you'd like some more?"

"If that's okay with you."

Picking up the bottle of wine they'd been sharing and realizing it was almost empty, he moved behind the bar again, carefully stepping around the shards of glass, and pulled out another bottle of wine.

"Château Cheval Blanc," he said, reading the label to her. "1996."

"Sounds fancy," Lily replied, resting her arms on the back of the stool she was now quite familiar with.

"We're about to find out."

He uncorked the bottle and made his way back to her, forgoing any wine glasses this time, and taking her hand in his, they headed out into the cool November night. The courtyard looked even more beautiful fully illuminated, with in-ground lights lining the edge of the lit pool and spotlights shining up from the base of each palm tree. A string of multicolored paper lantern lights added a nice touch above the outdoor bar, and the interior light of the hot tub made it that much more inviting. Their naked bodies shivered as they hurried to the pool, with Austin making a brief stop at the bar to grab a couple of towels from under it. Before stepping into the water, Lily asked Austin if it would be possible to kill all the lights. With how far removed they were from the ambient light of the city, she suspected the stars would really pop and make for the perfect romantic canopy. Austin agreed, and she enjoyed the view of his bare backside as he darted back to the courtyard entrance to flip a series of switches, each one shutting off a different series of lights until the yard was lit only by the bright stars overhead.

"A brilliant idea," he smiled, returning to her side. Shivering, they both braved the cold to admire the stars for a moment before stepping into the pool together, the warm water offering an idyllic reprieve from the cool autumn air.

Quickly twisting her ponytail up into a bun, she stepped deeper into the pool, stopping when the water reached her shoulders. She turned to find Austin just behind her, still carrying the wine bottle with the top well above the waterline. Even with the courtyard lights off, Lily could still make him out clearly, and she smiled at the sight of his body in the starlight.

"Your wine, my dear," he smiled, passing her the bottle. She pressed it to her lips and took a sip, not knowing what to expect.

"It's good," she decreed, and handed the bottle back to him. He let it pass in front of his nose a few times, taking in its boutique before giving it a try.

"It *is* good," he agreed, taking another sip. "It better be for two grand."

"You spent two grand on that?" Lily gasped.

"God, no," Austin replied. "It was a gift from Elon. I helped him out when SpaceX needed some high-end processors."

Lily shook her head in disbelief. "Wait… you know Elon Musk?"

"I mean, we're not best friends or anything, but we know each other, yeah," Austin explained, taking a swig from the bottle and passing it back to Lily.

"Do you know Bill Gates, too?" she asked, half jokingly.

"I just played golf with him last month," he answered flatly.

She searched his face and found that he wasn't playing around. Only now was she beginning to understand the importance of the man she'd fallen so hard for.

"I guess it pays to be brilliant," she said, enjoying more of the wine and feeling her buzz return.

"I'm far from brilliant," he laughed. "I just know computers."

"And business, and fashion, and home decor, and how to be charming, and how to please a woman," she rattled off. "Seriously, who are you?"

"I'm just a boy from Maine," he grinned.

"I've always wanted to go there," she confessed. "Lighthouses and fresh seafood? Yes, please."

"And winters that last half the year," Austin smirked. "But it's beautiful in the summer and fall, I'll give it that. I'd love to take you someday."

"Really?" she asked, moving in for a quick kiss.

"Really," he replied. "I have the perfect lighthouse in mind for you. You'd love it. I know all the best places for seafood, too."

"Mmm… that sounds like heaven," she purred. "Tell me about your life there."

They both hit the wine bottle again before setting it by the side of the pool. Austin wrapped his arms around her and she floated with her back against his body, listening as he recalled his upbringing. He was the youngest of three, he shared, and she wasn't surprised to learn his brothers were both successful in their own right. One was a real estate tycoon who owned dozens of rental properties, while the other was a restaurateur with a chain of restaurants running halfway down the East Coast. They'd both stayed in Maine to be close to their parents, he explained, who lived in a town so small, it was home to only two-thousand people and one traffic light. They'd been married for almost forty years, and he kept in touch with regular phone and video calls, visiting them twice a year. He had a niece and nephew he loved dearly, which explained many of the photos she'd seen around the estate.

They were halfway through the bottle when Austin began running kisses down her neck, and that's all it took to get her fired up again. Since the pool party, she'd caught herself fantasizing about this more than a few times, and she wasn't about to pass up the chance to make it a reality. She'd never had sex in a pool—or anywhere particularly noteworthy—but the idea had always excited her, and she was more than ready to act on it if Austin had another go left in him. As he kissed her neck softly, she reached for his cock and realized that wouldn't be a problem. He was already standing at full attention, and when she turned to face him, the look in his eyes told her that he was ready for more.

Lily led him to the side wall of the pool, and with her back pressed against it, wrapped her legs around him, moaning as he worked himself inside of her again. Holding her up by her bare bottom, he gave it to her slowly this time, leaning in for a long, impassioned kiss while sliding in and out of her. She sensed right away that this time was somehow different than before, but it took her a moment to identify how. Whereas the first time had felt like animalistic sex, this time felt more like…

Making love, she thought. *This is what making love feels like.*

In another first for her, she felt more than just a physical connection, but an emotional and almost spiritual connection as well. She ran her fingers through his hair while taking in the majesty of the stars above them, the beauty of the moment almost moving her to tears. Unlike before, there was no ribaldry between them now. When Austin spoke, it was with delicate praises rather than primal vulgarities.

She could feel his warm breath as he whispered into her ear, "You're so beautiful."

Holding him tightly, she buried her face into his shoulder and moaned as he continued to give it to her gently; a stark contrast from the pounding he'd given her earlier. She was surprised to find dirty talk much easier than any romantic line she could think of, and fearing she might spoil the moment by uttering the three words neither of them were ready for yet, she chose to stick with just her moans of approval. She knew she wouldn't be able to orgasm in this position, nor did she care—just feeling him inside of her was enough right now. After another passionate kiss, their eyes met and his face grew serious.

"Lilian," he began. His eyes were locked onto hers, and it felt like he was seeing directly into her soul. "I'm crazy about you."

"I'm crazy about you, too," she replied, running her hands across his broad shoulders. Their eyes remained fixed on each other as he carried her to the shallow end of the pool, where he carefully laid her down on the second step, making sure she was still covered with enough water to keep her warm. Positioning himself between her legs, he held himself over her by gripping the first step with one hand, the other hand working himself inside of her again. She gasped as he filled her completely and began thrusting, slowly building speed while remaining gentle.

"I just can't get enough of you," he breathed, looking down at her naked body.

She reached up and pulled him in for another kiss, wondering if this was the universe's way of rewarding her for the hardships she'd endured. She certainly never expected to meet a man as wonderful as Austin, and if they were to somehow end up together, those hardships would have all been worth it. With their bodies joined together in the warm water, their low moans made their way through the courtyard as they made love under the desert sky.

As she laid back on the steps, he unexpectedly pulled out of her, and swiftly moving his hands to her bottom, lifted her out of the water just enough to run his tongue up her slit. She responded with a whimper of pleasure, and he dipped his head back down for another taste. He really was a fast learner and had already figured out exactly how she liked it. Her body heaved in the water as he licked and sucked her clit, and when he slipped two twisting fingers inside of her, it took just seconds for her to cum again. Looking up at the stars, her body shaking from both the cool night air and the aftershock of the orgasm, she realized Austin's giving nature extended beyond his charity work. He seemed to genuinely love pleasing her and made a point of putting her pleasure before his.

Looking down at her nude body, he stroked himself while giving her time to recover. She found it both flattering and arousing that she excited him so much, and as she watched him in the starlight, she thought it might just be the hottest thing she'd ever seen. Needing to feel him inside of her again, she pulled him down by his shoulders to signal that she was ready, and given how wet she was from both the pool and her own cum, he slid back into her with ease. Her hands grasped his shoulders tightly while he gave her every inch of himself, yet he remained gentle, even as he neared his own finish. She could tell by his breathing that he was almost there, but before allowing himself the release, he leaned in to place a loving kiss on her forehead.

"I will never hurt you," he told her, looking deep into her eyes. His words made her heart flutter, and she reached up to brush his cheek, feeling his thrusts quicken.

"And I'll never hurt you," she said, returning his gaze. Rising just above the waterline, she ran her hand up her body, hoping the cue wasn't too subtle. "Give it to me, baby."

Sliding out of her, she watched his face twist as he stroked himself to orgasm, groaning as thick streams of cum shot up her body. She couldn't understand how he still had so much left in him and was looking at it in disbelief when he leaned in to kiss her forehead again.

"Thank you for an amazing night," he said softly.

"Is it over already?" she asked, stepping out of the pool to clean off using one of the towels Austin had grabbed. She knew she could have simply washed off in the pool, but she had every intention of enjoying more of it with him and didn't think he'd appreciate wading around in his own cum.

"Not by a long shot," he smiled up at her. "We still have half of that bottle left."

"Good answer," she shivered, hurrying back into the pool.

They spent the next hour enjoying each other's company under the stars, both allowing themselves to cross from buzzed to drunk as they finished the bottle of expensive wine. Austin revealed himself to be a playful, funny drunk, which was a welcomed contrast from the serious businessman she knew he was, and the laughs flowed as they let loose in the pool with plenty of breaks for kisses. There was a brief moment of alarm when Lily realized their sexual escapades had likely been captured on video. She expressed her concern over the estate's many security cameras, but Austin assured her the footage would be deleted the following morning and invited her to watch the process for her own peace of mind. He tactfully explained that the footage would be more damning for him, reminding her of his stance on scandal, and that was enough to put her at ease.

Floating in his arms, her back against his strong body again, they watched the stars together while sharing more banter and laughs. When a yawn by Austin triggered a yawn of her own, they knew it was time to call it a night and rushed back to the clothes they'd left strewn around the bar. Austin dried them both off using the surviving towel from the pool, and Lily still couldn't take her eyes off of his body as he dressed. She slipped her robe on and tied it at the waist before shaking her hair down and returning to the lighthouse Austin had made her, once again taken by his thoughtfulness. Despite being out of the pool, she still found herself floating from a night that couldn't have gone any better.

"Thank you for tonight," she said, all smiles as she held the wooden lighthouse. "You took this awful day and turned it into something really special."

The best night of your life, she thought.

He moved behind her and wrapped his arms around her waist.

"Let's go to bed, baby," he softly purred into her ear.

Baby. She melted every time he called her that, and she hoped it would last beyond the night. There was a slight moment of awkwardness as she fumbled through saying goodnight, unsure of the proper protocol for the situation.

"Well... I hope you get some sleep. I'm sure I'll see you tomorrow."

He spun her around by the hips and looked deep into her eyes. "I want you to be the first thing I see tomorrow. Come with me," he said, offering his hand.

With her lighthouse in one hand and her other hand holding onto his, she followed him into the elevator in the foyer, both erupting in laughter when she noticed that he'd drunkenly buttoned his shirt wrong. Still heavily intoxicated, they burst out of the elevator in hysterics and tried to stifle their laughter when they remembered how close they were to Winston's quarters.

"Shh," Austin playfully warned with a finger to his lips.

"Sorry, Winston," Lily jokingly whispered over her shoulder.

Stopping just outside of Austin's bedroom, he leaned in to kiss her again before opening the door and ushering her inside. "After you, my lady."

He flipped the light on and Lily gasped at the size of the master bedroom. Easily bigger than her entire apartment, its Southwestern theme matched the rest of the house with the same faux painting as the foyer, and positioned in the middle of the room was the largest bed she'd ever seen in her life. It was fitted with sheets and blankets in shades of terracotta, with cactus-green pillowcases adding a nice touch. Two large wooden nightstands stood on each side of the bed, both topped with matching lamps and small decorative items. Above the bed was a series of skylights with motorized shades allowing for moonlight or daylight, and another wagon wheel chandelier matching the ones she'd seen throughout the estate. The room was adorned with beautiful artwork in various mediums, as well as another glass display case protecting what appeared to be items of sentimental value. Long brown curtains dressed the room's large windows, and two double doors leading to the rooftop terrace featured sheer white curtain panels. Hanging from the long black metal curtain rod running above the doors were brown drapes, parted by black metal curtain holdbacks.

The enormous bedroom housed a walk-in closet big enough to get lost in, and a master bathroom just as big with beautiful marble tiling, matching his-and-her sinks, and a huge corner tub Jacuzzi beside a large glass shower stall. The bedroom also gave way to a small room that Austin referred to as his study, which looked like an appropriate name. A row of bookcases matching those in the library lined the back wall and shelved books along with other items she sensed were deeply personal artifacts from his life. In front of the bookcases sat a high-back leather office chair tucked behind a formidable wooden desk with a closed laptop in its center. Positioned in the corner of the room, a reclinable chair with an end table and lamp next to it suggested that's where Austin did the majority of his reading, and Lily smiled at the sight of it.

While she appreciated the brief tour of Austin's inner sanctum, his oversized bed was calling out to her weary body. She was exhausted from such a long, eventful day, and could tell she'd kept Austin up far beyond his usual bedtime. Remembering she'd left all of her things in the room she'd chosen on the third floor, Austin handed her a spare toothbrush and they continued to crack jokes as they brushed their teeth together, making good use of the bathroom's dual sinks. They shared a minty kiss before she left the bathroom so he could pee with privacy, and he returned the favor when he finished. She didn't realize just how badly she had to go, but after drinking nothing but wine all night, it only made sense.

She rejoined Austin by his bed, and he yawned as he peeled the blankets back for them. She crawled in first, eager to feel his skin on hers again, and cuddled up next to him when he took his place next to her. With his permission, she'd left the bathroom light on and the door cracked slightly, knowing she'd likely have to pee again before sunrise. Just enough light spilled in for her to make out his striking features, and with her head resting on his chest, she allowed her hands to explore his hard body again. He wrapped a strong arm around her and held her close, kissing her forehead before speaking to her as softly as his deep voice would allow.

"What an incredible night," he said, followed by a long moan of satisfaction.

"I'll say," she agreed, kissing his chest. The moment of silence following allowed Lily's overactive mind to drift to her past, and although she'd trusted Austin enough to give herself to him twice, she couldn't help but fear she was being played for a fool again. She was hit by a sudden swell of panic that threatened to ruin their night, yet even in his drunken state, Austin was still perceptive enough to pick up on her subtle change in demeanor, somehow feeling her internal conflict and addressing it head-on.

"What's wrong?" he asked, rubbing her back with his eyes closed.

"Nothing," she replied flatly. She kissed his chest again and whispered, "Get some sleep."

He opened his eyes and looked at her warily. "Nice try. Now spill."

She took a deep breath and released it as a heavy sigh. "I guess, I'm just..." she trailed off, unsure of how to phrase it. "Will you still be this sweet tomorrow?"

"And every day after," he smiled. When she didn't return his smile, he gently nudged her, and she found a solemn look on his face. "I don't want to get hurt either, you know. I'm trusting you not to hurt me. I need you to trust that I won't hurt you."

"Okay," she replied. "It's just hard. If you knew even half of what he put me through..."

"Tell me."

"It's a long story."

"I don't have anywhere to be."

"I'm afraid you're going to judge me."

"I have two million reasons not to judge you," he said, reminding her of his own mistakes.

"Fair enough," she conceded. "Strap in."

Chapter Six

The drive from Cleveland to Tucson took her just three days. She'd been so eager to start her new life with Ryan, she didn't want to waste time or money on any roadside attractions, stopping only when necessary. She kept her parents updated along the way, and she shared every leg of her journey with Ryan, who sounded genuinely excited for her arrival. However, within minutes of pulling into his apartment complex, she sensed something wasn't right. As planned, she'd called him to let him know she'd made it, yet it took him ten minutes just to greet her wearing a pair of ratty sweatpants, a stained white tank top, and a pair of tennis shoes that had seen better days. Between his questionable choice of attire, his mussed hair, and the heavy stubble peppering his face, it was obvious that he'd put no thought into the moment, whereas she'd stopped at a nearby gas station to change into something nice and freshen up. Even after a 2,000-mile drive, she wanted to look good for him, yet he hadn't bothered to put in the slightest bit of effort for her. Worse, he reeked of beer and cheap cigarettes, and was visibly drunk at only 2:00 pm, though trying his best to hide it. After a quick peck on the lips, he did help her carry a few of her belongings to his apartment, which she could smell before it even came into view.

Please don't let that stench be coming from his place, she remembered thinking as she followed him, only to realize his unit was indeed the root of the foul odor. The smell had been escaping through his screen door and two cracked windows, and she knew right away that he'd been lying about his cigarette smoking. When he ushered her inside, her mouth dropped in disgust at the sight of how he'd been living, and she immediately understood why he'd avoided showing her. From floor to ceiling, the entire unit was cluttered with junk, and she couldn't begin to count the beer cans strewn about. His claim of occasionally smoking a cigarette when nervous had been an outright lie, as cigarette butts and empty packs littered the apartment, making it quite clear that he had no problem smoking inside.

It was evident by the mess and its accompanying stench that the place hadn't been cleaned in years, and had quite possibly never been cleaned during Ryan's occupancy. Garbage littered every room, and she spotted several half-eaten slices of pizza that appeared to have been disregarded with a simple toss and left to rot. His kitchen sink was overflowing with dirty dishes, and she could tell by the rust stains on the pans that they'd been there for many weeks, if not months. His bedroom looked like an explosion of dirty laundry, pizza boxes, and empty alcohol bottles, and the stained full-sized mattress he'd been sleeping on was missing its bedding. He'd made no attempt to clear out space for her, and when she called him out on it, he claimed he'd been waiting for her so they could clean the place together. He had the audacity to frame it as a romantic endeavor; a project they could work on side-by-side, but after driving 2,000 miles, the last thing she wanted to do was deal with his mess. Unfortunately, he hadn't left her much of a choice, and she set to work cleaning while he pointed out what she was allowed to throw out, which wasn't much. She quickly learned that Ryan was a bit of a hoarder and held onto items of little to no value, convinced they might have some future use or worth. When he insisted on keeping an expired can of dog food she'd discovered in the back of a kitchen cabinet—even though he didn't have a dog—a heated argument ensued that almost ended with her driving back to Ohio. Between her frustration and his inebriation, their first official fight escalated quickly and ended when he saw how serious she was about leaving. They were able to kiss and make up, but it took Lily another four hours to make enough room for her things. During that time, Ryan hadn't been able to find any bedding, leaving her no choice but to run out and buy a set since she wasn't about to sleep on a filthy bare mattress. She chose to go alone, using her GPS system as a guide since Ryan was in no condition to tag along, and as much as she hated the thought, she didn't want to be seen with him until he cleaned himself up.

She returned to find that he hadn't done much other than smoke and drink, and after she'd made the bed, he insisted she join him for a nightcap to celebrate her first night there. She wasn't exactly in the mood for a drink, nor did the day feel like a cause for celebration, but she agreed anyhow, thinking it might calm her enough to sleep. Still upset by how her arrival had unfolded, she met Ryan on the bench just outside of his apartment since there was nowhere for them to even sit together inside. He did own an old recliner that he'd positioned in front of his television, and she assumed by its heavy wear that he spent a great deal of time in it, but it wasn't exactly built for two.

With the sun having set hours ago, the desert's cool night air warranted her winter jacket, while Ryan seemed just fine in the old sweatshirt he'd slipped on. Side by side, they cracked a beer and Ryan toasted to their future together; a future she was already questioning, considering their rocky day. She'd expected to pick things up right where they'd left off, but whatever magic she'd felt—or had imagined—just weeks earlier seemed to be missing entirely. Desperate to feel even a hint of it again, she hoped a few drinks with him would ease the tension that had been building since her arrival and possibly turn things around. She'd always hated beer, but choked it down while they sat and talked until they'd grown comfortable with each other again. When she delicately asked about his living conditions, he explained that he'd been so busy taking care of his ailing mother that he'd been neglecting his apartment. He apologized for the mess, claiming he hadn't realized just how gross it really was. He'd do better, he told her, and would help get the place in order.

Feeling better about things, they called it a night and settled into bed, and for the first time, Ryan tried advancing on her. She denied his attempt, telling him she was too tired from the long day, which wasn't a total lie. After driving for six hours just to spend eight hours cleaning the pigsty he called home, she wasn't exactly feeling sexy or amorous. Really, she wanted to wait until she felt a stronger connection with him and at least some sort of spark again. Lily could tell he was frustrated, but he acquiesced quickly and passed out, likely from the alcohol in his system. She passed out soon after in the same clothes she'd been wearing, having been too exhausted to unpack her things.

The following morning, she woke to hear Ryan crack open a beer, and when she asked why he was drinking at only 9:00 am, he told her it was just to help shake his hangover. "A little hair of the dog," he'd joked, and she was willing to overlook it since he seemed to be making good on his word, grabbing a trash bag and stuffing it with the garbage he'd strewn about the small, one-bedroom apartment. Following suit, she began filling a trash bag as well, and it wasn't long before they were both completely stuffed. Within just one hour, they'd filled six bags, but the amount of work left was almost overwhelming. When Ryan cracked another beer and saw the look she'd given him, he assured her that he needed just one more to shake the rest of the hangover. It was when he was in the middle of lighting a cigarette that their second fight broke out. She'd nicely asked if he could please refrain from smoking inside since the smoke was unbearable, to which he argued that it was still his apartment, and that he should be free to do as he pleased in it. She countered that if she was going to be living there and helping with the rent, he should consider it her apartment as well, therefore giving her some say in how things would be run. This didn't sit well with him, and he stormed out of the apartment to sulk. She let him cool down as she continued to clean, and he eventually apologized, agreeing to only smoke outside.

After many hours and several trips to the dumpster, they'd managed to take a good dent out of the mess, but she knew it would take a few more days to have it looking like a home. There was still a ton of garbage to be tossed, along with items she considered junk, yet Ryan found value in. Getting him to part with those items wasn't easy and resulted in a few small fights, but he did let go of more than she expected, although under protest. When a third beer was cracked and she asked what happened to the "just one more" line he'd given her, he promised her it was the final one and seemed to make good on that. When he was still drinking the same beer three hours later, she grew suspicious and discreetly touched the can, finding it not only full… but cold. This led to another blowout since he'd obviously helped himself to another beer when she wasn't looking, and she knew there had likely been more than just this one. "It's a cleaning party!" he'd joked, trying to make light of the situation, but she found no humor in it and insisted he lay off the booze for the remainder of the day. Seeing how upset she was, he agreed to that, and she was relieved to find his next drink was a bottle of water.

By the end of the day, she was impressed by how much they'd accomplished, and with the work leaving her sweaty and gross, she knew she was overdue for a shower. She realized that would have to wait since his shower was so disgusting she refused to step foot in it, and discovered just how hard Tucson's water was as she diligently scrubbed away what appeared to be years worth of calcium buildup. Pleased by the job she'd done, she felt herself relax as the soothing warm water ran down her tired body, transporting her to a whole other world. Her eyes closed, she enjoyed the scent of her lavender body wash as it offered a nice escape from the apartment that was looking better, but still reeked of cigarettes, beer, and rotten food. She knew it would take a few weeks, if not longer, to get the place smelling better.

She yelped when the shower curtain suddenly opened and Ryan stepped into the shower with her, uninvited and unwelcome. She tried concealing herself the best she could while screaming at him to get out. He laughed, saying it was too late and that he'd already seen her, but she'd bolted from the shower, reaching for her towel to properly cover up. She'd been so lost in her own thoughts that she hadn't heard the bathroom door open, and she was livid that he'd violated her privacy in such a way. If he was going to see her naked, it was to be on her terms and her terms only, not because he'd intrusively barged in, forcing her to see him nude as well. She still found him quite attractive, and from the quick glimpse she'd caught, his body was nice enough, but when it came to seeing each other fully exposed, he'd just ruined the romantic vision she'd had in mind.

Gathering the clothes she'd been wearing, she'd hurried into the bedroom to dress, and still fuming from Ryan's stunt, had moved to the bench outside to calm down. A fully clothed Ryan joined her moments later, still unable to comprehend why she'd been so upset and offering a half-hearted apology. She tried explaining why it was so inappropriate, but gave up when it was obvious he just wasn't getting it and headed back inside to get more cleaning done since she was too upset to sleep. Setting her sights on the pile of dirty dishes spilling out of his sink and onto the kitchen counter, she managed to clean half of them before the hot water ran out, which she took as her cue to get some sleep. She poked her head outside to tell Ryan she was heading to bed, and by the time she'd changed into her satin pajamas, he was ready to join her.

They laid awake talking, which she enjoyed and felt they needed more of, and for the first time since her visit weeks earlier, she felt a bit of their chemistry return. His words were a bit slow and slurred, which she knew was a part of his medical condition, but it wasn't much of a hindrance and she found herself enjoying their open communication. When he moved in to kiss her, she didn't stop it and was glad he'd at least had the foresight to brush his teeth. She could still smell the cigarettes on his breath, but it wasn't overpowering, and for a moment, she was able to forget about his squalid lifestyle.

That moment was ruined when he clumsily began groping her breast. She pushed his hand away just to have it return a second later, and when she pushed it away again, he moved his hand between her legs instead. When she asked him to stop, explaining that she wasn't ready for that level of intimacy yet, he ignored her and persisted, growing more forceful with every deflection she made until she finally sprang out of bed in a huff. An argument followed, with Ryan claiming that seeing her naked had got him so worked up that he couldn't control himself.

"You got me so fucking horny," he'd told her, his erection poking through the fly of his boxer shorts. "You owe it to me."

Aghast, she pointed out that he should have never seen her naked in the first place, and with that, the argument grew into another fight, culminating with Ryan stomping out of the room. When an hour went by and he still hadn't returned, she found him sitting in the living room, playing video games in his favorite worn-out arm recliner. She said nothing, choosing to let him pout while she went to bed, knowing she'd need the sleep to spend yet another day working on the apartment. The majority of her belongings were still in her car, and she was eager to get them inside since the complex didn't seem to be in the safest area.

Lily woke the next morning to discover Ryan had fallen asleep in the recliner with his video game paused. He stirred when he heard her in the kitchen preparing something to eat, which was never easy given its condition, but she managed to piece something together, and like she'd been doing, chose to eat outside to escape the apartment's lingering odor. She was debating whether or not the move had been a mistake when Ryan joined her on the bench a few minutes later, yawning as he took a seat next to her. To her surprise, he didn't get upset when she asked him to hold off on lighting his cigarette until she'd finished eating, and he took a swig from his water bottle instead. He put the cigarette back in the pack and apologized for his behavior the night before, which she accepted, but with the condition he never put her in such an uncomfortable position again. He'd had to apologize for his behavior a few times now, and she was growing tired of it, but she kept that part to herself. At this point, her concern was why she'd been there for three days, yet Ryan still hadn't gone to work. When she asked him about it, he told her he'd requested time off to help her settle in, and quickly turned the question around on her, asking when she planned to start looking for a job. He reminded her that she'd agreed to split the rent with him, and that with her help, he could save up for a car faster. She assured him she'd be looking for a job the moment the apartment was in order, which seemed to motivate him to help clean. There were a considerable amount of things he was still reluctant to get rid of, but sensing her mounting frustration, finally allowed her to toss some of it, even helping her carry it to the dumpster.

While finishing the dishes she'd started the previous night, she asked Ryan to start vacuuming the living room floor now that it was finally visible again. However, when the final dish had been washed and dried and she still didn't hear the sound of a vacuum cleaner, she poked her head into the living room and lost it at the sight of Ryan in his recliner, game controller in his hands, his eyes fixed on the television screen. Irate yet trying not to lose her cool, she asked through gritted teeth why he hadn't started on the floor, to which he replied he needed a break and would get to it shortly. When an hour went by and he hadn't moved from his seat, she reminded him about the floor and he told her he'd get to it soon. He avoided eye contact, focusing on his game with his water bottle and a bag of chips by his side. Out of frustration, she unearthed his dusty vacuum cleaner and began vacuuming the floor herself, only to have him yell at her for making too much noise. It didn't dissuade her from continuing, and in some sort of weird stand-off, he refused to budge from his seat, even when she rammed it with the vacuum. In what seemed to be an act of defiance, he spent the rest of the day playing his video game while she worked on the apartment by herself, finally making enough room for her belongings. He didn't help her carry them in, and he grumbled in irritation as she repeatedly walked in front of the television to set her things down in the bedroom behind him.

It took another four days of work for Lily to get the apartment looking presentable, and over those four days, Ryan had offered very little help, spending the majority of his time glued to his cell phone or playing video games. He'd join her in bed every night, often well after she'd fallen asleep, and she'd had to swat away his wandering hands on more than a few occasions. When he finally asked why she wouldn't "put out," as he eloquently phrased it, it gave way to the conversation they'd been needing to have. She expressed her concern over their relationship, which felt anything but romantic, and told him she'd been considering a return to Ohio since things hadn't exactly been going well there. He didn't feel like her boyfriend, she explained, nor did he feel like the same man she'd met when she'd visited a few weeks prior. This seemed to be the wake-up call he needed as his behavior immediately made a turn for the better, and for the next several weeks, things were much smoother between them, improving so drastically she finally allowed him the intimacy he'd been pushing for. She would have preferred their first time to have been forgettable. Instead, he'd made it quite memorable, but only for how disappointing it was. Fumbling around in the dark, he'd had a difficult time maintaining an erection, which he'd blamed on his small vessel disease, and after apologizing for his lackluster performance, had promised the next time would be better. Of course, she was understanding and told him not to lose any sleep over it, but the whole experience had been an awkward letdown. Unfortunately, the sex didn't improve, with Ryan continuing to suffer from the same problem while giving the same excuse. During their time together, he'd only been able to finish once, and with great difficulty, while she never came close to reaching orgasm.

Despite the sexual dysfunction, things continued to go well between them, and she soon forgot about their turbulent start. When he still hadn't returned to work, he told her that the time off had given him a chance to reflect on how unsatisfied he'd been as Circle K's regional manager, and that he'd resigned to consider other options. Since she knew he was capable of more, she was on board with this decision, but only because he'd assured her that he had enough in his savings to cover his half of the rent for another few months. Meanwhile, she'd found employment with a local cleaning company, OCD Cleaners, figuring whatever job she was assigned would likely be a breeze after dealing with Ryan's apartment.

Things began to crumble shortly after taking the job. She'd return home every day to find Ryan planted in his recliner, fixated on either his cell phone or video games with beer cans littering the floor beside him. When she questioned him about his job search, he told her he'd been researching possible employment avenues, which is why he'd been on his phone so much. He was still deciding what path he wanted to take in life, he explained, and asked her to give him more time. Despite his apparent lack of ambition, he knew how to turn on the charm when needed and could be quite convincing, always finding a way to pacify her concerns. His drinking, on the other hand, wasn't so easy to overlook, and seemed to be growing worse. She'd been able to put up with the beer, but when he switched to vodka, he became a different person, and that person wasn't somebody she wanted to be around. Each day she arrived back at the apartment to find him more drunk than the previous day, and she began finding reasons to come home late. She'd managed to befriend a coworker, and the two would occasionally grab a bite to eat when their shift wrapped up at the Hilton she'd recently been assigned to. It was the same Hilton she'd stayed at when she'd visited Ryan, but the memories she'd made with him there were now being tarnished by his current behavior, and at risk of being ruined entirely.

After two weeks of deliberately arriving home late, she knew it was time for a talk. To her surprise, Ryan admitted that he had been drinking too much, and promised he would reel it in, which she appreciated. The following day, however, she returned to find him drinking again, and when she confronted him about it, he reminded her that it was a Friday, which had always been his day to have fun. He invited her to share a drink with him, but she had no interest and tried coaxing him from the bottle by suggesting they go out to dinner. She pointed out that she'd been there for over two months, yet they really hadn't done much together and would like to see that change. He dismissed the idea and continued drinking, and as the evening progressed, grew so drunk she no longer recognized him. Worse, he began acting aggressive and seemed to be looking for a fight, even accusing her of cheating on him because she'd arrived home late again. She'd already explained that she'd stopped at the store to pick up a few groceries, and he'd even seen her carry them in, yet for some reason, he had it stuck in his head that she'd been out with another man.

"At least tell me his name!" he slurred, angrily pacing the living room. "Is he better than me? I hope he was worth it!"

The sudden accusation came out of left field and left her as confused as it did upset. She begged him to calm down, scared not just by his erratic behavior but by the deranged look in his eyes, yet there was no getting through to him. At some point, his words became so slurred they were no longer discernible, and she was relieved when he finally passed out in the recliner.

She'd hoped that was an isolated incident, but the following morning, she woke to hear a can open in the living room. Jumping out of bed, she stormed in and smacked the beer out of his hand, sending it to the floor where, it spilled onto the carpet. When it hit her what she had done, she steeled herself for his wrath, fully expecting him to come at her. Instead, he looked at her with confusion and asked why she was so upset, at which point she realized he had no recollection of the night before. Since he'd been blackout drunk, she was forced to recount his actions, and in doing so, relive the whole ordeal. He apologized, claiming he couldn't believe he'd acted in such a way, and explained that it was the culmination of the stress that had been building since she'd arrived weeks earlier. He went on to express how inadequate he felt, and how he worried he wasn't skilled enough to land a job that could afford the lifestyle she deserved. At one point, he even began to cry, which tugged at her heartstrings and bought a degree of forgiveness. She stressed that she didn't need a lavish lifestyle, and didn't care how much money he made as long as he treated her well. After pointing out that the fastest way to lose her would be to continue drinking, he agreed to an alcohol-free weekend and promised to spend every sober second of it with her. Pleased with how their talk had gone, they hugged it out and she set to work cleaning up the beer that had spilled. Ryan disappeared to fill his water bottle, returning moments later to apologize again, and to thank her for being so understanding.

With the entire day ahead of them, Lily asked if they could finally do something memorable together, and Ryan seemed to like the idea. They settled on the *Reid Park Zoo*, which happened to be close by, and the weather couldn't have been better for it. Ryan brought his water bottle so he could rehydrate from his night of drinking, and he suggested she bring one as well since the desert could still parch a person even in the winter months. The trip started off great, both sharing smiles and laughs while taking photos with each other and the animals, and they even splurged on lunch at the *Flamingo Grill*, the zoo's little restaurant. Lily couldn't stop giggling when Ryan ordered from the kid's menu, and they ate outside while watching the Chilean flamingos.

As the day wore on, Lily noticed Ryan's eyes had grown distant, his face appeared flushed, and he'd begun slurring his words. When she asked if he was okay, he told her that his small vessel disease was having a flare-up but it wasn't cause for concern. By the time they arrived home, however, his symptoms had grown worse, and she noticed his mood was beginning to take a dour turn. It almost seemed like he was…

Drunk.

It hit her like a blow to the gut. She watched as he positioned himself in front of the television again, taking a swig from his water bottle while waiting for his game to load. She'd never cared for video games, considering them a waste of time, but took a seat on the floor next to him to watch him play. Ryan didn't question her sudden interest and seemed excited to share his game with her, even asking her if she'd like to try it, to which she politely declined, insisting she was fine simply watching. When he got up to use the bathroom, she ran the water bottle under her nose and couldn't quite identify the smell, but knew it wasn't water and took a small sip, instantly recognizing it as straight vodka and recoiling in disgust. At that moment, everything suddenly fell into place and made sense. A mixture of emotions washed over her as she realized just how deceptive Ryan had been, and how foolish she was for not having seen it sooner. From the first moment they'd met, every sip of "water" he'd taken had been a lie designed to conceal his drinking, and if he'd been working that hard to hide it, she knew the problem had to be serious.

The revelation left her conflicted. She was furious at his deception, yet wanted to be sensitive to his problem. If he was an alcoholic, screaming at him wasn't going to help, and leaving him for it seemed rather heartless. She caught herself wondering if she would have gotten involved with him had she known about his drinking, but tried to let that thought go since it wasn't going to help, either. He was an intelligent guy with a lot of potential, and even though their relationship had its share of issues, she now understood that they mostly stemmed from his drinking. If she could help him quit, she was sure it would improve things between them drastically.

When he returned to his seat, she gently confronted him by saying she'd discovered the vodka after helping herself to a sip of what she believed to be water. With a deep sigh and a look of embarrassment, he admitted he had a problem yet refused to call himself an alcoholic, claiming he could put the bottle down any time he chose. This led her to ask why he hadn't since he'd promised her an alcohol-free weekend, and when she sensed his discomfort would lead to an argument, she reached for his hand, assuring him that she was worried about him and only wanted to help. He told her he appreciated the concern and was sorry he'd lied to her, but claimed this had been an isolated incident and denied having used the water bottle trick before, insisting this had been his first time and would be his last. Laying on his charm again and using his good looks to his advantage, he claimed to have social anxiety and needed the vodka to face the crowd at the zoo. Skeptical of this excuse and convinced this hadn't been his first time passing vodka off as water, she tried to remain calm while she continued to gingerly press him on his drinking. If his problem was manageable, and he wasn't an alcoholic, then he shouldn't take umbrage with her pouring out the rest of the alcohol in the home, she posited. Shooting from the recliner in a rage, he began angrily pacing the room while screaming about the alcohol being his property, and how she'd live to regret it if she touched it. When she asked what that was supposed to mean, he didn't mince words, telling her she'd end up in the hospital if she ever touched any of his things again. As with the alcohol, he'd done a good job keeping this side of himself from her, but his blackout the night before had suggested it existed.

"Did you really just threaten me?" she asked, knowing she needed to tread lightly.

"You're the one who threatened me!" he countered, arguing that she'd threatened to pour out his alcohol, which, in his twisted view, was tantamount to destroying his property. She was quick to point out that she'd never threatened that, and had simply presented the idea as a means to sobriety.

"Let's see you pour this out!" he'd yelled, swiping his bottle from the floor and chugging the remainder of it.

She'd pleaded with him to keep his voice down, worrying the neighbors would hear, but there was no reaching him. Fearing for her safety, she grabbed her keys and dashed out the door with an enraged Ryan following behind her.

"That's right!" he screamed maniacally, his words slurred and his face red. *"Go fuck your little boyfriend!"*

"Just go back inside!" she begged, knowing they were causing a scene.

"You don't get to tell me what to do!" he spat, pinning her against the side of her car with balled fists.

Her heart pounding, she feared he was going to strike her, and believed he might have had he not noticed several residents peering out from their doors and windows, curious as to what was unfolding in their parking lot. Having always been the quiet bookworm, being thrust into this unwelcome spotlight filled her with embarrassment and shame. She could feel herself shrink, and even turned her head to the onlookers in a futile attempt to conceal her identity. Realizing his shouting had brought witnesses, Ryan marched back inside, and Lily quickly sped off in humiliation. In her hurry to leave, she'd grabbed only her keys, leaving her with no real escape from the situation. Remembering her cell phone was in her pocket, she tried calling her coworker, Jeanine, but there was no answer, and with nowhere else to go, drove to a nearby supermarket where she sat alone in her car, debating a return to Cleveland and what she would tell her parents if it came down to that. She'd planned on applying at the University of Arizona the following month, and was confident she'd be accepted, but if she was going to stay in Tucson to chase this dream, it was looking like she'd be doing it without Ryan. She did care about him, but their living situation didn't exactly offer an ideal environment for her studies. As with high school, she wanted to graduate at the top of her class and wouldn't settle for less, but to accomplish that, she couldn't have Ryan as a distraction. Either he needed to shape up quickly, or she needed to find somewhere else to go.

It was pushing midnight by the time Ryan called her. Having fallen asleep in her back seat, her first reaction was to ignore the call in favor of more sleep. However, it occurred to her that Ryan might damage her belongings if he thought she was with another man, and with that in mind, she answered his call, letting her annoyance be heard in her voice. She wasn't surprised by how drunk he was, and almost hung up when he began begging her to come home, apologizing through his sobs and promising to do better. He wasn't upset with her, he assured her, he was upset with himself for screwing up the one good thing he had in his life. He didn't want to lose her, he slurred, and if that meant he had to quit drinking, that's exactly what he was going to do. Rubbing her forehead, she groaned while deciding what to do. He seemed sincere enough, but given his level of inebriation, she knew there was a good chance he wouldn't even remember the conversation. Still, if he really did quit drinking, which seemed to be the root of their problems, it might bring the peace she needed to focus on her schooling.

She returned home with the intention of leaving again if Ryan couldn't control himself. Luck was on her side, as she found him passed out in bed with his water bottle in its usual place on the floor beside him. As quietly as she could, she picked it up and carried it to the kitchen where she considered pouring it out, but settled on burying it deep in the fridge instead, figuring if Ryan found it missing and got violent, she could bail herself out of trouble by telling him where to find it. With that done, she crawled into bed next to him. He wrapped his arms around her and pulled her close to him, mumbling what sounded like some sort of apology before passing out again.

When the morning came, Lily watched him roll over to reach for his water bottle, only to find it missing. He scanned the floor with a look of confusion, even peeking under the bed, and when he couldn't find it, groggily asked her if she'd seen it. She used this as her opportunity to address his drinking again and asked if he had any recollection of his phone call the previous night. Of course, he could only remember following her to the parking lot and nothing beyond that, and after filling him in, she asked if he would honor his promise to quit drinking. If he had to choose between her and alcohol, he replied, the decision was easy, he just needed a few days to wean himself off of the booze. Seeing her confusion, he reluctantly admitted that he was an alcoholic and explained that he couldn't just stop drinking right then and there or he'd risk potentially life-threatening withdrawals. The admission was huge, and she was sure to praise him for it. Curious, she asked how long he'd been an alcoholic, and he replied that it hadn't been long. He'd started drinking shortly before her visit, he told her, because he was so nervous to meet her face-to-face. After seeing how beautiful she was in person, he continued, he kept drinking solely for the courage it gave him to talk to her. While flattering, she wasn't sure if she bought his story, but didn't want to rock the boat when they were making such enormous progress.

She pushed for him to seek treatment at a rehabilitation center, but that's where he drew the line, refusing outside help and insisting he could achieve sobriety on his own. They went back and forth on this until she finally agreed to do things his way, and she assured him she'd help to the best of her ability. Together, they worked out a path to sobriety, and the first step was to pour out all the liquor in the home, leaving only the beer. Ryan asked to pour it out himself, believing it would empower him and give him the strength he needed to kick the addiction, and Lily was fine with that as long as she was there to oversee it. In the kitchen, she showed him where she'd put his water bottle and watched as he poured it down the sink, followed by the rest of his stash from a kitchen cabinet. She was sure to express how proud of him she was, and her support seemed to mean a lot to him. With the apartment stripped of all liquor, she drove him to the store for the beer he needed to sober up. The irony of that wasn't lost on her, but from what she knew about alcoholism, Ryan's plan to get clean did make sense. He would do it over the course of twelve days, he explained, by drinking twelve beers that day, eleven the following, and working his way down to just one on the twelfth and final day. After that, his body would no longer need the alcohol and he'd be a brand new man again, he promised. His determination was convincing, and she was overjoyed by the prospect of finally seeing him sober.

They spent the day together, with Lily keeping a close eye on Ryan to make sure he paced himself and drank only the twelve beers they'd agreed upon. To his credit, he was able to control himself and seemed genuinely eager to reclaim his sobriety. She insisted he go to bed when she did, fearing he might cave to temptation if left alone, and he didn't put up a fuss. For the first time in weeks, they stayed up talking, with Ryan sharing his feelings as he held her. She hadn't realized just how lonely she'd been, and just how much she needed the time with him. Yes, he'd still spent the day drinking, but since he'd been limited to just beer, his temperament hadn't changed, and he'd stayed charming and sweet.

The following day posed a challenge. With the weekend over, Lily had to return to work, leaving Ryan alone for a large chunk of the day. He promised her he'd be fine, but she still insisted on taking the beer with her and leaving him the eleven he'd been designated for the day. Not only was he fine with this, he thanked her for looking out for him and even kissed her goodbye as she left for work, sending her out the door with a smile. They'd agreed to spend the day texting each other, hoping it would help keep Ryan in line, and to Lily's surprise, she found herself enjoying it. It was reminiscent of the time they'd spent talking before she'd moved there, and it reminded her of how funny he could be.

For the next four days, Ryan managed to stay the course, and in a welcome contrast from the previous weeks, she'd return home to find him a bit more sober than the day before. Over those four days, their relationship improved drastically, and with that improvement came a sense of optimism. Of course, his sobriety wouldn't fix all of their problems as he still needed to find a job, but it gave her hope that she could attend school while living with him. That hope was dashed when Friday came, bringing with it a nightmare that would change the course of her life.

Like she'd been doing, she finished her shift and hurried home to check on Ryan, only to find him missing. With how good their communication had been throughout the week, his unexplained absence left her with a bad feeling, and her concern grew when her phone calls and text messages went unanswered. She paced the apartment, unsure of how to handle the situation, when a sudden knock on the front door stopped her in her tracks. Thinking he may have gone for a walk and locked himself out, she rushed to open the door and was greeted by an attractive middle-aged woman who stood tall and proud, elegantly dressed in what looked to be an expensive belted pantsuit and holding a Louis Vuitton handbag. Her angled bob hairstyle made her pearl earrings stand out, and the pearls around her neck seemed to be a part of the same matching set.

"And you would be?" the woman asked, lowering her sunglasses to look Lily over.

"Lily Ward," Lily had replied. "And *you* would be?"

Both visibly surprised by the sight of each other, the woman introduced herself as Shannon Carter, Ryan's mother, and Lily immediately lowered her defenses, mentioning that Ryan wasn't home but welcoming Shannon into the apartment, regardless. The conversation that followed was one Lily would never forget.

"Wow," Shannon said, looking around the place in disbelief. "I've never seen this place so clean. I take it this was your doing?"

"It was," Lily nodded.

"So I'm going to assume you're Ryan's girlfriend, then?"

"I am," Lily answered. "He's never mentioned me?"

"I haven't spoken to him in almost three months," Shannon replied. "I've been calling and texting him but I haven't heard back. I thought I'd swing by to check on him while I'm in town."

“In town?” Lily asked.

“I drove down from Phoenix,” Shannon explained.

“Ryan told me you live here in Tucson.”

“Not for eight years,” Shannon laughed.

“You’ll have to forgive me if I seem a bit confused by all of this,” Lily had told her. “You’re not what I’d pictured at all.”

“And why is that?” Shannon questioned, looking just as confused as Lily.

Ryan had painted her as sickly and frail, Lily had explained, and claimed he’d been caring for her in recent months, yet the woman standing before her was anything but ill. She seemed healthy, strong, and very independent.

“I see he’s still up to his old tricks,” Shannon groaned.

“Excuse me?”

“Look,” Shannon began with a sigh. “You’re a beautiful young woman with your whole future ahead of you. I don’t know how you met Ryan, but I already know he’s been lying to you. I love my son unconditionally, but he’s got more than a few issues he needs to sort out before he can start dating.”

“We’ve been working on those issues,” Lily was quick to reply.

“I doubt you know half of them,” Shannon scoffed. “He got his looks from me. The rest, I credit to his con man of a father. Is he still drinking?”

“That’s one of the things we’ve been working on. He’s in the middle of quitting right now,” Lily replied proudly. “He’s almost sober.”

“Ha!” Shannon cackled. “I’ve heard that before a dozen times.”

Lily’s heart sank. “He told me his drinking has been a recent thing.”

“He’s been a drunk for a decade,” Shannon shared. “I’ve tried getting him help, but he refuses. I’ve threatened to take this place from him if he doesn't sober up, but even the threat of homelessness doesn't work."

"Take this place from him?" Lily repeated in confusion.

"Oh, sweetie, who do you think pays the bills here?"

Lily shook her head. "What are you talking about?"

"I've been keeping the roof over his head for the last six years because his drinking is so bad, he can't hold down a job."

"He was working as the regional manager for Circle K," Lily corrected her.

"Regional manager? That's a new one," Shannon laughed. "He worked there for three days last year. They fired him for showing up drunk. They also suspected he'd been stealing lottery tickets but couldn't prove it."

Lily's heart began to race, unsure of whom to believe. She thought back to all the times Ryan had mentioned his position at Circle K, and couldn't imagine it being a complete fabrication. He'd seemed so genuine, and so dismayed that he couldn't take the time off to fly to Cleveland. Surely, his mother had to be wrong.

"I'm sorry, but you must be mistaken. He was the regional manager there," Lily stated confidently in an attempt to defend him.

"You don't want to believe it. I understand that. None of you ever want to believe it," Shannon replied, followed by an exasperated sigh.

"None of who?"

"None of the women Ryan sponges off of," Shannon had told her. "You're not the first, and I know you won't be the last. It's what he does. Hell, he sponges off of me, too, only I allow it because I don't want him to end up a homeless drunk. I know I need to cut the cord, but I just can't bring myself to. I figure if I help him out with this apartment, at least I'll know where he is and won't have to search the streets for him. No mother wants to worry about where their child is sleeping."

"I… I don't know what to say…" Lily stammered, trying to process everything she was hearing.

"He's a con man, just like his father," Shannon continued. "It pains me to say that, but it's true. If you knew what was good for you, you'd pack your things and get out now. This is only going to end badly for you."

"We've addressed his issues and are working them out," Lily said, doubling-down on her position. The conversation was making her uneasy, and felt one-sided without Ryan there to defend himself. "He's sobering up, and he's been looking for another job."

"Sobering up," Shannon laughed sarcastically. "By drinking more 'water,' right?"

"Look, I know about the water bottle thing and I've been keeping an eye on it. I can't speak for his past, but I can speak for right now, and right now, he's doing great."

"Speaking of which, do you even know where he is right now?" Shannon asked.

"I'm sure he just walked to the store. He'll probably be back any minute."

Shannon used her cell phone to note the time and replied, "It's 6:00 pm on a Friday. I guarantee he's at that bar down the street. What's the name of it?" She snapped her fingers as it came back to her. "The Wooden Nickel, that's it. That's always been his go-to dive bar because he can't drive and it's only a mile away."

"What do you mean, he can't drive?"

"Because of his accident," Shannon replied. Seeing Lily's look of confusion, she explained that three years prior, Ryan had hit a man while driving blackout drunk. The man survived, though barely and with permanent damage, and Ryan had served a brief stint in the county jail. With no job to pay his hefty fine, Shannon was left to foot the bill, and Ryan had promised to pay her back when he sobered up and got back on his feet. That never happened, however, and his license had remained revoked.

Lily felt her face grow warm. Everything Shannon was saying was adding up, but she didn't want to believe it. All she could bring herself to reply was, "I don't know anything about that. I just know he's doing better now."

"Well, forgive me for being skeptical, but I've heard that before. If he is doing better, then I'm happy for him. It's all I've wanted for years now. How's he been doing with the gambling?"

"Excuse me?" Lily asked.

"Oh, no. You don't know about the gambling," Shannon groaned.

"I have no idea what you're talking about."

"And you've lived here for how long?"

"Almost three months," Lily nervously replied.

"Have you ever mentioned having any money? A savings account or anything?"

Lily's heart beat faster as she recalled the times she'd told Ryan about the money she'd saved up for her schooling. "Yes, I have."

"Then it's probably too late," Shannon sighed. "I'm so sorry, Lily. Had I known about you, I would have warned you sooner. There's a good man in Ryan somewhere, but his addictions bring out the worst in him."

By now, Lily was in a full-blown panic. "You really think he'd touch my money?"

Shannon paused for a moment, seemingly reluctant to condemn her son more than she already had.

"I'd be willing to bet it's already gone. I could be wrong. I hope I'm wrong. I just know he gravitates towards women with money so he can use it to fuel his addictions."

"So he uses women for money," Lily blurted, done with the sugar-coating.

"I don't know if it's intentional, but the last six all moved in here with money and left with nothing."

"The last six?" Lily spat. Ryan had mentioned very little of his previous relationships, only sharing that it had been some time since his last one, and that it had ended amicably.

Shannon took a step closer and said in a hushed tone, "Check under his mattress. It's where he likes to hide things." She cleared her throat and added, "I need to get going. I was only down this way to do dinner with the district attorney. We're old friends. I figured I'd pop by to check on Ryan before I left. I'll stop by The Wooden Nickel on my way out, and if I find him there, I'll be sure to send him home."

"Thank you," Lily replied, walking her to the door.

"You really seem lovely," Shannon said. "I wish we could have met under better circumstances, and I hope I'm wrong about Ryan this time."

She saw herself out, leaving Lily panicked and shaking. She stood frozen for a long moment, her mind racing from the allegations lobbed against Ryan by his own mother.

Check under his mattress.

Those words replayed in her mind, sending her bolting into the bedroom, where she dropped to the floor to look under the bed. She was disgusted to find a collection of empty vodka bottles and losing scratch tickets, but aside from those and a few dirty socks, there wasn't anything too incriminating. She felt a wave of relief as she returned to her feet, but that relief vanished when she realized Shannon had said "mattress," not "bed." Filled with a sense of dread, she took a deep breath, closed her eyes, and slowly lifted the mattress while silently praying to find nothing underneath. Opening her eyes, what she discovered was a betrayal unlike anything she could have ever imagined.

In the weeks since she'd moved in, she'd wondered why she'd hadn't received much mail, but had been so preoccupied with Ryan's drama, she hadn't had a chance to follow up with it. She typically didn't receive much mail anyhow, and it certainly wasn't enough to warrant having it forwarded through the post office, but she could always rely on her monthly bank statements. None had arrived in her time there, or so she thought, which she hadn't realized until she found them hidden under Ryan's mattress along with credit card offers and approvals in her name. He'd torn into the bank statements, and as she looked them over, she burst into tears at how much money he'd stolen from her. He'd managed to access her savings account, which likely wasn't too difficult considering they lived together, and over the course of three months, had blown almost all of the money she'd set aside for her schooling. She'd arrived with close to twenty thousand dollars, yet her recent bank statement was showing a balance of only five hundred dollars. Heartache turning to blind rage, she flipped the entire mattress over, sending it crashing into a nightstand and breaking a lamp.

Turning her attention to the credit card offers and letters of approval, she learned that Ryan had opened several lines of credit in her name, and she was sure he'd already maxed out whatever cards he'd been sent. Not only had he drained her savings account, he'd likely destroyed her credit as well, since several of the cards had been approved for rather large amounts that she knew she could never pay off with her current job. Frantic, she called her bank and angrily paced the bedroom as she waited to be transferred to their fraud department. She reported it, and was told they'd investigate it, but since most of the transactions didn't require any sort of authorized signature, the fraud would be difficult to prove since they had no signatures to compare. If they at least had a signature that didn't match hers, the fraud would be easier to identify. Her bank suggested she file a police report for the fraud, but assured her they'd still look into it and would be in touch. In the interim, they'd be canceling her debit card and changing her savings account number to prevent any further transactions, which she appreciated, but it meant she couldn't spend any of the money she did have left. They would be mailing her a new card along with her new savings account number once she provided them with another address, and knowing she certainly couldn't have any sensitive information sent to Ryan's address again, she did the only thing she could by having them mail everything to OCD Cleaners where, hopefully, her boss would pass it along to her.

Fuming, she stormed around the apartment as she pieced everything together. Ryan hadn't been using his phone to look for a job, he'd been using it to gamble her money away. He hadn't even been looking for a job because he didn't need to. His mother had been paying all of his bills while he'd been pocketing Lily's half of the rent to spend on lottery tickets and booze, likely knowing that when she eventually found out, he'd simply replace her with another sucker. While she'd been spending her days cleaning filthy hotel rooms to help keep a roof over their heads, he'd been sitting at home without a care in the world and had likely already begun searching for his next victim. Furious, she ripped his gaming console from its place on his small entertainment center and threw it against the wall with all her might, where it left a hole in the drywall before crashing to the floor. Standing over it with her chest heaving in anger, she stomped it to pieces while screaming obscenities aimed at Ryan. She was about to stomp it into smaller pieces when she heard the sound of the front door opening and turned to face the man who had left her as broken as the console she'd just smashed.

"What the fuck?" he'd shouted, seeing what she'd done. Rushing across the room, he pushed her aside and dropped to his knees to assess the damage, and after realizing there was no salvaging his beloved video game system, slowly rose to his feet with a crazed look in his eyes. Understanding the magnitude of her actions, she tried backing away but had nowhere to go and braced herself for the punch she knew was coming. She tried to dodge his fist, but it came too quickly, connecting with her left eye and dropping her to the floor. What followed was an assault so brutal, she'd never be able to recount it in full detail. After sending her to the floor with one powerful blow, she cried out in pain as he repeatedly kicked her in the ribs, screaming like a man possessed while he continued his attack.

"You bitch! You fucking bitch!" he yelled. Climbing on top of her, she could smell the alcohol on him as he proceeded to bash her head into the floor. Slipping in and out of consciousness, she pleaded with him to stop, but her words were lost on him. She passed out when he dealt another blow to her left eye, and she woke to find everything a blur, her vision wrecked from his relentless onslaught. With her left eye swollen shut, she had to rely on her right eye and found Ryan sitting in his recliner, nonchalantly sipping a beer as if nothing had ever happened.

When she tried to speak, she found her lower lip split and realized he must have hit her in the mouth at some point. "I'm… I'm… calling the…"

"Cops?" Ryan had finished for her. "Using what? This?"

He held up her phone, which he must have pulled from her pocket after she'd lost consciousness.

"How could you do this to me?" she sobbed, her entire body aching. She tried rising to her feet, but collapsed onto the floor again.

"Stop being so dramatic," he said, refusing to make eye contact. "You did this to yourself."

"You stole all of my money!" she hissed. A stabbing pain accompanied each breath she took.

"I don't know what you're talking about," he replied, lighting a cigarette and taking a long drag. Smoking in the apartment was his way of adding insult to injury.

"You won't get away with this," she warned, crawling to the bedroom. The mattress had been returned to its proper position atop the bedspring, telling her Ryan knew what she'd discovered. She expected him to follow her in, yet he didn't budge from his seat. Using the bed, she was able to get on her feet again and made her way to the closet to start packing as quickly as her battered body would allow. She jumped when she heard his voice from behind her.

"Going somewhere?"

Trembling, she turned to face him, her right arm raised defensively. "Please… I'm begging you… just let me leave."

"Oh, I'm not going to stop you," Ryan laughed. "Hell, I'll even help carry your shit to your car." He tossed her phone on the bed and motioned that she was allowed to take it. "But just know that if you call the police, I'm going to tell them you went nuts and tried attacking me after you destroyed my property."

"They'll never believe you," she said, swallowing hard. "Look at me. Look at what you did to me."

"You're lucky you're even alive," he warned, taking a step closer. "You're going to get the fuck out of here, and if you call the cops, I'm going to find you, I promise you that. I have all of your information. All of it. Debit card number, driver's license number, social security number… Hell, I even have your AAA membership number."

She burst into tears and fell to her knees again, a sharp pain coursing through her with every sob. "You ruined my life," she cried. "I can't believe you did this to me. What did I ever do to you? Nothing! All I did is care about you, and look at what you did to me!"

"Go ahead and play the victim," he spat, the intoxication slurring his words. "You've been cheating on me for weeks now. You deserve what you got."

"Cheating on you?" she asked, looking up at him with her one good eye. "Are you crazy? I've been going to work! Going to work while you've been here gambling with *my* money!"

"I was trying to secure our future!" he countered angrily. "Just one big win and we wouldn't have ever had to work again! I came close a few times, you know. If I had just a bit more time, I could have won millions."

Lily wheezed as she struggled to breathe, feeling like she'd been hit by a car. "You're insane. An insane drunk. You're paying me back every penny you stole, you piece of shit."

"That was *our* money," Ryan insisted. "If you're my girl, what's yours is mine. That's just how it works."

"What? No, it's not! That was my money, and if you won't pay me back, I'll have your mother—"

She was cut off by a slap across the face so hard that she saw stars and almost passed out again. Standing over her, Ryan grabbed her by the hair and forced her to look up at him.

"If you ever talk to my mother again, I will fucking kill you," he growled. "I will find you, and I will fucking kill you. I know she was here earlier. I don't know what she told you, but I'm sure it was a bunch of bullshit." He released her hair and pushed her down to the floor. "But she's my mother and I love her, so stay away from her unless you want a real problem."

A real problem, Lily remembered thinking. *As if what he just put you through isn't a real problem.*

"I'm going back to the bar," Ryan continued, "And when I get home, I want you and all of your shit gone."

Lily tried wiping the tears from her eyes and winced, her left eye swollen shut and throbbing in pain.

"I… I have nowhere to go… you ruined me…" she said meekly.

"I'm sure whoever you've been seeing will take you in," Ryan grunted.

"I haven't been seeing anyone!"

"Yeah, sure. You better be gone when I get back," he said. "And if you touch any of my shit, I really will ruin you."

With that, he stormed out of the room. She heard the front door open and close, but waited a few minutes to make sure he was really gone before making her way to her feet again. Limping to the bathroom, she caught her reflection in the mirrored medicine cabinet and burst into tears again at the sight of what Ryan had done to her. Her left eye was a bruised, swollen mess, and she had a thick gash running down the middle of her lower lip, presumably from where he'd either punched or kicked her during his attack.

Weak and in agony, she packed what she could, which wasn't much given her condition. She grabbed only her essentials and limped to the front door, only to fall to pieces again at what she found outside. The beautiful decorative ceramic lighthouse her grandmother had given her had been completely shattered, having been thrown to the ground by Ryan as his final act of cruelty. Out of the few decorative lighthouses her grandmother had passed down to her, this one had been Lily's favorite, and it had been her grandmother's favorite as well. Given its immense sentimental value, she'd cleared out a spot to display it on a shelf in the living room. On his way out the door, Ryan had clearly taken it from the shelf to smash it where he knew she would find it. Heartbroken, she fell to her knees and wept, attempting to collect the pieces in hopes of gluing it back together. Even with her blurred vision, she could see there was no saving it and gave up, leaving the pieces there and continuing on to her car.

She drove to the same supermarket she'd parked in the night Ryan had promised to stop drinking, knowing it was a safe enough place for her to gather her thoughts. She parked in the back of the lot, worried a passerby might notice her bruised face, and as her adrenaline began to subside, she realized just how much pain she was really in. She had to fight back tears since the sobs accompanying them were so agonizing, but the emotional damage he'd caused hurt even worse. She'd put her trust in him and he robbed her blind, destroying any chance she had of enrolling in school and leaving her without a home. Sitting in silence, wheezing with each breath, she debated how to handle the unthinkable situation she'd been placed in, but the pain made reaching any decision impossible. She couldn't think clearly enough to plan her next move, and noting a buildup of metallic-tasting fluid in her mouth, opened her car door just enough to spit out an alarming amount of blood. Accepting that she needed medical attention, she reached for her phone to search for the nearest hospital and began the drive there, forcing herself to stay awake and feeling a small sense of relief when she made it safely.

Inside, the receptionist took one look at her condition and rushed her into an exam room where she was admitted for a concussion, two broken ribs, and severe lacerations to her mouth and left eye. Her doctor informed her that he would be notifying the police since her injuries were indicative of domestic abuse, and knowing Ryan couldn't be allowed to get away with what he'd done, she didn't fight him on it.

If you call the cops, I'm going to find you, I promise you that.

Ryan's words replayed in her mind as she recounted the attack to the officer, who hadn't arrived until the following morning. With Ryan knowing where she worked, it wouldn't be hard for him to find her and retaliate, but she was willing to take that risk if it stopped him from hurting another woman. Along with the assault, Lily was sure to report Ryan's fraud as well, hoping to recoup at least some of the money he'd stolen. After taking her statement and handing her the victim notification paperwork containing her police report number, the officer told her the case would be passed on to a detective who would follow-up with her soon. She didn't realize "soon" meant that same day, and was surprised when the detective showed up that evening to dive deeper into the incident. She recalled the attack the best her memory would allow, as well as the events leading up to it, while the detective listened sympathetically, taking notes and asking for additional details. Before leaving, he snapped a few photos of her injuries and commended her on the bravery it took to come forward. Too many women, he reminded her, refuse to name their assailant out of fear, which only leads to more victims. He recommended a restraining order and walked her through the process of obtaining one, and with his investigation underway, he told her he'd be in touch, asking where she'd be staying should he need to speak with her again in person. When she told him she had nowhere to go, he referred her to *Sister José Women's Center*, assuring her she'd be safe there until she found somewhere to call home. She thanked him for his compassion and understanding and managed a small, polite smile on his way out the door.

Alone in her hospital room, she rubbed her lighthouse pendant as she tried to focus on some sort of plan. She was grateful that during the attack, her prized necklace had remained around her neck and hadn't broken loose. She'd already replayed the savage beating dozens of times in her mind, and although it wouldn't be easy, she knew she needed to block it out so she could move forward and figure out her next move. Ryan had blown most of her money, but he hadn't blown all of it. From her bed, she was able to verify her checking and savings account balances again, and combined, they left her with almost one thousand dollars to her name. That was enough to make it back to Ohio, should nothing go wrong along the way, but as desperately as she needed her mother and father, she was too ashamed to return home. She'd always considered herself too smart to end up in a situation like this, and the humiliation was enough to keep her quiet about it. She knew she shouldn't blame herself for what had happened, but it was hard not to take at least some responsibility when she'd ignored all the warning signs and had stayed with Ryan far longer than she should have. She'd landed herself in this position, and it was up to her to get herself out of it.

One thousand dollars wasn't much, but it was better than nothing. It occurred to her that she couldn't spend any of the money she had left anyhow until her new debit card arrived and made a mental note to ask her boss to be on the lookout for it. She had another paycheck coming her way soon, and with it, she might have enough money to rent a place of her own if she could find an apartment cheap enough. She knew the biggest hurdle would be her employment history since she'd only been working for OCD Cleaners for a month, and most legitimate leasing agents required at least six months of employment. She'd cross that bridge when the time came, but for now, she just needed to rest and heal.

She was released the following day with a list of recovery instructions, and with nowhere to go, she called the shelter the detective had mentioned. Of course, they were completely full and had no room for her, so she spent the day in her car, thankful summer hadn't arrived yet. It was nearing May now and still quite hot, but from what she'd heard, the months to come would be far worse. She'd found a spot to park under a tree, with the shade offering her a degree of relief from the desert sun, and used the only cash she had in her purse to buy enough non-perishable food to, in her estimation, last until her new debit card arrived. She'd filled a couple of water bottles at a convenience store for free and passed the time searching for affordable apartments online using her one good eye since her left eye was still swollen shut. She was in the middle of looking at an apartment possibly in her price range when she received a text message from Ryan:

Where are you? I'm sorry. Come home and let's talk this out.

In an instant, her heart rate skyrocketed and chest began to heave, pain shooting through her with each and every breath. She was on the verge of a panic attack and she knew it, but managed to calm herself with the reminder that she was safe and out of harm's way. His message meant he hadn't been arrested, but she had no way of knowing if the police had talked to him yet. She couldn't believe he'd even had the audacity to message her after what he'd done, and with nothing kind to say to him, she blocked his number.

Sleeping that night wasn't easy since her back seats were full of her belongings, leaving her to sleep seated upright in her driver's seat, but she was able to get a few hours. She was dreading her weekly meeting at OCD Cleaners, but it was Monday morning, and there was no avoiding it. Cleaning herself up the best she could, she winced in pain as she changed into her work uniform and chose to wear sunglasses to hide her bruise. A coat of heavy lipstick almost concealed the gash on her lower lip, but she knew anyone standing close enough would see it. As predicted, all eyes were on her that morning, yet nobody dared ask why she was wearing sunglasses during an indoor meeting. Nobody, that is, except for her boss, Jose, who she'd asked to speak with in private after the meeting adjourned.

"You get smacked up?" he'd crudely asked when the other workers had cleared the room.

Never one to lie, Lily replied that she'd rather not talk about it and told him she was expecting an important piece of mail from her bank, asking him nicely if he could pass it along to her when it arrived, and apologizing for the inconvenience. He wasn't thrilled that she'd had her personal mail sent to his business without his permission, but realizing she was having a rough time, softened a bit and agreed to keep an eye out for it. She thanked him, and on a whim, she asked if he knew of any cheap apartments for rent. To her surprise, Jose replied that his sister was the property manager of a few apartment complexes and jotted her number down on a piece of paper.

"You're new here, but you're doing a good job so far. I'll put in a good word for you," he said, handing her the number. "Her name's Veronica."

Vulnerable and needing the kindness, she fought back tears as she thanked him, and knowing how temperamental he could be, hurried out the door before his mood could change.

She wore her sunglasses her entire shift, both out of shame and out of fear somebody would see her face and ask questions. Jeanine, the coworker she'd befriended, did sidle up next to her at one point to ask what the sunglasses were all about, to which Lily replied she'd clumsily ran into a tree branch. She hated lying to the one friend she'd made, but Jeanine was smart enough to piece everything together, regardless.

"It hit you in the mouth, too?" she'd replied. Seeing Lily shrink in humiliation, she was quick to add, "Just don't go back to him, girl. You deserve better."

When her lunch break came, she returned to her car and called the number Jose had given her. Unlike Jose, Veronica was an absolute pleasure, and Lily felt completely at ease with her right away. Over the next several minutes, Veronica had made her so comfortable that Lily allowed herself to share a bit of what had happened and stressed the urgency of finding a place to live as soon as possible. In a move that was surely against company policy, Veronica told Lily to embellish her work history on her rental application, instructing her to list OCD Cleaners as her employee for the last year, not month.

From there, she could probably get Lily into their Grant and Alvernon complex as long as Lily passed their background check and could come up with the deposit, which Lily could afford—although barely—with her upcoming paycheck. She'd have to live in her car for the remainder of the week, but that felt like a breeze compared to what Ryan had put her through. If she could survive that, she felt like she could survive anything, and spent the rest of her lunch break filling out the online application Veronica had sent her. As soon as she submitted it for review, she called Veronica back and they scheduled a viewing of the apartment for that very day at 6:00 pm. She rarely scheduled viewings after 5:00 pm, Veronica had told her, but knowing what a pinch Lily was in, she'd made an exception.

The apartment wasn't much to look at, which was putting it nicely, but Veronica had been upfront about that from the start. Veronica, on the other hand, was every bit as sweet in real life as she had been on the phone, and Lily found herself just as comfortable around her in person. When Veronica asked to see what Lily was hiding under her sunglasses, Lily took them off with a sigh and Veronica let out an audible gasp. Wrapping her in a warm embrace that Lily hadn't realized she'd needed, Veronica gently patted Lily on the back as she cried in her arms, unable to contain the emotions she'd been trying to fight back.

"There, there," Veronica had said tenderly. "It's okay. Let all out. We'll get you into this place, I promise. If you can come up with the deposit, I'll take care of the rest."

Lily couldn't thank her enough for her kindness, and agreed to hand over the deposit when she got paid that Friday. The wait wouldn't be easy, but her work cleaning the Hilton helped pass the time she would have otherwise spent bored in her car. She could also bathe there, which was nice, and when Thursday came, Jose called her to let her know the mail she'd been waiting for had arrived. She rushed over to his office to pick it up, eagerly tearing into the envelope for her new debit card that would finally allow her to buy a bit more food. She was careful not to overspend, knowing that if she could get into the apartment, it would likely take her very last dime. The following day, she was able to use her new debit card to deposit her paycheck, and with just enough money to cover the deposit, eagerly met with Veronica at the apartment. Lily's credit check had returned a perfect credit score, which made sense since the credit cards Ryan had opened in her name were still so new. She knew that if she didn't get a handle on that situation soon, however, her credit score would quickly plummet and made a note to call the various credit card companies she was now indebted to. She'd been smart enough to pack the offers and approval letters she'd found under Ryan's mattress, making it easier to know who she owed money to.

After signing a one-year lease, Lily was handed the key to her apartment and couldn't stop thanking Veronica for her help. She knew things were going to be tight financially, but it was worth it to be free of Ryan and to have a quiet place to study when she enrolled at the university. Unless she could get approved for a student loan, her schooling would have to wait a bit longer since Ryan had blown all of her tuition money. Between her bank and the police department's investigations, she hoped she'd see some of that money again, but she knew the odds weren't good. Thinking of how long she'd worked to save up that money just to have it stolen by the man she'd trusted hurt just as much as the physical pain he'd inflicted on her. She felt herself begin to crumble but held herself together, knowing that if she was going to make it through this, she needed to stay strong.

Most people were overjoyed when handed the key to their very first place, but the excitement she should have felt for her new apartment was nonexistent. While it fit within her budget—although barely—it was still overpriced for its rundown condition, and it didn't seem to be in the best area. It didn't take long for her to unload her vehicle, and in doing so, she realized just how much she'd forgotten at Ryan's. In her haste to leave, and with her mind still reeling from the attack, she hadn't done the best job packing, and had left behind far more than intended. Unfortunately, some of her favorite books had been left there in her hurry, while some had to stay because they were too heavy to carry with her broken ribs. She debated asking an officer to accompany her there so she could get the rest, but knowing she'd have to see Ryan if she did, she wrote everything off as a lost cause. The detective had informed her that if her case went to trial, she'd be asked to testify and would have no choice but to face Ryan again. She knew if that did happen, it would be months away, giving her time to heal both physically and emotionally. For now, she wasn't ready to see him, nor would she be anytime soon. Just the mere thought of him disgusted her.

Taking a look around her scant apartment, she found herself wishing she had enough money leftover to make the place feel like home. It looked and felt empty but it beat living in her vehicle, and while she didn't have a bed, she was looking forward to at least being able to lie down since she'd been sleeping in her upright driver's seat all week; her back seats too full for her to recline it. The stained, ratty carpet didn't look inviting, but she was able to make it work using a small pile of clothes for a pillow and her coat as a blanket. She awoke in the middle of the night in a panic, still traumatized by what Ryan had put her through, and suspected it might be weeks, if not months, before she could sleep soundly.

She was still in a tremendous amount of pain, and although the swelling in her eye had subsided enough for it to open again, it still looked awful. The cut on her lower lip had scabbed over, making it even more noticeable, and her head still hurt from Ryan driving it into the floor. She looked and felt like a mess, but she was determined to pick herself up and start anew. She chastised herself for having moved in with Ryan in the first place since she hadn't known him well enough. She thought she had, but learned the hard way that spending just four days with somebody wasn't nearly enough time to truly know them. She'd been so caught up in the romantic notion of starting a life with a handsome, charming man in the new city she loved so much, her better judgment had fallen by the wayside. It was a mistake she'd never make again, and one she was deeply embarrassed by. After what Ryan had done to her, leaving her beaten and broke, she didn't think she'd be able to trust any man again. Starting over in a city where she had no friends or family as a support system wasn't going to be easy, but it beat returning to Cleveland in defeat, and she was determined to make it work, one way or another. Nobody could ever find out what happened. She would carry the secret with her, and use the lesson she learned to make better decisions going forward. Time would heal her wounds, and hard work would rebuild her bank account.

She would persevere. Ryan had made it easy to avoid men, and without any romantic entanglements, she could focus solely on fixing her life. A part of her feared she may never allow another man into her life after how thoroughly Ryan had gutted her. The psychological damage he'd inflicted would affect her for the rest of her life, and she couldn't imagine feeling truly safe with any man ever again.

Feeling used and worthless, she cried herself back to sleep.

Chapter Seven

"Oh my God, Lilian, I am so sorry," Austin said. "I can't believe you went through all of that."

"Maybe now you understand why I've been so weird around you," Lily replied, one arm draped across his body. There was just enough light spilling into the room for her to see his face, and his eyes looked like they'd grown damp. If she didn't know any better, she'd swear her recount had made him tear up.

"That's the most horrific story I've ever heard," Austin returned, pulling her into him. "The thought of anyone hurting you makes my blood boil. Please tell me this creep is behind bars now."

"I wish," Lily sighed. "The case was dropped a few weeks ago."

"What? You've got to be kidding me."

"His mother mentioned being friends with the district attorney here," Lily explained. "I think she used that connection to get the case thrown out."

"So this maniac who almost killed you is still out there somewhere?" Austin said with a troubled look.

"Unfortunately," Lily replied. "And who knows who else he's hurt by now."

"Please tell me you at least got your money back."

Lily groaned. "Not a single penny. My bank said there was no way of proving I didn't make the transactions myself. They saw that most of the charges were from gambling websites and probably assumed I was the one with the gambling problem."

"That's outrageous."

"I know. I was hoping to find my name forged somewhere, but Ryan was clever and avoided transactions that required a signature."

"Do you think he still has the rest of your stuff?"

"I don't know. I doubt it. Why?"

"Because if you want it back, I'm willing to go over there with you to get it. I can't promise I won't knock the guy's block off, though."

"You're sweet," Lily smiled, "but I can live without it. I've replaced most of it by now anyhow."

"Well, the offer stands." After a long moment of silence, Austin added, "You're safe with me. I hope you know that."

"I wouldn't be here if I didn't," Lily purred, kissing his chest. She did feel safe around him. Protected, even. In his arms, she felt like nothing could hurt her, and it was one of the many things she loved about him.

"Do you believe everything happens for a reason?" he asked.

"I don't know," she replied. "I used to. But now? I don't know."

"I don't know either," he said. "But I can't help but wonder if our paths crossed for a reason."

"Yeah?"

"Maybe we were destined to meet to help each other heal," Austin continued. "Silly, I know."

"It's not silly," she smiled, kissing his chest again. They did share similar stories, both having been burned financially by lovers who were supposed to be trustworthy yet ended up cheating them out of money.

"Thank you for opening up to me," Austin said. "I'm sure that wasn't easy."

"It wasn't," she admitted. "You don't think less of me, do you?"

Austin rolled onto his side to face her. "Think less of you?"

"For being so stupid," she replied, looking away sheepishly.

"Baby, you're far from stupid," he told her. "And you're even tougher than I thought. You could have gone back home to your parents, but you chose to stay here and go through everything alone. I can't even imagine how hard that must have been."

"One could argue that I was too weak to face them," Lily countered.

"You're anything but weak. You still haven't told them what happened?"

"No. I'd rather they never find out. I knew they'd want to send me a birthday card, so I had my mail forwarded to my apartment, that way I didn't have to give them my new address. That definitely would have raised questions. Speaking of which, I'm sure they'll send me a Christmas card, too. Is it okay if I get my mail forwarded here? If it's asking too much, I completely understand."

"Go right ahead. And I almost forgot that Christmas is coming up," Austin said. "I'd love it if we could spend it together."

"Really?" Lily asked excitedly.

"Really," Austin smiled.

They talked until the sun began to rise and fell asleep holding each other. Given how late they'd stayed up, they slept until almost noon and were both relieved to wake without a hangover. After making love again, they showered up together and made their way to the kitchen, where Austin insisted on making them breakfast. She was impressed by his culinary skills and devoured the bacon and cheese omelette he'd whipped up, which was every bit as good as the French toast he'd prepared as well. She thanked him by washing the dishes, and once Austin had finished a few business calls, it was time to get the rest of her belongings as planned. Since most of Austin's vehicles were luxurious two-seaters and didn't have enough room for the boxes she'd packed, it gave him a chance to drive the classic 1952 Chevy pickup truck he'd bought a few years prior. He confessed he'd only driven it a handful of times, and Lily preferred it to the other vehicles since it didn't draw as much attention. As they drove past her dead car, Austin assured her that he'd already called his mechanic and he'd be out to take a look at the vehicle later that day.

It didn't take long to load the truck with the few boxes waiting for them at Lily's apartment, and they were making sure the boxes were secure when Austin received a phone call he seemed eager to answer.

"Hey, baby? This could be important. Do you mind if I take it?" he asked with an apologetic look. "I'll try to make it quick."

Baby. She melted when he called her that, and she was glad it had carried over from the previous night. She'd worried he'd behave differently after sobering up, possibly even regretting the intimacy they'd shared, but from the moment he'd opened his eyes that morning, he'd been showering her with affection. She wasn't sure if they were a couple now and tried not to overthink it, choosing to just let it develop organically.

"Of course," she smiled. "Take all the time you need."

To her surprise, Austin didn't walk away for privacy, and seemed to have no problem conducting business in front of her. She took it as a sign of trust, but still tried to give him space and did her best not to eavesdrop, although it was hard not to overhear the conversation. Austin looked excited, and from what she was able to piece together from the one side of the call she was hearing, an opportunity he'd been waiting quite some time for had finally presented itself. She watched as he leaned against the truck, looking just as handsome as always in a white polo shirt tucked into khaki slacks and a pair of brown leather loafers that likely cost into the thousands.

"Okay, well, I appreciate the consideration, and I look forward to seeing the facility," Austin said, wrapping up the call.

"Good news?" Lily asked, making her way back to him. Still leaning against the truck, he pulled her in for a kiss.

When their lips parted, Austin looked at her with a smirk and asked, "How does France sound?"

"Excuse me?" Lily laughed.

"That was Jean-Marc Chery, the CEO of STMicroelectronics. They're a huge European semiconductor manufacturer, and one of my biggest competitors. It appears Jean-Marc is considering selling one of their manufacturing plants in Crolles, France. I've wanted it for years, but he hasn't been willing to let it go. We scheduled a tour of the facility on January 2nd."

"That's great!" Lily smiled. "I'm so happy for you!"

"It sure would be nice to have some company on the trip," Austin grinned.

"Why, Austin Matson, are you inviting me to France?" Lily playfully asked.

"I am," he replied.

Lily groaned. "I'd love to, but I'm broke and don't even have a passport."

"The entire trip is on me. He wanted me to fly out next week, but I pushed it to January so we have time to get you one. We'll start the application today and have it expedited. Shouldn't be a problem."

"We're going to France!" Lily shrieked in excitement, leaping into his arms.

"We're going to France," he laughed.

"You're not messing with me, right?" she asked, stepping back to examine his face.

"Oh, we're totally going," he beamed. "I was thinking we could spend Christmas in New England with my family and ring in the new year together in Paris. From there, we can head to Crolles to check out the facility. Of course, we can always stop in Cleveland to see your family as well, or spend Christmas there if you prefer. Totally your call."

"You're sweet, but I'd rather spend Christmas with your family. There's less explaining to do that way," Lily chuckled. "I've always wanted to visit Maine, and it'll give me a chance to meet the people who raised such an amazing man. You don't think it's a bit too soon to introduce me to your parents, though?"

"Do you?" Austin asked. "Because it feels right to me. And they're going to love you, believe me."

"Do I get to have fresh seafood and see a real Maine lighthouse?" Lily asked excitedly.

"It'll be a bit out of season for seafood, but I'm sure we can find some. And I know the perfect lighthouse. You're going to love it."

"I can't believe this. It's like my dream come true. You really think your parents will like me?"

"What's not to like?" Austin smiled. "I'll call them tonight to let them know we're coming."

Lily leapt into his arms again and covered him with kisses while he laughed, and after thanking him a dozen more times, she settled into the truck for the ride back to the estate, this time sliding across the bench seat to sit next to him. He seemed to like that and appeared proud to have her by his side. She'd never felt so genuinely wanted by any man, and couldn't stop smiling as they talked the entire ride home.

They returned to the estate to find Austin's mechanic had arrived to take a look at Lily's vehicle. He was wiping his hands off with a rag when they pulled up, and he nodded at them in greeting as they rolled by him into the garage. They met him outside where he broke the news that she'd need a new engine, and given the age and mileage of the vehicle, he recommended she scrap the car entirely since it had long outrun its expected lifespan. In tears and unwilling to let it go, Lily asked how much a new engine would cost, at which point Austin interjected that it was a lost cause and time for her to say goodbye.

Seeing how much the car meant to Lily, the mechanic spoke softly and apologetically while offering to scrap the car for her, but when Lily still couldn't bring herself to part with it, he suggested she take a few days to think it over. They thanked the man for his time, and after watching him disappear down the driveway, Lily turned to Austin in defeat.

"I'm screwed," she groaned, covering her eyes with her palm. "Of course. Of course," she repeated, "this would happen now. What am I supposed to do? I have no job, and I don't have enough saved up for a car."

To her surprise, she wasn't as upset as she thought she'd be, which was likely due to Austin's invitation softening the blow. It was hard to be too upset about anything with the thought of their upcoming trip still fresh in her mind.

"Follow me," Austin said, guiding her back into the garage. "Do you know how to drive a stick?"

"I'm the daughter of a mechanic," she reminded him. "Of course, I know how to drive a stick."

"Good, because only a few of these are automatics," Austin said, admiring his collection. "Pick one."

"Excuse me?" Lily asked.

"Pick one," he smiled. "Any one you want."

Lily let out an audible gasp. "Austin… you can't be serious."

"I promised to get you back on the road and I'm a man of my word."

"No, Austin, I could never. It's too much. I'm not going to let you give me—"

"Whoa!" Austin laughed. "Give you? In time, maybe. For now, I was thinking you could pick whatever one catches your eye and I can just add you to my insurance policy."

Lily stood in stunned silence for a moment. "Austin, I… I don't know what to say."

He looked at her with a wide grin. "Just say you won't scratch it."

The culmination of his generosity brought tears to her eyes. He'd taken her into his home, invited her with him on an all-expenses-paid trip of a lifetime, and was now offering her the use of a luxury vehicle from his prized collection.

"I can't," she said. "You've done too much for me as it is. I'd feel like I was taking advantage of you, and I'd never want you to think that I was."

Seeing how emotional she'd grown, Austin wrapped her in his arms and pulled her close. "It's not taking advantage if I'm the one offering."

"I know, but it's just—"

"Shh," Austin said, using his thumb to wipe away the tear escaping down her cheek. "Baby, you've had so many awful things happen to you, it's about time you have some good things come your way. Please, just accept them. After everything you've been through, you deserve them."

"I'll never be able to repay you for your kindness," Lily sniffled.

"We help each other out," Austin smiled. "It's what we do. Right?"

"Right," Lily agreed, wiping her eyes and returning his smile.

"I'd like to think you'd do the same for me if our roles were reversed."

"In a heartbeat," she said. Wiping her eyes again, she added, "I don't know what I did to deserve you."

"And that's exactly how I feel about you," he replied. Lightening the mood, he turned to his collection again and smirked. "So… which one will it be? The Ferrari? You seemed to like that one."

"What's the least expensive one?" Lily asked, and jokingly continued, "Do you have an old Ford Tempo hiding in here somewhere?"

"How about we just get you a unicycle?" Austin laughed, playing along.

"Stop!" Lily giggled, swatting his arm.

"Oh, come on, you'd look so cute on one. "We can teach you how to juggle while riding it and get you in the circus."

"Austin!" Lily burst, laughing so hard she snorted.

"Hey, you said you need a job!"

He knew how to make her laugh, she'd give him that. He showed her around the collection, pointing out the features of each vehicle to help her make her decision, and after mulling it over, she daringly asked if she could drive the same 1952 Chevy they'd just taken for a drive. She explained that, like her father, she loved classic vehicles and didn't need all the bells and whistles found in a new car. More features meant more problems, she told him, using a saying she'd borrowed from her dad.

"I had a feeling you'd choose that," he grinned. "It suits your modesty."

"It's still going to turn some heads," she replied, "but mostly from classic car lovers, which I'm okay with."

"She's a beauty," he said, slapping the back of the truck. "I'll get you on the insurance today."

"This is huge," she smiled, and gave him a peck on the lips. "Seriously, I owe you. I can get a job now and start saving for my schooling again."

"About that," Austin began. "How would you like to work for me?"

"You're kidding, right?" she asked. "I know almost nothing about computers. I mean, I can use one just fine, but that's about it."

"Actually, I was thinking more of a secretarial position. I've been looking to reduce my workload so I can enjoy life a bit more, and it would help to have somebody else fielding phone calls and emails for me."

"I thought Winston handled that?"

"He does what he can. He offered to help, so I gave him a business phone, but with his eyesight starting to go, it's not as easy for him anymore, and it's not what I hired him for anyhow."

"No?" she asked, realizing she wasn't entirely sure what Winston's official position was.

"I hired him to look after the estate when I'm away on business, which is often. I know I have all of these security cameras and alarms, but I still like having somebody in the house while I'm gone. It just feels safer to me. He also helps out in other ways, like polishing the cars and sorting my mail. Little things around here, you know? I give him free room and board, along with a weekly salary for his help. This phone right here?" Austin continued, pulling his cell phone from his pocket. "This is my private phone. My business phone is upstairs in my study, and I guarantee you I have fifty missed calls already."

"I don't know," Lily sighed. "You really think we should mix business with," she paused to motion between them, "whatever this is?"

"We make a great team," Austin countered. "I think we'd work well together."

"I have no secretarial experience," she pointed out, "but I'm a quick learner and think I could figure it out."

"I wouldn't have offered you the job if I didn't think you were more than capable," Austin smiled. "And it wouldn't take long for me to teach you everything you need to know. What calls and messages to look out for and what ones to avoid. You know, basic stuff like that. It's simple, really, and would give you a chance to rebuild your savings. I pay very well."

"Wow, I, yeah, I would love that," Lily stammered, taken aback by his continued generosity. "Can I still tidy up around here, too? This place still needs to be cleaned, and I know the property inside and out by now."

"If you want to, sure," Austin said. "And, of course, I'll pay you for that as well. We'll rebuild your savings account in no time."

Lily hesitated for a moment, worried she was being viewed as a charity case. Austin could see her overthinking and assured her that, no, he wasn't offering her these things out of pity, but out of trust. She'd proven herself to be a hard, reliable worker, he explained, and that made her a valuable asset. She was touched by his kind words and his appreciation for her work ethic. In her time cleaning the estate, she'd always arrived early, often stayed late, and had never missed a day, which hadn't gone unnoticed by Austin.

The following few weeks were simply incredible. Austin had invited Lily to share his bedroom, and they'd often talk late into the night in between making love. Mornings came with more lovemaking, both seemingly unable to get enough of each other. She'd never experienced such an immense attraction, and she would still get butterflies when his steel-blue eyes locked onto hers. She had no idea sex could be so good, and felt it was due to the deep emotional connection they shared. When Lily had playfully suggested they have sex in every room of the estate, Austin had replied with "challenge accepted." They knocked three bedrooms off the list that same day, with Austin never leaving her disappointed. He was an exceptional lover, always making sure she finished before him, and unlike the men in her past, wasn't in a hurry to leave when he'd had his fill. He was big on cuddling, which she certainly hadn't expected from such an imposing man, and she always felt safest wrapped in his big, strong arms. He was more than her lover, he'd quickly become her best friend, and somebody she could share everything with. Their time together made her realize just how pathetic her relationship with Ryan had been. It was a night and day difference, with Austin always putting her needs first, and going out of his way to make sure she was comfortable. It wasn't one-sided, though, as they both looked out for each other, which she came to realize was how a healthy relationship should be. Knowing that most relationships start off great, a part of her feared things would begin to sour as the days passed by. Her experience with Ryan had left her so traumatized that she worried Austin would change for the worse, and she kept looking for signs of a dark side he might be hiding from her. Their communication was so good that she was able to express these concerns with him, and as the weeks wore on, he proved to be every bit as genuine as she'd hoped.

Winston was overjoyed to have Lily there and was the biggest supporter of her blossoming relationship with Austin. He'd often comment on how nice it was seeing the both of them so happy, and would watch their interactions with a smile. Austin had needed a good woman, Winston had confided in her, and he had undoubtedly found one in Lily. He'd never seen him so smitten, and he loved the childlike playfulness she'd brought out of him. It was a welcome change from how business-oriented he'd been over the years.

She was surprised by how well she took to the secretary position, and it helped that Austin was such a wonderful teacher, walking her through her new secretarial duties with patience and reassuring praise. Austin hadn't exaggerated the number of calls and messages he received, but Lily quickly learned which calls to prioritize and which messages were spam. Austin was a wonderful boss, acting more like her colleague than her superior, and allowed her to set her own work schedule, which was nice. Using a headset featuring a microphone, she devised a time-saving system that allowed her to clean the estate while taking calls and messages, which seemed to impress Austin.

The similar schedules had them both wrapping up work by the mid-afternoon, which afforded them the rest of the day together. Lily loved spending time with him, and could tell the feeling was mutual. There was never a shortage of things to do, and every day seemed to bring some new adventure. When they weren't crossing more of the estate's rooms off their list—including the library where Lily's fantasy finally became a reality—they were exploring the city hand-in-hand, visiting parks, restaurants, and art galleries while counting down the days until their big trip. Lily's passport had been approved, and Austin's family was eagerly anticipating their visit. Austin had confessed that she would be the first woman he'd introduced to his mother and father, which she was honored by, but it put a lot of pressure on her not to disappoint.

Austin hosted another student workshop, which so closely mirrored the previous month's, she was hit by a sense of déjà vu. He clearly had these workshops down to a science, and like before, she loved watching him interact with the children. Five parents showed up this time, all women, and Lily could see their disappointment when Austin introduced her as his girlfriend, even pulling her in for a kiss to drive the point home. She loved how proud he was of her, and how eager he was to show her off. He didn't need to use his wealth or connections to make her feel special—his little gestures alone did a fine job of that. Holding her hand through another pool party meant more to her than anything material ever could.

When the day of their trip arrived, Lily woke ready to go. She'd excitedly packed the night before and had everything ready and waiting for her, which Austin seemed to appreciate. It didn't take him long to pack, and since Winston's driving days were over, Austin hired a chauffeur to drive them to the private jetport in a limousine, insisting they start the trip off in style. He wanted her to remember every moment of it from start to finish, and since she'd never been in a limousine before, it was an experience she'd never forget. They enjoyed a glass of wine along the way, which helped calm Lily's nerves since she still wasn't a fan of flying. She knew that would have to change if she was going to be with a jet-setter like Austin, who flew often for business and social events.

She smiled when she saw they'd be flying out of *Million Air*, a private jetport she'd driven by dozens of times while cleaning the Hilton by the *Tucson International Airport* just down the road. The name had always struck her as silly, but now that she understood it as a place for the rich to charter private jets, it suddenly seemed fitting… and clever. The chauffeur helped with their luggage, and after meeting the pilot of their luxurious private jet, it wasn't long before they were in flight. The jet featured an array of impressive amenities, including a fully stocked bar they helped themselves to, indulging in more wine while careful not to overdo it since neither of them wanted to greet his parents drunk. Austin drank at a slower pace than Lily, knowing he still had to drive once they reached the airport in Bangor, Maine, where he had a rental car waiting for them.

Feeling the effects of the wine, impassioned kisses led to Lily straddling Austin in his oversized leather seat, and the dress she'd chosen to wear hadn't been coincidental. Unbeknownst to Austin, she'd intentionally selected the shortest dress she owned, knowing they'd have the jet to themselves and hoping he'd be up for a little in-flight fun. Of course, she should have known he would be since he hadn't denied her advances yet, and was eager to take her at every opportunity.

"On, no!" she suddenly exclaimed.

"What's wrong?" Austin asked with a look of worry.

"All that planning and I still managed to forget something."

"What did you forget?"

Slowly hiking up her dress, Lily flashed him a wicked grin. "I forgot my panties."

"You little minx," he laughed. Looking at her freshly shaved slit, his eyes grew hungry. "I guess I'll have to punish you for being so forgetful."

"Mmm… and how will you do that?" she played along, grinding herself into him.

"By making you ride my cock, that's how," he spoke in the amorous growl she'd grown to love.

"Oh, no, how truly awful," she smirked, unclasping his belt and snaking it out of his pants. "Anything but that." Undoing his pants had become second nature by this point, and she shuddered as she settled onto his shaft. "God, you're so big."

"You say that every time," he smiled.

"Because it's tr-tr-true," she stammered, gripping his shoulders tightly as she began to ride him.

"That's it," he said in his deep, authoritative voice. "You take that cock."

"Oh, fuck," she breathed, moving up and down with her hands still clutching his shoulders.

"I want these," he said, tugging the top of her dress down. She could do without panties, but given her bust size, she rarely went without a bra. She let it fall to the floor beside them, freeing her breasts and watching Austin's eyes grow wide.

"You're just so perfect," he groaned, and for the first time, she thought he might finish before her. She wouldn't have cared if he did, but he managed to gain control of himself and she continued riding him as they rocketed across the sky. She lowered herself slightly so he could mouth her breasts, which was something she enjoyed as well.

They'd always been sensitive, and having them touched while he was still inside of her was almost enough to make her cum.

A burst of mild turbulence made Lily yelp but added to the thrill. Austin was a sexual powerhouse and could always outlast her, but she sensed the excitement of their mid-air tryst was too great for him to last much longer. She beat him to the finish line and hoped the pilot couldn't hear her cries of pleasure as the orgasm shot through her, with Austin's following seconds later. Although the jet boasted a number of extravagant features, a shower wasn't one of them, leaving Lily to clean up using the sanitary wipes she'd packed. Yet again, they'd neglected any form of birth control, and like always, neither of them made any mention of it. Lily couldn't help but wonder if maybe, on some subconscious level, they both wanted a child.

She was hit by a sudden case of fatigue that she ascribed to her lack of sleep the previous night. She'd been so excited to get the trip underway, she hadn't slept very well and apologized to Austin for her yawns. At his insistence, she reclined her seat to take a quick nap yet ended up sleeping the remaining three hours of the flight, waking when she felt the jet begin to make its descent into Bangor, Maine. The excitement of their arrival woke her in a hurry. Given the time of year, it was already dark out when they landed, but Lily had expected that and knew she'd have plenty of time to see everything in the week they'd be there. Austin had welcomed her help with the planning, and they'd both decided that flying into Maine on the 22nd and departing on the 29th would give them enough time to enjoy the state's top attractions.

Austin had stressed the importance of packing for the weather, reminding her that a Maine winter was every bit as cold as an Ohio winter, if not colder, and that winter meant the same thing in France as well. With that in mind, she slipped out of the thin dress she'd been wearing in favor of jeans and a sweater, with a heavy winter jacket on top of that, yet still shivered when she stepped into the cold Maine air. Tucson had spoiled them both, as Austin was shivering as well, despite being bundled up in a thick wool peacoat.

After moving their luggage from the jet to their rental car, Austin surprised her by driving her past Stephen King's house, which happened to be close to the airport. While she wasn't the fan Austin was, she did appreciate his work and got a kick out of seeing his home, which was lit well enough for her to see it in its entirety. Looking at it with fascination, she wondered if there was a specific room he'd designated for writing, and if he was in there peeking out at them. The place was quite the tourist attraction, with another car pulling up behind them to take pictures. Lily was guilty of snapping a few photos herself and was sure the famed author had grown used to it by now.

The drive to Austin's parents' place took a little over an hour, and although it was too dark to see much of anything, she still enjoyed the ride. When he'd told her he'd grown up in a small town, he hadn't been kidding as evidenced by the houses growing fewer and farther between as the drive progressed. They had a bit of a scare when a couple of deer darted across the road in front of them, but Austin had prepared for that by staying alert, hitting the brakes as the deer disappeared into the surrounding woods.

"We're here," he announced when they turned down a long, unpaved driveway. Recessed from the road, the home awaiting them was quaintly beautiful, and Austin explained that it had come a long way over the years. Growing up, the house had been much smaller, he explained, and he'd had to share a bedroom with one of his brothers. His parents had built a spacious addition to accommodate his grandmother in her later years since the assisted living facility she'd been living in was bleeding her dry. Since her passing, his parents had been using the addition as guest lodging, which was ideal for occasions such as this. The home's cedar shingles had been upgraded to vinyl siding after the construction of the addition, giving the place a newer feel despite being built five decades prior. The house sat on twelve acres of land surrounded by woods, which worked well for his father, who was an avid outdoorsman, and Austin mentioned a small pond could be found at the far end of the property.

"You made it!" a woman's friendly voice sounded while they were pulling their luggage out of the vehicle. Lily turned to find an older yet youthful woman waving from the home's front porch with an excited look on her face.

"Hi, Mom!" Austin replied. A second later, they were greeted by a deliriously excited black dog that was so full of energy, it almost knocked Lily over when it barreled into her.

"Amos!" a man's voice bellowed. Austin's father had stepped onto the porch as well, both to greet them and to rein in his boisterous labrador retriever.

"Meet Amos," Austin smiled, setting the luggage down to give the dog the attention he was craving. An animal lover, Lily followed suit and showered the dog with affection while he ran circles around them both, panting in pure elation of the unexpected guests.

"That's enough, Amos!" the man's voice roared again.

"He's fine," Austin laughed.

"Well, hello, Amos," Lily smiled as the dog continued to dart between them, eagerly taking in their scent.

Picking up their luggage, they made their way to the porch where Austin's mother and father were waiting for them, and Lily was immediately taken by how kind they seemed.

"And you must be Lily!" Austin's mother beamed, wrapping her in a welcoming embrace. Stepping back, she looked Lily over with a smile. "I'm Pamela, but everyone just calls me Pam. Austin wasn't kidding. You're beautiful!"

"Thank you," Lily blushed. "You are, too!"

Austin's father greeted her with a simple handshake and a polite grin. "And I'm Mark, but everyone just calls me Mark," he joked. "It's nice to meet you." Extending his hand to Austin, he added, "Welcome home, son."

Moving inside to escape the cold, Lily found the interior of the home warm with country charm. After setting their luggage down in the addition, Lily was treated to a brief tour of the home, with Austin's mother sure to point out the family photos along the way.

"There's no way that's you," Lily gasped when his mother showed her a picture of a teenage Austin. Chubby and short, the boy in the photo bore almost no resemblance to the man standing next to her now.

"Right?" Austin laughed. "Let's just say I had a bit of a growth spurt."

He hadn't always been strikingly handsome, which likely explained his enormous character. She found the most naturally handsome men were often the most boring as they relied solely on their appearance, but because Austin wasn't born with his good looks and grew into them later, he had to develop a big personality to get by. The revelation made him even more attractive, which she hadn't thought possible.

After showing Lily the home, they settled in for a late dinner, and any nervousness Lily had felt quickly vanished. She couldn't believe how sweet his parents were and how comfortable they made her feel. They took a genuine interest in her, asking her about her upbringing in Cleveland and listening attentively as she recounted her move to Tucson and how she'd met Austin through her work as a cleaner. She left out any mention of Ryan, choosing to focus on how wonderful Austin had been treating her, and how lucky she was to have him. His parents swelled with pride, yet still humbled him with embarrassing stories from his childhood. It was all in good fun, of course, and the dining room was alive with laughter as they enjoyed the lasagna his mother had prepared for the occasion. Lily's lighthouse necklace hung outside of her sweater and it didn't go unnoticed by Pam, who complimented its beauty and gently pried into its significance. Lily explained that it had been handed down by her grandmother, who had also passed on her love for lighthouses, and went on to share how excited she was to finally see a real New England lighthouse.

"You've definitely come to the right place," Mark joked.

Thanking them for dinner, Lily insisted on washing the dishes, but Austin's parents wouldn't allow it. They appreciated the offer, but as a guest in their home, Lily was expected to simply relax and enjoy herself. Thanking them again, Austin and Lily excused themselves for the night and retreated to the addition. They went to bed shortly after, knowing they had a packed schedule the following day and wanting to get an early start. Austin had promised her seafood and a lighthouse, and he seemed hellbent on making good on those promises. His parents were early risers as well and invited Austin and Lily to join them for breakfast. Wonderful hosts, they were sure to ask how they'd slept and if they'd been comfortable enough, to which Lily assured them everything had been perfect.

"At least it looks like Christmas here," Lily said, gazing out the window at the snow covering the ground. "It's hard to get into the Christmas spirit in Tucson. It just doesn't feel right when it's seventy degrees and sunny, you know?"

"Yeah, I can see how that would be weird," Austin's mother agreed.

"The forecast is calling for snow on Christmas this year," his father chimed in.

"A white Christmas!" Lily exclaimed. "Oh, I'd love that. I've never been a fan of snow and ice, but I make an exception on Christmas."

"Agreed," Austin nodded. "Christmas in the desert just isn't the same."

Bundling up, Austin and Lily stepped into the cold to start their day, with the first stop being the lighthouse Austin was excited to show her. It was only a twenty-five minute drive, and Lily squealed with excitement when it came into view. Located at the end of a long jetty known as the Rockland Breakwater, the lighthouse wasn't what she was expecting, but certainly didn't disappoint. She'd envisioned a conical red and white tower jutting up into the sky, but this particular lighthouse emphasized the "house" part, looking more like a traditional New England home with white siding and green window shutters. The brick light tower was located at the rear of the keeper's house and faced the surrounding harbor, serving as a guide for passing ships of all shapes and sizes.

To reach the lighthouse, one had to walk the long jetty that extended nearly one mile and was made of large granite rocks that had been carefully selected and placed to form a path cutting through the ocean. In the summer months, this ocean walkway saw a lot of foot traffic from the locals and tourists who braved the path's crevices for a closer view of the lighthouse waiting for them at the end. It was a great way to get some exercise and fresh air while enjoying a scenic view of the harbor, but people rarely made the trek in the cold winter months.

Standing on the shore, Lily excitedly announced that she wanted to walk the jetty, which Austin hadn't expected since she was already shivering.

"You realize it's even colder out there, right?" he asked, nodding at the distant lighthouse. "It gets windy."

"I can handle it!" Lily assured him. "Come on, let's go!"

"It's a longer walk than it looks," Austin reminded her. "It's almost a mile one way."

"It sounds like you're making excuses not to go," Lily teased.

"Hey, I'm down if you are," he chuckled. "I just wanted you to know what you're getting yourself into."

Gloved hand holding gloved hand, they slowly traversed the jetty, cautiously avoiding the gaps in the large rocks that could easily break an ankle, or even a leg, if one were to misjudge a step. Along the way, Austin recalled watching his father and grandfather fish off the side of the jetty when he was just a child. The memory was vague, as he'd been very young, but what he could remember seemed to mean a great deal to him.

"Okay, you were right, it's way colder out here," Lily said with chattering teeth.

"We can always turn around," Austin offered.

Lily looked over her shoulder at how far they'd walked, noting they were halfway to the lighthouse. "No, I'm good. I got this."

Despite the cold, made worse by the wind, they pressed on, determined to finish what they'd started. Given the uneven surface and gaps caused by the rocks drifting over time, it took them twenty-five minutes to reach the lighthouse, but they agreed the walk had been worth it. The lighthouse offered a bit of refuge from the wind, and Lily ran her fingers along the side of it in admiration.

"It's beautiful," she said, staring up at it. Looking around the harbor, she added, "This whole place is beautiful."

"It's always been one of my favorite places," Austin smiled, watching a schooner sail by.

They circled the lighthouse so Lily could see it in its entirety, and she couldn't help but notice how many initials had been carved into the side of it. She looked at Austin with a mischievous grin. "Can we?"

"I can see the headlines now," Austin laughed. "Tomorrow Tech CEO Austin Matson caught defacing historic Maine landmark."

"Oh, come on, don't be a wimp," Lily smirked.

"Hey, I didn't say no," he replied, returning her smirk. Pulling his keys from his pocket, he made sure nobody could see before carving their initials into the lighthouse.

"There," he said, taking a step back to admire his work. "AM + LW."

"My turn," Lily said, taking the key from him. "Partners in crime, right?"

"Partners in vandalism," Austin chuckled, taking another look around to make sure they couldn't be seen.

He watched with a smile as Lily outlined their initials with a heart.

"There," she said. "Much better."

Standing next to their handiwork, Austin wrapped her in his arms and kissed her. They both smiled as they rubbed the tips of their red noses together.

"We'll have to look for it the next time we visit," Austin said, taking another look at their carving. Shivering, he joked, "Preferably when it's warmer out."

"You really are a wimp when it comes to cold weather, huh?" Lily laughed, using her phone to take a picture of their initials wrapped in a heart.

"There's a reason I moved to the desert," he reminded her.

Lily tucked her phone away and her face grew solemn. "Thank you for bringing me here. You have no idea how much this means to me."

"Thank you for coming with me," Austin smiled. "I love seeing you this happy."

Lily grinned wide. "You know what would make me even happier?"

"Let me guess," Austin replied, playfully rolling his eyes. "Seafood?"

"Can we? Can we? Can we?" she asked, excitedly hopping up and down.

Austin rolled up his sleeve and peeled his glove back to look at his watch. "Yes, actually, we can. We should get there right on time if we leave now."

"Get there?" Lily questioned with her brow raised curiously.

"You'll see," Austin winked. "Now let's get out of here before I freeze to death."

As much as Lily loved taking playful jabs at Austin over the cold weather, she'd had enough of it as well and was ready for warmth. On the walk back to the car, Austin explained that the buoys they'd been seeing were used to indicate where lobster traps had been placed, and Lily listened with fascination as he detailed how lucrative and cutthroat the lobstering industry could be. While rare, he went on, people had been murdered for touching somebody else's traps, so it was best to leave them alone.

Finally reaching the car, they cranked the heat and held their hands to the vents to warm themselves. From the lighthouse, it was another twenty-five minute drive to Camden, Maine; one of the state's wealthier cities. Camden was home to its own beautiful harbor, and along that harbor were inns, restaurants, and small shops that catered primarily to tourists. Given the time of year, business wasn't exactly booming, and most of the restaurants were closed for the season. Austin guided them to the one restaurant open for business, and when she stepped inside to find they were the only patrons with a bare-bones waitstaff, it was clear that Austin had used his name and wealth to pull some strings.

"Is this your brother's restaurant?" Lily asked, recalling that one of his brothers owned a chain of restaurants.

"It's not," Austin answered, looking over the menu. "He doesn't really deal in seafood. His restaurants are known more for their pizzas and burgers."

"Did you pay them to open just for us?" Lily leaned over their table to whisper, covering her mouth with one hand.

"Why, Lilian Ward, I have no idea what you're talking about," he smiled.

They'd been seated by a large window offering a breathtaking view of the harbor, and Lily couldn't get enough of the moored boats gently rocking in the water. It was like a moving postcard, and although she knew photos wouldn't do it justice, she still couldn't resist snapping a few, even taking photos of the exquisite lobster dinner she'd ordered. They took their time, enjoying their meals that had been prepared to perfection, and Austin was sure to tip their waitress quite well before they left. After an unforgettable lunch, they drove back to Bangor to do their Christmas shopping, getting the majority of it done at L.L. Bean; a chain founded in Maine that specialized in high-end clothing and outdoor gear and had achieved nationwide success. There, Austin carefully picked out a selection of clothing for his family, along with a few magnets for the collection his parents kept on their refrigerator. Even though Austin had offered to pay, Lily insisted on using the money she'd earned working for him to buy small gifts for his family as well. He'd been paying her quite nicely, and had even given her time off to enjoy their trip together. Austin's mechanic had given her a few hundred dollars for her car so he could part it out and sell the rest to a scrapyard, which had put some extra money in her pocket.

After a full day of shopping, they'd worked up an appetite again and Austin delighted in showing her one of the restaurants his eldest brother owned that happened to be in the area. He'd messaged his brother in advance to tell him they'd be dining there, and he was thrilled when he'd replied that he was working until closing and would see them when they arrived. It was a short drive, yet a far cry from the seafood restaurant they'd dined in earlier. This place catered to the blue-collar working man, and had an almost rockabilly vibe to it, leaning heavily on a music theme with an assortment of records and guitars hanging as decor. Signage promoted karaoke nights on Fridays and Saturdays, with a small stage located at the back of the dining area for drunken performers. A long bar adorned with chrome ran the length of one wall and offered a variety of alcohol that likely fueled the majority of the singers.

"You son of a bitch," a slender man with graying hair greeted Austin when he walked through the door. Fearing an altercation, Lily felt her adrenaline spike.

"Careful, that's our mother you're talking about," Austin smirked. Realizing who Austin was speaking with, Lily breathed a sigh of relief. "Lily, I'd like to introduce you to my brother, Steven."

"It's so nice to meet you!" Lily smiled, offering her hand.

"Wow, you're really hot," Steven grinned, but his joking tone made it funny. Inappropriate, yet funny.

"Why… thank you?" Lily laughed.

Steven turned his attention back to Austin and looked him over. "Bro, you're looking jacked. How many days a week are you averaging in the gym these days?"

Guiding them to an open dining booth, the two caught up for a bit, both making a point to include Lily in their brotherly banter. Like she had with their parents, she felt completely at ease around Steven and realized a warm, inviting nature was something that seemed to run in their family. They invited Steven to sit with them for dinner, but as the owner of the restaurant, he had important duties to attend to and had to get back to work.

"That gray hair is from working in the restaurant business," Austin explained. "It's not as easy as people think. It's actually one of the hardest industries to break into. Most restaurants don't last long. A year or two, tops, and then they're gone."

"I've heard that," Lily nodded. "But he seems to be doing just fine."

"He is now," Austin agreed. "He had a bit of a rocky start, but things finally took off and he's doing great."

Along with a friendly, welcoming nature, success was something else that seemed to run in their family. Looking over the menu, Lily settled on a cheeseburger and a Diet Coke, while Austin followed suit and ordered the same. She loved the laid back atmosphere, and the clientele were definitely her kind of people. Austin dared her to hit the karaoke stage, to which Lily replied there wasn't enough alcohol in the world to get her singing. Not in front of a group of people, anyhow.

Steven would pop by their table when he could to check up on them, and the more she saw of him, the more she could see the family resemblance. Unlike Austin, however, Steven had dark brown eyes, was a few inches shorter, and easily sixty pounds lighter. She knew Austin had another brother as well, and if he was anything like the rest of the family, she was eager to meet him.

"We should probably get going," Austin said shortly after they'd finished their meals. Noting the time, he continued, "If we get home too late, Amos will bark and wake my parents up. That would be all bad."

"Yikes. We better get this show on the road," Lily nodded. "Thank you for dinner. Thank you for the entire day!" she corrected herself. "Today has been simply amazing."

"It has, hasn't it?" Austin agreed, smiling wide. "Oh, and Steven comped our dinner, so let's be sure to thank him for that."

Before heading out the door, they were sure to flag down Steven to tell them they were leaving and to thank him for dinner. He apologized for being so busy and told them he looked forward to spending more time with them on Christmas. After saying their goodbyes, Austin and Lily headed back to his parent's place, and hit by a bout of extreme fatigue she credited to their busy day, Lily slept through most of the drive, waking when Austin gently nudged her to announce their arrival.

With the following day being December 24th, they opted to spend a relaxing day inside. Unfazed by the cold weather, Austin's father ventured out to hunt while his mother invited Lily to help her in the kitchen, preparing food for Christmas. Austin sat at the dining room table using his laptop to handle some of the work emails he'd received, and from the smile on his face, he seemed to enjoy watching his mother and Lily interact so effortlessly. They got along great and exchanged stories and recipes while Christmas music played softly in the background, adding to the holiday feel.

Later that day, Austin and Lily retreated to the addition for a heated game of Scrabble, and after Austin managed to eke out a win, Lily was able to best him in a rematch. They spent what was left of the day working on a puzzle, with a break to join his parents for dinner, and realizing there was no way they could finish it that day, they left it to work on over the remainder of their stay. Being Christmas Eve, they wrapped the gifts they'd bought and waited until Austin's parents had gone to bed to quietly slip them under the beautiful Christmas tree in the living room. Taking a few steps back to admire the tree's decor and lights, Lily noticed the stockings his parents had hung on the wall before they'd retired for the night, all of them bearing the names of their family members.

"Oh, how sweet!" Lily gushed, realizing they'd included a stocking for her, even taking the time to sew her name onto it. The gesture was so touching, Lily's eyes welled with tears. She held Austin's arm and rested her head on his shoulder as they stood in the warm glow of the lights.

"They really like you," Austin told her quietly.

"Yeah?" she asked, looking up at his handsome face.

"Yeah," he smiled, and gave her a kiss. "Come on. Let's get some sleep."

Calling it a night, they sneaked back to the addition and snuggled up in the cozy guest bedroom. She fell asleep with Austin holding her, which had become the norm, and woke bright and early with Lily rolling onto Austin to cover him with kisses.

"Merry Christmas, baby," she smiled.

"Mmm… Merry Christmas," Austin purred, still half asleep. She was sure he could sense her arousal, but he shut her down by expressing how uncomfortable it would be having sex under the same roof as his parents. She could understand that since she wouldn't be comfortable with it either if their roles were reversed, so they settled on taking a shower together instead. Clean and clothed, they met his parents in the kitchen for a light breakfast, and they'd just finished eating when Amos—who had been lying under the table—signaled that the rest of Austin's family had begun to arrive. With a deep bark, he hurried to the front door with his tail wagging, knowing they were about to have company.

"You ready to meet my other brother?" Austin asked Lily with a smile.

Moments later, the front door burst open and Lily was introduced to Jason and his beautiful wife, Holly, along with their two children, Annabelle and Ethan, who were both squealing with excitement. The youngest of the two at only four years old, Ethan stopped dead in his tracks at the sight of Lily and looked at her with utter fascination.

"A chocolate girl!" he exclaimed.

"Oh my God," Holly groaned, covering her eyes in embarrassment while Austin's parents looked at each other awkwardly.

Jason, on the other hand, found it hilarious and roared with laughter. He delicately explained to Lily that living in a small, predominantly white community, she was the first black person Ethan had ever seen, and after offering an apology, asked that she please take no offense to the comment. Understanding that it was said out of innocence, Lily found humor in it as well and knelt down to Ethan's level to speak with him directly.

"Hello, Ethan," she smiled.

"Hello," he replied, looking her over.

"Do you like chocolate?" she asked.

"Yes!" he said, excitedly bouncing up and down.

"Well, I'm not chocolate, but I hope you still like me anyway," she grinned.

Moving into the living room, the children squealed in excitement again at the sight of the Christmas tree and the gifts spilling out from under it. They were aching to dig in, but were told they had to wait until Uncle Stevie arrived, which, they were assured, would be soon. Making use of the living room's ample seating, they made themselves comfortable and passed the time with conversation centered around Lily. She seemed to be the star of the show, with Annabelle taking an immediate liking to her and sandwiching herself between her and Austin on the sofa, looking at Lily as if she were some sort of celebrity.

Lily wasn't surprised to find Jason and his family every bit as remarkable as she'd expected. An inch or two shorter than Austin, he shared the same brown eyes as Steven, which they both seemed to get from his mother. Austin's steel-blue eyes that she loved so much were a gift from his father and set him apart from his brothers. Jason was also extremely charming, which likely explained his gorgeous wife who, as a third-grade teacher, had quickly bonded with Lily over their shared love of teaching. Lily was asking Holly what to expect of her schooling when Amos began to bark, announcing Steven's arrival. Austin's parents got up to welcome him and ushered him into the living room.

"Merry Christmas!" Steven smiled, setting down the two large gift bags he'd been carrying.

The kids sprang from their seats, knowing it was almost time to tear into the presents they'd grown impatient waiting for.

"Merry Christmas!" they echoed in unison, rushing to give him a hug.

"I'm sorry I'm late; the snow slowed me down a bit," Steven said. Everyone had been so lost in conversation, they hadn't noticed the snow that had begun to fall outside. Lily hurried to the nearest window to take in the wintery view.

"Now this feels like Christmas," Lily said, grinning wide. Austin sidled up next to her to admire the snowfall as well, which seemed to be getting heavier by the minute.

"Merry Christmas, baby," he said, followed by a quick kiss.

"Aw, how cute," Steven's voice sounded from behind them.

"Shut it," Austin grumbled in jest.

"It's good to see you again," Lily greeted, turning to face Austin's oldest brother. She was surprised when he gave her a familial hug, and she welcomed it with a smile.

"Merry Christmas, Lily," he said, returning her smile. "Are you sick of Maine yet?"

Lily laughed. "Oh, goodness, no! I love it here. I mean, I'm not a fan of the cold, but this place is beautiful from what I've seen so far."

"Presents! Presents! Presents!" the kids sounded loudly, eager to get things underway.

"Okay, okay," Austin's parents laughed.

The family agreed that the kids should open their gifts first, and they got no complaints from Ethan and Annabelle. They spent the next hour opening their presents with wrapping paper flying across the room as the kids tore into them. Annabelle was old enough to read the labels that had been carefully placed on each gift, and having been assigned the task of passing them out, was sure to announce which ones had come from Santa and which ones had come directly from the family. Lily couldn't believe the number of gifts they received. Clearly spoiled but sweet enough children to deserve it, they took the time to appreciate each one before opening the next.

"This one is from grammy," Annabelle said, handing Ethan a gift that he wasted no time opening.

"Oh, cool!" Ethan beamed, holding up his new Spider-Man socks.

"And this one is mine from Santa," Annabelle smiled, quickly unwrapping the toy pony set and excitedly prancing around the room with it. She looked up at nothing in particular and said, "Thank you, Santa!"

"Boy, you two must have been really good this year!" Lily smiled.

"Oh, they're just the best," Holly chimed in. "We got so lucky with them."

"It's not luck, it's called good parenting," Austin's dad said.

Lily was almost moved to tears when Annabelle passed a gift to Ethan and said, "This one is from Auntie Lily."

She watched with bated breath as Ethan ripped it open and was relieved by his reaction.

"Look! Look at what Auntie Lily got me!" he smiled, proudly showing everyone the official L.L. Bean teddy bear she'd picked out for him.

Sitting next to her, Austin could see how emotional she'd become and squeezed her hand supportively. He flashed her a grin and quietly whispered into her ear, "I knew he'd like it… Auntie Lily."

A tear did escape her, but she wiped it away before anyone could see it. From the first moment they'd arrived, she'd been made to feel like a part of the family, which she hadn't expected and appreciated more than she could ever express. She didn't look like them, and with the slight urban accent she'd worked to bury but occasionally resurfaced, she knew she didn't sound like them, either. Yet, they treated her like she was no different, welcoming her with open arms as if they'd known each other for years. Not even two months prior, she'd planned on spending a depressing Christmas alone in her trashy little apartment, but here she was, surrounded by these wonderful people who'd invited her into the fold and were overflowing with kindness and love. After everything she'd been through, that kindness and love felt like a godsend.

When the kids opened the last of their gifts, it was time for the adults to exchange theirs. Austin's mother was in charge of passing out these and explained that, as their guest, Lily was to open one of hers first. She hadn't expected to receive any gifts and nervously accepted the wrapped gift box, knowing all eyes were on her.

"This is from me," Pam said, smiling affectionately.

Carefully unwrapping the box, Lily opened it to find a gorgeous sweater knitted in light pink yarn, and she held it up to admire it.

"I love it!" she exclaimed, smiling wide. "And it's my favorite color!"

"I hope it fits," Austin's mother said with a slight look of concern. "I guessed your size from a few pictures Austin sent me."

"I can tell it will. Thank you so much!" Lily beamed, holding the sweater to her face to feel its softness.

"Isn't she talented?" Austin remarked, admiring the sweater as well.

"Wait, you made this?" Lily asked his mother in shock.

"I did," she smiled, pointing at her knitting basket nestled next to the sofa.

"Oh my goodness, Pam, this is just… wow! I can't believe you made this for me!" Lily rose to her feet to give her a hug, thanking her again for such a thoughtful gift.

"Grammy makes the best sweaters," Annabelle said, still thoroughly intrigued by Lily, who she'd been paying more attention to than her new toys.

The family took turns exchanging gifts, with several more handed to Lily that included a hooded sweatshirt with "Maine" embroidered on the front from Jason and his family, and a case of cheap beer from Steven that had the family erupting with laughter. He didn't know what to get them, he confessed, and had stopped by the only open convenience store along the way to pick out their "gift" that he'd crudely wrapped with a brown paper bag and some duct tape he'd found in his truck. Lily loved his sense of humor and thanked him for the beer regardless, knowing she'd never drink the bottom-shelf swill.

The gifts from Austin and Lily were a huge hit, with everyone loving the clothing from L.L. Bean and expressing their gratitude with smiles, thanks, and hugs. Annabelle was quick to slide on her new fleece slippers that were a perfect fit, which was a small Christmas miracle since Austin had no idea what size she was and had gone with his best guess. Pam got a kick out of the magnets they'd picked out for her and assured them they'd be displayed on the fridge by the end of the day.

With all the gifts opened and appreciated, Austin's mother passed out the stockings and invited everyone to dig in. Lily found hers stuffed with a selection of candy, along with small, individually wrapped gifts that also included a couple of magnets, one reading "Maine" with a lighthouse next to it, and the other reading "Maine" as well, this one with a lobster under it. She was sure to thank Pam, and she asked Austin if they could display the magnets on his fridge as well.

"Our fridge," he corrected her with a smile, "and absolutely!"

The turkey still had another hour in the oven, which gave Lily time to call her parents. While the kids returned to their toys and Austin's family caught up, Lily excused herself to the addition and steeled herself with a deep breath, dreading the conversation she was about to have. She'd planned on waiting until after Christmas to tell them about Ryan, but she knew they would ask her how she was spending her Christmas, and she couldn't bring herself to tell yet another lie. Nervously pacing the room, she gave her parents the short version of events, leaving out the vicious beating she'd suffered at Ryan's hands. It was simply too painful to relive again, and she knew it would cause them undo stress they certainly didn't need. She couldn't imagine any parent wanting to hear about their child landing in the hospital in the way she had. They'd insist she come straight home, and they would never stop worrying about her.

Omitting the horrific incident that had left her so traumatized, she told her parents that Ryan lived like a slob and had a drinking problem that made him too hard to live with, so she'd moved into her own apartment and had been getting by just fine with her cleaning job. She almost told them about his gambling problem and how he'd stolen her money, but decided against it as it was just one more thing they'd worry about. Instead, she shifted to the wonderful man she'd met who had invited her on the trip of a lifetime, to which they gently reminded her that she'd once referred to Ryan as wonderful, too. They asked her to remain cautious so she didn't end up in another uncomfortable situation, and both urged her to take her time with Austin. She expected the lecture and knew it would have been much longer had she mentioned having already moved in with him. There were several things she just couldn't tell them yet, and those would have to come in time. They were thrilled to hear from her, however, and agreed that she sounded happy, which assuaged some of their worries. They were sure to wish her a Merry Christmas and express their love, and after returning both, she promised to keep in touch before rejoining Austin and his family. The timing was perfect as they were just settling in for dinner.

"How did it go?" Austin pulled her aside to ask quietly.

"Good… I think," she replied, taking in the abundance of delicious food spreading across the table. "I'll tell you about it later."

Their bellies full, Lily insisted on helping with the dishes, and this time, she wouldn't take no for an answer. Pam pushed back but acquiesced and cleared the rest of the table, scraping some of the unfinished food into Amos' bowl as a Christmas treat, which he scarfed down in a hurry. Austin helped by drying the dishes while his father, who had already done his work by hunting and carving the turkey, relaxed with the rest of the family in the living room.

The kitchen and dining room cleaned, they spent the next hour mingling, with Lily reconnecting with Holly to continue their discussion on teaching. They got along swimmingly, and Lily could see her becoming a close friend if they weren't separated by 3,000 miles. They came from two very different backgrounds, yet seemed to share a tremendous amount in common and promised to stay in touch through social media. Lily had never been big on social media, dismissing it as a distraction and a waste of time, but if she were being honest, it was because she didn't have enough real-world friends to justify a social media presence, and she had no interest in building a network of people she didn't know and would likely never meet. She had a Facebook profile she rarely checked, but seeing that life with Austin would introduce her to new people, effectively expanding her social circle, she made a mental note to do a better job keeping up with her account.

Steven was the first to leave since his drive home would take around an hour, and possibly longer, if the roads were bad. The snow had continued to fall throughout the day but, thankfully, they didn't get as much as the forecast had predicted. Jason and his family stayed a bit longer since they lived nearby, and like she had with Steven, Lily was sure to thank them again for the generous gifts as they were leaving. Annabelle made her promise to come back, to which Lily replied that another visit would be up to Uncle Austin, not her.

"We'll be back," Austin assured Annabelle. He looked at Lily and smiled wide. "We'll definitely be back."

The house quiet again, Austin and Lily thanked his parents for a day they'd never forget and retired to the addition to chip away at the puzzle they'd started. They'd just sat down when Austin excused himself, returning a moment later with a wrapped box he presented to a very surprised Lily. She hadn't expected anything from him, and slowly opened the box to find a stunning silk robe—again in light pink—that felt every bit as expensive as it looked.

"Oh, my… Austin, this is beautiful!" she gasped.

"I have to admit, it's just as much for me as it is for you," he said with a suggestive grin. "I can't wait to see you in it."

"How did you know I wanted a robe?" she asked, genuinely curious as to how he'd hit such a perfect mark.

"Because I actually listen when you speak," he laughed. "It's what you do when you care about somebody."

Lily cocked her head and thought for a moment. "I did mention needing a new robe, didn't I?"

"You did," he smiled. "You mentioned it in passing, but it stuck with me. You said you'd forgotten yours at that scumbag's place."

She loved how he refused Ryan the dignity of addressing him by his name. "I can't believe you remembered that." She looked down at the robe and sighed. "Austin, this is just too much. I kind of considered this trip my Christmas gift. You didn't need to get me anything on top of it."

"Please," Austin scoffed playfully. "Like I wouldn't get my girl something for Christmas. Are you crazy?"

"You're too perfect," she said, pulling him in for a kiss. "And I might have something for you, too."

"Really, now?" he questioned with a smile.

"Like I wouldn't get my man something for Christmas," she returned in jest. "Are you crazy?"

He laughed, and she insisted he take a seat on the sofa while she disappeared into the guest bedroom to find the gift she'd hidden in her luggage. She met him a minute later with a small gift-wrapped box topped with a silver bow and nervously presented it to him, watching just as nervously as he delicately unwrapped it to find what was clearly a ring box. He looked at her curiously for a second before opening the box as slowly as she'd opened hers.

"Oh my God," he breathed, his blue eyes wide at the sight of the silver signet ring with a thick band and a remarkably detailed lighthouse engraved on its face. At the top of the lighthouse tower, a small diamond had been set, and several small engraved lines shot from it, giving the lighthouse the appearance of shining into the sky. "Lily… this is just…"

"Don't worry, I'm not asking you to marry me," she said, taking a seat next to him on the sofa and placing her hand on his leg. She swallowed nervously, and with a solemn face and tone, offered the meaning behind the ring. "You know how much the lighthouse thing means to me," she began.

"I do," he said, noting how serious she'd grown and matching it, covering her hand with his.

"This is probably going to come out all wrong," she muttered, "but in a way… you've become my lighthouse. I had nothing left. No job. No car. No money. I'd lost just about everything, and in that moment of darkness, you came in like a beacon of light, offering me protection and guiding me to safety." She paused to choke down her emotions and wiped away the tears that had started to form. "You're my shining light. You're my lighthouse, standing big and tall. If I ever feel lost, that bright light of yours will always guide me home. I… I think I…"

She felt herself shaking, and he must have felt it too. In a move that was his way off offering her assurance, he gently squeezed her hand.

"It's okay, baby," he said softly, giving her the courage to continue.

She wiped her eyes, sniffled, and blurted, "Austin Matson, I think I might be hopelessly in love with you."

A look of relief washed over him. "Lilian Ward, I *know* I'm hopelessly in love with you."

"Really?" she asked, wiping her eyes again.

"Really," he said, moving his hand to delicately brush her cheek with the back of his fingers. "I never believed in love at first sight… and then you came along, and, I swear, Lilian, the moment I looked into those big, brown eyes of yours, I knew I was in deep."

She looked at him and was surprised to see tears in his eyes as well. She sniffled again and smiled. "Are we in love?"

"We're totally in love," he beamed with the biggest grin she'd seen yet.

She moved onto his lap for a long, passionate kiss, both repeating "I love you" as their chests heaved with passion. When their lips parted, she pressed her forehead to his.

"You don't think the ring is stupid?"

"Baby, this is the sweetest thing ever," he said, looking at the ring. He'd set it on the small end table next to them and picked it up to admire it again. "I love it. I absolutely love it. And don't think I didn't notice how perfectly it matches your necklace."

"Yeah, that wasn't easy," she laughed. "I managed to find a jeweler who made it for me using my pendant as a reference."

"Custom made? Babe, this couldn't have been cheap. You didn't have to—"

"I did," she stopped him. "I most certainly did. It's my way of showing you how much you mean to me."

Austin slipped it onto his finger and was shocked to find a perfect fit. "How the hell did you know my ring size?"

"I didn't," Lily laughed. "I felt bad doing it, but I poked through some of your things hoping I could find a ring that would tell me your size. I couldn't find one, so I gave the jeweler your height and guessed your weight, which wasn't easy given all of that muscle," she smiled, squeezing his arm. "He took a shot in the dark and it looks like he nailed it."

"I'll say," Austin agreed, twisting the ring and nodding. "It really does fit perfectly."

"It's almost like it was made for you," Lily joked.

"I see what you did there," he smiled.

"It occurred to me that you're probably not a ring guy since I've never seen you wear one and couldn't find any in your bedroom—"

"*Our* bedroom," he corrected her, just like he always did when she referred to the room as his.

"*Our* bedroom," she smiled, and continued, "so there's a chain in the box as well, in case you'd rather wear it as a necklace. I mean, you don't need to wear it at all if jewelry isn't your thing…"

"Are you kidding me?" he replied. "It's staying right here on this finger and it's never coming off. It's my new favorite thing."

"What about your Ferrari?" she quipped.

"*Pfft,* that old thing?" he smiled. He looked at the ring again and his smile grew larger. "This is the most valuable thing I own now. I mean that, too."

She felt her heart swell with love for this incredible man she'd fallen so completely for. Still sitting on his lap, they shared another heated kiss that Lily abruptly broke when she feared her arousal was growing too hard to control. She knew how Austin felt when it came to getting frisky in his parents' home and wanted to respect his boundaries, which wasn't easy given how turned on she was. Those boundaries seemed to have flown out the window, however, as Austin was every bit as turned on as she was and couldn't restrain himself. Carrying her to the bed, they made love while trying to remain quiet, which was a new experience for them since they'd always been so vocal. Given Austin's sexual prowess, it never took her long to finish, and she buried her face in a pillow to muffle her cries when the orgasm hit. As was typically the case, Austin still had plenty of energy left and kept going until she came again, biting her fist to silence herself this time since the pillows had flown off the bed at some point. He finished inside of her and collapsed by her side, completely drained and breathing heavily.

"Yeah, Mom and Dad can never find out about that," he chuckled.

"Oh, darn, I was going to tell them over breakfast," Lily laughed, reaching over the side of the bed to retrieve the fallen pillows.

Pulling the blankets over them and drawing her close to him, he held her in his arms and kissed her shoulder. "I love you so much."

"Mmm… I love you too," she returned, smiling. "My lighthouse."

"My chocolate girl," Austin purred, to which Lily burst out laughing.

"How funny was that?" she said, still laughing.

"I just about died of embarrassment," he chuckled. "You know, you're probably the first black person to ever step foot in this house."

"I kind of gathered that," Lily replied. In her best backwoods Southern drawl, she joked, "You don't get many of my kind 'round here."

Austin rolled on top of her and covered her naked body with kisses while she giggled.

When the morning came, Lily met Austin's parents wearing the sweater Pam had knit, which fit perfectly and was just as comfortable as she'd expected. She thanked Pam once again and set off with Austin to explore a bit more of the state. Another cold, snowy day, they did most of their sight-seeing from the car and returned that evening to finish the puzzle, making sure to snap a few photos of it for posterity.

They spent the next two days at his parents' place, making the most of the time they had left there. Bundling up, they invited Amos with them and ventured across the twelve acres of land to the small pond Austin had told her about. There, they broke in the ice skates they'd bought, with Lily laughing at how unsteady Austin was and holding onto him so he wouldn't fall. He confessed that he hadn't skated in over twenty years, but quickly got the hang of it again and they were skating hand-in-hand in no time as Amos ran alongside them, panting in excitement.

Back inside, Austin spent some time with his father while his mother introduced Lily to knitting. She'd always wanted to learn, and Pam proved to be a wonderful teacher, even giving Lily a few balls of yard and some knitting needles so she could practice on her own. When the 29th came, they said their heartfelt goodbyes and promised to return for another visit in the summer. Having bonded over the course of their stay, Lily teared up as she hugged his mother goodbye, and she left with no shortage of memories and Maine memorabilia. They drove back to Bangor and returned the rental car, and from there, they made their way back to another private jet, this one even larger than the first.

"Paris, here we come!" Lily smiled.

Chapter Eight

Lily spent the majority of the flight practicing her knitting, with a break halfway through the flight to take Austin for another ride. She was exhausted by the time they touched down in Paris, where Austin had a driver waiting for them at the *Charles de Gaulle Airport*. The short, portly chauffeur handled all of their luggage for them, placing it onto a luggage cart and pushing it to the waiting limousine, while Austin and Lily followed behind. After helping them into the car, the chauffeur loaded their luggage into the trunk and drove them to the historic *Ritz* hotel, known for being one of the most luxurious retreats in the world. Austin had intended this to be a trip they'd never forget and had spared no expense, booking the renowned Suite Impériale, a palatial 2,500 square foot suite featuring an enormous living area, two bedrooms—each with its own bathroom—a dining room, and a kitchen. The suite radiated opulence with carved woodwork highlighted by gold leafing and gold fixtures throughout, including gold-plated swan faucets. The artwork alone was enough to leave Lily speechless, with walls adorned with paintings from famous artists from centuries past. Several elegant chandeliers hung from the ceiling that Lily suspected were worth a small fortune themselves.

The suite had been occupied by many important historical figures over the years, and it offered a breathtaking view of *Place Vendôme*, the grandiose city square built as a monument to the glory of King Louis the Great. In the center stood the famous *Vendôme Column*, a bronze column erected by Napoleon Bonaparte that was made from the cannons of the Russian and Austrian armies he'd defeated. It was dark by the time they arrived, and every bit as cold as it had been in Maine, but they couldn't resist stepping onto the balcony to admire the view of the lit square. Lily, a history lover, knew a bit about the area and was able to recount some of the history, which Austin seemed to enjoy.

Austin invited her for a drink in the impressive bar they'd seen downstairs, but fatigued and nauseous, Lily simply didn't have it in her.

"Sweetie, I think I might need to just lie down instead. I don't know what's gotten into me lately. I've been exhausted. I'm sure it's just from all the excitement. Would you be upset if I got some rest and we checked out the bar tomorrow?"

"Not one bit," he smiled. "I'm beat, too. I just want to show you a good time."

"Every minute I spend with you is a good time," she smiled back. "I still can't believe we're in Paris! This really is a dream come true for me. I just can't thank you enough."

After taking a warm shower together in one of the suite's lavish bathrooms, Lily found herself too tired to bother with clothes and simply crawled into bed naked. They'd already had fun on the jet, but she could tell Austin was ready to go again. He knew she wasn't feeling well, however, and out of respect, he didn't try to initiate anything. He seemed perfectly content just holding her, and they talked until Lily fell asleep in his arms, which didn't take long. She slept straight through the night, waking to find Austin in the living room on his laptop.

"I'm so sorry," she said, rubbing her eyes. "I overslept."

"Nothing to be sorry about," he smiled, standing to give her a quick peck on the lips. "This is your vacation. You're allowed to sleep in. How are you feeling?"

"Much better, actually," she grinned. "I'm ready to see Paris!"

"Good, because I'm ready to show it to you," he chuckled. "But how about some breakfast first? I'm starving over here."

Realizing they hadn't eaten a real meal since they'd landed, Lily agreed breakfast was a good idea and sat next to Austin to go over the room service menu he had waiting for her. Given his build, she knew how much he could eat and couldn't believe he'd waited for her to order. He'd helped himself to a few snacks to tide him over, he told her, but he couldn't bring himself to eat without her. It was their first official day in Paris, he continued, and he wanted to start their day off right by enjoying a meal with her. She found that remarkably sweet and smiled as they pored over the menu together.

They made their choices, and the breakfast arrived shortly after, brought to them on a cart pushed by a gentle young attendant who introduced himself as Pierre. He politely asked them how they were enjoying their stay as he laid out their breakfast, and the food looked nothing short of amazing, with everything cooked fresh and delivered quickly so it would arrive warm. Eggs, bacon, an array of fresh fruit, and, of course, croissants and beignets had been neatly arranged before them, along with a selection of juices and teas. Austin was sure to tip Pierre handsomely before they dug in, stuffing themselves for the day ahead.

Bundling up, they spent the entire day visiting all the major tourist attractions while Lily took as many photos as she could. Starting with the Louvre Museum, they spent four hours basking in the work of history's most renowned artists, with Austin joking that Lily had said "oh my God" more times than she had in bed with him.

"Oh my God, it's The Coronation of Napoleon!"

"Look! It's Liberty Leading the People, oh my God!"

"Oh my God, Death of the Virgin!"

"Oh my God, oh my God, oh my God… Austin, it's the Mona Lisa!"

Austin covered his mouth and muttered, "Quick, stuff it under your shirt. I'll make sure nobody's looking."

She laughed and playfully swatted his arm. He was impressed by her knowledge of fine art, and he couldn't stop smiling as he watched her react to each piece.

"It's so surreal seeing these in person," Lily gasped. "I've seen them in books and prints so many times, but seeing them—" she cut herself off as another piece caught her attention. "Oh my God, The Astronomer!" she squealed, rushing over to it. "Austin, this has always been my favorite painting!"

While Lily appreciated the artwork, Austin appreciated her reactions and seemed to spend more time watching her than he did admiring the paintings and sculptures carefully placed about the sprawling French museum.

From the Louvre, they made their way to the Arc de Triomphe before heading to Notre-Dame Cathedral, which they weren't allowed to enter since it was still undergoing reconstruction from the fire that claimed so much of it a few years prior. She was fine with that, and excited just to be in its presence. Standing in the cathedral square amongst the other tourists, she looked up at it with wonder.

"You know, most people think the Eiffel Tower is the most popular attraction in Paris, but it's actually this cathedral," Lily said.

"Really? Wow, I would have thought it was the Eiffel Tower for sure," Austin replied. "Boy, it sure does pay to read, doesn't it?" he remarked, referring to the knowledge she'd collected from the books she'd read over the years.

"I actually overheard somebody say it a few minutes ago," Lily smirked, to which Austin burst out in laughter.

"You got me," he said. Looking at his watch, he added, "Speaking of which, we should probably head to the tower now. I could eat again, and there's a nice restaurant up there. Two of them, actually. It would be nice to get there before the sun sets so you can get a better view of the city."

Arriving at the tower, they chose to use the stairs rather than the elevator and began their ascent to the first level. Lily was a little concerned by how worn out she was just from climbing the three hundred steps.

"Remind me to start working out with you," she joked at one point, pausing to rest for a moment before continuing on.

Reaching the first level, which was home to the *Madame Brasserie* restaurant, Lily was surprised to see how busy it was. Given the time of year, she hadn't expected the place to be so packed. Austin explained that this restaurant offered quick, simple dishes, primarily for tourists, and that the second restaurant, located on the next level, was a bit fancier and required a reservation, which he'd booked weeks earlier. Lily perked up when he mentioned the restaurant's name.

"The Jules Verne?" she repeated excitedly. Jules Verne was one of her favorite childhood authors, and she recounted how she'd read *Journey to the Center of the Earth* by flashlight over the course of two late nights in the makeshift fort she'd constructed using her bedding. With a burst of energy, she resolved to make it up the remaining three-hundred steps it would take to reach the restaurant.

"We can always take the elevator," Austin reminded her.

"No, the stairs are fine," she replied. "The first flight taught me that I could use more exercise."

"Fair enough," he said. He looked concerned when she stopped to rest again halfway up the stairs. "You okay?"

"I'm fine," she breathed, and offered him a reassuring smile. With a chuckle, she added, "I'm just out of shape."

When they reached *The Jules Verne* on the tower's second level, Lily gasped with wide eyes as she looked around the restaurant. The height of decadence, it sat 410 feet above the ground and its walls of windows offered a sweeping view of Paris.

"Austin… this is just…" she muttered, trailing off at a loss for words.

"Right?" he smiled, enjoying her reaction.

They were greeted warmly by a receptionist who asked if they had a reservation, and after Austin gave his name, they were led to the table he'd reserved which was seated next to one of the many windows, allowing them to take in the city as they ate. Shedding their winter jackets, they draped them over the back of their chairs and settled in to dine. The food was sumptuous, so much so that Lily couldn't stop expressing it with every bit.

"Baby, you have to try this chicken. Mmm. Oh… oh, this is just incredible. Here, try a bite of this rice. I wonder how they seasoned this? I'd love to ask the chef. Seriously, this chicken is unbelievable."

Those were just some of her utterances, and Austin couldn't stop smiling, clearly amused with her response to the meal that she knew wasn't cheap. Their lobster dinner in Maine was expensive, but she knew it was a drop in the bucket compared to this. With just enough room left for dessert, they shared a chocolate soufflé so rich, it was all they could do to finish it.

"Thank you," Lily said, reaching across the table to take Austin's hand and smiling at the lighthouse ring that hadn't left his finger. "I know I keep saying it, but thank you. This whole trip has been like something out of a dream."

"It has, hasn't it?" he agreed. "And thank you, too. I didn't know it was possible to be this happy. I know we haven't been together for that long, but I can't imagine going back to a life without you. I thought I was happy before, but you've made me realize that I was just content. There's a big difference. I realize that now."

"You're sweet," she said, leaning over the table for a kiss. "I love you so much."

"I love you, too. With all of my heart." He paused for a moment and a devilish grin spread across his face. "My chocolate girl."

She laughed at what had become their inside joke, and when he told her he had a little surprise for her, she looked at him questioningly. "A surprise?"

"Follow me," he said, rising from his seat and offering his hand. He guided her to the kitchen where he introduced her to Frédéric Anton, the award-winning chef who was known the world over for his culinary creations. He recognized Austin right away and greeted him with a friendly hug and a kiss on the cheek.

"Austin, my friend!" he spoke with a heavy French accent. "It is so nice to see you again!"

"You as well," Austin smiled. "I'd like you to meet my girlfriend, Lilian Ward."

"It's a pleasure to meet you, ma chère," he said, grinning wide. "You are très beau!"

Lily knew just enough French to know he'd complimented her beauty and felt herself blush.

"Thank you," she replied, looking away modestly.

"I asked Frédéric to prepare our meal himself," Austin told her. "He's one hell of a chef, isn't he?"

"Frédéric, everything was just amazing!" Lily gushed. "I don't think I can look at food the same again," she joked. "Everything is going to taste so bland now!"

Frédéric laughed and seemed genuinely flattered by the compliment. Seeing that he was in the middle of preparing another meal, they thanked him again and let him get back to work.

"An old friend of yours?" Lily asked while they made their way out of the kitchen, hand in hand.

"I've been here a few times," Austin chuckled.

"And how many women have you introduced him to?" Lily asked with a hint of bitterness in her voice. Old fears rushed back, and she worried she just was another in a long line of women Austin had romanced in what was known as "The City of Love."

Austin stopped them abruptly and looked hurt by her words.

"Just you, Lilian." She knew he was serious by his use of her full name instead of a pet name. With sincerity in his eyes, he explained that he'd done business in Paris several times over the years, and the restaurant had provided the perfect place to woo investors and potential clients. He assured her that he'd never stepped foot in the city with another woman and would never dream of bringing her somewhere he'd brought another lover. He was quick to remind her that his previous girlfriend was still sitting behind bars, and that there really hadn't been anyone significant before her.

"Austin… I'm so sorry," she replied, feeling truly awful about what she'd said. He'd proven many times over that she wasn't just some conquest, and that he had no hidden agenda, yet echoes of the trauma Ryan had left still reverberated within her. She thought they were gone, but it seemed they still remained, buried deep down. "I guess I still—"

"Stop," he said, cutting her short. "You don't have to explain. I get it. I really do."

"Yeah?"

"Yeah," he smiled. "Now let's get to the top of this thing, shall we?"

"I don't know if I can handle more stairs," Lily laughed, relieved she hadn't spoiled their fun.

"You're in luck," Austin smirked. "There's a lift that will take us to the third level."

"Oh, thank God."

The open top of the tower offered an incredible aerial view of the city, along with a champagne bar. Austin bought them an entire bottle, and with bubbling flutes, they clinked their glasses together.

"Cheers," Austin smiled.

"Cheers."

It was already cold, and with the sun setting, they knew it was only going to get colder. Still, they could manage it, and they both agreed that as cold as it was, it still wasn't as cold as their visit to the lighthouse in Maine. Austin had timed their day perfectly as they'd arrived just in time to watch the sunset, allowing them a view of the city during the day and at night. They watched the transition as they enjoyed their champagne, and before long, the city had become a sea of lights. They were having fun trying to spot the locations they'd visited earlier, and were able to find a few when a young man approached Austin with a bewildered look, as if he wasn't quite sure if he had the right person.

"Austin Matson?" he asked with an American accent. "It can't be."

Austin tensed as he looked the man over, and Lily could see him relax after deciding the man was harmless. "I'm sorry, do I know you?"

"I apologize for interrupting," the man said, raising his hands to show he wasn't a threat. "But you *are* Austin Matson, right?"

"I am," Austin nodded. The man seemed innocent enough, yet Lily instinctively stepped behind Austin for protection, knowing how quickly things could sour.

"No way!" the man belted, smiling ear to ear. "Oh, man, I thought it was you but I wasn't sure. It's different when you see somebody in real life, you know?" When Austin said nothing, the man nervously swallowed and continued, "I'm a huge fan, that's all. I'm an engineer at MIT, and you're pretty much royalty there."

Austin laughed and offered the man his hand. "It's always nice to meet a fan, especially one who's a computer engineer. Thank you for the kind words."

"My name's Cody. I'm here visiting with my fiancée." He turned and motioned to the woman standing just behind him, who stepped forward to introduce herself as Desiree. "We thought Paris would be a great place to ring in the new year," Cody explained.

"Great minds think alike," Austin replied, shaking Desiree's hand with a smile. "This is my girlfriend, Lilian Ward."

Lily shook their hands with a smile and congratulated them on their engagement. She noticed people had begun to look at them, likely overhearing Cody's comments and realizing they were in the presence of somebody important. After all, while he wasn't somebody who'd be recognized in every household, Austin was a celebrity, having appeared in countless magazines, television interviews, and internet shows over the years. Austin seemed to sense how uncomfortable she'd become, and since they were both shivering from the cold anyhow, he took it as their cue to leave.

"Listen, we have to get going, but thank you once again for the kind words," he told the young couple, "and I wish you an amazing life together."

They still had half of their bottle of champagne left, and not wanting to bring it with them, Austin asked Cody and Desiree if they'd like the rest of it. Cody was elated and asked Austin if he'd be kind enough to sign the bottle, to which Austin happily agreed. Desiree dug through her purse for a pen, and Austin autographed the bottle's label.

"Oh, man, I have the perfect spot for this in my office," Cody said excitedly. "Can I get a picture with you real quick if it's not too much trouble? I'm sure I've already bothered you enough…"

"It's no trouble at all," Austin smiled. Lily stepped aside and Cody took her place while Desiree readied her camera. For a more amiable appearance, Austin slung his arm around the young man's shoulders and flashed a thumbs up, grinning wide. Cody held the bottle up as proof it had been given to him by Austin Matson, and after a three-second countdown, Desiree quickly snapped a couple of pictures.

The unexpected photo shoot drew more attention from those nearby who stood wondering who Austin was, but they hightailed it out of there before anyone else could approach, hurrying to the elevator to make their descent down the tower.

"I'm sorry about that," Austin said when the elevator doors had closed. "I get that from time to time. It doesn't happen too often, but it happens."

"You have nothing to be sorry about," Lily replied. "It's part of dating the famous Austin Matson."

"I'm only famous in certain circles," Austin chuckled. "I'm mostly known by computer geeks like me."

She'd never admit it aloud, but a part of her found his fame attractive. Given his looks, success, and celebrity status, there was no question that he had his pick of women, yet he'd chosen her. She couldn't help but feel special.

"To be clear, we're taking the elevator all the way down, right?" Lily asked, half-jokingly. Exhausted from the excitement of the day, she didn't think she had more stairs left in her, even if they were downward steps.

"That's the plan," Austin smiled, leaning in for a quick kiss.

Their driver was waiting for them below, and because the man had driven them around the city all day, waiting patiently for them at each stop, Austin was sure to tip him well.

Returning to their suite tired and aching, Lily fought the urge to lie down, knowing that if she did, she wouldn't get back up and would likely sleep through the night again. She'd already felt badly about heading to bed so early the night before, so she brewed a pot of coffee while she took a cold shower in an attempt to liven up. It worked, and by the time she'd finished her cup of coffee, she'd perked up enough to enjoy more of the day. As he had the previous night, Austin suggested they check out the bar downstairs, and wanting to experience as much of Paris and this extravagant hotel as she could, she agreed to join him for a drink.

"You've got to be kidding me!" Lily cried when she saw the name of the bar. Named after another literary legend, *The Bar Hemingway* was a tribute to Ernest Hemingway; a Ritz regular who frequented the hotel's bar so often, they'd decided to rename it in his honor. The entire bar not only served a wide selection of high-end alcohol, it also served as an homage to the American author and war reporter who had penned some of history's most revered works. The walls were adorned with pictures of the iconic writer, along with several of his handwritten letters and postcards. Decor taken directly from Hemingway's life, particularly his passion for the sea, hung on the walls as well, and complimented the room's atmosphere nicely. Wood paneling, seats upholstered in fine leather, and sepia lighting gave the inviting bar more of a lounge feel, while also acting as something of a museum.

The bar wasn't particularly busy. Lily counted six people seated about the room, and the bartender, a petite dirty blonde wearing a white jacket reading "The Bar Hemingway" on its left breast pocket, welcomed them in with a warm smile. Austin and Lily chose to sit at the bar so they could chat with the barmaid, who quickly identified them as American and switched her language accordingly, introducing herself as Anne while handing them a drink menu. Austin settled on a simple rum and Coke, and when Lily couldn't decide what to order, Anne asked if she could create one just for her. Lily agreed, and to get started, Anne asked her a few simple questions. She still carried a thick French accent, yet her English was surprisingly good. Lily surmised it was from years of serving American tourists.

"Do you like fruity drinks?" Anne asked.

"I do," Lily nodded.

"Any fruits you don't like?"

"Not that I can think of, no."

"Do you like your drinks sweet?"

"Yes."

"Are there any particular liquors you don't like, or that don't agree with you?"

"I don't know," Lily shrugged. "I'm not a very experienced drinker. I'm sorry."

"That's nothing to apologize for," Anne replied with a smile. "You've given me everything I need to know."

Lily watched in awe as the master mixologist scooped a bit of ice into a stainless-steel tumbler followed by a selection of juices and liquors. She shook the concoction vigorously before carefully pouring it into a cocktail glass and affixing a stemmed rose to the side.

"Enjoy," she smiled, sliding the glass over to Lily and setting to work on Austin's drink.

"Austin… this is a real rose," Lily remarked, feeling the petals and leaning in to smell the beautiful pink flower.

"Every lady gets a real rose in her drink," Anne told Lily, overhearing her comment. "It's our tradition here."

"How cool is that?" Lily said, admiring her drink.

"You going to try it, or are you going to just stare at it?" Austin chuckled.

"I'm waiting for you," she smiled. Jokingly, she added, "It's called being polite."

Austin's drink arrived a moment later, and as always, they clinked glasses before indulging.

"Well?" Austin asked, eager for her verdict.

"Holy crap," Lily blurted. She took another sip and looked at their barmaid approvingly. "Anne, this is unbelievable. I have no idea what you put in here, but it's fantastic!"

"Why, thank you," Anne replied, taking a bow.

"Is there even any alcohol in here?" Lily asked, taking one more sip.

"Oh, yes," Anne laughed, and repeated with a mischievous look, "Oh, yes."

Austin took a sip of his drink and complimented Anne for the perfect job she'd done with his as well.

"Vous êtes les bienvenus," Anne replied, slipping back into French. Greeting a patron who'd stepped up to the bar, Anne left Austin and Lily to enjoy their drinks.

"This place is magical," Lily said, looking around the bar. "Not just this bar, but this whole city. It's everything I dreamed it would be, and so much more."

"I've always wanted to bring somebody special here," Austin replied, taking another sip of his rum and Coke. "I just never thought I'd find that person."

"Well, I hope you find her someday," Lily joked, grinning wide.

As quick-witted as ever, Austin didn't skip a beat.

"Me too," he smirked. Lily laughed and playfully swiped his arm.

They'd just ordered another round of drinks when something caught Lily's eye.

"Wait. Is that… Is that Hemingway's typewriter?" she gasped, spotting a vintage typewriter atop a small table in the corner of the room.

"I believe so, yes," Austin nodded. "One of them, anyhow."

Lily bolted from her stool and hurried over to it with Austin trailing behind. She studied it in fascination, wondering aloud how many books and articles the typewriter had produced with Hemingway's hands. It sat uncovered and unguarded, and it took every ounce of self-control she had not to run her fingers over it. Standing so close to such a historic piece was a sensation akin to what she'd felt viewing the artwork at the Louvre, and she showed it the same level of respect.

Austin glanced over his shoulder and noticed their drinks were ready. Even though the bar felt safe enough, neither of them wanted to leave the drinks unattended and returned to their seats. Austin enjoyed another rum and Coke, while Anne had made Lily a repeat of the drink she'd enjoyed so much.

"Well, I'm officially drunk," Lily announced when she'd finished her third. The drinks had gone down so smoothly, she hadn't realized just how much alcohol was in them.

"I'm right there with you," Austin replied with an intoxicated grin that turned suggestive as he asked, "Want to go back to our room?"

"I'd love that," she smiled. Anne presented the bill with a polite smile and Lily snatched it from her hand before she could pass it to Austin. "I got this."

"Babe, I don't—"

"Nope," she interrupted, pulling her bank card from her pocket. She'd slipped it in there next to her phone before they'd left the room, knowing she'd be paying their tab. "You've paid for more than enough. Let me treat you to something for once."

She gasped when she realized the bill was for a staggering two hundred dollars. Austin chuckled, seeing the look of shock on her face.

"That's what I was trying to tell you. Drinks here? Not cheap. I got this, baby, don't even worry about it," he smiled, reaching for his wallet.

"No, no, I said I'm paying, and I meant it," Lily insisted, handing Anne her card. After Ryan's theft, she'd learned to keep a better eye on her account, checking it weekly to make sure there weren't any unauthorized transactions. Because of this, she knew she had just enough money to cover the bill and Anne's tip, but it would be cutting it close. She'd be left with a few dollars, if that, but given how much money Austin had spent on her so far, it only seemed fair.

"Sweetie, I told you I'd cover everything," Austin griped.

Lily's phone sounded with a text message alert from her bank, warning her of a potentially fraudulent transaction and asking if she was really making a purchase in Paris, France. She typed "yes" to accept the charges, and the transaction was successfully processed.

"I couldn't live with myself if you covered everything," Lily replied, stuffing her phone back in her pocket. She dodged Austin's attempt to steal the pen from her before she could sign the receipt.

"In that case, allow me to thank you for the drinks," he smiled, "and to give you a two-hundred dollar bonus when we get you back to work."

"Austin, don't you dare!" Lily protested with a laugh.

Amused by their banter, Anne thanked them both for their patronage and bid them goodnight. Austin and Lily thanked her as well, and their repartee continued with drunken giggles as they made their way back to their suite. There, Lily dimmed the lights and pushed Austin onto the bed, insisting he stay put, and he waited patiently while she ducked into the bathroom to slip into the silk robe he'd given her for Christmas. She'd been waiting for the right moment to wear it, and it seemed like a fitting ending to the incredible day they'd spent together. It was a perfect fit, and wearing nothing underneath, she left it untied as she returned to Austin, who had already stripped down to his black boxer-briefs.

"Yeah, that was a good investment," he joked, looking her over with a satisfied grin.

"You like?" she asked, twirling around to give him a full view of the robe with glimpses of her naked body underneath.

"Oh, I like," Austin growled, his blue eyes burning with desire. She could tell he wanted her, and she wanted him every bit as much.

Slowly crawling onto the bed like a cat, her arms extended, back arched, and behind raised, she approached him while biting her lower lip seductively, which she knew drove him crazy.

"There's my big, strong man," she purred, climbing on top of him and playfully flicking his Clark Kent curl. Straddling him, she could feel how hard he was between her legs, and she reached down to free his cock.

"God," he breathed, shuddering at the feeling of her hand wrapped around his erection. She was so wet that despite his size, he still slipped inside of her with ease. "You are just so sexy."

He was always sure to tell her how beautiful she was, and how sexy he found her, which didn't go unrecognized or unappreciated. With his hands firmly gripping her bare ass, he controlled their rhythm, lifting her up just to bring her back down on his length, his eyes locked onto hers and his teeth clenched. Her turn to take charge, she sunk deeper onto his cock, grinding her clit into him in what had proven to be a surefire way to cum. It didn't take long, and the orgasm was so intense it took everything out of her. Falling on top of him, he gripped her ass again and thrust his hips up and down, ramming himself in and out of her.

"Oh... oh, fuck!" she cried, her voice trembling. "Baby... baby, you feel so good!"

"Yeah?" he asked through gritted teeth.

"Yeah! Give it to me, baby. I want it. I want it!"

"I'll fucking give it to you," he growled, and in a display if strength, flipped her over in one fluid movement, pushing her robe up to take her from behind. She loved it when he took her like this, and she wrapped her arms around a pillow, moaning loudly as he plowed into her. She came again, biting the pillow to soften her cries, and when he felt her orgasm had run its course, he slipped out of her to flip her over again. Placing her legs on his shoulders, he slid himself back inside of her and began to thrust, his pace building as he drew closer to his own finish.

However, when he reached down to hold her breasts like he always did in this position, she was alarmed to find the usual pleasure replaced by discomfort. The sensation she typically felt wasn't there, and an aching pain greeted her instead. It wasn't severe enough to interrupt them, but it was enough to elicit a mixture of concern and confusion. She pushed it aside, sensing he was close, but she knew she'd be investigating this unsettling turn when they were through.

"Baby... I'm... I'm..." he panted.

"Do it, baby," she breathed. "Cum for me."

Slipping out of her, her legs returned to the bed, and she watched as he jerked himself. Seconds later, an eruption of cum coated her body, making its way up to her neck with a few drops landing on her face. Her robe had fallen open around her, and she was relieved to find it hadn't been hit.

"Oh my God," he groaned, collapsing onto the bed next to her.

"Damn, baby," she said, looking down at her body in disbelief. "I think that was your most yet."

"I'd apologize if I was sorry," he grinned. Rolling onto one arm, he looked her over and added, "God, that's hot."

"I look like a Jackson Pollock painting," she chuckled.

"Quick, let's display you in the Louvre," Austin joked. "You're my work of art."

Still drunk, the two burst into laughter. Lily slipped out of the robe and hurried to the bathroom, feeling his "artwork" run down her body, and made it to the shower before any could drip onto the floor.

"I'm going to rinse off real quick," she told him from the shower.

"Okay," she heard him say. "I'd join you if I could walk. That kicked my ass."

"Just lie there and relax, baby. I'll be right out."

For the first time, she was glad he didn't join her. Washing herself clean, she gently felt her breasts and noted how sore they were. Between the random bouts of fatigue, nausea, a missed period, and now this, she knew something wasn't right. Searching her mind for an answer, a realization hit her like a freight train.

Oh, fuck. You're pregnant.

It made sense. They hadn't been using protection, and recalling the first time they had sex, the timeline seemed right. A gamut of emotions hit as she processed this unexpected development, starting with regret. They should have been using some form of birth control—they were both smart enough to know better. With their traditional values, her parents wouldn't be happy with an unplanned pregnancy out of wedlock, and she dreaded the lecture they were sure to give. The pregnancy could interfere with her schooling as well, and for a moment, she considered pushing her enrollment back a year. She brushed that idea aside knowing she couldn't keep postponing it, and although attending the university while pregnant wouldn't be easy, she was sure she could make it work. Regret turned to concern over Austin's reaction. She knew he wanted children, but he was in the middle of a potential acquisition that would require his attention for the next few months, if not longer. Concern gave way to guilt for the alcohol she'd drank on the trip, and she desperately hoped it wouldn't hurt the baby's development. She vowed to abstain from drinking, which wouldn't be hard since she rarely drank anyhow, and she had no problem ringing in the new year without it. The final emotion to hit was happiness, and an overwhelming happiness at that. She'd always said that if she were to ever get pregnant, she wanted it to be with a man she was head over heels in love with, and Austin definitely fit that bill. Looking back, she knew she was already in love with Austin when they'd crossed the intimacy line, and she believed that he had been in love with her at that point as well. Their baby had been conceived out of love, and with that realization, she smiled wide.

She returned to the bedroom to find Austin half asleep, which wasn't a surprise given their long day, the drinks, and his orgasm. He apologized for being so tired, and after helping him to his feet, the two properly readied themselves for bed. With their teeth brushed, they exchanged a kiss, professed their love for each other, and crawled back into bed to snuggle. Austin was out within minutes, but with all the thoughts racing through her mind, Lily knew sleep wouldn't come as easily for her. She was going to be a mother. Would the baby be a boy or a girl? What would they name the child? What would the child look like? For nearly two hours, she lay awake envisioning the new future she was facing, and that Austin was facing, too. She'd have to tell him, but she thought it best to wait until they returned to the States. Soon, their trip would become business, and she didn't want the announcement of a baby distracting him in any way. She needed the confirmation of a pregnancy test first anyhow, and that would likely have to wait until they arrived home as well since she was just about out of money and didn't think she'd be able to sneak away to buy one even if she wasn't. Austin had been by her side the entire trip, and she didn't see that changing since he was in charge of their transportation.

At some point, Lily drifted off to sleep and woke to the smell of breakfast. She'd told Austin that he didn't have to wait for her to eat, and it was clear that had registered with him. She was glad he'd already ordered and the food had arrived as she'd woken with quite an appetite, and by the way Austin was tearing into his meal, the same could be said for him.

"Morning, sunshine," he greeted, standing to give her a quick peck on the lips.

"Hey, baby," she groaned, tying her robe and taking a seat across from him in the suite's spacious living area. Their breakfast had been placed on the table between them, and it appeared similar to the breakfast they'd enjoyed the day before, with the addition of crêpes topped with banana and strawberry slices.

"Rough night?" Austin joked, pushing his laptop aside.

"Those drinks were stronger than I thought," Lily replied. "I'm a bit hungover, embarrassingly enough."

"It was worth it though, right?" he asked.

"Oh, without question." She loaded her plate with food and dug in, commenting on how delicious the crêpes were. Even hungrier than she'd thought, she reached for another.

It's because you're eating for two, she told herself. Along with a hangover, she'd woken with her breasts still aching, and they seemed to be a bit swollen. She knew these symptoms typically accompanied pregnancy, and they only bolstered the idea that she was pregnant.

"The chefs in this city really know what they're doing, don't they?" Austin said, taking another bite of his eggs.

"I'll say," she agreed halfheartedly, her mind still on the pregnancy. "What's on the agenda for today?"

"I'm glad you asked," he replied. "I'm sure you'd love to do some shopping while you're here. I was thinking we could spend the day checking out some of the stores in the area. There are a few boutiques nearby I think you'd enjoy."

He never pried into her finances, but she was sure he was aware they weren't good. It would be window shopping only for her, but she was fine with that. She'd gone so long with so little, she'd grown used to it.

"I'd love that," she smiled.

"And to celebrate the new year, I thought it would be fun to head to Champs-Elysées Avenue," Austin suggested. "Apparently, there's a huge celebration there every year. Fireworks and everything."

"Oh, that sounds fun! Count me in."

"I'll grab a bottle of champagne to bring with us. It should be a blast," Austin grinned.

If there was a chance she was pregnant, she wasn't going to risk any alcohol and made up an excuse, thinking fast. "Baby, with this hangover, the last thing I want to think about is alcohol."

"Aw, come on. You'll be fine by tonight, I'm sure."

"I'm so dehydrated, I'll be sticking to water. Last night was enough for me," Lily said. However, Austin pressed the issue.

"Just one glass won't kill you. We can't ring in the new year together without at least one glass of champagne."

"We'll see," Lily said, forcing a smile. It wasn't much of a reply, but it bought her time to think of another excuse. With the entire day ahead of them, she was sure she could think of a way around the champagne problem.

When Austin had suggested they spend the day shopping, he hadn't been kidding. She'd never known a man to like shopping, and she suspected the day was more for her than it was for him. As with everything they'd experienced, he seemed to enjoy watching her excited reactions to everything Paris had to offer. They made their way around the city, stopping everywhere from large department stores to small luxury boutiques specializing in overpriced clothing, jewelry, and accessories with their driver waiting patiently while they browsed. She'd always made an effort to dress nicely, but she kept it within her budget, finding clothes that looked far more expensive than they truly were. She could credit her entire wardrobe to discount stores, clearance racks, and even thrift stores, and had no interest in the latest designer trends. While her friends were sporting Coach handbags, hers had come from Walmart, and it served its purpose every bit as well. Her lack of interest in material things, along with her frugal nature, was how she'd been able to save so much money for her schooling. Money, of course, that was long gone, thanks to Ryan.

If only he could see me now, she thought, and quickly scolded herself for it. She didn't need to be thinking of him, and she certainly didn't need to gloat. Still, it was hard not to compare her old life with Ryan to her new life with Austin. She'd gone from living in squalor with a man who treated her horrifically to living in luxury with a man who treated her like a queen.

Stepping inside *Galeries Lafayette*, a Parisian chain known for their selection of haute couture, they were greeted by the biggest names in fashion, with clothing priced into the thousands. She recognized a few of the names, like Chanel, Dolce & Gabbana, Gucci, and a few more, but the rest were well outside her scope of fashion knowledge.

"Let's take a look at some of those dresses," Austin said, leading her into the Versace department—one of the few names she'd heard before. Following beside him, they landed at a selection of elegant dresses, and Austin invited her to browse them. It seemed silly since she couldn't afford any, yet she couldn't stop herself from taking a look. She didn't think any woman placed in this position could resist at least sneaking a peek.

"Oh, Austin… wow," she gasped, fawning over a red draped gown that had caught her attention. Made of liquid viscose jersey, it featured a cowl neck with shoulder straps, a front leg slit, and a gathered bodice. She gently brushed the fabric with the back of her fingers and found it was unlike anything she'd felt before.

"You like that one, huh?" Austin asked

"It's the most beautiful dress I've ever seen," she breathed.

"You have good taste," he smiled.

Curious as to how much a dress like this would cost, she found the price tag and blurted, "You've got to be kidding me. That's outrageous!"

Austin shrugged. "They don't come cheap."

"Four thousand dollars? That's robbery!"

"That's actually cheap compared to some of the other dresses here," Austin pointed out.

A saleswoman approached with a polite smile and asked Lily if she'd like to try on the dress, to which Lily politely declined.

"Thank you, but we're just browsing," Lily told her. "And it's not my size anyhow."

Looking her up and down, the woman replied, "Oh, we have more, and I believe we do have your size. I can get it for you if you'd like. It would look amazing on you."

"You're sweet, but we're just browsing, really. Thank you, though," Lily said.

"Well, if you change your mind or if you see something else you'd like to try—"

Austin interrupted the woman. "She would like to try it on, yes."

"Austin!" Lily hissed, tugging his arm. As much as she loved him, she didn't appreciate him answering for her. "I don't want to try it on. What are you doing?"

"Please," Austin replied, "indulge me. I'd love to see it on you."

"Why? It would just be a waste of time. It's too expensive. I can't—" Suddenly realizing where Austin was going with all of this, she cut herself off, feeling stupid for not having realized it sooner. "No," she told him sternly. "Absolutely not. You are *not* buying me this dress."

"Baby, please," he pleaded. "It's a beautiful dress. You're a beautiful woman. You were made for each other."

Upset, Lily felt her face grow warm and asked the saleswoman to give them a moment. She didn't have to ask twice, as the woman had felt the tension between them and had been itching to step away.

"Austin Matson, shame on you," Lily chided when the woman was out of earshot. "I appreciate everything you've done for me so far, but I am not letting you buy me that dress. You've done too much already."

"Babe, please," Austin pressed. "There's no better dress for New Year's Eve."

She already felt uncomfortable enough with the money he'd spent on her. The entire trip had already cost him thousands, and it was only halfway through. If she allowed him to buy her the dress, she'd never be able to live with herself for a myriad of reasons. He'd been used for his money once, and if she continued accepting his lavish trips and gifts, she feared he would grow to resent her, seeing her as just another gold-digger. Moreover, she couldn't help but think of the people struggling financially worldwide. While she'd be prancing around in a four thousand dollar dress, parents across the globe would be worrying how they were going to feed their children, and that thought didn't sit well with her. It was the type of excess she loathed and wanted no part of.

You had no problem wearing that robe, and Lord knows how expensive that was.

That thought filled her with guilt. It also made her feel like quite the hypocrite. She shouldn't have accepted it, nor should she have accepted the expensive meals or chauffeured rides around Paris. The money Austin had spent on their suite alone likely cost more than the average family made in a year, and that realization sickened her. She recalled driving through Austin's gated community only three months prior and shaking her head at the unnecessarily extravagant homes. Now, she was living in the grandest of those homes and residing among the wealthy, watching tens of thousands of dollars being wasted on frivolous things. She was disgusted with herself for becoming the very thing she'd always frowned upon, yet it was impossible not to enjoy all the luxury she'd been introduced to.

"I don't want it," Lily groaned. "Maybe we can find a cheap knock-off somewhere. Besides, it will be too cold to wear it tonight anyhow.

"You're right," Austin began, raising his index finger in thought, "but you know what? It would be perfect for our business dinner with Jean-Marc in Crolles on Tuesday. Maybe if we distract him with your beauty, his negotiating skills will slip and we can get a better deal on the facility."

Lily felt a wave of inadequacy washed over her. "My dresses aren't good enough?"

"Your dresses are great and all, but we might want something just a bit fancier for whatever restaurant we'll be dining at. I'm sure he'll want to meet somewhere nice."

It hit Lily that a life with Austin brought a heavy amount of compromise. She'd never planned on falling so madly in love with a man worth so much money, but she had, and although she'd stepped into their relationship knowing the lifestyle he lived, it was only now that she was beginning to understand it. She should have known that even her most expensive clothing—the costliest being an eighty-dollar dress she'd splurged on after a long deliberation over its price—wouldn't gel with his ostentatious life. Sure, her wardrobe was fine for around the house, but she could only assume he'd ask her to join him for future business meetings, and possibly even interviews as well. It made sense that he'd want her attire to be a bit more flashy. She couldn't show up to an important event wearing a shirt from a second-hand store while he was dressed in an Armani suit. She would have to find a way to reconcile that, but now wasn't the time.

She swallowed hard and looked away. "I'm uncomfortable. I'd like to leave."

Seeing her discomfort, Austin realized he'd pushed too hard and had overstepped. "I'm sorry. I didn't mean to make you upset. I thought you'd look nice in it, that's all." He cleared his throat and feigned a smile. "Let's get out of here."

"Thank you," she said, feigning her own smile back.

Galeries Lafayette was a department store for the wealthy, but it felt more like a mall, featuring a wide selection of eateries. When she couldn't decide on where to eat, Austin asked if *la Maison Le Bourdonnec*, a restaurant catering to meat eaters, would be okay since his muscle mass required a steady intake of protein. The place smelled so delicious that Lily was on board with the idea, and they settled in to enjoy their meal. Austin's T-bone steak didn't stand a chance, and Lily's burger didn't last long, either. Austin excused himself to use the restroom, and Lily picked away at the rest of her fries in his absence. When ten minutes passed and he still hadn't returned, Lily began to worry, and she'd just stood to search for him when he finally resurfaced.

"I'm so sorry," he said. If she wasn't mistaken, he seemed a bit winded, but Lily didn't pry. He leaned in for a quick kiss and explained that he'd had an unexpected phone call that he had to take, but had turned his phone off for the remainder of the day.

Austin asked if they could visit a few more departments, and although she'd completely lost interest, Lily agreed to stay longer just to make sure things were okay between them. She forced excitement at the overpriced merchandise and watched as Austin dropped five thousand dollars on a new Zenga suit—a brand she'd never heard of but would now equate with wealth. He insisted on buying a bottle of champagne to ring in the new year, and she managed to talk him down from a bottle priced at one thousand dollars to one priced at two hundred. When she felt the fatigue and nausea setting in, she asked Austin if they could return to the hotel so she could rest up for the night ahead. Afraid he'd begin worrying about her health and start asking questions, she told him she just wanted to shake the rest of the hangover so they could make it downtown later for the big celebration. He understood and agreed it was a good idea, adding that he wouldn't mind resting a bit as well.

Back in the suite, Lily headed straight for bed and was out within minutes. She woke only briefly when she felt Austin slide into bed next to her, and she purred when he wrapped her in his arms, their disagreement over the dress long forgotten. She fell back into a deep sleep and woke to Austin gently nudging her shoulder.

"Babe? It's ten o'clock. If you still want to celebrate, we should probably start getting ready."

"It's ten?" Lily asked sluggishly. She'd intended on taking a quick nap, but had slept for over three hours. "I can't believe I slept that long."

"Are you feeling better?" Austin asked, seated next to her on the edge of the bed.

"Yes, actually," she replied, rubbing her eyes. "Much better."

"Good," he smiled. "Only two hours until the new year!" Hopping off of the bed, he looked at her with a mischievous grin and offered his hand. "Come here. I have a surprise for you."

Helping her out of bed, he guided her into the living area where a gift-wrapped box sat on the sofa, a huge silver bow affixed to the top.

"Austin?" she asked, looking at the box. "What is this?"

"Open it," he smiled. "It's for you."

Still half asleep, she didn't have the energy to protest and unwrapped the box while Austin watched excitedly. She felt her face grow warm again when she saw "Versace" stamped on the box, already knowing what she was going to find. Opening the box, she was greeted by the red dress she'd rallied against and threw the box back on the sofa in anger.

"I can't believe you," she groaned, shaking her head. "I'm so mad at you right now."

"No, you're not," he said, playfully batting his eyes and flashing his charming smile.

"Stop trying to be cute," Lily snapped. "I'm being serious. I specifically asked you not to buy me this dress. I pleaded with you not to buy it. You steamrolled right over me and did it anyway. I don't want it." Looking around the decadent suite, she continued, "I don't want any of this. This isn't me, Austin. I'm a simple person. I like simple things. The four thousand dollars you spent on that dress could have fed… I don't know how many people!" she said, throwing her hands up angrily.

"I'm… I'm sorry," he said, taken aback by her reaction. It was apparent that he hadn't expected this response. "I was just trying to do something nice for you."

"Is that it? Or is it that my clothes aren't good enough for your business meeting? Because if that's the case, I get it. I don't expect you to wear your five thousand dollar suit while I'm sitting next to you in a twenty-dollar dress from Ross. I'm not an idiot. I understand. All I'm saying is, we could have found a nice dress for way cheaper."

"Yeah, but it wouldn't have been *this* nice," Austin said, looking at the dress sitting in the open box.

"You just don't get it," Lily groaned again, covering her eyes in frustration. "I'm not comfortable with the idea of wearing four thousand dollars. I think of all the good that money could do for people and it makes me sick. If I wore this dress, I'd feel like I was flaunting money at people who are struggling just to keep their lights on. It's like a slap in their face. We could have found a nice enough dress for one, maybe two hundred dollars and donated the rest of this money to people who need it. And, yeah, I know what a moralistic prig I sound like right now, but I'm not about to sacrifice my integrity over anything material, no matter how alluring it might be."

"Do you know how much money I pay in taxes alone?" Austin roared, his face turning red. "Do you?" he repeated. "It's well into the millions every year, and that money does more for people than volunteering at a soup kitchen ever could. For Christ's sake, I donated an entire hospital wing, Lily! I don't even know how many lives that's saved. And don't get me wrong here, I'm not trying to make myself out to be some sort of a hero, but with the money I shell out every year, I have no problem buying nice things for myself and for my loved ones. The property tax I pay every year alone would make your head spin. And all of these vehicles I own? Don't even get me started on the taxes I've paid on those. So, yeah, forgive me if I indulge in life's finer things. I worked for them. I earned them. I've paid more than my fair share, and I'm going to enjoy them."

It was her first time seeing him angry, and though his voice was raised and his brow furrowed, she realized she wasn't afraid of him, which came as a relief. As kind and gentle as he was, she knew he had to get angry at some point, and she worried he may have an aggressive side he'd kept hidden from her. Ryan would have pushed her up against the wall by now, but Austin had kept his distance and remained unthreatening. As she studied his face, she realized he now looked more hurt than angry. His words had hit her hard, as she'd never considered just how much he did contribute to society. While she'd proven to be good at saving money, she was no economics major and suddenly felt foolish for her uneducated stand. In less than a minute, he'd managed to reverse her opinion on the matter, leaving her embarrassed on her soapbox. Humbled, she stepped down from it and once again covered her eyes with her hand, this time out of humiliation.

"Oh, Austin. You're right. Of course, you're right." Ashamed and fearing she'd ruined the special night he had planned, she burst into tears. "I feel so stupid. I didn't know any of that."

"You'd be surprised how many people don't," he said, rushing over to console her with a heartfelt embrace.

"You've gone out of your way to do all of these wonderful things for me, and this is how I act. Oh, God, I'm so embarrassed," she sobbed.

"Hey, now, it's okay." He spoke softly, rubbing her back soothingly as she cried. "Really, it's okay. I'm sorry I raised my voice. I just get so heated when people think I just spend money without giving anything back when the reality is, I give back every time I spend money."

"I know you give back," she sniffled. "I just didn't realize the extent of it."

"I worked hard to build my empire," he said. "I'm allowed to enjoy the fruit of that labor without guilt. And you know what? You are, too."

He was making a lot of sense, and she couldn't argue with his sound reasoning. "I'm so sorry, Austin. Please, forgive me."

"There's nothing to forgive," he smiled. "Feeling guilty about wearing such an expensive dress while people are going without is one of the many reasons I love you. You're a good person, Lilian Ward. The best. I shouldn't admit this, but it was honestly a bit attractive when you turned the dress down. Most women would have accepted it without hesitation, and too many of them wouldn't have even thanked me after. You're wired differently, and that's why I'm so crazy about you."

"God, you're always so sweet, even when I don't deserve it," she said, pulling away to wipe her eyes.

"Now, I want you to do something for me, and if you say no, I won't push back. I'll let it go, and that will be the end of it."

"Yes?" she sniffled.

"I want you to put that dress on so I can finally see you in it. The woman had to guess your size, so I'm hoping it fits."

"How did you even get this?" she asked. The question had barely escaped her when the answer hit. "Oh, you sneaky little punk. There was no phone call earlier, was there?"

"Why, Miss Ward, I have no idea what you're talking about," he replied, grinning wide.

She knew he'd likely paid big money to have the store deliver it to the hotel and had waited for her to fall asleep before bringing it into the suite.

"I need to keep a closer eye on you," she chuckled.

"So? Will you try it on for me? Like I said, if you're still not comfortable with it, I'll return it with no questions asked."

"I guess there's no harm in that," she conceded. "Give me a moment."

Delicately lifting the dress from the box it had been neatly folded into, she disappeared into the bedroom and slipped into it, finding it a perfect fit. Stepping in front of the room's full-length mirror to see how it looked, she couldn't stop smiling. It highlighted her feminine curves in all the right aways, and the slit offered a glimpse of the legs she'd received so many compliments on over the years. Always humble and never one to boast, she had to admit that she looked good, though she would never say that aloud. She popped into the bathroom to retouch her makeup and fix her hair, and after taking one last satisfied look at herself, she was ready for the big reveal.

"Okay, close your eyes," she said, standing just out of sight behind the bedroom door.

"Closed," he replied.

Moving into the living area again, she stood before him and took a deep breath. "Okay, now you can look."

Austin opened his eyes, and they grew wide, his mouth falling open. He stood in stunned silence for a moment, slowly looking her up and down. Finally, he spoke.

"Lily… my God. You're breathtaking." Looking her over again, he continued, "You're the most beautiful woman on the planet, I'm sure of it."

"Stop," she blushed with a dismissive wave.

"I mean it," he said. "I've been all over the world and have seen countless women along the way, but none have even come close to your beauty. I'm just… wow. I'm sorry, I just can't stop looking at you."

"Well, I'm glad you like it," she beamed, overjoyed by his reaction.

"What do you think?" he asked. "Should we keep it?"

"I don't know," she sighed. "It is lovely, but the price still makes me a bit uncomfortable."

Closing the distance between them, Austin pulled her in for a kiss that grew deeper and more passionate by the second. She could tell by his labored breaths that he wanted her, and she wanted him just as much. Guiding her to the sofa, he brushed the box away with such force that it went flying across the room, and spinning her around, he positioned himself behind her. She hiked the dress up as she knelt on the sofa, and with no panties standing in the way, he had no problem sliding inside of her. She could hear the rattle of his belt buckle as he pumped in and out of her like a piston, his hands on her hips, and her fingers digging into the back of the sofa. The sex was so sudden and unexpected that it added a whole new level of excitement, and for the first time, they both came together.

"God," he breathed, tucking his shirt back into his pants and clasping his belt. "That was incredible."

"It always is," she said, panting. She could feel him dripping from between her legs and hurried to the bathroom to clean up.

"I guess we're keeping the dress, then?" Austin smiled when she rejoined him a moment later.

"Yeah, no way I'm returning a dress I had sex in," Lily laughed. "How messed up would that be?"

"Very," Austin agreed. "But I'm sure people have done it."

"Ew," Lily winced. "Now I'll have that thought stuck in my head the next time I buy a dress. Thanks, baby."

"Think nothing of it," he joked, glancing at his watch. "We need to get going soon if we're going to make it downtown in time."

"Shoot, you're right. Let me get changed real quick. As much as I'd love to wear this," she said, running her hands down the dress, "I'd rather not freeze to death."

She changed into a more appropriate outfit, Austin grabbed the bottle of champagne he'd bought earlier, and with their winter coats and gloves on, his driver dropped them off downtown. Their short yet heated fight over the dress had been erased by their make-up sex, leaving no tension between them as they joined the crowd on Champs-Elysées Avenue. They'd made it through their first fight. She was sure there would be others down the road, but they'd proved their love was strong enough to persevere. Their excellent communication helped, and their unbelievable sexual chemistry certainly helped as well.

The historic French avenue was swarmed with locals and tourists who had braved the cold to watch the light show at the Arc de Triomphe with the fireworks set to pop off at midnight. An hour until the countdown, they passed the time mingling with others, and given the size of the crowd, it was a given that at least a few people would recognize her affluent boyfriend. Austin was approached several times for autographs and pictures, and he was happy to accommodate, greeting everyone as if they were an old friend and taking a genuine interest in their lives. He really was a sweet, gentle man who could make friends everywhere he went, and before long, they'd formed their own little group to ring in the new year with. Austin cracked the bottle of champagne he'd brought and pulled out two small plastic champagne flutes from his coat pocket in preparation for the countdown, and Lily nervously watched as he filled them. She still hadn't found an excuse for why she couldn't drink, and with less than five minutes until midnight, she didn't have much longer to think of one. Seeing that a couple of their new friends were holding empty cups, Austin invited them to enjoy the champagne as well and poured them each a generous amount.

With only one minute left, Austin set the champagne bottle down at his feet and dug his cell phone from the breast pocket of his coat.

Lily assumed he was going to use it to record the momentous occasion, and was confused when he began dialing somebody instead.

"Who are you calling?" she asked, fighting irritation. They'd waited all day for this moment, and she was worried he'd miss it over a phone call.

"I'm calling Winston," Austin smiled. "I want him to ring in the new year with us. He's all alone there, you know? Nobody should be alone on New Year's Eve."

At that moment, Lily fell in love with him all over again. Of course, he should call Winston and include him in the celebration.

"That's so sweet of you," she smiled, shaking her head in disbelief at the incredible man who'd stolen her heart.

"It's only 4:00 pm there, so he should answer. He's usually—" he stopped abruptly when Winston answered the phone, and he put him on speaker so Lily could talk to him as well. "Winston! I know it's not midnight there yet, but it's about 30 seconds away from hitting here and we want you to celebrate it with us."

"Oh, Mr. Matson, that is so thoughtful!" Winston replied.

"I have you on speaker. I apologize for the noise. We're at the Arc de Triomphe and the place is mobbed!"

"I can hear you just fine," Winston said. "Everyone seems to be having fun."

"Hi, Winston!" Lily smiled. "We miss you!"

"And I miss you both as well," Winston replied. "Everything is just fine here at the homestead."

"The countdown is about to begin," Austin said, noting the large digital numbers that had been projected onto the Arc. "We're all going to count down together, okay?"

He'd just finished his sentence when the countdown began, and as the digital numbers ticked down, everyone in attendance shouted each passing number. The street was so filled with noise Lily couldn't be sure, but she thought she heard Winston counting down with them.

"Ten! Nine! Eight! Seven! Six!"

Lily looked at her champagne flute nervously again and fought the urge to announce her pregnancy. Telling Austin at the strike of midnight would have been perfect, but it still felt a bit premature. Austin had important business to handle first, and she still needed to take a test.

"Five! Four! Three!"

As the countdown continued, their small group formed a semicircle, their drinks lifted as the final seconds ticked away.

"Two! One! Happy New Year!" everyone roared in unison.

"Cheers!" Austin belted, his deep voice standing out above the crowd. He clinked his champagne flute to hers like she'd expected, and when he closed his eyes and threw his head back to gulp it down, Lily quickly tossed her champagne over her shoulder, leaving her with just the empty flute. The champagne covered the man standing behind her, and turning to face him, she mouthed the words, "I'm so sorry!" with a wince. He scowled at her and moved away, and as luck would have it, Austin missed the entire incident.

"Happy New Year, baby," Austin smiled, leaning in for a kiss. "I love you."

"Happy New Year, sweetie," Lily returned with her smile just as big. "I love you too."

Together, they repeated the sentiment to Winston, and reminded him that they'd be home in less than a week. When they got there, they'd be sure to fill him in on their adventures, they told him, and with that, they rejoined the group they'd formed to continue the celebration. Austin refilled her flute, but since there were no cheers or toasts this time, it was easier to discard. She waited until he was making small talk with a member of their party and simply poured it onto the street, grateful she'd talked him into a cheaper bottle. They stayed for another twenty minutes before the cold got to be too much, and after saying goodbye to the people they'd befriended and gifting them the remaining bottle of champagne, they worked their way back to the waiting car.

They spent their last day in Paris taking in a few more sights, and as the sun was beginning to set, Austin surprised her with tickets to *Paquita*, an operatic ballet hosted by the *Opéra Bastille*, a newer opera house known for its modern architecture. Austin had bought them the best seats in the house, and given their strict dress code, it gave Lily a chance to wear her new dress again at Austin's suggestion. Suspecting they'd be rubbing shoulders with Parisian socialites, she took her time getting ready, making sure her makeup and hair were perfect before carefully painting her nails red, which Austin agreed was a nice touch. She didn't wear heels often but remembered packing one of the two pairs she owned, though she couldn't remember what color she'd grabbed. Rummaging through her luggage, she was relieved to find she'd packed her black pair since her other pair were pink and wouldn't have matched. With her long, black hair, the black heels served as a nice bookend while giving her another three inches of height. Austin joked that wearing them, she'd no longer have to stand on her toes to kiss him. He changed into his new suit, and her reaction was similar to his reaction to her dress... minus the impassioned sex.

"Oh, baby," she smiled. "It's a perfect fit. You look so handsome!"

"Thank you," he said, adjusting his tie. "But all eyes will be on you tonight." He paused to admire her and grinned wide. "You'll be the belle of the ball."

That was no exaggeration. As they made their way into the opera house, at least a dozen men and women approached to compliment her beauty. There were plenty of stunning women in attendance, all dressed to the nines in designer attire, yet all eyes seemed to be on her. She credited it to her vibrant red dress, which stood out among the crowd, and she was flattered when a fashion photographer asked if she'd pose for a photo with Austin. They needed more pictures together and stepped aside to allow a few shots, both offering sincere smiles for the camera. The photographer asked for her name and jotted it down on a small notepad he pulled from his pocket. With a polite grin, he thanked them for the photos and disappeared into the crowd.

The show was phenomenal and went off without a hitch, earning a standing ovation from everyone in attendance. It was a perfect way to end their stay in Paris, but by the end of the show, Lily was exhausted, nauseous, and ready for bed. Back at the hotel, Austin advanced on her but quickly realized she wasn't feeling well and settled for holding her again, just as he had their first night there.

"I'm worried about you," he said. "You've been under the weather a lot lately."

"It's just all the excitement, baby," she assured him. "And I'm not used to walking around so much. I really want to start working out with you when we get back."

"I really need to get back to it," Austin groaned, playfully patting his stomach. "I rarely go this long without exercise. I feel like I've gained ten pounds on this trip."

"Oh, please," she laughed. "You're still built like a brick."

"Well, I won't be for much longer if I don't get back to the weights soon."

"I'd love you even if you had a dad bod," Lily smiled.

"Yeah?"

"Yeah."

"Okay, in that case, let's have a kid so I can let myself go," he joked. "I wouldn't mind spending less time in the gym. I can get my exercise by chasing around a little one."

Lily feigned a chuckle and swallowed nervously, knowing that little one might come sooner than he expected. "Funny, babe."

"Sorry, bad joke," Austin said, worried he'd made her uncomfortable. "I know it's too soon for that. It's easy to forget that we've only been together for a few weeks since I'm so comfortable around you. I feel like I've known you forever."

"I feel the same way," Lily smiled, turning to give him a kiss. "Maybe we really were destined to meet."

They woke early to pack for the third and final leg of their trip. They'd be taking a train to Crolles, which Lily was thrilled about since it gave her a chance to see more of France while offering a nice break from flying. Between the flight to Maine and the flight to Paris, they'd spent close to fourteen hours in the air, and they still had a long flight home in four days. Austin left a hefty tip for the maid service, and with the use of a luggage cart, they took the elevator down to the lobby to check out of the hotel. As the receptionist slid the bill over to Austin, Lily couldn't help but steal a glance and almost fell over. The four-day stay had set Austin back sixty thousand dollars, yet he'd signed the receipt like he was paying for a cup of coffee.

Their driver had become a familiar face over the course of their stay, waiting patiently for them at every stop, and for his excellent service, Austin handed him an envelope Lily could only assume was padded with money. The five-hour train ride gave Lily time to take in the scenery, and it also gave her time to update her social media. She hadn't logged into her Facebook account in so long, it took her a few minutes to remember her password, and she couldn't stop smiling at the friend requests waiting for her from Austin's family. She eagerly accepted the requests from his mother, two brothers, and Holly, and messaged each of them to thank them for their hospitality, generosity, and kindness. Her life had become much more interesting with Austin in the picture, and she was excited to finally have pictures worth sharing. Browsing through the photos she'd taken along the trip, she updated her page with pictures from their time in Maine along with pictures of their adventures in Paris. She didn't have many Facebook friends, just a few old high school friends and a handful of relatives, and she was sure they'd do a double-take when they saw the photos.

Austin saw her scrolling through her pictures. "What's been your favorite place so far?"

"The lighthouse," she said, looking at the photo she'd snapped of their initials surrounded by a heart.

"Really? I was expecting the Louvre or the Eiffel Tower. The Ritz. Maybe even the opera. The lighthouse, huh?"

"Easily," Lily smiled. "Your parents' place is a close second."

Austin smiled, and she sensed her answer meant a lot to him.

"The lighthouse would have been my answer, too."

Crolles was a much smaller city than Paris, and she welcomed the break from the hustle and bustle. It was a quaint place nestled in southeast France with scenic mountain views, and Austin had booked them a room in a small hotel since luxury hotels weren't an option there. They had a cab service drive them to the hotel, and with the amount of luggage they had, it barely left room in the car for them. Austin sat in the front seat while Lily, being far smaller than him, squeezed into what little space was left in the backseat. Thankfully, the ride to the hotel was short, so she didn't have to stay there for long.

Their room paled in comparison to their suite at the Ritz but was still quite nice and more Lily's style. With a few hours to kill before their meeting with the CEO of *STMicroelectronics*, they passed the time exploring the charming little city, though finding a driver wasn't as easy as it had been in Paris. It took a few calls before Austin found Andre, a heavyset man with a thick beard who was willing to drive them around since there were no rental car agencies in such a small city. He spoke in broken English, but they managed to understand him as he guided them around the city, pointing out local hot spots along the way. Lily was sure to snap photos of the snow-capped mountains, the rolling hills, and unique architecture before returning to their hotel. They found Andre so pleasant, Austin offered him a job as their driver for the remainder of their stay, to which Andre happily accepted, agreeing to wait for them while they prepared for their big meeting with Jean-Marc Chery. Slipping on her dress, Lily noticed it fit a bit tighter around her breasts than it had the previous night. Their swelling had increased, and the dull, throbbing ache was still there, but it wasn't unmanageable. She did her hair and makeup the same as she had the night before, and since her nails were already painted, it was one less thing to worry about. Austin changed into his Zenga suit and expensive Italian loafers, and it occurred to Lily that between them, they were wearing ten thousand dollars' worth of clothing. With a final look in the mirror, they met Andre in his waiting car and made their way to *L'Envol des Saveurs* where they'd agreed to meet Jean-Marc. While not as fancy as some of the restaurants they had dined in, it was still quite lovely and offered more of a laid-back atmosphere. It wasn't very busy, which Lily liked, and they were able to spot Jean-Marc right away. They were relieved he was waiting for them inside so he didn't see them pull up in Andre's old car that had seen better days. Image was important, and stepping out of a car with heavy rust spots and a dented fender wouldn't have looked good.

"Well, if it isn't the great Austin Matson," Jean-Marc greeted, rising from the table he'd claimed.

"It's nice to finally meet you in person," Austin smiled, shaking his hand. "I'd like to introduce you to my girlfriend, Lilian Ward."

"It's a pleasure to meet you," Lily smiled.

Jean-Marc kissed the back of her hand and looked her over. "The pleasure is all mine. You look resplendent."

If Austin's plan really was to woo the competing CEO with her beauty, it seemed to be working. He couldn't take his eyes off of her as they took their seats, and as they browsed the menus they'd been handed, Lily caught Jean-Marc stealing glances at her. While they ate, Lily listened as the two men talked business. An older man in his late sixties, Jean-Marc told Austin that he was considering downsizing to reduce his workload and overall responsibilities. He wanted to enjoy life, he said, and spend more time with his loved ones. Austin understood and appreciated that, and with the negotiation underway, Austin squeezed Lily's leg under the table. On the ride over, they'd decided that would be the cue for her to turn on her charm, hopefully distracting Jean-Marc enough to weaken his negotiating skills. Looking at him suggestively, Lily bit her lower lip while tugging her dress down to offer a better view of her cleavage. Her breasts were already large, but with the swelling, they'd grown even larger, and Jean-Marc seemed to enjoy the view.

"That's… it's a bit lower than I was hoping for," Jean-Marc replied in response to the number Austin had spit out. His fumbling of words told them their plan was working.

"It's a fair number for just that one manufacturing plant," Austin insisted. "The transition alone is going to set me back quite a bit. A lot of changes will have to be made."

Lily knew that was a bluff. Austin had confided in wanting the plant for how smoothly it operated, and for what little work it would take to transition it into a Tomorrow Tech facility. He sold the bluff well, and she respected the negotiating tactic.

"Yes, but you'll recoup that money in no time," his business adversary countered. "Let's do a bit better on that number."

"I'll do one and a half, and that's the best I can offer," Austin replied firmly. Pretending to look for the salt, Lily rose from her seat just enough to lean over the table with her breasts on full display.

"I… that's… I think that could work, yes," Jean-Marc stammered.

Success, Lily thought with a smile.

"Okay, well, if I take a look around the place and like what I see, consider it a deal," Austin told him.

The two men shook hands and spent the rest of the dinner working out the transition. Austin insisted on paying and agreed to meet Jean-Marc the following day for a tour of the manufacturing plant, and with that, they parted ways. To avoid being seen stepping into Andre's car, Lily and Austin lingered for a moment as they waited for Jean-Marc to leave first. It seemed so shallow and silly, yet Lily understood the reasoning.

"That was the quickest negotiation I've ever had," Austin laughed, settling into the backseat of Andre's car.

"You did it!" Lily beamed proudly. "I'm so excited for you!"

"*We* did it," Austin amended. "I couldn't have done it without you. See? We do make a good team."

Seeing how easily Jean-Marc had been distracted, she was glad she hadn't told Austin about the pregnancy yet. She wasn't sure if the news would distract him enough to blow the negotiation, but she figured it was better safe than sorry. She resolved to tell him when they got back to the States and had recovered from their trip.

"The meeting went well?" Andre commented over his shoulder. "That is good. Congratulations."

He dropped them off at the small hotel, promising he'd be waiting for them the following day at 1:30 pm sharp, and with the tour scheduled for 2:00 pm, that gave them plenty of time to sleep in and enjoy a nice breakfast together. Crawling into bed, they celebrated their victory by making love and spent the rest of the night talking until they both drifted off to sleep.

The following day, Andre was waiting for them as promised and drove them to the *STMicroelectronics* manufacturing plant where Jean-Marc was waiting for them. The facility was so large that it took two hours for them to complete the tour, and Austin was so impressed with how flawlessly Jean-Marc's operation ran, he sealed the billion-dollar deal with another handshake. The investment was a huge move for Austin's Tomorrow Tech, and he knew it would be making business headlines worldwide. The momentous purchase wasn't as easy as signing a piece of paper, and Austin informed Lily that it would take weeks, if not months, for the acquisition to be finalized. Still, it was a done deal, and although Jean-Marc was hesitant to let it go—especially to his biggest competitor—he confessed that if it had to go to anybody, he was glad it was Austin. After meeting Austin, he continued with high praise, he knew the manufacturing plant would be in good hands, which came as a relief since the facility had become such a valuable part of Crolles' economy. With Austin at the helm, he knew the employees would be treated well, and their jobs would be secure. After a final handshake, Jean-Marc assured Austin that he would get the necessary contracts drawn up and would send them over once his legal team had reviewed them. They thanked Jean-Marc for his time and professionalism, and rejoining Andre in the car, invited him to lunch with them. Given how long the tour and subsequent dealings were, they'd all worked up an appetite, and they left it up to Andre to choose the restaurant. He introduced them to *Au Perchoir*, a wonderful little eatery with an impressive selection of dishes, and they sat and listened as he recounted his life in Crolles. He'd spent his entire life there, and he gave them a brief rundown of the city's history while they enjoyed their lunch.

Filled with surprisingly good food, Andre drove them back to the hotel where they said their goodbyes, and just as she knew he would, Austin tipped him well. Having accomplished what they'd come for, they spent the rest of the day at the hotel and had another overstuffed cab bring them to the train station the following day. On the train ride back to Paris where they'd be boarding another private jet bound for the States, Lily passed the time reading, updating her social media again with pictures of Crolles, and daringly going down on Austin. They'd been seated in the back, and with very few passengers on the train, she knew she could get away with it. She was surprised Austin let her since he was always so worried about scandal, but given how excited he was by the thrill of it, it didn't take him long to finish.

Back in Paris and having seen most of what there was to see there, they had another cab take them to the airport and, using money as incentive, recruited the driver's help with their luggage. The private jet Austin had chartered was similar to the last, and every bit as luxurious. With another thirty minutes to take-off, Austin asked Lily if she'd like to change their flight plan by adding a stop in Cleveland to visit her family. She considered it, and appreciated his offer, but decided they'd had enough excitement for one trip. Having promised his family a return visit in the summer, Lily suggested they visit her family then as well, flying into Cleveland to spend time with them before moving on to Maine. Austin liked that plan and admitted that he was itching to get home, too. He explained that a big reason he'd hired Winston and invited him into his home was to have somebody there to look after the estate in his absence. However, given Winson's age and declining health, he was growing less comfortable leaving him alone for extended periods of time. He'd been checking in on Winston every day of their trip, he told her, which Lily hadn't known and found remarkably sweet. He was selfless, he was kind, he was generous, and he was hers. Leaning in for a kiss, she professed her love for him and settled in for the long flight home.

Chapter Nine

They'd been gone less than two weeks, yet they'd experienced so much, it felt like longer. Winston greeted them with a warm embrace and a big smile, eager to hear about their journey, and Lily delighted in showing him the photos she'd taken. As much fun as they had, it felt good to be home, and Lily was ready to get back to work so she could recover the money she'd spent along their trip. Austin asked if she'd be willing to take on a larger role in his business, explaining that Tomorrow Tech's acquisition of the STMicroelectronics manufacturing plant in Crolles was going to be big news in the tech industry, and as such, he expected a flood of press inquiries once the word of the buyout broke. While still serving as his personal secretary, she'd also be in charge of his public relations, fielding messages from the press and arranging interviews, and she'd be listed as his public relations manager on Tomorrow Tech's corporate website. It was a promotion that came with more responsibility, more pay, her own business phone and office, and would also come with a two thousand dollar sign-on bonus. Austin likely knew she had overspent on the trip, and the bonus was his way of padding her bank account. She refused it but he insisted, claiming the bonus would have gone to whoever else took the job had she not accepted the position. Dubious but desperately needing the money, she agreed to take it knowing it would take a dent out of her tuition. Pregnant or not, she still had every intention of attending the university and would be applying that May. Austin had offered to use his connections to get her in without an application, but this was something she wanted to do on her own.

Working as his secretary, she could still tidy up the estate, but working double-duty as his secretary and public relations person, there was simply no way she'd have time to continue cleaning the estate as well. They'd find a new cleaner soon, they agreed, once Lily had settled into her role as his public relations manager. Within hours of updating the corporate website with Lily's new title and contact information, she began receiving phone calls and emails regarding Austin's purchase of the Crolles STMicroelectronics facility. Word had spread much faster than they thought it would, and the industry was swirling with questions. Was Austin buying just the one manufacturing plant, or was he buying STMicroelectronics entirely? Was Tomorrow Tech merging with STMicroelectronics, or was it absorbing them completely? Rather than answer each individual inquiry, Lily thought issuing a statement on Tomorrow Tech's corporate website would be the better way to go. Austin agreed, and left her in charge of writing it. It was a lot of pressure, but Austin loved what she came up with, and after a few minor changes, he put the statement online, officially announcing the acquisition of the manufacturing plant in Crolles.

Austin told her to pick whatever bedroom she'd like to use for an office, and, of course, she chose the bedroom nearest the library. Together, they replaced the bedroom furniture with office furniture of her choosing, and over the next several days, Lily handled a barrage of interview requests that she vetted per Austin's instructions. Requests from small media outlets, online shows, or print publications were to be politely declined so they could focus on the larger ones that would reach a broader audience. Austin's time was valuable, and he didn't want to waste it doing interviews that nobody would even see. Major nationwide news outlets got an automatic approval, along with the top tech magazines, and online shows were only approved if they had a big enough audience.

Austin hadn't exaggerated when he told her the new position would keep her busy. They agreed on a 9:00 am to 5:00 pm schedule

Monday through Friday, and for two weeks after their return, the phone calls and emails were relentless. Her pregnancy weighed heavily on her mind, but given how busy they both were in the wake of the acquisition, she knew she'd have to worry about it when things died down a bit. By the time her work day was through, she was completely exhausted and often needed to lie down for an hour or two to recharge. Every day, she would tell herself to run out and buy a pregnancy test when her shift ended, but by the time her work was through, she was too drained to make the drive into the city. Troubled by this and worried he was working her too hard, Austin offered to reduce her hours but not her pay. Lily insisted she could handle it and was just suffering from a severe case of jet lag, reminding him that some people can recover in one or two days, while others need one or two weeks. It didn't seem like he bought that excuse, but he left it alone after she assured him she was fine and would bounce back soon. Meanwhile, the aching in her breasts had grown worse, and they'd continued to swell to the point where Austin had finally noticed.

"Babe? Is it just my imagination, or did these get bigger?" he'd chuckled, pointing at her breasts. They'd just finished making love and were lying naked together when he'd made the comment.

"A little," she'd lied, knowing that they'd grown almost one full cup size. "They tend to swell when it's getting close to my time of the month."

"Hmm. I never noticed that," Austin had replied, shrugging it off. With a joke, he'd added, "Does that mean next week is blowjob week?"

"Very funny," she replied.

With this exchange, Lily knew that she'd put it off long enough. Between her aching, swollen breasts, the nausea, bouts of exhaustion, and another missed period, she no longer thought she was pregnant, she *knew* she was, and she also knew she would have to tell him soon.

If she waited much longer, she was going to start showing, and it wouldn't take long for him to piece it together. She decided the best way to tell him would be to surprise him with a positive pregnancy test that she'd gift wrap and present to him in some romantic fashion. She envisioned preparing a lovely candlelit dinner for them, with soft music playing in the background, after which she'd slide the box across the table to him, nervously awaiting his reaction. With the negotiation of the Crolles facility complete and the purchase in motion, the pregnancy shouldn't interfere with his business going forward. He'd still have six or seven months to oversee the transition anyhow, which seemed like enough time to rebrand the plant. Jean-Marc had the facility running so efficiently, there really wasn't much more that needed to be done. Even with that, she wasn't entirely sure how he'd respond to the news. Because of the strong connection they'd forged so quickly, it felt like they'd known each other far longer than they really had. He might think it was too soon to bring a child into the equation, and he wouldn't be wrong, yet, somehow, it still felt right. If she knew him as well as she thought she did, and if their love was as genuine as she believed, she could see him being elated by the news. After all, he had mentioned wanting children on more than one occasion, and it's not like the child would be a financial burden. Having the weekends off and the following day being a Saturday, Lily resolved to drive into the city to pick up a long overdue pregnancy test.

She slept in yet still woke up exhausted, feeling as though she could have slept another eight hours. Her breasts were so sensitive and sore, she winced as she squeezed them into her bra and added larger ones to her shopping list. She'd have to drive further into the city for them, but she couldn't keep forcing her painfully swollen breasts into bras she'd clearly outgrown. In jeans and a loose t-shirt, she told Austin she was running to the store to grab some feminine hygiene products, which she knew was enough to silence any man. He didn't question it, and after a quick kiss, she climbed into the 1952 Chevy pickup to find the nearest pharmacy. She didn't need fancy, expensive bras since her breasts would likely return to their normal size after the pregnancy, so she settled for a Walmart knowing she could get everything she needed there for cheap. Along with a few new bras and an at-home pregnancy kit containing two tests, she found a small gift box, wrapping paper, and a white bow she felt would make for a nice presentation. She used a self-checkout lane to spare any awkward small talk with a cashier, and triple-bagged her items so Austin wouldn't see her purchases when she returned home. With her mission complete, she hurried back to the estate and breathed a sigh of relief when Austin wasn't there to greet her. He was in the gym, Winston informed her, and after brushing by him with a polite smile, she rushed upstairs to take the test.

Locked in the bathroom, she laid the test out on the counter and read the instructions, which seemed simple enough. Peeing wouldn't be a problem since she'd had to go since leaving Walmart and had held it the entire ride home. Dropping her pants, she took a seat on the toilet to relieve herself and made sure the test strip got its fair share before placing the test on the counter to work its magic. Even though she knew what the results would be, she still couldn't shake her nerves and paced the bedroom as she waited for the two pink lines to appear, confirming the pregnancy. Worried she might look too soon out of impatience, she glanced at the time and decided to give it five minutes before checking. She spent those five minutes walking back and forth across the bedroom while playing out Austin's possible reactions in her mind. Would he recoil in horror, insisting they weren't ready for a child? Maybe. Perhaps he'd spring from the table in excitement and whisk her into his arms, covering her with kisses while expressing his joy. Five minutes felt like an hour as she watched the minutes slowly pass by, and when they had finally passed, she bolted into the bathroom for the positive reading she knew she'd find.

Only, it wasn't positive.

She groaned in frustration, knowing she'd somehow taken the test incorrectly or it had been defective.

I guess that's why they give you two, she thought as she tore open the second test. Returning to the toilet, she managed to squeeze out the few drops needed and set it beside the first test to await the results. Rather than pacing the bedroom again for another five minutes, she sat on the bed and passed the time by checking her social media, which she'd been using to keep in touch with Austin's family. Seeing that his mother had responded to her previous message, she replied back with an update on life in Tucson, and by the time she sent it, ten minutes had gone by. Hurrying back to the bathroom, she was sure she'd find the two pink lines confirming her pregnancy, yet the second test was negative as well. Confused and upset, she decided the entire kit must have been defective and buried the tests as far as the bathroom's small wastebasket would allow, along with its packaging.

Friggin' Walmart and their cheap, generic tests, she grumbled to herself, grabbing her purse. Downstairs, she peeked into the gym to find Austin still at work, which gave her a chance to run out again with no questions asked. Since another test was all she needed, she drove to a CVS this time knowing there was one much closer than Walmart, which might land her back at the estate before Austin had finished with his workout. She decided to play it safe by grabbing two name brand kits, each kit containing two tests with digital readouts this time, and she also bought a large bottle of Gatorade she planned to chug along the drive home. With no self-checkout, she was forced to face a cashier who was a younger woman with enough courtesy to comment on the weather instead of the pregnancy tests.

"Thank you for not making it awkward," Lily chuckled, breaking any tension between them.

"I got you," the young woman smiled.

Back in the Chevy, Lily cracked open the bottle of Gatorade and tucked the tests into her handbag since they were small enough to fit discreetly. If she did run into Austin when she arrived back at the estate, she would tell him she'd left her phone at the pharmacy and had run back to get it. Fortunately, she was able to avoid that lie since he was still in the gym when she returned home. That didn't surprise her since his workouts often took two hours and were always followed by a protein shake in the kitchen, which took another few minutes to prepare and drink. She had his routine down well enough to know she still had time to take at least one more test, and with the Gatorade already making its way through her system, peeing wouldn't be a problem.

Ripping open the first kit, she read the instructions twice as she sat on the toilet with her pants down, ready to go. They were the same as the first kit, requiring her to pee on the exposed test strip, which seemed basic enough. With a frustrated exhale, she relieved herself while holding the strip in the stream long enough to soak it thoroughly, but didn't empty her bladder completely in case she had to take one more test. Satisfied that she'd wet the strip as instructed, she set the test on the counter to do its thing like she'd done twice already. She took a seat on the bed again, mindlessly browsing the internet until five minutes had passed, and returning to the test, she was shocked to find another negative reading. "Not pregnant" was displayed on the readout, which was just as confusing as it was frustrating. She knew she was pregnant, yet for some reason, the tests were all coming back negative. Lily could only assume it was due to some hormonal issue, and she decided to give it one more go, emptying her bladder with yet another test strip held in the stream.

When this one came back negative as well, she stood looking at the results for a moment in disbelief. Four tests had all come back negative, and struggling to understand why, she used her phone to call up Google. She typed in "why would a pregnancy test" when the search engine completed her question for her before she'd even finished typing it.

"Why would a pregnancy test give a false negative?"

Google placing this inquiry at the top of their search suggestions told her countless others had made the same search, and that somehow made her feel a bit better. It meant it was a common problem, and according to the search results, it was likely the result of low hCG, which was a hormone produced during pregnancy. This could be caused by a number of reasons, a list of websites told her, and a visit to a doctor for a blood test was recommended since they were far more accurate than a urine test. Lily groaned, knowing a gift-wrapped box with papers containing her blood work results would be far less romantic than a simple over-the-counter pregnancy test. Austin would open the box and she'd have to explain what he was looking at, which wasn't exactly what she'd had in mind.

Knowing she couldn't stuff more negative pregnancy tests into the bathroom's small wastebasket without Austin seeing, she shoved them into her handbag to bury in the kitchen's larger wastebasket when he wasn't around. She still had the other kit containing two more tests in her handbag as well and decided to take another one the following morning. If she took one the moment she woke, she hoped her hCG levels might be high enough for a positive readout. Of course, she had no idea if there was any science to that, but the logic seemed sound enough.

She'd just set her handbag by the foot of the bed when a sweaty Austin appeared, stopping to give her a quick kiss on his way into the bathroom to shower up. They'd made plans to spend the rest of the day together, and while she always loved spending time with him, she knew it would take the best of her acting ability to feign enjoyment. She was sure the negative results were caused by her low hCG levels, yet she couldn't take her mind off of the four tests that hadn't gone as planned. While Austin was rooting through the bedroom's enormous walk-in closet for an outfit, she ducked into the bathroom and quickly rummaged through the small wastebasket for the first two tests she'd buried. Pulling them out, she looked for even a faint sign of a second pink line, yet both tests still showed only the one. With a frustrated sigh, she buried them again and spent the remainder of the day with Austin, trying hard to push the tests from her mind with little success. At one point Austin—who was remarkably perceptive and could always seem to feel her energy—asked if she was okay, to which she replied she was just experiencing cramps courtesy of her monthly visitor, and that it was nothing to worry about.

She took a fifth test the following morning while Austin was still asleep, heading straight to the bathroom the moment she woke, thinking her hCG concentration would be high enough for a positive reading. When that test came back negative as well, she threw it against the wall in frustration and gripped the counter with white knuckles, her chest heaving in anger and her mind racing. She was supposed to take one test, wrap the positive reading in a box, and surprise Austin with it. It should have been that simple, but the universe had a way of throwing unexpected monkey wrenches into her plans. Now, she was going to have to find a doctor and take a blood test, which presented a whole new challenge. With her work schedule, there was no way she could squeeze in an appointment without requesting time off. She knew Austin would grant it, but he'd surely want to know why she needed it, and she hated the thought of lying to him. She considered coming clean by telling him what was going on, but held onto the idea of surprising him over a romantic dinner. Blood work results wouldn't garner the same reaction as a positive pregnancy test would, but it suddenly hit her that an ultrasound would work just as well. Realizing she'd just found the perfect alternative to a positive pregnancy test, a wave of relief washed over her. She'd skip the blood work entirely and surprise Austin with an ultrasound of the life they'd created. Smiling, she climbed back into bed, and cuddling up next to him, she fell back to sleep thinking of possible baby names.

It was back to work the next day, and after failing the sixth at-home test, she used her lunch break to find an obstetrician. The first two she called weren't accepting new patients, and the third couldn't fit her in for another three weeks. Not wanting to wait that long, she finally found an office that could squeeze her in that Friday afternoon, which created a new problem. Austin had an interview scheduled with CNN that day, and he'd be conducting it via satellite from a local TV station. As his head of public relations, Lily was expected to be there, and she knew Austin would be disappointed if she wasn't. With a groan, she scheduled the appointment anyhow, knowing it was the only chance she had of getting the ultrasound without having to wait three weeks. If the appointment was quick, and she hurried to the studio the moment she had the ultrasound results, she might be able to make it for the second half.

When their work day was through and they were able to spend time together, Lily requested that Friday afternoon off, claiming she had an appointment with her gynecologist. It was just a simple check-up, she told him, and nothing to be worried about, but there was a slight overlap with his interview. It was the only time her gynecologist had, she explained, and if she had to reschedule, she might not get in for weeks. She told herself that replacing the word "obstetrician" with "gynecologist" wasn't too big of a stretch, but she still hated lying to him and hoped he would understand when the big reveal came. Austin granted her the afternoon off like she knew he would, and although she could tell he was a bit bummed about her missing the preparation and the subsequent interview, he assured her that her health always came first.

The work week dragged. The six failed pregnancy tests weighed heavily on her mind, and by the time Friday rolled around, she was so eager to see the obstetrician that she showed up to her appointment an hour early. Right away, she understood why Doctor Reinhart had earned so many five-star reviews online. She was a remarkably pleasant woman with kind eyes and a warm smile, and Lily felt completely at ease with her right away.

"So, I hear you want to skip a blood test and go with an ultrasound," the doctor said, looking over Lily's paperwork.

"That's right," Lily replied from her seat on the examination table.

"And what makes you think you're pregnant?" Doctor Reinhart asked.

"Well, last month, I noticed an aching in my breasts. It wasn't too bad—a dull throbbing, really," Lily explained. "It's gradually grown worse. They're so sore now, it hurts just to touch them. I've also been getting nauseous throughout the day and have been experiencing these horrible bouts of fatigue. One minute, I'm fine, the next, I can barely keep my eyes open and have to lie down. I've also missed two periods now. There have been a few drops of blood, but that's about it."

"I see," the doctor nodded. "Yeah, that sounds about right. Mostly."

"Mostly?" Lily asked.

Doctor Reinhart left that question alone as she began to prepare Lily for the ultrasound, instructing her to lie down, slide her pants down a bit, and lift her shirt. They made small talk as the doctor applied the cold ultrasound gel before wheeling the machine closer to Lily.

"And about how far along do you think you are?" the doctor questioned.

"I'd say… Two months?" Lily guessed. "Maybe closer to three now."

"Okay," Doctor Reinhart smiled. "Let's take a look, shall we?"

The doctor slowly moved the transducer across Lily's belly and lower abdomen, her eyes fixed on the display monitor. Lily's eyes were glued to the monitor as well, excited to see the developing fetus, but she couldn't quite make out what she was looking at. Doctor Reinhart made several passes with the transducer, and Lily began to grow impatient when a few minutes had passed without a word from her.

"Well?" Lily prodded. "How's it look? Is it healthy?"

"Miss Ward, I'm sorry, but I'm just not seeing anything," the doctor replied.

"What do you mean?" Lily asked nervously.

"Let me give it another pass," Doctor Reinhart told her. "Bear with me here."

She repeated the process of running the transducer across Lily's belly and lower abdomen, moving it a bit slower this time and making several more passes rather than one. When Lily noticed a concerned look on the doctor's face, her heart began to pound.

"What's the matter?" Lily asked, swallowing hard. "Is there something wrong with it?"

The doctor set the transducer back in its cradle on the machine and pushed the entire unit against the wall where it had initially been stationed.

"Can you do me a favor and sit up, please?"

"Okay…" Lily replied, moving to a seated position on the edge of the examination table. "What's going on?"

"I need you to take your shirt off, please," the doctor replied. "Your bra, too. I need to examine your breasts."

"What? Why?" Lily asked, taken aback by the unexpected request.

"It's standard procedure and will only take a moment. Please," the doctor urged. "I'll make it quick, I promise."

With a sigh, Lily peeled her shirt off and set it aside. With shaking hands, she unclasped her bra, freeing her swollen breasts, and set it on top of her shirt.

"I see you have a small scar here," the doctor said, pointing out the faint scar on Lily's right breast. "Can you tell me about that?"

"I had a tumor removed a few years ago."

"Was it cancerous?"

"No, thankfully."

"Does this hurt?" the doctor asked, gently pressing Lily's bare chest.

"A little, yes," Lily nodded.

The doctor applied a bit more pressure. "And this?"

"Ow, yeah, okay, that hurts."

"I'm going to press them just a bit harder. Is that okay?"

"Okay, just… okay." Lily wasn't looking forward to it and steeled herself with a deep breath.

"On a scale of one to ten, how would you rate—"

"*Jesus!*" Lily yelped, recoiling in agony as the doctor pressed her fingers deeper into her breasts. Lily's pain seemed to tell the doctor all she needed to know, and she quickly removed her fingers from Lily's breasts.

"I apologize for the discomfort," Doctor Reinhart said. "I'm done, I promise."

"Oh, thank God," Lily muttered, still reeling from the pain.

"Miss Ward, I'm sure you're aware of how swollen your breasts are. It's hard to tell with your complexion, but they look a bit red as well."

"I noticed that," Lily said, unsure of where this was going.

"Even if you were pregnant, your breasts wouldn't be this sore," the doctor explained.

"Even if?" Lily shook her head in confusion. "What are you saying?"

"I'm sorry, Miss Ward, but I didn't see anything in there. We can still do a blood test if you'd like, but I can tell you right now that it would be a waste of time. You're simply not pregnant."

"That's not possible," Lily countered. "I know I'm pregnant."

"I'm sorry, I really am," Doctor Reinhart replied with genuine compassion. "I can tell you really wanted to be. Oftentimes, people want it so much that they convince themselves they are. I've seen it dozens of times over the years."

"This just doesn't make any sense," Lily said, desperately trying to wrap her mind around the doctor's words.

The doctor pulled a referral slip out of a drawer and jotted down a name along with a number.

"I need you to give Arizona Oncology a call right away," the doctor said, handing her the referral slip. "This is urgent, Miss Ward. Do not put this off. I want you to call them today."

"Why are you referring me to an oncologist?" Lily asked.

"Miss Ward…"

"Why are you referring me to an oncologist?" Lily repeated, her voice trembling and tears beginning to form. She knew the answer, but she sat in stunned disbelief.

Doctor Reinhart sighed and shook her head. "I'm so sorry, Miss Ward. This is the hardest part of my job. Please, call them right away."

"I... I... Okay," Lily stammered, looking at the slip of paper she'd been handed. She tried to hold herself together, but it was a lost cause. She fell to pieces, her chest heaving as she sobbed. "This is bad, isn't it? Like, really bad."

"It's certainly not good," Doctor Reinhart said, handing Lily a tissue and rubbing her back gently in consolation. In a soft, caring tone, she spoke to Lily like she was an old friend rather than a patient. "But there are a lot of treatments available, Lilian. We've made tremendous progress in dealing with this. Call Arizona Oncology and set up an appointment right away. They're usually pretty good about getting people in quickly."

Lily wailed. The doctor made no attempt at silencing her, wrapping her arm around Lily's shoulder instead and holding her while she wept. It took almost ten minutes for Lily to regain enough composure to put her bra and shirt back on, with Doctor Reinhart by her side the entire time. She appreciated how compassionate and understanding the doctor was in her time of need, and was sure to thank her before making her way back to the same receptionist who had greeted her on her way into the office. She wore sunglasses to hide her red, puffy eyes, and with no health insurance, she used her bank card to pay her bill in full. With the money Austin had been paying her, she was finally in a good spot financially and had been chipping away at the credit card debt Ryan had racked up while still managing to save for her schooling. She could manage this bill just fine, but she knew her future medical bills would be much steeper. She'd cross that bridge when the time came. For now, she needed to schedule an appointment with Arizona Oncology to find out how much trouble she was really in.

She broke down again in the truck, crying as she struggled to come to terms with what had just happened. She woke that day believing she was pregnant and excited to return home with an ultrasound to surprise her boyfriend with. Instead, she was tacitly given a cancer diagnosis with ramifications she was just beginning to process. She stared blankly at nothing in particular for a long while, realizing just how difficult this was going to be; not just for her, but for Austin as well. He certainly hadn't signed on for this, and it was going to be a lot for him to deal with as well. Remembering the referral slip she'd been tightly holding onto, she called Arizona Oncology and was relieved when they were able to see her so quickly, scheduling an appointment for that following Monday at 10:00 am. It would require more time off and telling Austin another lie, which she wasn't looking forward to.

Glancing at the clock and realizing she could still make it in time to catch the end of his interview, she hurried across town to the TV station broadcasting his appearance to millions of viewers around the globe. Identifying herself as his public relations manager and flashing the badge he'd made her, she crept into the studio as quietly as possible and watched as he finished discussing his purchase of the STMicroelectronics plant in Crolles, detailing what it meant for the future of Tomorrow Tech.

"Hey, baby," he greeted her with a smile once the cameras had stopped rolling. "How much of that did you happen to catch?"

"Enough to know that you nailed it," she smiled, burying her diagnosis as far down as she could.

"Yeah?" he asked, loosening his tie.

"Seriously, you did great. I'm sorry I missed some of it, but I'll be there for your next one, I promise."

"Oh, it's okay," he said, and leaned in for a kiss. "How did your appointment go?"

Knowing he would ask, she used it to set herself up for more time off. "Not good. I got there and was told the doctor was running late. I waited a half an hour just to have the entire appointment canceled on me. Apparently, there was some sort of family emergency and the doctor couldn't make it. They rescheduled me for Monday at 10:00 am. Is that okay?"

"Yeah, that's fine. Are you hungry? There's a new Italian restaurant that just opened downtown. I was thinking we could try it since we're already so close."

"I'd love that," Lily replied, doing a better job of masking her troubles than she'd expected.

CNN had provided a chauffeured town car for Austin's interview, and he dismissed the driver knowing he could ride back to the estate with Lily in the classic pickup truck he'd been gracious enough to lend her. He insisted on driving, however, which Lily was fine with, and they made their way downtown to check out the restaurant Austin had mentioned. Lily didn't have much of an appetite but still enjoyed the food, and gave no sign of the worry she was concealing. The whole ordeal was beginning to feel surreal to her, as if it was just some bad dream and wasn't a reality. Surely, she couldn't be sick, and if she was, it couldn't be that bad. She'd get it sorted out on Monday when they'd likely clear it up with a few simple treatments. Austin devoured his meal, and after he handed a generous tip to their waiter, they headed home with Lily sliding across the bench seat to sit by his side, resting her head on his shoulder as he drove.

They'd just stepped inside the estate when Lily's business phone rang. Austin listened as she handled a call from a company named "Atari," who she'd never heard of but had called hoping to speak with Austin directly. Austin nodded that, yes, he would take the call, and Lily passed him the phone. It was her turn to listen now, and seeing her curiosity, Austin put the call on speaker so she could hear the conversation.

"Austin Matson speaking," he announced.

"Austin Matson, it's a pleasure speaking with you. Wade Rosen here, CEO of Atari."

"Atari?" Austin chuckled. "There's a name I haven't heard in a while. To be honest, I didn't think you were still in business."

"We had a few rough years, but we managed to hang on and are rebuilding our brand," Wade replied.

"I remember tearing apart one of your Jaguar systems when I was a kid," Austin replied. "I wanted to see exactly what you were using for processors. The internet wasn't really a thing back then and there were lots of rumors circulating, so I found a used one for cheap and dug into it."

"Ah, yes, the gaming system that almost put Atari out of business entirely," Wade laughed. "Don't remind me. Let's just say that if I was around back then, that whole fiasco would have never happened."

As Lily listened in, she was able to piece together that Atari was a video game company from before her time that had a long, rocky history. They started off strong and paved the way for Nintendo, who usurped them to become the biggest name in the gaming industry, and teetering on bankruptcy, they had attempted a comeback with the release of the Atari Jaguar, a video game console that was supposed to catapult them back to the top of the gaming world. Only, the system was a complete dud, largely due to the misrepresentation of its computational power. Marketed as a 64-bit system, the console really housed two 32-bit coprocessors that, working in tandem, still didn't quite function as 64-bits like the company touted. Lily didn't really understand any of that, but she did understand the rest of the conversation. Atari had secured enough investors to attempt another comeback, and was in the nascent stages of designing a new home video game console. To make this happen, they'd need a supply of powerful yet affordable microprocessors, and with Austin's acquisition of STMicroelectronics, they were hoping he could help them out. Austin's initial response was a resounding "no," since he had no interest in the gaming industry and knew little about it. He did know there was fierce competition, and the chances of Atari's new system finding success were slim to none.

"I'm just not a video game guy, I'm sorry," Austin said, shaking his head.

"And we don't need you to be," Wade countered. "We just need you to supply us with the processors we need to make this dream a reality. We'd like to work out some sort of a deal with you. I was hoping we could buy the processors upfront at a bulk discount, while also making you a partner, giving you a small percentage of each console sold."

"I don't know," Austin sighed. "The Crolles plant we just acquired is already operating at max capacity. Your processors would have to come from one of our plants here in America. I don't know if we'd be able to produce the processors you'd need at a viable price. I'm sure the goal is to make this system as affordable as possible."

"Yes, exactly. We're hoping to keep it in the three hundred dollar range. If we can produce a system with more processing power than the competition, yet offer it at a fraction of the price, I think we'd have a good chance of breaking through and stealing the thunder from the industry's top names."

"I assume you're talking about Sony, Microsoft, and Nintendo," Austin said.

"Yes, exactly. Hell, Sony's new system is five hundred bucks. Microsoft's isn't much better. People don't want to spend that much on a gaming system. It's just too much."

"Look, there's a reason I haven't touched the gaming industry," Austin replied. "It's a cutthroat business. I might be able to supply the processors, but as far as a partnership goes, I think I'm going to have to pass. I mean, come on. No disrespect here, but Atari? You really think there's a chance Atari could become a household name again?"

"I do. One hundred percent. The nostalgia thing is huge right now. There are people buying retro video games and consoles at insane prices just to relive their childhood. Just the name 'Atari' alone will catch their eye. I'm telling you, we can do this thing."

"I don't know…" Austin groaned.

"We're willing to do this," Wade began. "We'll host a small retro gaming convention right there in Tucson, so you don't have to travel anywhere. That way, you can see firsthand how much weight the Atari name still carries."

"I guess what it comes down to is the processing power you'll need. I'm going to shoot you over my personal e-mail address so you can send me the technical specs. I'll look them over to see if what you're asking for is even feasible."

"I'll get them over to you right now," Wade assured him. "I know how busy you are, but if you could get back to me within a week, I'd really appreciate it."

"Will do," Austin replied.

When the call ended, Austin handed Lily back her business phone, and the two made their way upstairs for entirely different reasons. Exhausted and nauseous, Lily needed to lie down for a bit and told Austin she'd just been hit hard by her time of the month. He was eager to check his email anyway to see what Atari had in mind and told her he'd join her for a nap when he was through. With so much on her mind, she didn't think she'd be able to fall asleep but was out within minutes, waking some time later to Austin crawling in bed and wrapping her in his arms.

"How are you feeling, baby?" he asked softly.

"Mmm… better now that you're here," she purred, trying to return to life as usual. She'd convinced herself that she wasn't that sick, and that they'd caught the problem early enough for her to make a full recovery after just a few treatments.

"Good."

"Did you review the Atari specs?" Lily asked, turning to face him.

"I did. What they're looking for just isn't possible. The chips would be too expensive to produce. They want to keep the system around three hundred bucks, and that's probably not feasible with the price of the processors. If I sold them at a bulk discount like Wade asked, I'd be taking a huge loss and would have to partner with them to make any sort of profit, which isn't guaranteed. It's a risk I'm not sure I'm willing to take, given their track record. Their last video game console was a complete disaster."

"There's no way to cut costs somewhere?"

"I don't know… I mean… I just don't see how."

"What about that PlastiCPU thing?" Lily asked, recalling the drama with Jose.

"Oh my God!" Austin bellowed, excitedly jumping out of bed. "That could actually work! Lily… you're brilliant! I can't believe I didn't think of that. It would be much cheaper than silicon, reducing the price of the processors, and since the PlastiCPU processors don't produce as much heat as traditional processors, Atari wouldn't need to worry about a cooling system. That would make production even cheaper and could make this whole deal possible."

"Aren't you glad you keep me around?" Lily joked.

"I mean, I'd have to invest in some new equipment to manufacture the processors, but I was going to do that anyway," Austin said as he paced the room. He was thinking out loud more than he was addressing Lily directly at this point. "And if I partnered with Atari for a percentage of every unit sold, I could end up making a hefty profit. Hell, even if the system is a total failure, I'd still make a profit."

"Make it happen, baby," Lily smiled.

"I've never loved you more," Austin quipped, leaning in for a kiss. "Is it okay if I get started on this? It's going to take a lot of work."

"Go do your thing, handsome. I'm going to rest a bit more. This period is kicking my ass."

"Okay, baby. I'll be in my study and will leave my door cracked. Just holler if you need anything," Austin said, leaving her to sleep.

Lily slept straight through the night with no recollection of Austin crawling into bed with her, and she woke to find daylight peeking through the bedroom's curtains. Glancing at the clock on her nightstand, she was shocked by how long she'd been out. It was 7:00 am, and rolling over, she found Austin sound asleep next to her looking just as handsome as ever. Her entire body aching, she made her way to the bathroom to pee and rejoined Austin in bed where she quickly fell back to sleep. When she woke again, she saw a single pink rose had been placed on her nightstand in a beautiful glass vase along with a card reading "get well" and a small box of chocolates. Her breasts felt like they were on fire, but she still managed a smile and climbed out of bed to find Austin, pausing to smell the rose. She slipped on the silk robe he'd given her and made her way to his office where he was hard at work on his laptop, presumably hashing out the details of the Atari deal. He usually took Sundays off, but since Lily hadn't been feeling well, it looked like he was using the day to work on the logistics of what they were still referring to as "PlastiCPU" until they found a better name.

"Hey, you're awake!" he smiled, and she could sense relief in his tone. He stood to give her a kiss and brushed her cheek gently. "I've been so worried about you."

"I'm just a little under the weather, that's all. It's nothing to worry about. Thank you for the rose and the card, and those chocolates aren't going to last long," she said with a smile.

"You've seemed to be under the weather a lot lately," he pointed out. "I can't help but worry. I love you. It comes with the territory."

"You're sweet. I don't know what's gotten into me lately. I think I might have caught whatever bug is going around. I'll be okay."

Austin eyed her skeptically, and it looked like he was holding something back. After a long moment, he couldn't contain it and asked bluntly, "Lilian… are you pregnant?"

"What?" Lily laughed nervously. "Where did that come from?"

"You've been tired, nauseous, fatigued, and your breasts look even bigger than they did last week. I just want you to know that if you are pregnant, I won't be mad. Just the opposite, actually."

Lily fought back tears. Now more than ever, she desperately wished she was pregnant. Two days earlier, she was convinced she was, and her biggest concern was how Austin would take the news. Here he was, telling her how happy he'd be if she was carrying his baby, yet she was carrying cancer instead, the severity of which still remained unknown. It didn't seem fair.

"I didn't even think of that," Lily lied, and immediately hated herself for it. Their open communication was one of the things she cherished, and by lying to him, she was destroying that. However, she knew that a possible pregnancy could explain away her illness for the time being and buy her the time she needed to get well. Between Austin's acquisition of the Crolles plant and his blossoming relationship with Atari, the last thing he needed was a sick girlfriend. It could jeopardize his business plans, possibly leading to resentment, and she couldn't have that. She would tell him eventually, but now certainly wasn't the time. "I'll have to take a test soon."

"Is it weird that I'm hoping it's positive?" Austin smiled.

His words felt like a dagger stabbing into her heart and she could feel her breakdown coming.

"It's not weird at all," she replied, returning his smile with a forced one. "I'm heading to the kitchen for a bite to eat. You want anything?"

"No, I'm good, babe. I'm going to work on this Atari thing for a bit, if you don't mind. Maybe we can spend some time together this evening?"

"I'd love that," she said, turning to leave so he couldn't see the look of pain on her face. She was on the verge of bursting into tears and couldn't allow it in front of him. Hurrying to the privacy of the library, she curled up in what had become her favorite of the shearling armchairs and wept. She'd always found comfort in books, but it was hard to find any comfort in them now. She cried until she had no more tears left in her and sat for a long while, staring at nothing in particular while she regained control of herself.

You're going to be okay. They'll give you some medication and you'll be fine. Once you're better, you can have Austin's baby.

The library had also become where she would practice her knitting, which she'd still been keeping up with when time and energy allowed. She'd been sending pictures of her progress to Austin's mother, who always responded with praise and encouragement, along with pictures of whatever pattern she was working on. Lily had positioned a small knitting basket by the chair, and as a way of distracting herself from her troubles, she reached for the blanket she'd been attempting to knit. Knitting had a calming effect on her, and as the minutes passed, she became so engrossed in her work that she was able to forget about the exchange with Austin that had left her so crushed. She'd been so convinced that she was pregnant that discovering she wasn't had cut her deeply. Learning that Austin would have welcomed the pregnancy only added salt to the wound.

That evening, Austin challenged her to a game of Scrabble, which was something they'd both come to enjoy. Not only was it a way for them to engage in friendly intellectual competition, but it also gave them a chance to talk. Austin had decided to work with Atari, he told her, and he would be negotiating the deal the following day. Lily agreed it was a good business move since he had nothing to lose and everything to gain, and she shared pictures of the progress she'd made on the blanket she'd been knitting. She left out the blanket being for the baby she thought she'd be having, which is why she'd chosen gender-neutral white yarn. Austin took a genuine interest and seemed impressed by how far her skills had come. Before their game wrapped up, he mentioned he'd scheduled an interview with a potential cleaner the following day at noon, and would like Lily's help vetting the woman. Lily loved that he wanted to include her in the process but reminded him of her appointment at 10:00 am that might not land her back at the estate in time.

They called it an early night, knowing the following day would be a busy one for the both of them. Austin was hoping to finalize the Atari deal and secure a new cleaner for the four-story mansion, all while handling a heap of other work. Lily planned on squeezing in a couple hours of phone calls and emails before her appointment with Arizona Oncology, and returning to them when it was through. Austin was out quickly, but Lily wasn't so lucky and spent half the night tossing and turning, too worried about her appointment to sleep. She finally drifted off after convincing herself that Doctor Reinhart had likely misdiagnosed her. She was an obstetrician, after all, not an oncologist, and hadn't performed any real tests. There were a number of reasons her breasts could be sore and swollen, she told herself, and with that in mind, she was able to get a few hours of sleep before their alarm sounded, waking them both at 7:00 am.

"It's too early for this shit," Austin jokingly groaned, half-asleep. Rolling over, he gave Lily a quick peck on the lips.

"I second that," Lily grumbled.

The two started their day with a shower, though Lily chose to take hers alone. As much as she loved showering with Austin, he had a hard time keeping his hands to himself, and with how sore her breasts were, she didn't want to risk him touching them. She always loved when he washed her and looked forward to experiencing it again when the doctors cured whatever was ailing her.

By the time she was out of the shower, Austin had prepared a wonderful breakfast for them. With the estate being so large, he called her phone to invite her to the kitchen, and they enjoyed their breakfast together before parting ways to do their own thing. Austin wanted to get a workout in before his negotiation with Atari, and Lily already had phone calls and messages waiting to be returned. She was only able to work for a little over an hour before heading to her appointment, wanting to get there early like she had her appointment with Doctor Reinhart. She was eager to finally have answers and held out hope that the obstetrician had been wrong, and that she'd simply been fighting some sort of infection. Perhaps she'd caught something on their trip and it had been causing the symptoms she'd been experiencing.

Arriving at Arizona Oncology, she filled out the required paperwork she was handed and nervously rubbed her lighthouse pendant as she waited to be seen. A young female nurse with a kind smile invited her into an examination room, and a few minutes later, she was greeted by a woman who introduced herself as Doctor Ahmed. The two made small talk for a few minutes, getting to know each other and building rapport. Lily wasn't quite as comfortable around her as she was Doctor Reinhart, but credited that to the potential severity of the situation. Given the circumstances of the visit, she imagined it would be hard for anyone to feel truly comfortable. While going over her information, the doctor asked Lily to remove her shirt and bra so she could take a look at what she was dealing with. Like with the obstetrician, the oncologist felt Lily's breasts for signs of discomfort and had her rate her level of pain as she applied increasing pressure with gloved hands. This preliminary test was followed by a mammogram, which Lily was no stranger to. She'd had one a few years prior before getting the small tumor removed from her right breast, which she was sure to tell Doctor Ahmed about. After multiple X-rays of both breasts, the doctor informed Lily that she'd be performing a stereotactic breast biopsy along with a skin biopsy, which required using a needle to extract a tissue and skin sample that would be sent to a lab for testing. Despite Lily's fear of needles, she handled both well, and with the biopsies on their way to the lab, it was finally time for some answers.

"It's just some sort of infection, right?" Lily nervously asked, still trying to convince herself there was no major cause for concern.

"No, Miss Ward, this is not an infection. I could tell just from my visual exam that you have what's called 'inflammatory breast cancer.' The mammogram was to gauge the severity of it."

"What?" Lily hissed. "How is that possible? That can't be right. No, that just can't be right. I think I'd like a second opinion."

"And you're entitled to that, Miss Ward, but I'd like to review the results of the mammogram with you so you can see just how serious this is. I think once you see results for yourself, you won't be needing a second opinion."

"I mean, I didn't feel any lumps or anything," Lily muttered, shaking her head in disbelief. "I just don't understand."

"And that's the problem, which is why it often goes undetected for so long. With inflammatory breast cancer, there are no lumps. It's a widespread area of abnormality rather than a distinct mass. Here, let me show you."

Doctor Ahmed presented the X-rays that had been taken of each breast alongside images of healthy breasts for comparison, and Lily could spot the difference easily. Unlike the healthy breasts, her X-rays revealed large white patches of increased breast density, and in reviewing the images, Lily couldn't help but notice just how large those patches were. She began to tremble as she realized just how severe this was.

"This is bad, isn't it?" she asked. "Be honest with me."

The doctor sighed and hesitated for a moment. "Yes, Miss Ward, this is bad."

Lily fought back her panic. "How bad?"

"As you can see, it's spread to both breasts. Had you seen a doctor sooner, there might have been a chance of saving them, but—"

"Oh, God!" Lily shrieked, bursting into tears. *"Oh, God, no! No, no, no! Please! You aren't taking my breasts! Oh, God, this can't be happening!"*

Like with Doctor Reinhart, Doctor Ahmed didn't try to quiet her. Rather, she handed Lily a box of tissues and let her ride out her emotions while she mapped out their next steps.

"Miss Ward, given the severity of the cancer, removing them might not solve anything."

"W-w-what's that supposed to m-m-mean?" Lily whimpered, her chest heaving in panic.

"I can see the cancer has already metastasized. The skin of your breasts has thickened, meaning the cancer has spread to your skin. I'm going to order a bone biopsy to see if it's spread to your bones. Normally, I'd recommend an MRI first, but between the results of your X-rays and the skin thickening, I think it's best if we move right to the bone biopsy."

"This can't be happening," Lily said, her sobs turning into an almost maniacal laugh. "This just can't be happening. Oh my God, first Ryan, and now this. The universe hates me, I'm sure of it."

"I'm going to see if we can get the bone biopsy done this week. Meanwhile, we should have the results of today's biopsies within the next twenty-four hours. I'm going to put you on a combination of tamoxifen, doxorubicin, and docetaxel to help prevent the cancerous breast tissue from spreading. That should stop any further swelling, but it's not guaranteed. Everyone responds differently. Let me make a phone call to see how soon we can get the bone biopsy scheduled. I'd rather not leave you alone right now, so I'm going to make the call from here."

"T-t-thank you," Lily sniffled. The last thing she wanted was to be alone and appreciated the doctor's consideration. Lost in her own world, she didn't hear a word of Doctor Ahmed's phone call as she sat trying to digest the terrifying hand she'd been dealt.

"Miss Ward?" the doctor said. She had to repeat herself to regain Lily's attention. "Miss Ward?"

"Huh? Yes, I'm sorry," Lily replied, trying to shake herself out of her daze.

"They can get you in tomorrow at 3:00 pm."

"I… have to work," Lily returned, her mind still muddled from the realization that she might not make it out of this.

"I suggest you clear your schedule," the doctor said sternly. "You can't put this off. We need the bone biopsy results as soon as possible to determine the appropriate treatment."

"Yes, of course, I'm sorry. 3:00 pm is fine," Lily replied, trying to find yet another reason to request more time off.

"The results of today's biopsies should be ready by your appointment tomorrow. We'll go over them then." The doctor paused and looked at Lily with compassion. "I'm sorry, Miss Ward. Now, please go home and try to rest."

With Lily's prescription sent to the CVS nearest the estate, the doctor referred her to a grief counselor specializing in cancer patients and urged her to schedule an appointment. Lily thanked her but knew she wouldn't make the call as it would require even more time off, and she'd already been requesting too much already. Her first priority was to head to a post office to set up a post office box where she could have her medical bills sent. She had just enough money to cover this visit, but future visits were going to require a payment plan, and she couldn't have oncological bills arriving at the estate. She'd be able to intercept most of them, but all it would take was Austin or Winston beating her to the mailbox and she'd have some serious explaining to do. She was going to tell Austin about her condition, of course, but only when the time was right. With so much on his plate at the moment, she knew that time wasn't now. He was already busy enough with the Crolles plant, the negotiation with Atari, and his other daily business dealings. The last thing he needed was to manage a sick girlfriend on top of everything else. This was no common cold and would require a good deal of attention. As much as she'd love to have him by her side for her appointments, and as a shoulder to cry on, she couldn't involve him in this yet. As irrational as she knew it was, a part of her feared he'd leave her. After all, they'd only been together for a few short months. She knew his character well enough to know he'd never do that to her, yet a niggling doubt remained. She blamed that on the lingering trauma Ryan had left her with.

She found a post office near the estate and set up a post office box for herself as planned. It would be where her medical bills and records would be sent until she told Austin about her condition. From there, she stopped by the CVS her prescription had been sent to, remembering how a little over one week prior, she'd visited this CVS to pick up the two at-home pregnancy kits that had left her so disappointed and confused. She sat in the CVS parking lot for a half an hour, still trying to wrap her mind around the disastrous turn of events. One day, she was convinced she was carrying Austin's child. The next, she was sick with an aggressive form of cancer so severe, treatment might be a futile waste of time. It was a lot to process, and more tears flowed as she struggled to come to terms with it. It really didn't seem fair that she'd overcome so much just to be faced with this. With a heavy sigh, she took her first dose of medication, hoping it would slow the disease enough to give Austin the time he needed to wrap up his two big projects. Glancing at the time, she groaned at how late she'd be arriving home. The examination and subsequent testing had taken hours, and it was pushing 3:00 pm. As if she didn't have enough problems already, she now had to find another excuse for why her supposed gynecological exam took five hours.

Returning to the estate, she found Austin hard at work in his study, wearing one of his elegant three-piece suits. This told her he'd likely had a video call with Atari since he always dressed to the nines when conducting business. He smiled when he saw her and ushered her in.

"Hey, you're alive! I was just about to call you."

"I'm so sorry," Lily said. "It's been a day. The doctor was late again, this time by an entire hour, and then my parents called and my mom was talking my ear off. Ugh."

"It's fine," Austin smiled, rising to give her a kiss. "I'm just glad you're okay." His smile turned to a wide grin as he shared his excitement. "The deal with Atari is good to go. They agreed to my terms and will be giving me a small percentage of every unit sold. They're going to host a small convention here in April to build hype and to show me that their brand is still very much alive. We're going to intentionally leak rumors of a new system to get people talking. It's a solid plan."

"You look awfully excited for somebody who doesn't deal with video games," Lily teased.

"I don't deal with video games, but I do deal with money," he chuckled. "I mean, this partnership isn't going to make me billions or anything, but it will fund the new manufacturing equipment I need for the PlastiCPU production. It all kind of works itself out."

"That's great!" Lily replied with a smile as genuine as she could muster.

"Oh, and we have a new cleaning lady. Her name is Stella, and she starts tomorrow. I hope you don't mind that I hired her without you. I just didn't want to wait, you know? This place is way overdue for a good cleaning. Dust galore."

"That's fine," Lily said. "I wanted to be here for the interview, I really did."

"Don't worry about it, sweetie," Austin said, turning his attention back to his open laptop. "I have to finish finding the parts I need for the new production line. Maybe we can have dinner together in a bit?"

"I'd like that," Lily smiled, lingering for a moment to watch Austin at work. He was just so handsome and sweet, the thought of being too sick to spend a full life with him brought tears to her eyes. She turned to leave before he could see the forlorn look on her face and headed to the office they'd set up for her so she could catch up on the work she'd missed. She had a long list of calls and emails in need of response, and as exhausted as she was, she couldn't bring herself to put them off. She'd always been commended on her work ethic, and it was something Austin had professed to love as well. Even in the face of a life-threatening sickness, she wasn't about to slack off, but she did burst into tears a few times in between calls.

Done with work for the day, she spent some time researching her condition, hoping to find some glimmer of hope. Instead, she found only despair, as the prognosis was dire. Had she only visited a doctor sooner, there was a chance treatment would have worked and resulted in a full remission. Successful treatment at her current stage was highly unlikely, and if it had spread to her bones, treatment seemed entirely pointless since the chances of recovery were slim to none. She chastised herself for not seeing a doctor sooner, but she'd been so thoroughly convinced she was pregnant that she didn't consider it a priority. Still, when she'd had the tumor in her breast removed a few years earlier, the doctor had strongly recommended regular breast exams to catch any future abnormalities, and she'd been good about it until her move to Arizona. Since arriving in Tucson, she hadn't done the best job of keeping up with her health, and she was paying for it now.

She looked at the wooden lighthouse Austin had made her. She'd set it on her desk as an homage to their love, and while it usually made her smile, it brought nothing but pain now. With how strong their love was, she saw them getting married, having kids, and living a long, happy life together. She burst into tears again, knowing that might not happen now, but held out hope that she'd respond well to whatever treatment she'd be undergoing. That faint glimmer of hope was all she had, and she needed it to keep moving forward. She needed that hope to—

"Knock, knock," Austin's voice sounded from the doorway, interrupting her thoughts. She welcomed the intrusion as it snapped her out of her self-pity.

"Hey, handsome," she said, wiping her eyes. She hoped Austin hadn't seen her tears, but it had been too late.

"Baby? What's wrong?" he asked, stepping beside her to rub her back.

"Nothing, it's silly," she said, clearing her throat and straightening her posture.

"If you're crying, I'm sure it's not silly," Austin pointed out. "What's going on?"

"My doctor called. They think I might have a small cyst on one of my ovaries and would like to see me again tomorrow," Lily lied, making up a story on the fly. "They don't think it's anything major, but they want to make sure. Is it okay if I end my shift a bit early tomorrow?"

"Of course," Austin nodded. "In fact, I've been meaning to talk to you about that."

Oh, great, and now you're in more trouble, Lily thought. *He's pissed about the work you've been missing.*

Instead, Austin threw her a curveball. "I want you to know that you never have to request time off. If you need it, go ahead and take it."

"Are you sure?" Lily asked, both in surprise and relief.

"I know that, technically, I'm your boss, but I don't like feeling like I'm your boss, you know? I don't like feeling like I hold some sort of dominion over you. I'd rather view us as partners. Equals. I know how hard you work and that you only take time off when it's absolutely necessary. I trust you."

"God, how did I get so lucky?" Lily said, pulling him in for a kiss. "You're always so good to me."

"Well, yeah," Austin smirked. "You're my girl. I'm always going to be good to you." Snapping his fingers, he added, "Hey, did you ever pick up a pregnancy test?"

"I did," Lily replied. "Negative."

If she wasn't mistaken, Austin looked to be hiding disappointment. "Ah, okay. It's probably too soon for that anyway."

They invited Winston to share dinner with them, which was something they did often. He was like family, and knowing he didn't have anyone else, they tried to include him as much as possible. He was a character, and Lily always enjoyed his company. After a lovely meal prepared by Austin—who'd proven to be quite a good chef—Winston joined them for a game of Scrabble and surprised them by trouncing them both.

In bed that night, Austin held Lily as they talked, which was always her favorite part of the day. She felt so safe and protected in his strong arms that for a moment, she was able to forget about the trouble she was in and the long battle ahead. She could overcome anything with him by her side. Certainly, fate couldn't be cruel enough to bring them together just to tear them apart so suddenly, and in such an unforgiving way. She was going to beat this. She was sure of it.

Chapter Ten

Early as always, she arrived for her bone biopsy with high hopes. She had a mild panic attack when they told her they'd be inserting a needle into her sternum, and she found herself wishing she had a friend by her side. She'd met a few members of their gated community, but nobody she associated with on a regular basis, and certainly nobody she'd ask to a procedure of this significance. There was a lot riding on this since the outcome would determine her chance of survival, but she'd resolved to stay positive, refusing to allow any negative thoughts. Seeing how terrified she was of the needle, and that she had nobody to lean on, a kind nurse offered her a hand to hold, which Lily appreciated tremendously. The results of the breast tissue and skin biopsies had confirmed the cancer and revealed it to be every bit as aggressive as believed.

The extraction of the bone sample went smoothly, and thanks to the numbing agent they'd liberally applied, Lily felt only a slight sting. Like with the previous biopsies, Doctor Ahmed told her they'd have the results within twenty-four hours and would call her once they were in. The procedure didn't take long, and Lily was in and out within an hour. On the drive back to the estate, she debated calling her parents to let them know what she was dealing with, but decided to give it a bit more time. If there was a chance she could be treated and cured, she could avoid telling her parents altogether to spare them the worry. They would lose their minds and insist she return to Cleveland, but she loved Austin too much to leave him.

You might be leaving him either way.

She shook the thought away, upset that she'd allowed the pessimism. As difficult as it was, she needed to stay positive and had to believe she was going to make a full recovery. At the estate, she wasn't surprised to find Austin still hard at work, grumbling in his study about some technical kink he had to iron out. He could do it, he assured her, it was just going to take a bit more time. Leaving him to his work, she passed the time in the kitchen preparing a nice dinner for them. She always enjoyed cooking, though baking was more her thing, and it proved a nice distraction from her problems. The timing couldn't have been better as Austin appeared in the kitchen just as Lily was pulling the lasagna out of the oven.

"Baby, that smells amazing," he smiled, playfully smacking her bottom and pulling her in for a kiss.

"You don't look as stressed," Lily noticed. "I take it you solved the problem?"

"I did," Austin nodded. "Everything should be good to go."

"I knew you'd figure it out." She ran her fingers down his chest and purred, "My big, strong, brilliant man."

Needing time together, they ate dinner without Winston but saved a few slices of lasagna for him in the fridge. Austin wanted to discuss the current state and future of Tomorrow Tech, and asked Lily to begin research on Atari's long history in preparation for the convention in April. He'd be doing his own research as well, and thought it best if they both went into the event as knowledgeable as possible. As his public relations manager, she'd likely be taking questions about Tomorrow Tech's involvement with Atari, and there was a good chance she'd be asked about the gaming company's bumpy track record. She needed to emphasize Atari's successes while downplaying their failures, applying a certain level of spin with enough skill and tact to assuage any concerns regarding the new console. The PlastiCPU processors needed would be produced in a Tomorrow Tech facility in Detroit, Michigan, and Austin would be overseeing the installation of the equipment needed to manufacture them. It would take roughly two weeks by his estimation, and although he invited Lily along, he warned her that it would be strictly business and likely a boring experience for her. Once the production line was operating smoothly, Atari's new system was slated to begin production in August. They'd have a few weeks in between to visit Maine again with a stop in Cleveland along the way, which Lily was thrilled about since she'd get to experience New England in the summer, and Austin would finally get to meet her parents.

In bed that night, Lily allowed Austin the sex she knew he'd been waiting so patiently for. She adored him for never pressuring her, and for always being so understanding when she wasn't feeling well. She could tell he'd been aching for her, and she couldn't keep making excuses. Despite her condition, her sex drive was still alive and well, but she'd been avoiding intimacy in fear he'd comment on the discoloration of her breasts, which had grown far more visible. She also knew how much he loved feeling them, both with his hands and his mouth, and they'd become so tender, she didn't think she'd be able to mask the pain. She tried keeping her bra on, but as predicted, he wasn't having that and insisted she remove it. He loved seeing her naked, but she'd planned for that by turning the lights down low enough to hide any visual signs of her sickness. In an effort to protect her breasts from his touch, she teased him with her raised bare bottom as a cue for him to take her from behind and gently buried her chest into the bed so he couldn't reach them. With so much weighing on her mind, she knew she wouldn't be able to finish, which posed a problem since he always made sure she got off before him. He wouldn't stop until he knew she'd reached at least one orgasm, and with this in mind, she did what she had to do.

She faked it.

It was the first time she'd had to fake it with him since he was such an incredible lover, and she was immediately overcome by guilt. Since it had been over a week since they'd had sex, it didn't take him long to finish, collapsing by her side and falling into a deep sleep shortly thereafter. Sleep didn't come as easily for her. It was another restless night as she worried what the bone biopsy would reveal, and it was pushing 2:00 am by the time she drifted off. She woke completely exhausted and wished she could spend the day in bed, but she knew she had business to handle and an important phone call to take.

After getting some food in her and taking her morning dose of the medication she'd been hiding in her handbag, she spent a few hours in her office replying to emails and returning phone calls. Interview requests had slowed but were still coming in, and she knew they'd pick up again when word of the Atari deal broke. Austin had another interview scheduled for later that week, this time with Fox News, and unlike his interview with CNN, she promised to be there for its entirety.

The call she'd been anxiously awaiting finally came in at 1:00 pm. Doctor Ahmed had the results of the bone biopsy, but insisted on reviewing them in person. She asked Lily if she could meet her in her office at 4:00 pm, to which Lily nervously agreed, and from the tone of the doctor's voice, she suspected the news wasn't good. Austin giving her carte blanche to take time off from work whenever she needed came as a relief as it was one less lie she'd have to tell him. They were already piling up, and she hoped he would forgive her when the time came. She spent the next two hours focusing on work, knowing she needed to keep her mind as occupied as possible to avoid another breakdown. She'd been an emotional rollercoaster since her appointment with Doctor Reinhart, and it was taking its toll on her mental health. She spent the drive to Arizona Oncology sobbing uncontrollably in between fits of unhinged laughter, finding a twisted humor in how hard the universe had stuck it to her. She'd survived Ryan's heinous attack just to face a cancer so aggressive there was a very real possibility she'd see an early grave. She didn't know what she did to deserve it, and she cursed God aloud for delivering such an unfair sentence. Teasing her with a fairytale life with the perfect man just to take it from her so suddenly, and so cruelly, was simply unforgivable. At this point, she wasn't sure if she even believed in God, but it did feel like the universe had it out for her.

She had her self-pity in check by the time she reached Doctor Ahmed's office, and before stepping inside, she silently apologized to God for her outburst. If there was a higher power, berating it wasn't going to help. Although it felt like she'd been singled out, she knew there were plenty of others who'd been placed in this same unfortunate situation. She took a seat in the waiting area and tried to remain hopeful, telling herself that hope and positive energy might manifest itself into some sort of good news. While she waited for the doctor, she thumbed through one of the magazines that had been placed about to help pass the time, and she did a double-take when she found a picture of her and Austin together at the opera in Paris. The caption below the photo read, "Tomorrow Tech CEO Austin Matson strikes a pose with his beautiful date, Lilian Ward." Chuckling, she noted the publication she'd grabbed was *People Magazine* and made a mental note to grab a copy while she was out. Austin would get a kick out of it, and she wanted to clip the photo for her office. She was admiring how cute they looked together when she was greeted by Doctor Ahmed, who led Lily to her private office rather than an examination room to go over the bone biopsy results.

"So," the doctor began, taking a seat behind her desk where she had Lily's paperwork laid out. She motioned for Lily to take a seat as well. "I wish I had good news for you."

Lily's heart sank. "Just give it to me flat-out. Don't sugarcoat anything. How bad is it?"

"Unfortunately, Miss Ward, the cancer has made its way to your bones. If it's spread to your skin and bones, it's likely spread to your internal organs as well. At this stage, our treatment options are limited."

Lily sat frozen for a moment, too stunned to have any visible reaction.

"Are you going to take my breasts?" she asked in a faint, trembling voice.

"A mastectomy wouldn't accomplish anything at this point, since the cancer has already made its way to your bones. Generally, a mastectomy is to prevent the cancer from spreading to the rest of your body, and since…"

Doctor Ahmed continued speaking, but Lily heard none of it. The doctor's voice had become muffled and indiscernible, as if Lily was hearing it through a wall. She sat stock-still, feeling detached from not only the moment but reality itself, like she was trapped in some sort of a dream state. At some point, the doctor noticed that Lily was no longer present, and it took repeating her name three times to bring her back.

"…Miss Ward?"

"Am I terminal? Lily asked bluntly.

The direct question seemed to catch Doctor Ahmed off guard. "I… it's serious, but I'm not ready to call it terminal. Along with your current medication, we'd like to start you on chemotherapy right away. Once we see how your body responds, we can determine if the cancer is terminal."

Lily swallowed nervously. "I'm stage four, aren't I?"

"Yes, I'm afraid that's correct," the doctor replied.

"Then I'd like to thank you for your time, and I'll see myself out," Lily said, rising from her seat.

"Wait, Miss Ward, you can't just—"

"I've seen what chemo does to people," Lily said flatly, turning to face Doctor Ahmed. "I watched my aunt go through it. At stage four, I'm basically terminal. We both know chemo isn't going to help. If anything, it'll just kill me faster. I don't want to spend whatever time I have left with my fingernails falling off. My hair falling out. Soiling myself. Vomiting after I eat. Forgive me, but if I'm going to die, I'd rather die on my terms, with dignity and grace."

"Miss Ward, there's still a chance—"

"No, there's not," Lily interrupted again. "I could tell by the look in your eyes that there's no coming back from this. I'll keep taking the pills, but as far as the chemo goes? No thanks."

It was the doctor's turn to be stunned, and she sat in silence for a moment. "Miss Ward, please don't let your pride stand in the way of what could be a successful treatment."

"This isn't about vanity," Lily rocketed back. "It's about quality of life.

Though, if she were being honest with herself, vanity did play a factor. She took pride in her appearance, and she knew Austin found her beautiful. The thought of appearing disfigured and weak, especially around him, horrified her. The long, thick hair he loved so much would be gone, and she'd be stripped of the curves that drove him crazy. She would become a skeletal, hairless shell of her former self, too weak to walk on her own, and needing help just to use the toilet. That's how it had gone with her aunt, and she knew that's how it would go with her as well. She wouldn't be seen like that; not by herself, and not by anybody.

"Very well," the doctor conceded with a sigh. "I respect your decision. I'll keep refilling your prescription and will prescribe you medication for the pain as well. If at any point you change your mind about the chemo, please call me. Meanwhile, I'd like to schedule you for monthly follow-up exams to see how you're holding up. Can you do that for me, at least?"

"Fair enough," Lily said.

After telling the receptionist where to send the bill, Lily climbed into the 1952 Chevy and sat. She didn't move. She didn't cry. She didn't tremble. She simply sat and watched the shadows slowly making their way across the Catalina Mountains as the sun began to set, reflecting on the life she'd lived and how blessed she was to have met so many wonderful people along the way. She could scream and yell, curse God again, and cry until there were no tears left, but none of that would change the inevitable outcome she was facing. She was going to die. All she could do was try her best to enjoy the time she had left and not take a single second for granted. A stabbing pain hit her as she realized she would have to tell Austin, who would be completely gutted by the news. She'd seen her children in his eyes, and felt a great sorrow knowing she wouldn't live the life she'd envisioned. For nearly an hour, she sat and watched the blue sky change to pastel hues of orange, pink, and purple. The Southwestern sunsets were part of what had brought her here, and she wasn't sure how many more she had left to see.

On the drive back to the estate, Lily stopped at a couple of convenience stores before finding a copy of the *People Magazine* she'd been flipping through in Doctor Ahmed's waiting room. She vowed to live the rest of her days with as much normalcy as possible, not holed up crying and feeling sorry for herself. The Atari convention was in April, and she'd tell Austin about her illness after that. It was only seven weeks away, and he'd be gone for two of those managing the installation of the new equipment in Detroit. That gave her plenty of time to figure out how she'd break the news, which wasn't going to be easy. She scolded herself yet again for allowing herself to end up in this situation. She'd been neglecting her health, and reflecting on the months gone by, she realized the warning signs were there long before France. She recalled experiencing random bouts of fatigue shortly after meeting Austin, which is when she should have seen a doctor. She knew it was unlikely, but had to wonder if the second-hand smoke Ryan had subjected her to had triggered the cancer.

Austin was still working when she returned home, and he didn't seem to know she'd even left. She interrupted him for a kiss and asked if she could bring him something to eat or drink. Glancing at the time, he politely declined and asked if they could do dinner together in an hour. She agreed with a smile and made her way to the library in hopes of distracting herself with the knitting needles she'd grown so familiar with. Sadly, no amount of stitches could take her mind off of her diagnosis, and she set her project aside to allow her tears. Alone and surrounded by books, she wept for the future she wouldn't have with Austin and desperately wished they could grow old together. She'd pass, and given how long they'd been together, he'd likely move on quickly. He'd find another woman to grow old with, and they would inevitably have children. Lily would become a distant memory, and that thought only brought more tears.

She wasn't sure if it was just her imagination, and perhaps wishful thinking, but over the next several days, it felt like the pain and swelling in her breasts had subsided. The difference was marginal, but unless she was experiencing nothing more than a placebo effect, it seemed as though she was responding well to the medication she'd been given. The discoloration in her breasts had faded slightly, but she still made sure to dim the lights whenever they were intimate. At her monthly follow-up appointment, Doctor Ahmed noticed how well she'd taken to the medication and believed she might respond just as well to the chemotherapy. At her persistence, Lily finally agreed to give it a shot, but between how sick it made her and the hair she'd started to lose, she ended the therapy after just four treatments. Had she kept going with it, Austin would have surely noticed something was wrong, and with the Atari convention approaching, he didn't need to be worrying about her. He was also leaving for Detroit soon, and she didn't want her condition distracting him from the work he needed to do there. Doctor Ahmed urged her to continue, insisting she hadn't given it enough time, to which Lily explained the importance of the upcoming convention she was expected to attend. As Austin Matson's head of public relations, she didn't want to show up at the event looking sickly with clumps of hair missing. She'd consider giving the chemotherapy one more chance when the convention was over, Lily told her, but she wasn't going to make any promises.

Austin once again invited Lily to accompany him to Detroit, but since he'd stressed that it was going to be all work and no play, she thought it might be best if she stayed behind to do a deep dive into Atari's history like he'd asked. She'd already begun researching the company, but wanted to know them inside and out, so she wasn't blindsided by questions she wasn't prepared to answer at the convention. Of course, Atari CEO Wade Rosen was scheduled to attend the event and could answer questions as well, but she knew there would be times when he wouldn't be by her side and she'd have to handle questions herself. She didn't want to make Tomorrow Tech look bad by fumbling an answer to a question she wasn't ready for. Austin agreed that her time would be better spent at the estate and promised her another wonderful trip together when the convention wrapped and the PlastiCPU production was in full swing. They still hadn't come up with a better name for it, and had referred to it as "PlastiCPU" so many times that the name seemed to have stuck.

Lily drove Austin to Million Air, where he'd chartered another private jet, and she boarded it with him just long enough to give him a proper send-off with her mouth. Still completely crazy about each other, they promised to keep in constant communication, and with that, Lily returned to the truck to watch the jet take off, waving goodbye, although she knew he likely couldn't see it. She used his absence to focus on her health, thinking that if she cleaned up her diet and started exercising, she might see an improvement in her condition and prolong her life. She also spent a good deal of time researching homeopathic treatments, but didn't find anything that seemed credible enough to try. She stuck with her medication, and as the days wore on, she noticed a continual improvement in her symptoms. She still experienced bouts of fatigue that would force her to lie down for a bit, but those bouts weren't as severe or as often as they had been, and her nausea wasn't as frequent, either. The swelling in her breasts had receded, though not quite enough for her to wear her old bras, and the discoloration was only noticeable if you looked for it. Despite the abatement of her symptoms, Doctor Ahmed was quick to remind her that the cancer wasn't in remission, and urged her to resume the chemotherapy.

The estate didn't feel the same with Austin gone. He would send text messages to her throughout the day, and he called her every evening, updating her on the progress there in Detroit. In return, she would update him on life at the estate and the work she'd been doing on her end. He wished that she'd made the trip with him, he confessed, because sleeping without her by his side didn't feel right. She seconded that, missing the feeling of him next to her in bed with his strong arms wrapped around her, protecting her from the outside world. He'd had a few technical hiccups with the installation of the new manufacturing equipment, he told her, but had managed to get them sorted, and with everything running smoothly, he would be home soon to cover her naked body in kisses.

Eager to return to his life in Tucson, Austin arrived home two days earlier than expected, which Lily welcomed, and he wasted no time stripping her naked and playfully throwing her on the bed to have his way with her. Anticipating this, Lily had taken a dose of the pain medication she'd been prescribed, knowing he wouldn't be able to keep his hands off of her breasts. She was right, but the medication numbed her enough to make it bearable. She worried he'd feel the difference in her breasts as they were much denser and heavier now, but he was so aroused, he didn't seem to notice. With what they dubbed their "welcome home sex" out of the way, they spent time going over their notes on Atari in preparation for the upcoming event. While Lily had done her own research, Austin had done his as well, and they wanted to make sure they both had the same information.

Atari CEO Wade Rosen arrived in Tucson two days before the big day to finally meet with Austin face-to-face and to manage the twelve-hour event directly. It would be held at the *Tucson Convention Center* and would feature every Atari arcade machine, console, and game released since 1975. Truckloads of Atari products spanning five decades had been delivered to the convention center, as well as television monitors, display stands, signage, and promotional material. Austin and Lily had been invited to oversee the setup, and they were both impressed by the effort Atari had made. They'd pulled out all the stops, creating a gaming station for every console they'd released, along with the accompanying games for that specific system. Visitors were welcome to bounce from station to station, enjoying the various devices and games Atari had introduced over the years. They'd gone with a fitting retro theme, choosing decor from the first three decades of their history, and had blended them together seamlessly to create an almost surreal nostalgic atmosphere. The walls were lined with hundreds of Atari arcade machines, and eye-catching neon signs had been placed about. Adding to the fun, Atari had partnered with a local pizza business who would be supplying the event with pizza throughout the day. More food, snacks, and beverages would be available as well, allowing people to spend the entire day at the convention without having to leave to get a bite to eat. Atari had invested a lot of money in this event and watching everything come together, even Austin and Lily found themselves excited for it.

Both Atrari and Tomorrow Tech had issued press releases for the event that had garnered interest from every major news outlet. As Tomorrow Tech's public relations manager, Lily had reached out to local media outlets who would be covering the event as well. Atari had spent the last two months promoting the convention, and Austin had also been promoting it on Tomorrow Tech's corporate website. Nobody knew why Atari and Tomorrow Tech had teamed up, and the tech industry was swirling with speculation. Having just bought one of STMicroelectronics' largest manufacturing plants, rumors of Tomorrow Tech buying out Atari were beginning to float around. Of course, Wade and Austin had intentionally kept their deal under wraps, knowing the intrigue would bring more attention, which it had. They found Wade a joy to work with, and his energy was infectious. He was around Austin's age, and the two had hit it off right away, forging not just a partnership, but a friendship as well.

When the doors opened to the public at 9:00 am, neither Austin nor Lily could believe the number of people who'd lined up to enjoy the free event, and even Wade was shocked by the turnout. Nobody had anticipated such a large crowd, and by noon, the convention center was packed with those looking to relive their childhood. Nostalgia was bringing people in, and the entertainment was keeping them there. Parents of all ages were showing up with their sons and daughters, effectively introducing a whole new generation to the Atari brand. That had been Wade's plan all along, and it had worked perfectly. The smell of pizza and popcorn were in the air as people huddled around each station and arcade machine to play the games they'd grown up with while experiencing the games they never had a chance to play.

"A kid on my bus had this game and I remember being jealous because I didn't have it. I always wanted to play it but ever got a chance. I waited almost fifty years for this," an older man joked with what appeared to be his grandson by his side.

Throughout the day, they heard many stories like this, and each was told with a big grin. The event was a huge hit, with some people driving hours just to attend, and although Lily experienced a few dizzy spells along with her usual fatigue, she was holding up better than expected. She knew the day would be exhausting given her condition, but the energy radiating throughout the event was enough to keep her going. National and local press arrived to report on the convention and question the unexpected relationship between Atari and Tomorrow Tech. Rather than answer each reporter individually, Austin and Wade announced they'd be holding a press conference at 5:00 pm sharp, where they would reveal their exciting news and take questions from the media. A few reporters tried prying the news out of Lily early, but they got no leaks from her. She'd been sworn to secrecy, she told them, and would only answer questions regarding Atari's past dealings. As predicted, she was asked about the Atari Jaguar, Atari's last attempt at a home video game system that had crashed and burned in spectacular fashion, almost destroying the company entirely. Lily was ready and deflected the question by highlighting all of Atari's accomplishments with the reminder that every successful company has released one dud. That answer seemed to satisfy them, but there was one question from a CNN reporter that she hadn't prepared for and completely caught her off guard.

"Miss Ward, is it true that you're romantically involved with Austin Matson?"

On the spot and unsure how to answer, Lily chose honesty and answered that, yes, she was in a romantic relationship with the CEO. Off the record, she asked the reporter how he'd learned this, and he replied that he'd seen their photo in People Magazine. She'd shown Austin that photo and he'd been amused by it, so she didn't think he'd mind her officially announcing their romance. Throughout the day, she'd find Austin in the crowd and they'd shoot each other smiles, both elated by how well the event was going. When 5:00 pm rolled around, Austin and Wade held their press conference, revealing Tomorrow Tech's partnership with Atari, and they hinted at the development of a powerful new video game console. The media pushed for details, but the two CEOs remained tight-lipped, promising more news in the weeks to come. Those in attendance seem thrilled by the announcement, which Austin took as a good sign. Atari had proven that their name still packed a punch, and that a new gaming system might have a shot at competing in the market.

The event was going even better than planned, but all of that changed when Lily spotted an approaching face in the crowd that drove terror into her heart. Staggering backwards as she recoiled in panic, she bumped into Austin, who immediately noticed her trembling jaw and look of fright.

"I-I-need to leave," she stammered, turning to him. "I have to get out of here."

"Baby?" he asked quietly. "What's wrong?"

"Please," she pleaded with tears in her eyes, tugging at the arm of his suit. "I need to go. I can't be here. I—"

"Hello, Lily," Ryan's voice sounded from behind her. "I thought that was you."

Lily instinctively moved behind Austin for protection, her entire body shaking in fear. Ryan, who had emerged from the crowd, stood looking at her with a knowing grin and drunken eyes. He was holding hands with a pretty blonde who stood smiling as well, but she looked more confused than anything. Lily could only assume this was his new girlfriend, who would likely end up another in his list of victims. Ryan's other hand was gripping a water bottle, but Lily knew that wasn't water in the bottle.

"Just go!" Lily spat, peeking out from behind Austin while gripping his arm tightly. *"You're not welcome here!"*

"Oh, come on," Ryan chuckled. "You're not still upset about the breakup, are you?"

"This man attacked me!" Lily told Ryan's new love interest. "He beat me so badly, he put me in the hospital! Please… you need to get as far away from him as you can!"

"Attacked you?" Ryan scoffed. "That's a stretch. You were destroying my property, so I pinned you to the floor until you calmed down. Nice try, though."

"That's a lie!" Lily shrieked. *"There's a police report! There are photos! Photos of what you did to me! Of how badly you beat me!"*

"Let's just calm down," Austin said to nobody in particular, his hand raised while he looked around the room nervously. Lily realized her outburst had drawn attention from attendees, and all eyes were now on the unfolding drama.

"All lies," Ryan laughed dismissively. "I dumped you. You couldn't handle it so you made up that ridiculous story. That's all there is to it."

"Sweetie, you need to get away from this man," Lily begged the girl by Ryan's side. She spoke quickly and in fragments, knowing their time was limited. "He's a complete monster. He's just using you. I'm sure you've already seen warning signs. Don't ignore them like I did. That's not water in his bottle!"

"Just listen to how crazy she is," Ryan told the girl, shaking his head. "I told you she was nuts."

"I'm going to ask you and your girlfriend here to please leave," Austin said quietly, trying to diffuse the situation. Still holding his arm, Lily could feel him tense up.

"Leave? We just got here!" Ryan hissed. "We have every right to be here. We haven't done anything wrong!"

"That may be," Austin said, his voice growing stern, "but this is my event, and I'm telling you to get out."

"Man, fuck you," Ryan replied angrily, showing his true character. He pointed at Austin and asked Lily, "Who's this guy, anyway, your new man?"

Austin spoke through gritted teeth, his brow furrowed in anger. "I'm not asking you again. Leave. Now."

Not wanting any part of the drama, Ryan's presumed girlfriend broke free of his hand. "I don't know what's going on right now, but I don't want any part of it."

"Baby, come back!" Ryan called after her while she stormed off. "Baby!"

"You'd be wise to leave, too," Austin scowled. "Right now."

Ryan took a step closer to Lily, who shrunk in fear behind Austin. "I should have beat you harder," he told her in a low, menacing voice. "You fucking bitc—"

He was interrupted by a punch to the face so hard it sent him flying into an arcade machine where he fell slumped over, out cold from Austin's fist. Austin stormed over and grabbed him by his shirt collar, shaking him back to consciousness.

"If you come near Lily again, little man, I will fucking kill you," he growled at Ryan before slamming his head against the arcade machine, knocking him out again.

The crowd erupted with mixed reactions. While some people cheered, others were horrified, and a few parents quickly ushered their children out of the event with looks of disgust. Despite the convention's retro theme, these were modern times, and everyone in attendance had a cell phone. Those cell phones had been out in full force, capturing the incident as it played out, and Lily was sure the footage had already made its way online where it would live in perpetuity. Several news outlets had caught the incident as well, and reporters rushed Lily and Austin for details. Who was this man Austin Matson had punched, and what had he done to warrant it? These questions were at the forefront of everyone's mind, but neither Austin nor Lily were ready to answer them. Austin shot Lily a look of frustrated disappointment that broke her heart. She'd ruined the event, and she knew it. Everything had been running so smoothly, and in less than a minute, it had come to a grinding halt because she'd been unable to control her emotions. Had she just ran the moment she saw Ryan, this whole ordeal could have been avoided. Instead, she'd made the mistake of engaging with him and had allowed him to work her into such a frenzy that she'd completely flown off the handle.

Austin towered over Ryan's unconscious body, and unless Lily was seeing things, his ring had left an impression of a lighthouse on Ryan's cheek, just under his left eye. Lily would have found amusement in that if she wasn't so overcome with emotion. She was fully aware that she'd just ruined the event Atari had worked so hard on, and between the roar of the crowd and the grilling from the reporters, it was all too much to bear. Overwhelmed and hyperventilating, the room began to spin, and feeling faint, she grabbed the table next to her for stability. It didn't help, and she fell to the floor, passing out before she'd even landed. She woke on a stretcher, and as muddled and confused as she was, she knew being wheeled out of the event by paramedics was only going to add to this publicity nightmare.

"Stop," she pleaded faintly. "I can walk. I'm fine. I'm—"

She passed out again, and when she came to, she found herself in the back of an ambulance with everything spinning. She could feel a blood pressure cuff around her arm as she fought to stay alert, but kept slipping in and out of consciousness.

"Ma'am, do you have any medical conditions?" she heard a paramedic ask. "We need to know what medications you're taking. Ma'am?"

"I… I have cancer," she muttered before passing out again.

She woke in a hospital room with the feeling that several hours had passed. Somebody had dimmed the lights, which she appreciated, and as she slowly came to, she sensed that she wasn't alone.

"Hey, you're awake," Austin's voice sounded gently from beside her. Sliding his chair closer to the bed, he took her hand in his. "I've been so worried about you."

Lily swallowed and tried to remember what had landed her in the hospital. Searching her memory, she could only recall small fragments. "What happened?"

"You passed out," Austin replied, speaking softly. "Your blood pressure was extremely low."

Lily groaned as her memory began to return. "Oh, God. I ruined everything. You must hate me. I'm so sorry, Austin. I feel—"

"Shh…" Austin quieted her. "You didn't ruin anything. This is my fault, not yours."

"It's not your fault," Lily said, squeezing his hand. "I let him get under my skin. I started shouting. None of this would have happened if I'd just kept my mouth shut."

"Stop. He deserved it, and that girl deserved to know who she was dealing with. I'm sure you did her a huge favor. This falls squarely on me. I lost my temper."

"You punched him," Lily said as the memory came back to her. "You punched him right in the face."

"Not my proudest moment," Austin sighed.

"I shouldn't say this, but it was kind of hot," Lily smirked. "I've never seen that side of you before."

"And I'm hoping you'll never see it again," Austin replied. "It takes a lot to get me that angry. Still, I should have controlled myself. When he started saying those horrible things to you, I just lost it. I saw red."

"You were defending me," Lily smiled.

"The only time you'll see me fight is if I'm defending somebody I love."

"So you don't hate me?"

"Don't be silly. My heart is completely yours."

"I bet Atari is pissed," Lily winced, remembering Austin's new partner.

"I explained what happened. Wade said he would have done the same thing. Besides, bad publicity is still publicity, right? I think that's how the old saying goes."

"I bet the media is having a field day with this," Lily cringed. "How bad is it?"

"Actually, the media is on our side here. It didn't take long to unearth the police report you filed and—" Austin paused to choke back his emotions. "And the pictures of what he did to you."

"You saw the pictures?" Lily asked, looking away in shame and embarrassment.

"You told me it was bad, but I had no idea," Austin replied, swallowing hard. "God, Lily, I am so sorry that happened to you."

"Please tell me the media didn't release those photos," Lily said.

"I made sure that will never happen."

"Thank you."

"The media is painting me as some sort of hero," Austin chuckled. "Go figure."

"You are a hero," Lily smiled, squeezing his hand again. "You're my hero."

"Wade called me about an hour ago. He said the event resumed as if nothing had ever happened, and everyone is still having a blast. Despite the hiccup, he still considers the convention a huge success."

"Well, that's a relief. I thought the whole show was ruined. What happened to Ryan?"

"The paramedics looked him over once he got back on his feet. Wade told me he looked embarrassed and got out of there in a hurry."

"Wade told you? You mean, you weren't there?" Lily asked, confused.

"No, baby, I rode over here in the ambulance with you."

She remembered her admission in the ambulance, and her heart began to pound. "You were in the ambulance?"

"I was," Austin nodded. There was a long moment of silence, followed by a gasp as he began to silently weep, his chest heaving with each sob. "Baby…" he began, stopping to sniffle and wipe his eyes. "How long have you been sick?"

"I… I found out after we got back from Paris. I thought I was pregnant."

"I thought you were, too," Austin admitted. "I kept waiting for you to break the news."

"I'm sorry," Lily shrugged.

"Baby, you have nothing to apologize for. I just… I can't understand why you didn't tell me about this. We're supposed to be partners."

"I know. It's just… you have the Crolles facility to worry about, and now this deal with Atari. I didn't want to be a distraction. I know how important your business is. I was going to tell you after the convention, I swear."

"You should have told me the moment you found out," Austin said. "Jesus, I can't believe you've been going through this alone. Do you really think my business is more important than you? Than your health? Sweetie, you're the most important thing in my world. You. My business will never come before you."

"I guess I was just worried it would screw up your plans."

"I was doing just fine without the Crolles facility and without this Atari partnership," Austin reminded her. "I didn't need either of them. What I do need is you." There was another long pause before Austin spoke again. "How bad is it?"

"It's bad," Lily replied, her voice trembling as her eyes welled with tears. "Stage four."

"Oh, God!" Austin cried, bursting into tears. This time, they weren't silent. "Oh, God, no. No, no, no."

It was the first time she'd seen him truly cry. He was such a powerful, imposing man that a part of her wondered if he was even capable of it. She knew that was silly, but with the way he held himself, both in stature and composure, seeing him weep was both surreal and heartbreaking. They held hands tightly as they cried together, with his tears making hers fall harder.

"How... How did this happen?" Austin asked when he'd regained enough composure to speak. "I mean... so fast?"

"An aggressive form of breast cancer. Had they caught it in October or November, I might have had a chance. It's spread to my skin... my bones... my whole body."

"No," Austin said, shaking his head. "No, this can't be right. This can't be happening."

"I'm dying, Austin," she told him bluntly.

"No, you're not," Austin wept. "You're going to be okay. We're going to get a second opinion and you're going to be okay."

He rested his forehead on the bed's handrail and sobbed while Lily ran her fingers through his hair.

"Baby…" she spoke in a hushed tone. "At least I got to experience true love before I go. Thank you for that. For everything."

A long moment passed before Austin spoke. "Did they tell you how long…"

He trailed off, unable to finish the question, but Lily knew what he was going to ask.

"No. I've responded well to the medication they put me on, but it's just going to prolong the inevitable. I could have two years. I could have two months. We really don't know."

"What about chemotherapy?"

"Have you seen what chemo does to people? I don't want you to remember me like that."

"You have to at least try it," Austin said, wiping his eyes again.

"I did try it. It made me so sick, Austin. I told my doctor I'd give it another chance, but I'm done with it. At this stage, the chances of it working are slim to none anyhow."

"Try it again? For me?" Austin asked.

"No, honey. I'm not going to spend my final days having you help me with every little thing because I'm too weak to do them myself. I don't want to worry about vomiting on myself in front of you, or how my wig looks because I lost all of my hair, or—"

"I need you to listen to me," Austin interrupted with a firm grip on her hand. "You will always be beautiful to me. My love for you isn't superficial. I love you for who you are. I love you all the way to your soul. I just found you, Lilian. I can't lose you. I just… I can't. Please, let's get a second opinion, maybe even a third, and let's get you back on the chemo."

"Okay," Lily conceded. "I love you, lighthouse."

"I love you, chocolate girl."

Given her condition, Lily was kept overnight for observation, and Austin refused to leave her side. He made sure she got at least some food down before they turned on the television to pass the time and settled on the first major news channel they found. It didn't take long for their story to air, and they chuckled when the news anchor cleverly referred to the Atari convention as a "knockout event." Footage of Austin's knockout blow was shown, having been recorded by an attendee's cell phone camera, and the accompanying story painted Austin's act as heroic. He'd been defending his girlfriend's honor, they reported, after she'd been confronted by her abusive ex-lover. To Lily's surprise, they aired a picture of Ryan along with his full name and the allegations of abuse made by Lily in her police report. Austin offered to pull some strings to get the case against him reopened, but Lily didn't want to be dragged into a courtroom, especially in her condition, and decided his public humiliation would be punishment enough. Austin disagreed but let it go, not wanting to upset her by pressing the issue.

"He's probably going to have the imprint of a lighthouse on his face for a while," Austin joked, lightening the mood.

"I saw that!" Lily laughed.

Austin used his clout to have another bed brought in, but only after the nurse assured him that it was a slow night and they had enough to go around. With the nurse's help, they pushed the two beds together and filled the gap with blankets, allowing Austin to spend the night next to Lily. She needed his big arms around her more than she knew, and after taking her evening dose of medication, she fell fast asleep to the feeling of his warm body pressed against hers.

In the following weeks, they saw four more oncologists hoping for either a differing diagnosis or prognosis, but the verdict remained the same. Lily returned to her chemotherapy and was driven to her appointments by Austin, who sat by her side through the treatments.

Each treatment took so much out of Lily that she had to spend the rest of the day in bed, too sick to move. Austin doted on her, always at her beck and call to wait on her hand and foot, which riddled her with guilt. He'd put his business on the back-burner to focus all of his attention on her wellbeing, which only made her feel like a burden and was exactly what she didn't want. He offered to hire a live-in nurse to help with her daily care, but she didn't feel she was ready for that just yet. After losing close to thirty pounds and half of her hair, she gave up on the chemotherapy entirely and hoped to rebuild at least some of her strength. The cancer hadn't been responding to it, and Doctor Ahmed conceded that further treatments likely wouldn't change that. Austin was deeply conflicted by this. He saw how sick the treatments made her and it broke his heart, yet he urged her to continue in hopes there would be some sort of a breakthrough. With even her doctor agreeing that it was a lost cause, Lily stood firm, refusing additional treatments and accepting that she was now considered terminal. Austin didn't take this well and began searching for alternative treatments, refusing to give up hope. He reached out to his high-profile connections, asking them to keep their ears to the ground and report back to him if they heard of any successful unorthodox treatments.

With her birthday coming up, Lily asked to take the trip they'd been in the early stages of planning before her illness. She still hadn't told her parents about the cancer and had been waiting to tell them in person since a phone call didn't seem like an appropriate way to break the news. The severity of the situation felt like it warranted a face-to-face talk, which Austin agreed with. After a stop in Cleveland, they would continue on to Maine like they'd talked about so she could see their lighthouse again and spend the 4th of July with Austin's family. After all, she had promised little Annabelle that she would be back. Austin was reluctant to agree given how sick she was and felt it would be best if she stayed home resting, but when Lily worded it as her final wish, he couldn't say no and chartered the private jet.

"Just to be clear, this is *not* your final wish," he told her. "You're going to have many more, and I'm going to try my best to make them all come true."

"Austin… look at me," she replied, gesturing to her frail body. "You have to know I don't have much time left. I want to make as many memories with you as I can before I go."

"You're not going anywhere," he said, fighting back his emotions. She knew he hated when she talked like this, but one of them had to be realistic. She was still taking the oral medications she'd been prescribed, but that was mostly to manage a few of her symptoms, and they were beginning to lose their efficacy. The chemotherapy was a bust, and if anything, it stole a good chunk of whatever time she had left. She regretted having agreed to the treatments, but it was too late now, and all she could do was try to make the most of each passing minute.

She made sure to pack her yarn and knitting needles so she could work on her blanket in-flight and brought a few new books with her as well. She would have loved to have passed the time by riding Austin, but he'd shown almost no interest in her sexually since learning of her condition. Although he'd never admit it, she knew he saw her as frail and sickly, which she was, and he expressed concern over accidentally hurting her if he got too carried away. She understood that since he'd been known to manhandle her in the bedroom—something she always loved—but she also knew that a dying woman wasn't exactly a turn-on. If the roles were reversed, she didn't think she'd be able to have sex with somebody who was terminally-ill, either.

They landed in Cleveland on a Saturday afternoon, four days before Lily's June 28th birthday. They'd planned their arrival knowing her parents typically had weekends off, which would give them time to process Lily's diagnosis before returning to work, and it would also give Lily a few days to rest and recover so they could celebrate her birthday properly. Her parents were excited about the visit since they hadn't seen their daughter in over a year, and they were looking forward to finally meeting Austin as well. They already adored him for defending her the way he had, both having seen the footage of him leveling Ryan with just one punch.

Austin had a driver waiting for them who drove them through the city, with Lily reminiscing along the way.

"That's where I fell off the monkey bars and broke my hand," she recalled as they drove by her old elementary school. "There's the street my best friend used to live on. We haven't talked in years." Passing a grocery store, she smiled wide and nudged Austin, who seemed to genuinely love hearing her stories. "That's the first place I ever worked. I bagged groceries and helped stock the shelves. It sucked."

Lily called her parents to let them know they were just minutes away, and when they pulled up to the small home, both her mother and father were waiting outside. They both smiled wide when the chauffeur opened the rear door and helped Lily out of the car, but their smiles quickly faded once they got a better look at her. They approached to greet her, but before they could speak, Lily stopped them to introduce Austin. When he stepped out of the car dressed in a blue polo shirt tucked into pressed dress slacks, his parents looked a bit taken aback by his size.

"Mom, dad, I'd like you to officially meet Austin Matson," Lily beamed. "Austin, this is my father, Darnell, and this is my mother, Tymeka."

"It's a pleasure to meet the both of you," Austin smiled, shaking their hands. "I've heard so much! All good things, of course."

"And it's a pleasure to meet you as well," Darnell replied, yet his eyes remained locked on Lily.

"Yes, a pleasure," Tymeka said. Like her husband, she hadn't been able to take her eyes off of Lily, and her face was painted with concern.

"Gee, do I really look that bad?" Lily joked, hoping an injection of levity would lighten the mood. She knew she didn't look her best, but she didn't think her condition was that obvious. By the look her parents shot each other after seeing her, it was clear that she'd thought wrong. Like she'd been doing, she'd pinned her hair up and concealed it with a head wrap to hide how thin it was, and although it had started to grow back, she wasn't ready to be seen with it down yet. She was much thinner than when they'd seen her last, and she was sure her face looked gaunt and worn.

"Lilian…" her mother began, but she stopped herself, realizing the conversation would best be had inside. The chauffeur helped Austin with their luggage, who refused to let Lily carry anything other than her light handbag filled mostly with yarn. After handing the driver a wad of cash, the man thanked Austin and left, promising to return in a hurry should Austin need his service again.

Lily could tell her parents were itching to ask about her health, but didn't want to be bad hosts. They gave Austin a tour of their modest one-story home, and Austin was sure to compliment it with sincerity along the way, commenting on how cozy it was and how much he loved their choice of decor. He got a kick out of seeing Lily's old bedroom, which looked just as she'd left it, and he playfully ribbed her for the *Backstreet Boys* poster taped to her closet door.

"Shut up. I put that up when I was, like, five," Lily laughed.

"And you kept it up… why?" Austin chuckled.

The tour finished in the living room, where Lily's parents invited them to take a seat. Austin sat by her side on the sofa, and her parents took the two armchairs across from them. After a bit of small talk, it was finally time to address the elephant in the room. Sensing her parents didn't know how to ask, Lily approached the situation head on.

"I can tell you're worried about me," she began. "I know I've looked better."

"Lilian… what's going on?" her mother nervously asked, and Lily could tell she was bracing herself for bad news.

"I'm sick," Lily answered bluntly. "When I moved out, I didn't do a good job keeping up with my follow-up exams. You know, for that tumor I had removed? I was just so distracted with the Ryan situation, and then moving into my own place and barely affording rent. I was working so much, I just kept putting it off, and, well… I'm sick."

Her father cleared his throat and leaned forward in his chair. "Lilian, what are you saying?"

Austin squeezed Lily's leg in silent support.

"I have cancer," Lily sighed. "And it's bad. Really bad."

"Oh, God! Oh, God!" her mother shrieked. She covered her mouth in shock and Lily could see her hands shaking. "Lilian… how bad is it?"

"I'm terminal," Lily said. Seeing her mother's tears brought tears of her own. She sniffled and continued, "It spread to my bones. It spread everywhere. The chemo didn't work."

"Oh, Lilian," her father said with tears in his eyes as well.

Her parents rushed to her side, and Austin moved so they could sit next to her. They wrapped their arms around her and sobbed together, holding her tightly as they wept. Austin took her father's armchair and sat silently while they worked through the pain.

"This can't be right. Not you. Not my little girl. Not my beautiful little girl," her mother cried.

"Sweetie, did you get a second opinion?" her father asked. "Mistakes are made all the time. There's a chance—"

"I've seen five oncologists, Dad," Lily told him, trembling. "I've lost track of how many tests I've taken. They all say the same thing."

Her father looked at Austin pleadingly. "Is there anything you can do? Please. I can't lose my baby girl."

"I'm doing everything in my power," Austin finally spoke. "I've been hoping to find some sort of alternative treatment. There has to be something out there. Some way to cure this. I'm not giving up." A tear fell down his cheek. "She's the love of my life. I can't lose her. I just can't."

Many tears were shed in the hours that followed, with Lily's news casting a dark cloud over their visit. They attempted to eat dinner together, but none of them had much of an appetite given the circumstances, and conversation was sparse. Her parents were so thoroughly gutted by the news that they'd break into fits of tears, and Lily would try to console them the best she could. She'd come to terms with her illness, she told them, and had accepted her fate. It wouldn't be easy, but in time, they would have to accept it, too.

Lily and Austin spent the night in Lily's old bedroom and joined her parents for breakfast the following morning. She could tell they hadn't slept well, and the mood in the house remained dour. Needing an escape from the gloom, Lily borrowed her dad's car to show Austin around Cleveland, and her health held up well enough for them to visit both the *Museum of Natural History* and the *Rock and Roll Hall of Fame* before she needed to rest. Despite how somber they'd grown, Lily assured Austin that her parents liked him a lot and felt like she was in safe hands with him.

When her birthday came, Austin insisted on treating everyone to dinner in style by having a limousine drive them to *Dante*, one of Cleveland's finest restaurants. Lily wasn't thrilled by the idea but agreed to go, knowing her parents may never get a chance to dine in a restaurant of this caliber again. She'd packed her red Versace dress in hopes of stunning her parents with its beauty, and she burst into tears when she realized she'd lost too much weight for it to fit properly. It no longer sat snugly against her curves, but hung loosely around her instead, making her look waifish and ill. If she was trying to conceal her sickness, the dress had the opposite effect. Heartbroken, she settled for dress slacks and the sweater Austin's mother had knitted for her, which hid how frail she'd become.

Lily's parents dressed in the nicest clothes they owned and were overjoyed to ride in a stretch limousine for the first time. She loved watching their reaction as they looked around the interior in awe, commenting on its amenities. Lily realized it was the first time she'd seen them genuinely smile since learning of her condition, and for that alone, she had to thank Austin. The restaurant was spectacular and the food divine, but she could only get half of her meal down before hurrying to the bathroom to vomit, barely making it in time. She still hadn't recovered from the chemotherapy that had ravaged her entire body inside and out, and she knew she'd never recover entirely.

Returning to their table, she tried to mask her embarrassment and apologized for rushing away like she had. Austin leaned in to quietly ask if she was okay, or if they should wrap things up and head back to the house. Exhausted and nauseous, she needed to lie down, but in fear of spoiling the evening, she put on her best smile and assured him she was fine. She dug deep and powered through, eager for the bill to come so they could leave, and she breathed a sigh of relief when their server finally handed it to Austin. Her parents expressed their sincerest gratitude, thanking Austin for a wonderful night out, and Lily was sure to thank him as well. When they stood to leave, Lily followed suit only to be hit with a sudden lightheadedness that sent her falling into the table, toppling it to the floor and shattering the dishes so loudly that everyone in the restaurant turned to identify the cause of the commotion. Austin caught Lily before she fell to the floor along with the table, and she fainted in his arms, albeit momentarily. She was alert again within seconds, and well aware that everyone in the establishment was now looking at her. Embarrassed, she hurried out of the restaurant and into the waiting limousine outside where she was met by her parents a moment later.

"There, there," her mother consoled her, rubbing Lily's back as she sobbed.

"Did I ruin the night?" Lily asked through her tears.

"Of course not," her father assured her. "But it's time to get you home and in bed."

Austin joined them in the limousine and Lily cringed at how much money he must have dropped to cover the damage she'd caused.

"I'm sorry, baby," she told him, wiping her eyes.

"Nothing to be sorry about," Austin smiled. In jest, he added, "They tell me it happens all the time. A few times a day, actually."

His attempt at downplaying the incident worked. Lily chuckled, as did her parents, and the chauffeur drove them home so she could rest. Weak and worn, she was in bed within minutes of walking through the door with Austin crawling into bed next to her to once again search for a credible treatment. He truly believed a cure existed, and that it was a matter of finding it before the clock ran out. Lily's spill at the restaurant seemed to light a fire under him again, and he stayed up half the night on his laptop, scouring the internet for leads. His searches always ended in frustration as they only turned up quacks and charlatans claiming cures with no basis in actual science. It was always herbs, oils, crystals, or some other nonsense with no real clinical trials or peer-reviewed studies, and with no documented cases of successful treatment.

They spent their remaining time in Cleveland exploring more of the city when Lily's health allowed it. Her pain had increased, and to counter it, she'd been taking more pain medication than she was comfortable with. She preferred to do most of their sight-seeing during the day when her parents were working, and from the safety of the chauffeured town car in fear of another embarrassing incident like she'd had at the restaurant. Their evenings were spent with her parents, either in the living room talking or huddled around the kitchen table playing board games. When it was time for them to move on to Maine, their goodbye was long and emotional. As much as her parents wanted her to stay with them in Cleveland, they knew Austin could provide her the end of life care she was going to need. They simply didn't have the resources to accommodate the comfort and assistance she'd require, which broke their hearts, and they were deeply touched when Austin offered to move them into the estate so they could be by Lily's side. Their life was firmly planted in Cleveland, however, and they reminded him that they still had a house to finish paying off. As much as they would have loved to stay in his mansion to care for their ailing daughter, it simply wasn't a realistic plan. Austin understood and promised to fly them to Tucson whenever they wanted before stepping aside to let them shower Lily with more love. The moment was hard on both Lily and her parents, whose tears fell freely knowing it could be the last time they ever saw each other.

"Thank you for how well you've treated our daughter," Darnell told Austin as they lingered by the front door. "You're a good man, Austin Matson."

Austin shook his hand and accepted a warm embrace from Tymeka as she expressed her gratitude as well.

"This is just goodbye for now," Austin stressed. "You'll see us again. I'm not giving up. There's a cure out there and I'm going to find it."

On the jet to Maine, Austin searched for unorthodox treatments, jotting down the names of any doctor or researcher with even an ounce of believability. Lily spent the flight working on her blanket again, excited to show Austin's mother the progress she'd made. When they touched down in Bangor, they picked up the rental car Austin had reserved and began the drive down the coast to his parents' house. With the weather being so beautiful, they took their time to enjoy the scenery, even stopping for ice cream along the way, which was one of the few things Lily could keep down.

Austin's parents greeted them just as they had six months prior, waving from the front porch as Amos excitedly ran circles around them with his tail wagging. They met his parents on the porch and dropped their luggage to say a proper hello as Amos continued to lose his canine mind, slobbering and whining in excitement. While Austin took a knee to give the dog the attention he wanted, Pam welcomed Lily back with a warm hug, and Mark surprised her with a hug as well. Austin had told his parents about Lily's condition, so they knew what to expect, and she appreciated that they didn't treat her any differently than they had before. She didn't want to be looked at with pity, or to have exceptions made because she was sick.

They gathered in the living room to catch up, and Lily couldn't wait to show Austin's mother how far her knitting had progressed. Pam was quite taken with the blanket Lily had been working on, which she hoped to finish during their week-long visit. Austin filled his parents in on the Atari deal and his acquisition of the Crolles manufacturing plant, offering details the media hadn't shared, and was in the middle of recounting their wonderful time in Paris when Amos began to bark, alerting them to more visitors. Moments later, they heard the front door fly open, followed by, *"Auntie Lily! Auntie Lily!"*

Annabelle burst into the room and leapt onto Lily's lap, overjoyed that her new aunt had returned as promised. Austin winced, worried his niece might have hurt Lily in her excitement, but Lily saw his concern and mouthed that she was okay. Jason and the rest of his family entered seconds later, and Lily gently set Annabelle down so she could stand to greet them with a hug. Now that Annabelle had seen Lily on her feet, she realized that something wasn't quite right. She cocked her head as she curiously looked Lily over for a moment.

"You got skinny," she said.

"I did," Lily agreed, feeling the sudden tension in the room. "Your uncle has to fatten me up again."

"Are you sick?" Annabelle asked bluntly.

"Annabelle!" Holly barked, looking at her daughter sternly. "Don't be rude!"

"It's okay," Lily laughed. She knew Austin had told Jason and Holly about her condition and had left it up to them to tell the kids. Fearing they were too young to understand, they decided against telling them, choosing to see how the situation played out. "Yes, sweetie, I'm sick."

Annabelle looked concerned. "You're going to get better, though… right?"

Austin answered for her. "She sure is!"

Given the perfect weather, Annabelle invited Lily outside for a game of tag with Ethan. Austin didn't think it was a good idea, and Lily had her reservations as well, but she didn't want to disappoint the kids. Perhaps more than anything, she just wanted to feel normal again. Austin accompanied her outside to watch the fun, but she knew he really wanted to keep an eye on her. The children's laughter and smiles kept her going for the first few minutes, but she had to stop when she began to feel lightheaded. The last thing she wanted was to pass out in front of the kids, leaving them upset and traumatized. Thinking quickly, she asked them for a game of hide and seek instead, knowing it was more her pace. The kids were completely on board with it, squealing in excitement as they scurried off to hide.

"How are you holding up?" Austin quietly asked, leaning over the railing of the front porch.

Lily took a break from her countdown to assure him she was fine, and when the countdown was complete, it was time to find the kids.

"Ready or not, here I come!"

Jason and his family stayed until it was time to put the kids to bed. Annabelle didn't want to leave and asked if she could spend the night, which Lily found exceptionally sweet. She reminded Austin's adorable little niece that she was sick and needed to rest, but promised her a sleepover soon. Needing to rest wasn't an excuse as she really was exhausted and had to lie down. Retiring to the guest lodging, she seductively crawled into bed wearing only the silk robe Austin had given her, hoping it might elicit some sort of sexual response from him. Since ending the chemotherapy treatments, her sex drive had begun to return, but it typically came in short bursts every few days. She was experiencing one of those bursts now, but Austin wasn't taking the bait. She understood, but still couldn't help but feel unattractive. Only a few weeks prior, he couldn't keep his hands off of her, and now, he rarely even touched her.

"You don't find me attractive anymore," she sighed. "I get it."

"Where did that come from?" Austin asked, taken aback by her words.

"You haven't touched me in so long, baby. I just miss that intimate connection, that's all. You used to make me feel so sexy."

"I'm sorry," Austin said. "I still find you extremely attractive, and you're every bit as sexy now as when I first laid eyes on you."

"Then make love to me. I just want to feel you again. Please. Just for tonight, let's pretend things are like they used to be."

"I'm afraid of hurting you…"

"I'm not a porcelain doll, Austin. You're not going to break me."

"Are you sure?" he asked.

"Please. I need you."

For the first time since learning of her condition, Austin moved on her. It was slow and gentle this time, and with his steel-blue eyes locked onto hers, he quietly told her how beautiful she was. Hearing that while feeling him inside of her was just what she'd needed, and when they'd both had their fill, she fell into a deep sleep wrapped in his arms.

They spent the next two days seeing more of the state and doing things winter hadn't allowed on their first visit. They were both eager to return to their lighthouse, but wanted to save that for last as a sort of romantic farewell. Lily had asked to walk on a beach and Austin hadn't disappointed, taking her to Sand Beach in Bar Harbor; one of the state's ritzier cities and a summer tourist destination. Her frail body left her too self-conscious to wear a bathing suit, which was fine since she had no intention of swimming anyhow. Really, she just wanted to feel the sand on her feet and to collect a few seashells to display in her office. Austin found amusement in how particular she was, poring over each shell for just the right one, and she pocketed a few small stones as well, each varying in color and smoothed over by the ocean. She kicked off her sandals and hiked her sundress up to get her feet wet, splashing around in the shallow water while Austin filmed it for posterity, smiling wide as he watched her play. She noticed he'd been taking far more photos and videos this time around, and she had to wonder if he'd finally accepted her fate, capturing these moments, knowing they would be some of her last.

Austin's parents hosted a big cookout for the 4th of July, and the day couldn't have gone any better. Jason and his family showed up again, and Austin's eldest brother, Steven, made the drive to be there as well. As Austin's dad manned the grill, Ethan and Annabelle challenged Lily to another game of hide and seek, and Austin joined in on the excitement. Stuffed with burgers and hot dogs, the entire family drove to their larger neighboring city to watch the fireworks there, since Austin's hometown was too small to host its own fireworks show. The evening was incredible, and the kids watched the explosions with wide eyes while enjoying the ice cream Uncle Austin had treated them to. When the show wrapped up, Jason and Holly thought it best they leave from there since it was already past the kids' bedtimes, and facing an hour drive, Steven needed to get on the road as well. Since Austin and Lily were flying back to Tucson the following evening and wouldn't have time to see them again before they left, they knew the time had come to say their goodbyes. Lily knew the odds of seeing these wonderful people again weren't good, and she couldn't hold back her tears as they exchanged hugs.

"We're really having a sleepover next time, right?" Annebelle asked, her arms wrapped around Lily tightly.

"I'd love that," Lily said, kneeling down with tears streaming down her cheeks. Ethan and Annabelle couldn't quite understand why Lily had become so emotional, but the rest of the family knew why, and Lily sensed the situation was hard on them as well. Seeing how upset Lily was, Holly gave her another hug.

"You'll be in our prayers," she told Lily quietly. "Don't give up hope. We all love you."

Steven took Holly's place with a hug of his own, and she sensed he'd made a conscious effort to be gentle. Easily the most awkward of the brothers, Lily could tell he didn't quite know what to say. "You make my brother happy, and I love you for that. Stay strong and get better."

"Thank you," Lily sniffled, and wiped her damp eyes.

As she watched them leave, she was stuck with an overwhelming sadness, knowing these incredible people would just be fleeting characters in her short life. Austin felt her sadness and wrapped her in his arms, kissing her forehead softly.

"Let's go get some sleep, baby."

That was easier said than done, as she spent another restless night in silent contemplation. She thought she'd accepted her fate and had come to terms with it, but being in the company of such a warm, loving family who had been so welcoming left her yearning for a different fate; one where she could have that sleepover with Annabelle and grow old with Austin by her side. She'd been trying hard not to feel sorry for herself, but lying in a dark room in the middle of the night with nothing but her thoughts, it was hard to keep the bitterness at bay. She wanted to live, and the emotional pain of knowing she couldn't escape her fate hurt worse than the physical pain of her sickness.

She woke the following morning feeling awful, but since it was their final day in Maine and they'd reserved it for a visit to their lighthouse, she had no choice but to tough it out. There was no way she was going to miss out on seeing the lighthouse they'd claimed as theirs, especially in the summer. The lighthouse wasn't all that was on their agenda, as Austin thought Lily would enjoy the small shops of downtown Camden, which was another hot spot for summer tourists. They'd visited the coastal city of Camden on their first trip, but given the bitter cold, they hadn't explored much of it and many of the shops had been closed for the season anyhow. By the time they arrived, Lily was feeling much better thanks to the double dose of pain medication she'd taken. Austin wasn't kidding about the tourists, and given the beauty of the posh little city, she understood the attraction. By noon, Lily was worried that if they didn't make it to their lighthouse soon, she wouldn't have the energy to walk the mile it took to reach it, let alone make the walk back. To Austin's credit, she did enjoy Camden's array of unique shops, and she left with plenty of souvenirs, as well as photos of the city's gorgeous harbor. Recalling how much she loved their lunch on their first visit, Austin suggested they try another one of Camden's fine seafood restaurants, but Lily was too afraid of embarrassing herself again and asked that they go somewhere cheaper. The idea of spending one hundred dollars on a meal just for it to come back up didn't sit right with her, and she didn't have much of an appetite anyhow. They settled on a fast-food joint on the way to the lighthouse, and Lily was able to keep down what little her body allowed her to eat.

They arrived to find the Rockland Breakwater packed with tourists and locals, which made sense given the weather. Eighty-five degrees and sunny with a light sea breeze, it was the perfect day to walk the jetty and several fishermen could be seen casting their lures off of the rocky pathway. Lily smiled wide at the sight of the lighthouse and was eager to see if their carved initials were still visible, but noticing how worn she looked, Austin thought it best they admire the lighthouse from a distance rather than traversing the granite walkway. Lily wasn't having that and insisted she was capable of making the trek as long as they moved slowly, reminding Austin that they could simply turn around if she started feeling ill. She could tell Austin had his doubts, but knowing she had her heart set on seeing the lighthouse up close, he wasn't going to say no. Digging through her purse, she found her pain pills and took two more in hopes they'd help her aching body with the walk ahead.

Braving the cut granite rocks, they made their way toward the lighthouse one step at a time, with Austin keeping a close eye on Lily, ready to catch her should she fall. As people hurried by them, Lily felt badly for how slowly she was moving and tried to pick up the pace only to end up overexerting herself. She stopped to rest for a moment as Austin looked at her with concern.

"Baby, maybe we should head back. I'm worried about you."

"I'm fine," she said, catching her breath. "We're over halfway there. I can make it. I want to see it in the summer. I've been waiting months for this."

"This is my fault," Austin groaned. "We shouldn't have wasted energy walking around Camden. We should have just come straight here."

"Shush. I just need a second to recharge."

"Sweetie, I—"

"Please," she interrupted. "Let me finish this. I want to see our lighthouse. I don't know how much longer I have. This could be my only chance."

"Don't talk like that," Austin said.

"I'm sorry, but we have to face reality," Lily replied. "I'm getting worse, Austin. The painkillers are the only thing keeping me going most days. My other medication is useless now."

"I didn't know that. I wish you'd told me this sooner," Austin said with an exasperated sigh.

"I'm sorry. I didn't mean to make you angry."

"I'm not angry, I'm upset," he clarified. "There's a difference."

"Please," Lily said, taking his hand. "Don't be upset. This is our day to see our lighthouse," she paused and looked at the historic monument ahead of them with a smile, "so let's go see our lighthouse."

"How about I give you a piggyback ride?" Austin suggested.

"You've got to be kidding me," she chuckled, knowing her pride would never allow such a thing. "I can make it. Please. This is important to me."

Austin looked her over before glancing at the lighthouse, and she could tell he was gauging both her condition and the probability of her making the rest of the walk.

"Okay," he shrugged in defeat. "Let's go see our lighthouse."

Her pace slowed considerably as the little strength she had left faded, and she held Austin's arm tightly as they inched their way forward. They were almost there when Lily's body gave out entirely. She began to collapse, but Austin caught her and scooped her into his arms.

"I'm sorry…" she said weakly. "I really thought I could make it. I wanted… I wanted to see…"

"It's okay," Austin said. "We need to get you in bed. Let's go."

He turned to carry her back down the breakwater, but she faintly pleaded with him to stop. "No. Baby, no. We're so close. Please… please, just let me just see it. Let me… see it… this is my last chance…"

She could feel his conflict as he stood holding her in his arms.

"I'm probably going to regret this," he grumbled, and hurried toward the lighthouse. She could feel his strength as he effortlessly carried her, ignoring the stares from concerned onlookers. Given Austin's speed and power, they reached the lighthouse quickly, and he gently sat her down on one of the benches on the observation deck.

"We made it," Lily smiled.

Several people approached to ask if she was okay, to which Lily thanked them for their concern and assured them that she'd be fine after a short rest. They didn't look convinced, but seeing she was being cared for by Austin, they left the situation alone. Austin took a seat by her side and brushed her cheek gently.

"How are you holding up?" he asked.

"I've been better," she replied. She rested her head on his shoulder and looked up at the lighthouse in front of them, noting the seagulls flying overhead. "Thank you for this."

It took a few minutes for her to recharge enough to stand, and it still took Austin's help to get her on her feet. Holding onto his arm for stability, she slowly led them to the side of the lighthouse to look for the initials they'd carved into it months earlier. It didn't take her long to find them, as they were still quite visible, and she smiled wide at the sight of them. The moment was bittersweet, however, and her smile faded as she realized this was the last time she'd see the crude lettering enclosed in a heart. She fought back tears but lost the battle, feeling them roll down her cheeks as her lamentations got the better of her.

"What a perfect day that was," she said, running her fingers over their initials. "Cold, but perfect. I'd give anything to feel that alive again. I'm… I'm sorry I got sick."

"Hey, now," he replied softly, and wiped her tears away with his thumb. "There's nothing to be sorry about."

"Do you ever regret meeting me?" she asked bluntly.

"What? Never," he answered, shocked by her question. "You've made me so happy. The best memories of my life have been with you."

"I wish we could make more," she sighed.

"Stop. You know I hate it when you talk like that."

"I hope I can take these memories with me when I go." Realizing she was thinking aloud more than she was addressing him, Austin stood silently and let her thoughts pour out while he listened. "Maybe we can meet again—" she paused as she looked at the world around them, "after all of this. In our next life, if there is one. I mean, this can't be it, can it?"

"I don't know," Austin shrugged. "I hope not."

"If I do meet God, I'll be sure to put in a good word for you," she smirked.

Austin cleared his throat and his mood turned solemn. "Lilian Ward, I know I've told you this before, but I've been in love with you since the second I laid eyes on you. I can't imagine spending my life with anybody else. You're it for me. Those eyes of yours still make me melt, and I'm still excited every morning I wake up next to you."

He reached into his pocket for something, but before he could pull it out, a sudden dizzy spell took Lily down before either of them had a chance to react. Her fall wasn't graceful, nor did she have time to brace herself for the impact, and her head hit the metal railing surrounding the lighthouse with such force that it knocked her out cold. Slipping in and out of consciousness, she felt Austin pick her up and could hear him frantically calling her name, but everything felt as if it were happening in some sort of muddled dream state. Looking up at the sky while fading in and out, she was loosely aware of how fast he was moving as he carried her, yelling at people to get out of the way as he hurried back down the breakwater with her in his arms.

"Move! Move! It's an emergency!" she heard him cry. She could smell the salt water and hear the waves gently crashing against the jetty as he navigated the rocky pathway as quickly as he could.

"I see it…" she breathed in his arms. "I see it. The lighthouse. It's beautiful. I see it…"

"No!" he yelled pleadingly. *"We're not doing that! It's not your time yet! You stay with me, Lilian! You stay with me!"*

Only, Lily was no longer there in his arms, being rushed down the granite breakwater, she was back in her grandmother's hospice room, smiling at her grandmother as her grandmother smiled back.

"Come with me, Lily," her grandmother's welcoming voice said. "Let's go see a lighthouse. Let's go see it together. It's time."

With that, everything faded to black.

Chapter Eleven

"Am I dead?" she asked weakly, slowly opening her eyes.

"Oh, thank God," Austin sobbed, squeezing her hand before covering it with kisses.

"Where am I?" she croaked, her mouth so dry she could barely talk.

Austin helped her take a sip of water. "You're at Pen Bay Hospital. I got you here as fast as I could. Baby, you had me so scared. I thought I lost you."

"I passed out?"

"You did. And you hit your head, but you got lucky and there's no concussion."

"I'm so sorry," Lily said. "I really did think I could make it."

"Shh…" Austin gently quieted her. "At least we got to see our lighthouse, right?"

"We did," she smiled. "We did. I'm so glad we did."

A nurse interrupted to check Lily's vitals and ask how she was feeling. After noting that Lily's blood pressure had increased and that she seemed to be doing better, she left the two alone again to pick up where they'd left off.

Lily felt the bump on the back of her head and noticed that her head wrap was missing. She hated Austin seeing her without it and couldn't help but feel embarrassed.

"It fell off when you hit your head," Austin said. "I think it blew into the water. I'm sorry."

"Damn," Lily sighed. "I liked that one."

"You're just as beautiful without it," he smiled.

There was a moment of silence as Lily struggled to recall the events leading up to her fall.

"You were saying such sweet things to me. You reached into your pocket for something," she recalled.

"I did," he nodded. Letting go of her hand, he reached into his pocket again and pulled out a white ring box. "I was going to give you this. I was going to ask…"

He stopped and opened the box, presenting Lily with the most exquisite diamond ring she'd ever seen.

"Oh, Austin," she gasped, taking in its beauty.

"I was going to ask if you'd marry me."

"Austin, you can't… I don't… I can't…" she stammered. This was the last thing she'd expected, and it had caught her so completely off guard, she wasn't sure how to respond.

"I love you just as much now as I did the day we met. That love has never changed. It's never wavered. If anything, it's only grown stronger. I know this isn't exactly the most romantic setting," he said, looking around the room, "but I just can't wait any longer. It was all I could do just to wait until the lighthouse."

"Oh, no. You had this beautifully romantic proposal planned, and I completely ruined it," Lily replied, shaking her head in frustration. "I'm so sorry."

"If anything, you made it more memorable," Austin chuckled.

"Austin, this is the sweetest thing ever, but you can't be serious. Why would you want to marry me? You'd be a widow before our first anniversary."

"Because I love you with every fiber of my being, Lilian Ward. Marriage means loving each other through sickness and health. Through the good times and the bad. You're it for me, baby. I will never love another woman like I love you. And if we can't get you better," he continued, cleverly skirting around any mention of death, "I promise you that I will never marry again. You are my wife. You. Nobody else."

"Austin," she began, moved to tears by his words. "I… I don't know what to say…"

"Say you'll marry me. We don't have to have a big ceremony. It can be just the two of us if you'd like."

"All the healthy women in the world, yet you want to marry me…" she said, unsure how to answer.

"That should tell you something," he smiled.

He had a point. He had his choice of women, yet he wanted her knowing she was terminally ill and likely didn't have much time left.

"It tells me you're either crazy or you really do love me," she smiled. While the circumstances were far from ideal, the idea of marrying the man she loved so deeply proved too hard to resist. "Austin Matson, I would be honored to be your wife."

"Yes?" Austin beamed.

"Yes," she repeated, grinning wide.

Austin slipped the ring on her finger and had just leaned in for a kiss when his phone rang from his pocket. He silenced the call but his phone sounded again a moment later, this time with a text message alert.

"Sorry," he grumbled. "I forgot to put it on silent."

Pulling out his phone to mute it, she saw his brow raise curiously as he read the text message he'd received.

"Everything okay?"

"It's an old friend and business associate of mine, Beau Sullivan. He says I need to call him right away. It's about you."

"About me?" Lily asked.

"Yeah, this sounds important. I'm going to give him a call back, if you don't mind."

"Not at all," Lily replied. "He has me curious."

"Me too," Austin said as he dialed his friend, who answered after only two rings. "Hey, buddy. Listen, I'm sorry I missed your call. I'm in the hospital with Lilian. She's not doing too hot." There was a long pause as Austin listened to what his friend had to say. Lily tried to listen in but couldn't quite make out his words. "Yes, definitely," Austin finally spoke. "Can I put you on speaker so she can be a part of this? Okay, great. You're on speaker now."

"Hello, Lily," Beau's voice sounded from Austin's phone. "It's nice to talk to you, although I wish it were under better circumstances."

"Hello," Lily croaked. Hearing how dry she was, Austin helped her with another sip of water.

"I hear you're not feeling so well," Beau began. "I was just telling Austin that I think I found somebody who might be able to help you. His name is Doctor Stanislaw Burzynski, and he runs a clinic in Houston, Texas. Apparently, he's developed a way of treating cancer with an impressive rate of success. He's even cured terminally ill patients."

Skeptical, Austin beat Lily to the question. "If he's so successful, how come we've never heard of him?"

"I'll let him explain that, but trust me, the guy's legit. I wouldn't have reached out if I hadn't done my homework. His treatment works, and it's saved people in Lily's condition."

"Stage four?" Austin asked, making sure Beau knew just what they were dealing with.

"Stage four," Beau confirmed. "The guy's a miracle worker."

"And he's not just some crackpot?" Austin questioned, still dubious.

"He's the real deal, believe me. I just spoke with him directly and he's expecting your call on her personal line."

"I have my doubts, but I trust you," Austin said. "And if it turns out he can help Lily, I'll be sure to bump up your percentage."

Beau laughed. "No need for that, man. I can't imagine what you two are going through. I'd lose my mind if anything happened to Vivian."

"I take it things are going well?"

"We couldn't be happier. We're expecting our second child soon! Enough about that, though. I need you to call this guy right now. I just sent you his number. We'll catch up down the road."

"I appreciate you," Austin smiled. "And congratulations on the baby. Send Vivian my love."

"Will do. I'm wishing you a speedy recovery, Lily!"

"Thank you," Lily replied, this time a bit easier.

"Now call this guy and let me know how it goes. You'll be in my prayers."

Austin ended the call and looked at Lily. "Well?"

"I mean, it's worth a shot…" she muttered. "We might as well hear what the guy has to say."

"My thoughts exactly," Austin agreed, dialing the number Beau had sent him. He kept it on speaker so Lily could join the call.

"Doctor Burzynski speaking," a man greeted in what sounded like a thick Polish accent.

"Good evening, Doctor, this is Austin Matson calling. I believe you spoke with a dear friend of mine, Beau Sullivan."

"Ah, yes! I've been expecting your call," the doctor replied. "Mister Sullivan tells me your girlfriend is in trouble?"

"Fiancée," Austin corrected, shooting Lily a wink. "Her name's Lilian Ward, and she's here with me now. We have you on speaker, if that's okay."

"Yes, yes," the doctor said. "Good evening, Miss Ward."

"Good evening," Lily greeted. "Is it true that you can help me out?"

"Nothing is guaranteed," the doctor told her, "but my clinic might be able to treat you. It's certainly worth a shot, anyhow. If you'd be so kind, could you please tell me when you first experienced symptoms, when you were diagnosed, what treatments you've undergone, and what your current stage is?"

Lily gave him a brief yet thorough rundown of her condition while the doctor took notes, asking for additional information when needed.

"Do you think you can help her?" Austin asked, eager and hopeful.

"I think we have nothing to lose," the doctor answered. "The treatment is non-invasive and comes with minimal risk. It certainly won't make her worse or harm her in any way."

"Can you explain this supposed treatment?" Lily asked, still skeptical of the man's claims.

"Certainly. Here at my clinic, we use what are called 'antineoplastons' to treat all stages and all types of cancer. They're a blend of amino acids and peptides often lacking in cancer patients, you see. We extract peptides from healthy donors and administer them to those with cancer. It's a much more effective and far safer treatment than traditional radiation or chemotherapy, which are carcinogenic themselves. Fighting cancer with carcinogens has always seemed absurd to me. Granted, those treatments have their uses, but they should still be used sparingly and in conjunction with antineoplastons."

"And you've had success with this?" Lily questioned, still on the fence about the man's legitimacy.

"Remarkable success!" the doctor replied with pride in his voice. "I've been treating patients using this method for over fifty years now. Many people are alive because of it."

"I don't know," Lily sighed. "It seems like this would be major news."

The doctor laughed. "Trust me, it's made the headlines more times than I can count, but that was a bit before your time. News of my research and treatment have died down in recent years. I've been battling the Texas Medical Board and the FDA for over four decades now. There's big money in current cancer treatments, so they've been doing their best to silence me or paint me as some lunatic. Just search my name on the internet and you'll see for yourself. If it makes you more comfortable, I'll send you videos of my patients testifying before Congress to the validity of my work. I'll also send you dozens of other testimonials."

"I'd like that, thank you," Lily said. "And you've cured people with stage four cancer?"

"I have," the doctor replied. "If you trust me with your email address, I'll send you a more detailed explanation of my treatment, along with patient testimonials and information on my clinic here in Houston. You can review everything and decide if you'd like to proceed. I must say, however, that given your condition, I believe it's best if we start your treatment right away."

"How quickly can you get us all of that information?" Austin asked.

"I can send it over right away," the doctor replied.

Lily gave the doctor her email address, and they stayed on the phone with him until it arrived in her inbox. Confirming she'd received it, she asked Doctor Burzynski if she could have a bit of time to review everything so she could make a proper decision, promising to call him back by the end of the day. He assured her that was fine, and before ending the call, he stressed the importance of starting the treatment as soon as possible.

Lily forwarded the email to Austin so he could review it as well, and side by side, they digested the information the doctor had sent. Austin understood the science better than her, albeit marginally, and from his limited grasp of it, he found it valid. It was the videos of his patients' emotionally-charged testimonies before Congress that sold them on the treatment. An internet search revealed that the doctor hadn't been exaggerating, and that his controversial treatment had been major news in decades past. A heavy smear campaign had been launched against him, painting him as a charlatan; a snake oil salesman whose research hadn't been proven, and who had never cured a single person of any ailment. The Texas Medical Board and the FDA had fought hard to shut him down, even threatening him with imprisonment, but thanks to his persistence and the outcry from those he'd successfully treated, they finally had no choice but to leave him be. The smear campaign was ongoing, however, and his work continued to be buried for the threat it posed to the enormous industry that had grown out of traditional cancer treatments.

"I mean, even if the guy is a quack, what does it hurt to try?" Austin shrugged, having considered the material Doctor Burzynski had sent as well as their own internet searches. "It looks like the treatment won't make you worse. I feel like it's worth a shot."

"I can't believe I'm saying this, but I think I agree with you," Lily said. "The guy might be nuts, or he might be brilliant."

"Or both," Austin smiled.

Lily looked at the beautiful ring on her finger and found the peace she'd made with dying was gone, having been replaced with a burning desire to live. If she wanted a future with this incredible man, she had to fight for it, and she was willing to do whatever it took.

"I'm in," she nodded. "Let's do it."

"There's my girl," Austin said, grinning wide. "How's your head feeling?"

"It hurts, but I'll be okay."

He called Doctor Burzynski back, who insisted he meet with them as soon as possible, and since Austin already had his private jet on standby, he asked if the next day would work. The doctor was thrilled by this and agreed to meet with them at 10:00 am the following morning, which gave them time to grab their luggage, make the flight, and get a hotel room. Of course, the hospital wasn't happy about this since they wanted to keep Lily overnight for observation, but after laying on his charm, they agreed to release her under Austin's care.

On the way to his parents' house, Austin arranged the new flight plan with his pilot, offering him a hefty amount of money for the last-minute change. With their flight to Houston secured, they gathered their luggage as quickly as possible and Austin gave his parents a brief rundown of what was happening.

"There's a clinic in Houston that might be able to help Lily, but we have to leave right now. There's no guarantee it will work, but we have to take the chance," Austin hurriedly told them, carrying their luggage to the front door. "Oh, and I asked Lily to marry me. She said yes."

Lily showed his parents the ring, who stood trying to process the sudden, unexpected news.

"Congratulations," his mother said, looking a bit confused and troubled. She gave Lily a hug and looked at Austin with concern that she kept to herself, giving him a congratulatory hug as well. Lily sensed she would have cautioned him against marrying a terminally ill woman had she not been in the room, and she wouldn't have blamed her since it did seem utterly insane.

His father also offered his congratulations, shaking Austin's hand before embracing Lily with a smile. "We already feel like you're a part of the family, but I'm glad he's making it official."

Knowing it could be the last time she ever saw them, Lily used the opportunity to thank them for their hospitality and for always making her feel so welcome. She gave them both another emotional hug, expressing what a blessing it was to have met such remarkable people.

"I'm sorry to rush out the door like this, but we have a flight to catch," Austin told his parents. "I'll keep you updated on everything."

On the drive to Bangor International Airport, Austin phoned Winston to fill him in on their change of plans, asking him to man the fort a bit longer while they sought treatment for Lily in Houston.

Winston, who had been heartbroken over Lily's diagnosis, had remained hopeful for a cure and agreed the trip to Houston was worth the gamble. He wished them a safe journey and told Lily that she would continue to be at the forefront of his prayers.

Still recovering from her fall, Lily spent the majority of the flight quietly resting next to Austin and drifting in and out of sleep. Austin held her hand and would occasionally squeeze it to make sure she was still with him, and she'd squeeze back, letting him know that she was okay. It was the middle of the night by the time they arrived in Houston, and after renting a car, Austin booked them a room at the closest hotel they could find. It wasn't the nicest place since their options had been limited at almost three in the morning, and Lily could tell Austin wasn't impressed by the room, but she had no complaints and was just happy to have a bed to curl up in. He promised to find them better accommodations after their meeting with Doctor Burzynski, and with how long he'd been awake, he was out within minutes of crawling into bed.

They awoke with plenty of time to shower up and grab a bite to eat before heading to the Burzynski Clinic. Lily could tell Austin was still exhausted, and she felt bad for robbing him of his sleep. He'd been so worried about her that he hadn't slept on the flight and had only managed to get a few hours in the hotel before their alarms went off. With how important their upcoming meeting was, they played it safe by each setting an alarm to make sure they weren't late. They arrived fifteen minutes early as planned, and before making their way inside, they both agreed to remain on high alert, looking for any warning signs that might hint at some sort of deception. Doctor Burzynski surely knew he was dealing with a man of enormous wealth, and if he was a crook, he might play on their emotional vulnerability to sell them a bogus treatment just to line his pockets.

They were surprised to find the doctor waiting for them inside, and he greeted them both with a handshake and a genuine smile. Lily liked him right away, noting his kind, honest eyes, but tried to keep her guard up, knowing all good con men are likeable at first. She could tell Austin liked him as well, but was also trying to remain skeptical. Their doubts quickly vanished as Doctor Burzynski gave them a tour of his impressive clinic, which was much larger than they'd expected, and even introduced them to a few of his patients who were currently in remission thanks to his unique antineoplaston treatment. Before the tour even finished, Lily and Austin had silently agreed that this was their man. Making their way into Doctor Burzynski's office, he invited them to take a seat to discuss Lily's current health and the methods he'd be using to treat her. He did a wonderful job explaining the science behind the treatment using layman's terms they could both understand.

"Critics will tell you there's not enough scientific evidence that antineoplaston treatment works," the doctor told them in his heavy Polish accent. He stood and moved to the large filing cabinet behind his desk, opening the drawers to give them a glimpse of the files inside. "But these patients will tell you otherwise."

"Those are all the people you've cured?" Lily asked.

"Yes," the doctor nodded, "using either antineoplastons or a combination of antineoplastons and traditional medicine. Some of today's cancer treatments are quite effective and can work alongside the antineoplaston treatment for a higher success rate."

Austin looked at Lily, and they flashed each other a smile.

"We're sold," Austin said. "When can we get started?"

"I'd like to treat Lily using antineoplastons along with current medications, and I'd like to begin her treatment today."

"Wow… that's… that's wonderful!" Lily burst, grinning wide.

"Please, before we begin and before you get too excited, it's important to know that this is no miracle," the doctor began, specifically addressing Lily. "It's simply an alternative treatment that's had its successes and failures. This cabinet here?" he said, pointing to a smaller filing cabinet behind his desk. "These are the unfortunate failures. Regretfully, these patients didn't make it, despite my best efforts. It's important that you see not only the successes, but the failures as well. Thankfully, recent revisions to my treatments have increased the rate of success."

"I see," Lily replied. Showing his failures was a humbling move that bought him more credibility, as a fraud would have only shown positive results.

"I need to stress that it all comes down to individual genetics," the doctor continued. "Everyone is wired differently, so what works in one patient might not work in another. We'll keep tweaking your treatment until we find what works for you. I can't promise success. The unfortunate reality is, there are some people I just can't help. However, I will promise to do my absolute best and to never give up on you."

"I understand, and I appreciate your help," Lily nodded. "How long does the treatment typically take? Overall, I mean."

"This is no in-and-out procedure. The treatment will take time and could take months to yield results. Again, it all depends on the individual. Some patients see remission in weeks, while others take a year or more. We just have to see how well your body responds. The treatments will be frequent, so you'll have to remain here in Houston for the duration. This isn't something that can be administered long distance. We'll need routine testing to see how the treatment is impacting the cancer."

Lily swallowed nervously and looked at Austin. She hadn't expected the treatment to take so long or require such a lengthy stay in Houston.

"We'll have to talk it over to—" she began, only to be cut off by Austin.

"No, we won't. We'll move to Houston if that's what it takes."

Lily leaned in to speak with Austin quietly. "Baby, are you sure? I don't want to—"

Austin interrupted her again, this time to address the doctor. "We'll stay as long as necessary. If you can cure her, I promise you that your clinic will have all the funding it ever needs."

"I appreciate that," the doctor replied. "And like I said, I promise to do my very best."

"I'll throw in an extra ten million if you make her your top priority," Austin blurted.

The doctor put his hands up and shook his head. "Mister Matson, here at my clinic, every patient is my top priority. No patient is more important than another. Everyone receives the same level of treatment to the best of my ability."

Austin shrunk in his seat, and Lily could tell he was ashamed by his offer. Doctor Burzynski's rejection of it, however, told her she'd found the right doctor, and that he wasn't just some snake oil salesman looking to make an easy buck. He had integrity, and he truly cared about his patients.

"Yes, of course. I apologize," Austin said. "It's just… I love her so much, you know? I can't lose her."

"I can see how much you love each other," the doctor smiled. "We'll work hard to make sure you have a long life together. Let's get started, shall we? We'll worry about payment later. I know you're good for it. For now, I'd just like to get her registered and her treatment started. Time is of the essence."

After filling out a pile of paperwork, the doctor led Lily to an exam room to discuss her treatment in greater detail. The first injection of antineoplastons was administered along with a few traditional drugs used to treat her condition, requiring an observational overnight stay. She'd have to be monitored closely in case her body had an adverse reaction to the treatment, which she understood and was fine with. Austin used the time to browse real estate in the area, and before the day was done, had bought them a gorgeous home close to the clinic after taking a virtual tour of it online. They'd need a place to stay while she was receiving her treatment, and he wasn't going to have them living out of a hotel room. Lily marveled at how much easier life was with money, especially if that money belonged to somebody with good looks and a quick wit. In just a few hours, Austin had purchased a home outright, and he'd done it all from the clinic using just his phone and his charm. He was so charismatic and charming, he'd talked the realtor into meeting him at the clinic with the paperwork he needed to sign.

When Lily was released, they got to work making the new house a home. Although their stay would only be temporary, Lily's comfort was Austin's main concern, and he spared no expense furnishing the place, giving her the final say in both the furniture and the decor. He was able to work remotely from his laptop, and Lily insisted on returning to work as well to give her some semblance of normalcy. Lily continued her weekly treatments at the Burzynski Clinic, and once a month, she'd fly to Tucson with Austin to check in on Winston and the estate. They didn't like leaving Winston there by himself, but Austin was uncomfortable leaving the mansion unattended, and given the valuables it housed, Lily understood why. Between visits, they'd call Winston three nights a week to chat, hoping it would help fend off his loneliness.

Her hair had grown back, but after three months had passed with no improvement in Lily's overall health, Austin began to wonder if they'd been suckered. Lily was quick to point out that while there hadn't been any improvement, she also hadn't gotten any worse. Still, Austin's frustration grew, and he was on the verge of confronting Doctor Burzynski when a breakthrough happened. Calling them into his office, the doctor sat them down and smiled as he announced a reduction in Lily's cancer cells. She was in the early stages of remission, he told them, as her body had finally begun to respond to the treatments. Austin wept with joy while Lily sat in silence for a moment, too shocked by the news to have any outward reaction.

"It's… working?" she asked in disbelief.

"It's working," the doctor grinned. "Of course, this doesn't mean you're out of the woods. We still have many months of treatments ahead, and there's always a chance they could stop working. Still," he said, looking at her test results, "this is a very good sign. If your body is responding this well to the treatments, I have reason to believe it will keep responding just as well."

"Oh my God," Lily said, bursting into tears. "Austin… oh my God!"

She leapt into his lap to cover him with kisses while they smiled, laughed, and cried, overcome by emotions they couldn't contain.

"Please, just remember that we still have a long way to go," the doctor told them, reiterating that the remission may not last.

In the weeks to come, the cancer continued to recede and Lily noticed a tremendous improvement in her health. Her bouts of fatigue had all but vanished, and her fits of nausea had subsided as well. On their fifth return to Tucson, Winston wept at the sight of how good she looked, and was convinced God himself had intervened to save her. It was a divine miracle, he told them, and vowed to thank the man upstairs every day for bringing Lily back to them.

It took another six months of treatments for Doctor Burzynski to declare Lily cancer-free. With his help, she had become one of the few people to ever survive such an advanced stage, making it a historic moment worthy of national recognition. Not only did Austin make good on his word, providing the clinic with the funding needed to expand, he brought Doctor Burzynski's work back into the media spotlight. With his wealth and influence, Austin couldn't be ignored, and he was able to vindicate the doctor who had been painted as a fraud by mainstream medicine and the scientific community. The entire world had to recognize the legitimacy of the clinic, and after decades of refuting Burzynski's claims, the FDA was forced to acknowledge the validity of his methods.

Lily's successful treatment and subsequent interviews introduced millions of people to a therapy they never knew existed, saving countless lives in doing so. She became somewhat of a celebrity, known not just as Austin Matson's fiancée, but a champion in the fight against cancer. In an unexpected move that rocked the tech industry, Austin sold two of his manufacturing plants and used the money to help Doctor Burzynski open four new clinics, allowing the doctor's treatments to reach more people. Austin also sold their Houston home—which they knew was only temporary to begin with—and managed to sell it at a profit, which he insisted Burzynski keep as a thank you for successfully treating Lily.

Lily and Austin returned to Maine that summer, where they were married in an extravagant ceremony held just on the upper deck of the lighthouse on the Rockland Breakwater. Austin had used his influence to secure the entire jetty for the day, and had flown in Lily's parents for the event along with Winston, who he insisted fill the role of best man. The media was there in full force to report on the celebrity wedding, and Annabelle stole the show as the ring bearer. Austin presented Lily with a wedding ring even more exquisite than her engagement ring, which she hadn't thought possible, and he insisted the lighthouse ring she gave him serve as his wedding ring. He still hadn't taken it off and vowed it would remain on his finger for eternity and beyond. There were no dry eyes in attendance as Lily married the man who'd never given up on her; the man who'd stood by her side through everything, and whose commitment to her had never wavered, even for a second.

They spent their honeymoon in Maine, and Lily set aside a night for her sleepover with Annabelle, which they spent watching movies, snacking out, doing their nails, and, of course, talking about horses. Every second Lily had was a blessing, and she appreciated each day, taking nothing for granted. Her life had been spared, and she was going to make the most of it. When she returned to Tucson with Austin, she enrolled at the University of Arizona as planned and excelled in her studies. Doctor Burzynski had requested a follow-up every six months to make sure the cancer hadn't returned, and a year later, there was still no sign of it.

Austin and Lily welcomed their first child shortly after their second wedding anniversary. Knowing Winston had no surviving family, they named their little boy after him to keep his name and memory alive. Since the old man was like family himself, the boy would be raised knowing him as a great grandfather. The gesture moved Winston to tears.

Austin and Lily shared a disdain for cold weather, yet relocated to Maine after Lily had finished her schooling, earning her degree and graduating at the top of her class. Austin wanted to be closer to his family so they could be a part of the boy's life, and also wanted their son to experience all four seasons like he had as a child. With Lily's blessing, he sold his estate to a powerful hotelier who'd had his eye on it for quite some time. He bought them an extravagant ocean-side home in Camden, Maine, and great grandpa Winston came with them to oversee the home. Lily, who had become a national treasure at this point, had no problem landing a job with the local school district and was quickly named "Teacher of the Year." Austin's partnership with Atari was a huge success, and he was credited for making the company a household name again. Somewhere along the way, they learned that Ryan had been killed after laying his hands on the wrong woman and being shot by her father. Neither of them lost any sleep over it.

Their second child came, followed by a third. As Lily stood in the doorway, watching her children play in the snow, she caught her reflection in the window and mused at the gray that had started to show in her hair. After her diagnosis, she was convinced she would never grow old, yet here she was, doing just that. She smiled and waved at her beautiful children, who had been conceived out of love and given a wonderful life, ripe with opportunity. She had survived and had gone on to lead a life most would envy. She closed her eyes and silently thanked God when she felt Austin wrap his arms around her from behind. Together, they stood watching their children build the snowman they'd been working so hard on.

"I love you, chocolate girl."

"I love you, lighthouse."

In loving memory of Tymeka Rochell Ward, who lost her battle, but got to see a real Maine lighthouse before she went. She is deeply missed.